FLAT SPIN

A CORDELL LOGAN MYSTERY

FLAT SPIN

DAVID FREED

THE PERMANENT PRESS
Sag Harbor, NY 11963

For information, address:
  The Permanent Press
  4170 Noyac Road
  Sag Harbor, NY 11963
  www.thepermanentpress.com

Library of Congress Cataloging-in-Publication Data

Freed, David–
    Flat spin / David Freed.
        p. cm. — (A Cordell Logan mystery)
    ISBN 978-1-57962-272-5
        1. Pilots—Fiction. 2. Murder—Investigation—Fiction. I. Title.

PS3606.R4375F53 2012
813'.6—dc23   2011052956

Printed in the United States of America.

For Karoline and Jerry, who gave me life

and

Don and Mitch, who gave me wings

ACKNOWLEDGEMENTS

"There are three rules for writing the novel," the great William Somerset Maugham once said. "Unfortunately no one knows what they are." With all due respect to Maugham's literary genius, I believe that one of those rules is to be surrounded by smart, supportive friends and relatives who can both challenge and comfort a humble scribe as he lurches along that darkly self-doubting path that is a first novel.

I am indebted to many such wonderful people. Their myriad contributions appear tangibly on the pages of this book, even if their names do not.

My thanks to *El Jefe*, author par excellence and former Navy SEAL Chuck Pfarrer, whose courage and inspiration by example, generosity of spirit, and depthless humor over two-plus decades of friendship have hauled me out of more than a few shell craters of my own making.

I would be remiss without thanking my late, brilliant editor, Dale Fetherling, who read an early version of this book and offered constructive comments edged with always tactfully delivered, "What in the hell were you thinking?"-type notations. Ditto the skilled, ever-sage Dick Barnes, another of my mentors and former editors from the *Los Angeles Times*. Other talented, hawkeyed journalists were not afraid to weigh in critically when assessing my often tortured efforts, and are deserving of praise. Among them: Barbara Baker, Scott Duke Harris, and especially Barb Hallett, whose effusiveness after reading an early draft convinced me that maybe I was on to something. Thanks also to editor Anne Bensson, whose deft assessment of my deficiencies in plot improved the outcome immeasurably.

For their guidance on matters technical, I would like to express my appreciation to two longtime friends, Sergeant Arthur Ames, PhD (Los Angeles County Sheriff's Department, retired); and Captain Greg Meyer (Los Angeles Police Department, retired). Thanks also to Terry Harris, the most competent, certified flight instructor from whom any pilot could ever hope to learn—even if she does like working the rudder pedals with her bare feet.

Jill Marr of the Sandra Dijkstra Literary Agency is as loyal an ally and effective an agent as there is and I am fortunate to be represented by her, as I am to be published by Judith and Martin Shepard, who took a chance on me when others were unwilling. I'd also like to give a well-deserved shout-out to artist Lon Kirschner for his excellent book jacket design, and to Joslyn Pine for her meticulous copyediting.

To Doug Barr; Norm Draper; Steve Chawkins and Jane Hulse; Dennis Franklin; Howard Hilt; John Jarrett; Jim and Bev Kreyger; John and Cathy Maier; Jay Pfeiffer; Maggie Roiphe; Carl and Helen Schaukowitch; Bob and Edna Sizlo; Bruce Smith; Ty Smith; Scott Weiner; Steve Wick; the many members of the Bates, Freed and Kash clans; my amazingly talented sister, Lisa Pavelka, and her industrious brood; my warrior surrogate sons, Mathew Best and Mike Eggli; and my own awe-inspiring children, Rachel Ann and Army National Guard 1st Lt. Robert M. Freed, I am blessed by your presence and made whole by your laughter.

To my beautiful partner, Dr. Elizabeth Bates Freed, who, on more evenings than I care to admit, prodded me to "finish the damn book" after bringing me red wine and insisting that I read to her what I'd struggled to write that day, when I would've been only too happy to pursue other, less trying avocations (like, say, alligator wrestling), I remain forever yours.

Finally, to Aurelia Valley, a transformational high school English teacher from suburban Denver who struggled mightily to instill in her distracted, working-class students a love of prose and recognized some potential in one of them, encouraging him to explore the writer's life, I offer my belated gratitude. I only wish I could have thanked you before you were gone.

Live thy life as it were spoil and pluck the joys that fly.

—Martial, *Epigrams*, AD 86

Arlo Echevarria opened his door in flip-flops and a foul mood.

"You got the wrong address, dude. I didn't order any pizza."

The Domino's guy stood there mutely on the front step, cap pulled low, face obscured in the dim buttery glow of Echevarria's jelly jar porch light, cradling a pizza hot pouch in both arms like it was baby Jesus.

"What are you, deaf? I said you got the wrong address." Echevarria went to push the door closed, but the Domino's guy blocked it with his foot, drawing a blue steel semi-auto from the red vinyl pouch.

Echevarria yelled, "Wait a—"

Boom.

The .40-caliber hollow point splintered rib bone and mushroomed through Echevarria's left lung, blowing a kebab-size chunk of flesh out his back and dropping him like 164 pounds of wet laundry.

Boom. Boom.

Slugs two and three made pulp of Echevarria's liver and spleen. The coroner would deem all three wounds potentially fatal. Any cynical street cop, which is to say, any cop, would deem them all sweet, sweet shooting: three rounds, center mass, square in the 10-ring.

The Domino's guy tucked the pistol up under his shirt, then calmly gathered his spent brass, depositing each casing in the hot pouch before disappearing into a pleasantly temperate San Fernando Valley evening. The tang of cordite lingered on the breeze with the perfume of night-blooming jasmine.

A rookie and her field training officer, both working the night watch out of Devonshire Division, punched the at-scene button on their mobile data terminal six minutes after catching the "shots fired" call. They found Echevarria lying facedown, unresponsive, inside the entryway, blocking his partially opened front door. Hoping to save a life and impress her FTO, the rookie bulled open the door, sliding the body and smearing blood across the oak parquet floor, thus disturbing both a homicide scene and the on-call LAPD homicide detectives who would arrive later along with more than a dozen other uniformed patrol officers, all of whom raced to the scene to get their nightly dose of gore, even though the need for lights and sirens had long since passed, along with the decedent.

Several of Echevarria's neighbors told police they'd heard him yell, heard what sounded like firecrackers, and glimpsed the killer through their windows. They described him as five-foot-five and 180 pounds. Or five-foot-ten and 160 pounds. Or well over six feet, on the thin side, with a long loping stride—kind of like Gomer Pyle, who used to be on TV back when TV was worth watching. One witness said the shooter was a Latino in his late twenties. Another said he was Arabic in his thirties. Two witnesses said the killer was a Caucasian with a West Hollywood tan. Still others described him as "Jewish-looking" or "the Italian-type" or even Indian—the tomahawk-chop-Geronimo kind, not the kind that worship cows and wrap goddamn bed sheets around their heads. Whoever murdered Echevarria was swarthy and clean-shaven. The witnesses all agreed on that. They also agreed on the getaway car: nobody saw one.

On Echevarria's coffee table, investigators snapped digital photographs of an empty pint bottle of Jameson Irish whiskey, three recently emptied takeout cartons from a Chinese restaurant on nearby Sherman Way, and a paperback copy of *Cover-up: The Secret of UFO Technology Transfer*, detailing American industry's covertly profitable relationship with space aliens. Wedged in the waistband of Echevarria's plaid flannel Costco lounge pants, under his blood-soaked "Don't Blame Me, I Voted for the Other Guy" T-shirt, they found a nine-millimeter Beretta, Model 92FS, standard U.S. military issue. The pistol held a full fifteen-round clip. The firing chamber was empty.

"Like tits on a nun," one particularly salty patrolman observed.

The paid funeral notice that ran in the *Los Angeles Times* six days later said Echevarria had "set off to see the Lord to receive the angel wings he'd deserved for so long." It said he was born in Oakland in 1961, that he'd earned a business degree from San Francisco State, and that he'd built a successful international marketing company in the Bay Area before taking early retirement and relocating south to LA, there to enjoy the balmier weather, Dodger baseball, and serving his favorite charities, none of which were specified. Survivors included his "devoted wife and soul mate," Savannah, and a twenty-year-old son from a previous marriage who worshipped him "for the exceptionally caring parent that he was." No mention was made of Echevarria having been gunned down and gone off to see the Lord in flip-flops and Costco lounge pants. His passing, it was noted, had been "sudden and unexpected."

Of course, anyone who knew the real Arlo Echevarria knew the obit was mostly all bullshit.

Especially the unexpected part.

ONE

We were turning final when the engine died.

My student was a frosted blonde divorcee named Charise MacInerny with all of six hours in her private pilot's logbook, who'd decided that learning to fly was an excellent way to show her plastic surgeon ex-husband that she was still every bit as alluring as that gold-digging, cheerleader-turned-pharmaceutical sales rep slut he'd dumped her for. Charise swiveled her ridiculously blue Malibu Barbie eyes toward me, wide with horror, and said, "Fucking do something!"

My plane, the *Ruptured Duck*, was 300 feet above ground level, half a mile from the runway and dropping faster than the Dow in October. Charise had extended too far downwind in the pattern and surrendered too much altitude, while I'd been stupidly mesmerized by the postcard pretty coastline and shimmering sea of diamonds beyond, wondering how the hell I was ever going to pay for the 2,000-hour overhaul due on the *Duck's* power plant.

"I have the airplane," I said in my nothing-rattles-me-I'm-a-certified-flight-instructor voice.

I grabbed the copilot's yoke with my right hand, yanked the carburetor heat control with my left, and brought the nose up to sixty-five knots indicated—best glide speed in a Cessna 172. Then I reached down between the seats, keeping my eyes outside the cockpit to maintain spatial orientation, and groped the fuel selector valve: it was turned to both tanks. The gas gauges registered more than half-full—plenty of go juice—yet the engine was deader than a resolution the morning after New Year's Day.

Charise was hyperventilating. "I don't want to die, Logan!" she yelled into the boom microphone of her headset. "Please don't let me die! Oh Jesus oh Jesus oh Jesus oh mother of JESUS!"

"Chill out, Charise. It'll be OK."

Or, quite possibly, not.

Ahead of us was a BMW dealership, a lumberyard, and a parking lot jammed with yellow school buses—not the most forgiving locales to attempt what we aviators euphemistically like to call an "off-airport" landing, and what TV anchors refer to as a "lead story." In a flash, I envisioned myself at the top of the evening news: *An incompetent flight instructor and his comely student died today when their single-engine airplane* . . . If the crash didn't kill me, the humiliation of my own inattention would.

I glanced down at the mixture control, which is what I should've done to begin with. The red knob was pulled all the way out. Instead of easing back on the black throttle control knob to reduce airspeed, as she was supposed to have done, Charise had inexplicably pulled the fuel-air mixture, effectively starving the engine of gas. I shoved the red knob forward hard enough that I thought for a second the metal shaft might snap in half, retarded the throttle control to a quarter-inch, then reached across Charise's supple thighs with my left hand and cranked the ignition key.

The little four-cylinder Lycoming thrummed to life with a death-cheating growl.

I eased back on the yoke, rolled in some trim and dumped full flaps as I kicked the rudder and banked the *Duck* hard left, keeping one eye on the airspeed while clearing the roof of the Rancho Bonita Athletic Club by less than ten feet. We turned final with an eight-knot crosswind and touched down on Runway One-Seven left like a butterfly with sore feet. If the theater critics in the tower were watching, they never said a word.

"Cessna Four Charlie Lima, where are you parking today?" the controller asked pleasantly as we rolled out.

"Charlie Lima's going to Premier Aviation."

My answer was met with scratchy static through the headphones. After a few seconds, the controller asked again: Where were we parking? He obviously hadn't heard my response to his question. The *Duck's* ancient, unpredictable communication radios were acting up yet again. I smacked the audio panel where I always smacked it with the heel of my hand, keyed the mic button on my control yoke and said, "Charlie Lima to Premier Aviation."

"Cessna Four Charlie Lima, roger. Exit on Echo, cross One-Seven left and contact ground, point six."

I repeated his instructions back to him, tapped the toe brakes and jockeyed the plane off the active runway. After we crossed Runway One-Seven left, I stopped short of the parallel taxiway and dialed in 121.6 on my number-two radio.

"Rancho Bonita ground, Cessna four Charlie Lima, clear of One-Seven left at Echo, taxi Premier."

"Cessna four Charlie Lima, taxi as requested."

Charise was gulping air like a gaffed tuna. Her eyeliner had run with her tears, painting a thin black stripe down each cheek. The effect reminded me of one of those annoying street mimes always trying to feel their way out of imaginary boxes.

"I've never been that close to death," Charise said, "and I don't want to ever be again!"

"Well, Charise, I believe it was Cicero who once said, 'Anybody is liable to err, but only a fool persists in error.' We learn from our mistakes, make sure we don't repeat them."

She was looking at me with her mouth open. "You're saying it was *my* fault?"

"You pulled the mixture control, Charise. The engine doesn't like that. The engine will take its ball and go home."

"Well, maybe I did or maybe I didn't, but if I'm not mistaken, Logan, I believe *you're* the flight instructor. You should've *instructed* me. I mean, my God, what am I paying you all this money for?"

She wiped the tears from her cheeks, smearing the black streaks and transferring eyeliner onto her fingers, then noticed her fingertips and panicked anew. She reached into the backseat, retrieved a gold compact from an alligator skin clutch and went to work on her face with a silk handkerchief, attacking her smudged cheeks like a monkey scratching itself. She was wearing wedge sandals with four-inch cork heels and $350 blue jeans that looked like they were sprayed on. Her low-cut knit top was cream-colored and two sizes too small, accentuating a set of baby feeders that either her ex,

Dr. Nip/Tuck, designed or the Lord did when Mrs. Lord wasn't looking. Her lips were alluring little bee-stung pillows. The skin under her chin was pulled Miss Teen USA tight. Whatever Charise MacInerny may have looked like before the advent of modern cosmetic surgery, she was definitely slammin' now.

"To tell you the truth," she said, angling her little mirror this way and that, making sure she'd scrubbed off all the errant eyeliner, "I'm not sure this whole flying thing is right for me. I mean, you actually have to *remember* things."

There was a time when I would have told her she was wrong, that nearly anybody can learn to be a pilot. And even though I knew full-well after our first flight lesson that Charise MacInerny's near-total lack of hand-eye coordination, not to mention smarts, placed her solidly outside the "nearly anybody" envelope, we would have gone up again and again. At forty-eight dollars an hour, another hundred an hour for the plane rental, plus fuel, I would have taken her for all she was worth. And, after she'd logged about fifty hours and had yet to solo because the idea of having to actually take off and land a small airplane all by herself still freaked the living Botox out of her, I would have politely suggested that perhaps she was better suited to other, more earthbound recreational pursuits.

But that was the old me. Before I regrew that thing priests call a conscience and the Buddha calls enlightenment. Don't get me wrong. The new me still needed the money as much as the old me. Even more so. There comes a point in life, however, when you realize it's not always about the bucks. It's only about the bucks most of the time.

"Well, Charise, there are always sailing lessons."

"*Sailing lessons?* Are you kidding? I get seasick in the Jacuzzi."

She touched up her lips with one of those liquid lipstick pen things, making sure the coverage was perfect with a dab of her manicured pinkie finger, then shed her headset and brushed out her gilded cougar mane.

I steered the *Duck* into an open tie-down spot along taxiway Bravo in front of Premier Aviation, one of two fixed-base operations on the field catering to mostly rich, corporate flyers. I turned off the avionics master switch and leaned the mixture until the engine sputtered and quit. After we got out of the airplane, I braced the nose wheel with a pair of black rubber chocks sitting on the tarmac.

Charise handed me her logbook without a word. I wrote down the date, the aircraft type, the plane's tail number, the total time we'd flown that day (1.2 hours), the amount of instruction she'd received (1.2 hours), and the number of touch-and-go's we'd made (7). In the "Remarks and Endorsements" section I nearly wrote, "Came perilously close to buying the farm," but instead put, "Practiced emergency procedures." Then, for grins, I jotted, "We'll always have Paris."

The old me might've suggested we go grab an umbrella drink on the beach after sharing so harrowing a near-death experience. Maybe we would've ended up at her place or, God forbid, mine. I was no Brad Pitt, but I was no Meatloaf, either. I still owned my own hair and all my teeth. The plumbing still worked just fine, thank you very much. I was a solid six-one and 190 pounds, a mere five pounds more than I'd been back in the day, snagging footballs for the Air Force Academy and studying Sartre, a rare Humanities major on a campus thick with geeky aeronautical engineers. But, like I said, that was the old me. I signed the entry and handed her back her logbook.

"Well," I said, "at least it wasn't boring."

"You can say that again."

"At least it wasn't boring."

She smiled and kissed me on the cheek. It beat a firm handshake any day of the week.

"Take care of yourself, Logan."

"Don't go changing, Charise."

I watched her glide into the parking lot where a tall, tanned man in his late thirties was leaning against a silver Lamborghini Diablo convertible, smoking a cigarette. He wore a dark-colored suit with a crisp white dress shirt and a rep necktie striped blue and gold, cinched way too tight. His dark hair matched the gloss of his wingtips. His eyes were cloaked behind a pair of cool guy Ray-Bans.

A personal injury attorney. Had to be. There has to be more puke-inducing ways to earn a living than chasing ambulances, I thought to myself, though none came readily to mind.

He flicked away his smoke as Charise approached. She showed him what I'd written in her logbook. He nodded like he almost cared, then flashed me a stony smile as he held open the passenger door for her on his $200,000 road rocket. After she was comfortably settled in, he gingerly closed the door, then hustled around to the driver's side, glancing my way to make sure I was still watching. He hopped in, fired up the Lamborghini and roared out onto Mayfield Place, grinding the transmission as he upshifted. Charise never looked back.

Oh, well.

I took my time tying down the *Duck*. Over at the commercial terminal, a turboprop taxied in and disgorged its passengers. High overhead, a turkey vulture wheeled unsteadily in the morning air. Two black SUVs drove onto the ramp and parked beside a Dassault Falcon 7X. A large, middle-age woman in sweat pants, who looked very much like Rancho Bonita's most famous resident, the star of a wildly successful TV talk show and publishing empire, stepped out of the lead SUV. She chatted up one of her personal assistants while others transferred a queen's procession of designer luggage onto the jet.

I wanted to yell, "You go, girl!" but somehow restrained myself.

Had I been able to afford my own personal assistant, I might've checked in to see what was next on my busy schedule. Truth was, I needed no reminder to know that I had nothing going the rest of the day. Or the rest of the week, for that matter. I was fresh out of students, with no immediate prospect of any new ones. If I were a religious man, which I'm not, at least not in a conventional sense, I would've prayed that my monthly retirement check from Uncle Sugar was waiting in my mailbox when I got home. A breakfast burrito loomed large on my radar, then maybe a nap.

The last thing on my mind was murder.

Two

It was not yet nine A.M. and already eighty degrees when I walked in off the flight line that morning. Weird weather for early November if you live in North Dakota. Not so weird for the central coast of California.

Inside Larry Kropf's cavernous hangar, where Marine mechanics once toiled over gull-winged Corsair fighters destined for war in the Pacific, it was dank and cool. The place smelled of grease and history. Larry was balanced on a step stool, leaning precariously into the engine compartment of a V-tail Beech. All I could see of him were his elbows and the north end of his ass crack, peeking out the back of his low-riding, navy blue work pants.

"Somebody's in your office," he said without looking up. "Been there awhile."

"Did they bring balloons?"

"Say again?"

"Publishers Clearing House. I'm a Super Prize finalist. This could be it, Larry. My ship has docked at last."

Larry hitched up his pants and descended the stool gingerly, grimacing with each painful step while pushing his Buddy Holly glasses back up his nose with a finger thick as a Wisconsin brat. He was a wide man with furry forearms and a Grizzly Adams beard dense enough to hide small animals. His nose was flat and veined, tenderized by one too many bar fights and far too much tequila. Stretched across his cannonball belly was an oil-smeared gray T-shirt that said, "Guns Don't Kill People, Postal Workers Do."

"Didn't see no balloons," he said, rummaging through the drawers of a rolling tool chest stationed beside the Beechcraft's wing.

"No balloons? Then screw 'em. I *was* gonna subscribe to *Cat Fancy*, up my chances of winning, but they can forget about it now."

"Good. Then maybe you can finally pay me that back rent you owe me."

"I'll get you your money, Larry, as soon as I can. You know I'm good for it."

"Only thing I know is, you haven't paid me a dime in two months, Logan. Not to mention that spot weld I done on your exhaust stack and that's been, what, four months?"

"Three months. But who's counting, right?"

"I got bills to pay, too, OK?" Larry said. "I got a knee needs replacing. I got a kid needs braces. Five grand to get her teeth fixed so when she turns sixteen, I can stay up all night debating whether to take a shotgun to her pimply little prom date after he brings her home four hours late, or de-ball him with a pair of channel locks."

"You know, Larry, I'm no psychotherapist, but I believe those would be called *issues*."

"What about the fucking money you owe me, Logan? What about *those* issues?" He grabbed a socket wrench from the tool cabinet and climbed back up the step stool, pissed and in pain. "You know, Logan, I used to think you were a funny guy. *You* obviously think you're a funny guy. But your bullshit's getting pretty goddamn old. You're a grown-ass man. Stiffing honest people. You should be ashamed of yourself."

I was. And then some. If I'd had the dough, I would've paid him every penny I owed him right then and there. But what little I had in the bank was barely enough to cover next month's rent on my apartment, let alone the rent I owed Larry for the cramped, converted storage room I sublet from him in his hangar and called a flight school. The *Ruptured Duck*, my four-seat 172 with its unreliable radios, hail-dimpled wings, and faded orange, yellow and white color scheme that practically screamed 1973, the year the plane came off Cessna's Wichita assembly line, was the only inanimate object I owned of any value, and I'd already borrowed against it—twice.

"Look, I've got a government pension check coming in," I said. "We're talking $920. I'll give you half as soon as I get it."

"Sure you will." He shook his head with disgust and disappeared once more into the Beech's engine compartment. "You need to find yourself a job, Logan, a *real* job, cuz this flight instructor gig obviously ain't working out too good for you."

What can you say to the truth? I said nothing.

"I hear they're hiring over at Sears," Larry said.

"They're always hiring over at Sears," I said.

⊙══╪══⊙

A banner the size of a toboggan hung from the wall above my desk. In red, white and blue letters, it said, "Above the Clouds Aviation—Flight Training, Whale Watching and Aerial Charters." I'd paid a graphic artist sixty-nine bucks to design and print it out, splurging for three colors instead of two. The artist offered to throw in some smiling cartoon whales jumping out of the water and cute little psychedelic-colored biplanes zipping through rainbows and around cotton ball clouds, but I figured the FAA would take one look at all of that extraneous garbage, assume I was smoking crack—like the artist—and revoke my pilot's license. I stuck with the basics.

A woman was standing below the banner, flipping through my "Babes and Bombers" wall calendar, smirking at all the photos of hot chicks posing with hot warbirds. The calendar had been a birthday gift from Larry, back when I could still afford to make the rent, before the economy took a dump and prospective student pilots disappeared like shadows from a passing cloud. She looked up as I entered.

"I know you," she said with a cloying smile.

Some faint new lines around the eyes. A slight softening under the jaw. Not bad for six years gone by. She wore a sleeveless gray silk pantsuit and a black lace camisole that showed more cleavage than I really needed to see. Her feet were clad in patent leather high heels with Wicked Witch of the West toes. A Kate Spade satchel hung from her right shoulder. Her hair was a shade redder than when I last saw her, and shorter. She wore a gold wedding band. No other jewelry. No makeup. She needed none. My ex-wife, Savannah Carlisle, was still every inch the heartbreaker I unfortunately remembered all too well.

"The devil must be wearing thermal underwear," I said.

Her smile faded. "What's that supposed to mean?"

"Outside your attorney's office. That morning we signed the papers."

"I said I'd see you again when hell froze over. I was upset that day, Logan. I'm sure you could understand, under the circumstances."

Her eyes were liquid mahogany, her gaze as penetrating as ever. I wondered if she could hear my heart slamming around under my polo shirt.

"You cut your hair," I said.

"And you didn't."

She approached me slowly, shoulders back, accentuating her breasts, maintaining eye contact while biting her lower lip—classic signals of carnal interest. I was hoping she was going to wrap her toned arms around my waist and admit how much she'd missed me, what a terrible mistake she'd made by leaving. The biggest mistake of her life. But as she drew closer, I could see that her pupils were barely dilated.

She reached out and gave my beard a playful tug.

"Very Grizzly Adams," Savannah said. "I think I like it."

"Whew. What a relief. The first thing I said to myself when I grew it was, 'Gee, I wonder what my insignificant other would think?'"

"Still the same sarcastic jerk. Some things never change, do they, Logan?"

I couldn't decide if I wanted to make love to her or crush her exquisite throat with my hands. A man doesn't lose so rare a woman as Savannah Carlisle without craving and loathing her the rest of his life.

"Still modeling?" I asked, doing my best to keep things civil.

"Nobody wants to see a forty-two-year-old woman walk the runway, not in a string bikini, anyway. Actually, I'm doing a fair amount of counseling these days." She dug a business card out of her bag and handed it to me. In Ye Olde English script it said, "Savannah Echevarria. Life Coach."

"That's rich. You, of all people, telling people how to manage their lives."

"You always did enjoy putting me down, didn't you?"

I would've apologized but I was in no mood. I parked myself behind my desk and shuffled through a stack of outdated airworthiness directives like it was important work.

"So," Savannah said, glancing around, "seems like you're doing well."

"Me? Top of the heap. Couldn't be better."

I was amazed my nose didn't go Pinocchio on me. All she needed to do was take one look around my stuffy, windowless "flight academy" to see that things could've been way better: A card table littered with a dozen dog-eared Jeppeson flight manuals. A cheap plastic fan and a couple of green plastic lawn chairs from Kmart. A decrepit, Vietnam-era metal desk and an Army surplus filing cabinet, olive drab. A computer so old, I had to just about shovel coal into it to make it work. I resented the hell out of her showing up, invading my space, inviting herself back into my world without fair warning. But it was my own fault. I'd left the door unlocked. In the sun-kissed, seaside enclave of Rancho Bonita, with its red tile roofs and Italian climate and verdant hills overlooking the Pacific—"California's Monaco" as the city's moneyed minions like to call it—most everybody leaves their doors unlocked. At least they claim to. Admitting otherwise would be to concede that Rancho Bonita, like Los Angeles—its bloated, apocalyptic neighbor 120 miles down the coast—has a crime problem. Heaven forbid anything should undermine property values in paradise.

"So," Savannah said, "what made you decide to grow out your beard?"

"Just trying to walk a different path, that's all."

"A different path. Sounds vaguely Buddhist."

"I dabble."

"Are you serious? Cordell Logan, a *Buddhist*?"

I shrugged.

"Don't tell me you've gone vegetarian, too."

Another shrug.

"A vegetarian. I don't believe it," Savannah said. "What happened to Mr. Meat and Potatoes?"

"You'd be amazed," I said, "what they can do with mock duck these days."

Let me be honest here. I struggle with the vegetarian thing. I mean, sometimes, a dude just *has* to have a *chile verde* burrito. But I wasn't about to admit that to a woman who'd walked out on me. I was the new and improved Cordell Logan. A better man without her. The man she could no longer have. That's what I wanted her to believe, anyway, even if it wasn't close to being in the same hemisphere as true.

"Definitely not the man I married," Savannah said.

"Not the one you dumped, either."

"I didn't dump you, Logan. You filed on me."

"Yeah, after you banged my boss."

Her eyes flashed fire. "Whatever I did, I did long after you forgot what the word *faithful* meant."

"You make it sound like I was some kind of womanizer."

"Did you or did you not sleep with that flight attendant?"

"If you'll recall, Savannah, we were separated at the time."

"Did you or did you not sleep with her? Yes or no, Logan?"

"I was drunk. I told you, she meant nothing to me."

"Well, she sure as hell meant something to me."

"Look, what I did was wrong. I admitted that then, I admit it now. But I didn't leave you, Savannah. I wasn't looking for a way out. You were."

She sank into one of my Kmart lawn chairs without asking if I minded and ran a hand through her hair.

"I didn't come here to open old wounds," she said, sighing.

"Old wounds? I don't see you for six years. Not a phone call. Not a Christmas card. Then you show up unannounced and expect us to have a friendly little chat? Catch up on old times?" I got up from my desk and stuffed some papers into the filing cabinet. "What the hell did you come for anyway, Savannah? Because, as

I'm sure you can appreciate, being a life coach and all, I really do have a life to get back to here."

"Arlo's gone."

"And you expect me to give a shit? The guy ran out on his first wife, Savannah. What makes you think he wouldn't run out on you someday?"

"I meant, he's dead."

Her words hung in the air like the rumble of distant artillery fire.

"Dead . . . as in *died?*"

She stared at her shoes. "Last month. I wasn't sure if you'd heard or not."

Arlo Echevarria. My old boss. The man she'd dumped me for. Dead. I wanted to punch my fist in the air. I wanted to dance like Snoopy come suppertime. I wanted to shout that the Buddha was right, that Karma is real! I looked back at my ex-wife from my make-believe paperwork, hoping the expression on my face didn't betray the sudden, unbridled joy I felt inside, and said instead, as evenly as I could, "What happened?"

"Somebody came to his door dressed like a pizza delivery driver and shot him."

My head was spinning. "You said *his* door."

"We moved to LA last year, after Arlo retired. My father helped us buy a place in the hills, above Sunset, but Arlo moved out after a couple months. He was just . . . He'd changed. We fought a lot. He was renting a little house up in Northridge. We were . . ." Savannah drew a breath and let it out slowly, "separated."

She unfolded a newspaper clipping from the *Los Angeles Times* and laid it on my desk. I snatched it up and skimmed it. A paid obituary. It was full of lies and half-truths.

"Who wrote this?"

"I did."

She waited for me to say something comforting. I slid the clipping back to her across the desk and picked at a splinter in my thumb.

"Christ, Logan, you act like it was nothing. Did you hear what I said? Arlo was *murdered*."

"Sorry for your loss."

She gave me a hard look and made a little huffing sound through her nose and mouth, like she couldn't believe anyone could be so callous, let alone a man to whom she'd once given herself so freely.

"You know, I'd forgotten what a complete bastard you can be." Her chin quivered. Then she began to sob.

The air inside my office started to feel heavy. I turned the table fan on low, watching it oscillate back and forth, the blades riffling the pages of my wall calendar, while she wept. I thought about all the pain she'd heaped upon me and how hard I'd tried to drink myself off the planet after we'd divorced. I had long ago accepted the reality that the wounds she'd inflicted having left me for Echevarria would fester forever. And yet, bitter as I still was, I actually found myself feeling sorry for her as she sat there in obvious pain. Which made me feel even more bitter.

I yanked open the top drawer of my desk. Inside was a thick stack of brown paper napkins from Taco Bell. *How the hell can any corporation possibly turn a profit when half the free world steals its napkins by the fistful?* I backhanded her one.

"You want some water or something?"

She shook her head no, dabbing her tears with the napkin.

"Then what *do* you want, Savannah? Why drive all the way up here from LA? Because I know it wasn't just to tell me Arlo's *gone*."

"I'd like you to tell the police what Arlo did for a living."

"He worked in marketing."

"His *real* job."

"That was his real job."

We both knew I was lying.

"Logan, the police are *never* going to find who killed him if they don't know who he really was, *what* he really did. I need your help. Please."

Something shifted in my gut, a moist sickness. *Some nerve, asking for my help after cutting off my balls.* I swallowed down the taste of bile and leaned back in my chair, my hands clasped nonchalantly behind my head.

"What are the police telling you?"

"That they're not getting anywhere."

Detectives assigned to the case, she said, had concluded that Echevarria's demise was the result of more than some random act of violence in a metropolis whose middle name is random violence. But given what meager evidence they had to go on, investigators had been unable to gain much traction, according to Savannah. No arrests had been made. No viable suspects had even been identified.

"People die in LA all the time," I said with a shrug. "Sometimes, for no reason at all."

"Arlo died for a reason," Savannah said. "I think it had to do with what he did, his work—his *real* work. Somebody out for revenge. If you could just talk to the detectives . . ."

She searched my eyes, waiting. I gazed at her evenly and gave back nothing.

"I told them that Arlo worked for the government," Savannah said. "They said they couldn't find any records other than when he was with the Army."

"Yeah, well, I wouldn't know anything about it."

"You know that's not true, Logan. You worked with him. You worked *for* him."

"That I did. In marketing."

Her jaw muscles tightened. She was getting nowhere, but she wasn't about to give up. "I want to show you something," she said, digging through her purse.

Outside, a regional jet began its takeoff roll down Runway Twenty-Six, its twin turbines rattling the walls of the hangar. I hiked the sleeves of my polo shirt a little and folded my arms across my chest, pushing my biceps up with the backs of my hands to give her a glimpse of what she'd given up for the likes of scrawny Arlo Echevarria, but she was too busy rummaging through her designer handbag to notice my *mas macho* gun show. She brushed a strand of hair from her eyes and tucked it behind her ear as she searched her purse. Why did she have to still be so goddamn gorgeous?

"I haven't been over to his house yet," Savannah said. "I can't. It's just too . . ." She cleared her throat, still going through her purse. "My father hired a company. They come in after somebody dies and pack up all their clothes, personal effects, clean up the mess. Can you imagine a job like that? Anyway, I was going through a box of Arlo's things the other night, and I found this."

She pulled out a wallet-size photograph from her purse and slid it toward me across the desk. I exhaled like I was doing her a big favor picking it up:

The photo was of Echevarria and me, taken in the Nubo-Sindian Desert. Our cheeks were streaked with camouflage face paint and eight days of Iranian dust. We were outfitted in battle dress devoid of rank or unit insignia. Sprawled at our boots was a bearded Arab, arms splayed above his head, his eyes half-hooded in death, the front of his white *dishdasha* man-dress splotched red from multiple gunshot wounds. In Echevarria's right hand was a Kalashnikov assault rifle with a collapsible stock and extended banana clip. His left hand was clamped affectionately on my shoulder. He was beaming at the camera like a safari hunter posing with a trophy lion, while I stared grimly into the lens, thoroughly exhausted.

I'd forgotten how slight Echevarria was. His combat uniform hung from his bony frame like a protestor on a hunger strike, yet there was no denying his raw physical appeal. The pale green eyes so inconsistent with the bronze Mayan skin. The high cheekbones. The aquiline nose. The lips curved perpetually in an impish little boy's smile.

"I showed that picture to the police," Savannah said. "They said they didn't know what to make of it."

I flipped it back across the desk. "Picture's a fake," I said.

"Fake? What're you talking about?"

"Going-away party. The guy on the ground worked in accounts receivable. Got a bookkeeping job with Halliburton in Baghdad. We squirted catsup on him, told him to lay there and look like roadkill so he could get an idea of what he had to look forward to. It was all a big joke."

"That's the biggest bunch of bullshit I've ever heard. That man is dead, Logan. Arlo killed him. Or you did."

I put my feet back up on my desk, clasped my hands behind my head once more and stared at her blankly.

"Logan, Arlo's *dead*. He's *dead*, OK? There's no reason to keep covering up everything. Why can't you just *talk* to me? That's all I'm asking. Be honest with me. For once in your life. I'm begging you. Please."

I'll admit it. I got off watching her grovel. Probably too much. But unless you've been there, sitting within tactile proximity of a woman who once carved your heart out and stomped on it like Carlo Rossi come grape harvest, you'd probably never understand.

"Was it the CIA? At least tell me that much."

I forced a chuckle. "That's one thing I always did like about you, Savannah. You always did have a healthy imagination."

She looked away, nostrils flaring, like a bull about to charge. "Do you really think I didn't notice? All the late night phone calls, the last minute 'business trips'? All the *lies*? It was no different with you than it was with him, Logan. How stupid do you really think I am?"

As dispassionately as I could, I said, "Arlo Echevarria ran a marketing company. I worked for him. I respected him. Until he stole my wife."

Savannah slung her bag angrily over her shoulder and stood, then slowly, deliberately, leaned toward me over my desk, her palms flat on the worn gray metal.

"I'm not going to tell you how much I despise you," she said, her mahogany eyes burning holes in my soul. "You can figure that out yourself."

For the second time that morning, I watched a beautiful woman walk out of my life. The only difference was, this one I cared about.

Only after she'd gone did I notice that she'd left behind the photograph of Echevarria and me.

THREE

I can't say whether there was a second gunman in Dallas the day JFK was assassinated, though anyone familiar with the elegant efficiency of your basic L-shaped ambush could take one look at the sixth floor sniper's nest and the stockade fence behind the grassy knoll on Dealey Plaza and draw their own conclusions. I can't say whether it was a flying saucer outside Roswell in 1957, or whether Elvis is alive and well and eating chili dogs with Marilyn Monroe on some obscure island in the Mediterranean. What I can say with certainty is that, until very recently, in the name of national security, the government of the United States relied on a select handful of men to do its dirty work in places and ways that never once made the network news.

The agency to which these men reported was classified Tier One Ultra and code-named Alpha, a purposeful tip of the hat to *Alfa*, Russia's most elite counterterrorism unit. Known only within highly compartmentalized circles, Alpha showed up on no Defense Department orders of battle. There was never a mention of it in any Congressional budget reports, nor on any blogs. No Tweets. Culled from the various branches of America's military and intelligence apparatus for their individual skills, elite operators assigned to Alpha surrendered all formal rank and title. They were referred to synonymously as "go-to guys." They were hunter-killers, these men, honed in the arts of asymmetric warfare and oblivious to the sovereignty of treaties or international borders. They proved an invaluable weapon in the fight against global terrorism. But they were not invulnerable to the vagaries of shifting political winds. The current administration, fearing scandal if word of Alpha's actions ever were fully known, quietly ordered the group disbanded within a month of Inauguration Day. White House officials past and present will deny there were ever any "go-to guys." But I know there were because I was one of them. And so, too, was Arlo Echevarria.

I'd be on the next Con Air flight to Super Max were I to divulge all that we did. That's how nondisclosure agreements work. Sign one, tell a few tales out of school, and the next thing you know, you're bunking with Robert Hanssen and stamping out license plates the rest of your life. So you'll excuse me if I'm a bit vague on operational details—target ID's, mission locations, and the like. What I can tell you, though, is how Echevarria and I worked together, how I initially revered him, and how, ultimately, I wished him dead.

For me, it began in college.

We were playing New Mexico at Albuquerque my senior year. With time about to expire before halftime, I snagged a pass cutting across the middle and turned to run upfield when the Lobos' 240-pound middle linebacker, a first-round NFL prospect with "I Shall Fear No Man But God" tattooed across his throat, separated me from my cleats. The football went one way; the major structural ligaments of my right knee the other. And so ended my collegiate gridiron career. Fortunately for me, playing football was not the only reason the Air Force put me through college.

Flash forward ten years. I'm flying A-10 Warthogs. The 'Hog sometimes gets a bad rap from other fighter pilots who drive ships with pointier noses, but there's no better platform when it comes to blowing up stuff. I blew up stuff real good all over the world— and got paid well to do it, too. Tanks. Republican Guardsmen. Miscellaneous terrorists. A total blast. Literally. Then, during an otherwise routine six-month physical, my friendly flight surgeon asked if I had any squawks. I made the mistake of telling him half-jokingly that I was considering applying for work at the Weather Channel because I could always tell when a low pressure system was moving in based on how lousy my surgically reconstructed knee felt. The doctor bent and prodded my lower leg this way and that, then concluded that the joint had atrophied beyond acceptable Air Force standards. I was ruled unfit to fly. At that moment, no longer a fighter pilot, I could've just as easily been ruled unfit to continue living.

I spent a month searching for the true meaning of life at the bottom of bourbon bottles, debating whether to resign my commission. The airlines were hiring like crazy back then. Most were so desperate for pilots they didn't care about something as trivial as a reconstructed anterior cruciate ligament. As long as you had a pulse and could more or less keep the dirty side of the airplane down, you were assured of a paycheck. For me, though, the notion of hauling software salesmen and colicky infants around in the back of a 737 held all the appeal of driving a Greyhound bus. I enjoyed being in the Air Force. I just needed a different career path. My superiors, as it turned out, were only too happy to accommodate me.

Soldiers and Marines are quick to point out that the Air Force is the most non-military of the military services. They call it the Air Farce. The Chair Farce. Civilians in Uniform. A country club with airplanes. Deservedly so. Most Air Force weenies can't tell the difference between a handgun and a howitzer. I was somewhat unusual in that regard. When you bounce from ranch to ranch as a foster kid on the arid plains east of Denver, you quickly learn that: 1) much of Colorado bears little resemblance to a Coors commercial and 2) shooting firearms is about all there is to do recreationally in such places unless you count goat roping and getting loaded and/or laid. Goats give me the creeps; booze, I discovered early on, brings out the bad in me; and street narcotics always seemed to me a stupid thing to do to one's physiology. But guns, ah, now those were another story altogether.

I loved the precision they demanded, their perfect utility. For my twelfth birthday, my foster parents *du jour* gave me an old single-shot, bolt-action .22 with a red cocking indicator and a battered walnut stock. It was the most animate inanimate object I'd ever seen, let alone owned. I worked every job I could get—digging irrigation ditches, shoveling snow, pulling weeds—to buy ammunition, and target practiced endlessly. Cans, bottles, rocks, birds on the wing, varmints on the run. After awhile, I could hit anything with consistency and at ranges that sounded more like bragging than marksmanship. Which helps explain why, after being admitted to the Air Force Academy, I consistently registered among the highest scores in school history with both pistol and M-16.

My performance on the firing range was not lost on my superiors when they sought to find me a suitable new job after clipping my wings. Such ability, they concluded, lent itself to the wonderful world of military informational gathering and assessment. What one's shooting skills had to do with flying a desk as an intelligence analyst was beyond me, but I didn't ask many questions. Most things in the military make no sense. And thus, with some initial reluctance, I accepted a series of ground-based assignments, first to the Air Intelligence Agency at Wright-Patterson, then to the National Air Intelligence Center at Lackland Air Force Base, until, finally, I ended up where I did, in the darkest shadows, on the blackest operations, a token zoomie in the land of snake eaters—among them a warrior of Mayan ancestry who one day would steal from me the only woman I'd ever truly loved.

○═══╬═══○

I was lounging on a rope hammock in my landlady's backyard, hoping the sun would bake away all thoughts of Savannah and her unannounced visit that morning. The plan wasn't working. I thought about going inside, maybe catching up on my reading, but when it's ninety-four degrees and your home is a converted two-car garage with a flat roof and no insulation or air conditioning, going inside isn't something you do voluntarily until well after sundown. So I just lay there. Even my feline idiot of a roommate, Kiddiot, the world's most worthless cat, was showing the effects of the heat. He was dozing in the oak tree above me with his tongue lolling lethargically out one corner of his mouth. His lanky orange and white limbs straddled the tree like some Bulgarian gymnast passed out on a balance beam. A mockingbird perched on the same branch not two feet away from him, singing every song in its vast repertoire, untroubled by the cat's proximity. Kiddiot's slothful reputation obviously had preceded him.

I slipped the photo of Echevarria and me out of my pocket and studied it for the umpteenth time. I'd lied to Savannah. The blood in the picture was as real as the dead Al-Qaeda operative who'd spilled it. He was a pharmacist from Damascus, mastermind of at least four jihadist bombings in Madrid and Islamabad. More than eighty innocents had met their end, courtesy of his handiwork. Any one of the attacks might've easily landed him atop Alpha's tasking board. But the Syrian pharmacist was definitely three strikes and you're out material: it just so happened that he was related by marriage to a prominent Arab-American politico with personal ties to the White House. The President's handlers were not keen on seeing *that* story above the fold in the *Times*. So telephone calls were placed on encrypted lines and options discussed—obliquely, to be sure, and always off-the-record. Make the evil pharmacist disappear.

Great patience and skill were needed to bag him—that and a $250,000 reward. In the end, his own daughter gave him up. He was not merely a crazy mad-dog bomber. As it turned out, he was also a member of the Disneyana Fan Club, an avid collector of all things Mickey. That alone was reason enough, the daughter would later insist, to drop a dime on Daddy. We helicoptered in on a moonless night and tracked him for almost a week before cornering him and two of his lieutenants in a wadi southeast of nowhere. When they tried to run, we shot all three with Kalashnikovs to make it look like the handiwork of local warlords. We photographed and fingerprinted the bodies to confirm their identities, then left them to rot in the sun.

The screen door swung open with a crash, disrupting my stroll down memory lane, as my landlady, Mrs. Schmulowitz, emerged from her modest 1920's bungalow, shuffling backward, all eighty-eight pounds of her, while struggling to balance an orange plastic tray with two glasses and what looked to be a pitcher of iced tea.

"Global warming, schmoble warming. This is nothing. Try August in Bensonhurst."

"Here, let me get that for you, Mrs. Schmulowitz."

I pocketed the photo as I bounded out of the hammock and steadied her by a bony elbow, commandeering the tray of drinks a half-second before she took a tumble.

"Always helpful Cordell, who never gives me trouble and pays his rent on time—and good-looking to boot," the old lady said, beaming at me. "You are one handsome man, you know that? The most handsome man I ever saw."

"You told me your first husband was the most handsome man you ever saw, Mrs. Schmulowitz."

"Don't get me started. My first husband, such a *shmendrick,* that man. A man more in love with a mirror you never saw in your life, may he rest in peace."

Mrs. Schmulowitz was pushing ninety and crooked like a question mark. Her sun-baked skin was the color and approximate texture of an apricot fruit roll. A retired elementary school gym teacher, she was the only octogenarian I ever saw whose preference in warm weather attire was Lycra bicycle shorts and a fire-engine red sports bra. Her hair was Einstein frizzy and thinning at the crown, but the years, so far as I could ever tell, had done nothing to dim her mind. Rhodes Scholars and stand-up comics only wished they were half as sharp as Mrs. Schmulowitz.

I carried the tray of drinks and set it down on a rusting wrought-iron patio table that could've stood a new coat of paint.

"Even money Tampa Bay chokes on Sunday," she said, pouring me a glass of iced tea. "Their passing game stinks, they can't stop the run, and that coach of theirs. They shouldn't fire him. They should *indict* him."

"Be honest, Mrs. Schmulowitz. New York could start Rudolf Hess at fullback and you'd still pull for the Giants."

"Hess? Hess was a *pitseleh,*" Mrs. Schmulowitz said. "Hermann Goering, now *there* was a fascist who had starting fullback written all over him." Gingerly, she lowered her arthritic back into a chair and exhaled, like air escaping a tire. "I'm making a nice brisket Monday night. With those green beans in the cream sauce you like—and, yes, I realize dairy with meat violates every kosher law in the book, but so does bacon and I think it goes without saying where we all stand on bacon, am I right? Anyway, you coming, yes or no? Be there or be square."

"Brisket? Green beans in cream sauce? Of course, I'm coming."

She double-clicked her dentures approvingly.

I'd signed the lease the previous summer after relocating to Rancho Bonita, where I'd vacationed one spring break in college and had wanted to live ever since. Every Monday night during football season, Mrs. Schmulowitz cooked me dinner. We'd sit together on a blue mohair sofa more shabby than chic, eating off of metal TV trays and watching the game on the world's only still-functioning black and white console television. Cocooned in a cabinet of real mahogany which she dusted every day, it was a twenty-one-inch Magnavox that took ten minutes to warm up and hummed like a transmission tower, drowning out the announcers. But Mrs. Schmulowitz never seemed to mind. She knew more about offense and defense then any announcer who ever lived. It was in her blood. Her uncle was Sid Luckman, the late great Jewish quarterback. Accordingly, Monday nights were spent with Mrs. Schmulowitz offering her own expert play-by-play commentary, when she was not speculating aloud as to whether certain players were members of her tribe based on the names stitched on the backs of their jerseys.

"What does it matter if they're Jewish," I'd say, "as long as they can play?"

"What does it matter? I'll tell you why it matters!" she'd respond, her voice rising with indignation. "It matters because the *goyim* of this world need to know that Jews can do more than balance the books and win Nobel prizes!"

Mrs. Schmulowitz sipped her iced tea. "So, no flying this afternoon?"

"Too hot to fly," I said, hoping I sounded convincing.

The old lady rubbed her eye, an unconscious gesture that suggested she doubted I was telling the truth. "You wanna talk hot? I'll tell you hot. Back in Brooklyn, we used to pour boiling coffee in our laps, just to cool off."

"Somehow, I doubt that, Mrs. Schmulowitz."

"Believe what you want, bubby. My third husband, he'd believe anything. Nothing but trouble, that man."

In the oak tree above us, Kiddiot uncurled his tongue like a roll of bubblegum and yawned.

"Listen, Bubeleh, tell me it's none of my business, but some kid came by today looking for you. Said he was from a collection agency. Tall, black, muscles out to here. I told him for his own good to get lost before I had my way with him."

"I'm having a few minor cash flow issues. Nothing to worry about. Business'll pick up."

Mrs. Schmulowitz reached over and patted my hand. "Of course it will. But, listen, if there's anything I can do between then and now, slip you a few bucks to tide you over, whatever, you give me the word, OK? Happy to help. And don't you worry none. I got more money than I know what to do with. My first husband, he saw to that, may he rest in peace."

I thanked her for her generosity and assured her that I was getting along just fine. Taking a handout from my landlady would have been about as low as I could go. I wasn't there. Yet.

⊙═╾╼═⊙

Kiddiot and I were napping on the hammock when my cell phone rang an hour later. He jumped off my chest and onto the grass while I groggily fished the phone out of my pants pocket. I was hoping it might be a new student or possibly a whale watching charter. Anything to generate a little income. It wasn't.

"My hot water heater just took a dump," Larry Kropf up at the airport said, "but I can't call a plumber. Wanna know why?"

"Well, your telephone's working, Larry, so I know *that's* not the reason."

"I can't call a plumber, smart ass, because I can't *afford* a plumber. The wife wants to run a load of clothes. The kid wants to take a shower. But they can't do either one because I got no hot water! So now I gotta replace the fucking heater myself and go to the plumbing supply place and buy all the fittings at least three times because nobody in the history of mankind has ever done a plumbing project without first getting the wrong parts at least twice. Plus, I gotta take time off from *making* money so I can *spend* money I ain't got! You know what I'm getting at here, Logan?"

"That retirement check's coming in any day, Larry, I promise."

"When're you gonna pay me what you owe me?"

"Soon as I can."

"What the hell does that mean?"

"It means have a little faith, Larry."

"Faith don't put food on the goddamn table!"

"Tell it to the Pope. You should see that guy's table."

"Sell the *Duck*."

"I sell my airplane, I'm out of business."

"You're out of business now! You got no students, Logan!"

I told him that running a flight school is a lot like fishing. Some days they're biting, some days they're not. Things could turn around for me tomorrow, I said. You just never know.

There was silence on the other end for a couple of seconds. Then Larry said, with more resignation than rage, "You got two weeks. Either you pay me what you owe me, in full, or you're out. You don't pack your shit up on your own, I call the sheriff and he packs it for you. I got other people interested in the space, Logan. Nothing personal. It's business. You understand."

"Yeah. I understand."

The line went dead.

The left side of my face burned from too much sun. The back of my head throbbed from too much Larry. For a moment, I considered taking Mrs. Schmulowitz up on her offer of a loan, just to tide me over. But the notion of it made my stomach spasm. I was forty-three, a divorced, dime-a-dozen flight instructor with a tired airplane and no students, sharing a converted garage with a cat that barely gave me the time of day. My life was in a flat spin.

I thought about calling around to some of my old superiors in the intelligence community. Maybe one of them might know of a job somewhere. After all, I'd left Alpha on good terms. Passed my psych evaluation on the way out with flying colors. My superior officers couldn't believe that anyone would ever willingly leave so coveted an assignment. I gave them some clichéd explanation about needing new challenges. In my resignation letter, I even managed to squeeze in a quote by Anaïs Nin that I remembered from my Academy days: "One does not discover new lands without consenting to lose sight of the shore." But the reality was, after a decade of covert ops, I was tired of all the secrecy and all the blood. I knew it was time to hang it up when I finally ran out of euphemisms to describe death in my after-action reports. You can write that the target was "voided" or "neutralized" only so many times before the words begin to lose their potency. Yet all of that only partly explained why I had wanted to move on. The demise of my marriage to Savannah also factored into my decision to quit. Echevarria, arguably my closest friend in Alpha, had stolen her from me while my fellow go-to guys did little more than watch. There's an old maxim among warriors: "Trust me with your life, never with your money or your wife." It was my fault, my brothers-in-arms reminded me: I'd been stupid enough to trust one of them.

I left Alpha angry. Six years later, I was still angry. But anger, like faith, as Larry reminded me, doesn't put chow on the table. His threat to kick me out of his hangar reinforced what should have been glaringly apparent to me long before: I needed a steady job.

I decided to head inside despite the heat and check the classifieds on Craigslist. I rolled out of the hammock and was bending down to strap on my sandals when my phone rang again.

FOUR

Gil Carlisle, my former father-in-law, had a West Texas drawl smooth enough you wanted to rub your cheek on it. He never raised his voice. He never had to. A self-made oil tycoon who had more money in the bank than some Third World countries, he almost always got what he wanted on his deceptive country-boy charm alone. And on those rare occasions when charm didn't do the trick, his platoon of $1,000-an-hour lawyers usually did.

"Bet you're wondering why I'm calling," Carlisle said over the phone.

"I know why you're calling, Gil."

Savannah had tried to get me to go to the police, to tell them what I knew about the real Arlo Echevarria. I knew when I said no she'd likely go sobbing to her daddy. Now daddy was calling, the master of silky persuasion, bent on convincing me to do what his daughter could not.

"You heard about Arlo, I take it?" he said.

"Savannah told me."

"A damn shame is what it is. I'll tell you what, Cordell, sometimes I just don't know what this world is coming to. I truly don't."

"It came to that a long time ago, Gil."

"Well, I suppose there's some truth to that, son."

The last time Gil Carlisle and I had spoken was when Savannah and I were lurching through the sudden death of our divorce. He'd called from his Lear jet en route to a business meeting somewhere in Europe to let me know how truly disappointed he was that things hadn't worked out between his daughter and me, and how he always genuinely appreciated having me as a son-in-law, even if he never did get around to inviting me to go dove hunting with him on his 3,000-acre spread outside Lubbock, what with his busy schedule and mine. Then he warned me, sweet as honey glaze on a side of mesquite barbequed beef, that if I ever tried to claim as community property so much as one thin dime of Savannah's trust fund, I'd find my ass in court faster than a three-legged sheep chased by a pack of coyotes. I told him I didn't give a shit about Savannah's money. He hung up without saying another word.

And now, here we were, years later, talking like all of it was water under the bridge.

"My little girl's hurtin', Cordell," he said. "Nothing worse on this earth than for a father to see his baby girl in pain. Rips your guts up. You'll do anything to stop that kinda pain. I mean, *any*thing."

Mrs. Schmulowitz emerged from her house lugging a galvanized watering can and began dousing the pots of pink geraniums that lined her back porch. I shifted the phone to my other ear and kept an eye on her to make sure she didn't fall off the top step.

"I'd appreciate you talking to the police, telling 'em what you know," Carlisle said.

"There's nothing I can tell them they don't already know, Gil."

"Savannah tells me otherwise."

"Savannah's mistaken."

There was a pause. Then Carlisle said, "Listen, Cordell, if I've learned one thing thirty years rootin' around out in the patch, making hole, it's that there's never been a sticky situation that couldn't be unstuck. How much we talkin' 'bout here?"

"Are you offering me a bribe, Gil?"

"I'm trying to pay you for your valuable time, you stubborn donkey, is what I'm trying to do! Hell, I'll have the money wired direct to your bank account if that's what you want. All you gotta do is go talk to the police. An hour out of your day. That's it. Don't sound too sticky to me now, does it?"

"I'm not interested in your money, Gil."

"Well, then hell, hoss," he laughed, "you're the only one."

I was certain he'd checked out my credit report before calling. He knew damn well I was interested in his money. Given my financial straits, I was interested in just about anybody's money. With the possible exception of Mrs. Schmulowitz's.

"OK, here's the deal," Carlisle said, "I'm flying out to El Molino tonight for a business meeting. I'd sure like it if you could find the time to come on up a spell. We could do breakfast, pow-wow this thing. There's a little café right there at the airport. Food's real tasty. Ate there awhile back."

"I'm not much of a breakfast eater," I said.

"All right. Lunch, then."

"It's a long way to go for lunch, Gil."

"Not for a crackerjack pilot who's got his own airplane."

My head ran through everything I had to do tomorrow: Get up. Look for a job without success. Sink deeper into depression.

"Unfortunately," I said, "I'm pretty booked tomorrow."

"Well, I don't doubt it, a man of your many talents. Look, Cordell, I'm just gonna cut right to the chase. How does twenty-five grand sound? You fly up to El Molino in that little ol' plane of yours, enjoy a nice meal on yours truly, you're back home come siesta time. No strings attached."

Twenty-five grand. With no strings attached. I could pay off Larry and still have enough left over to cover the engine overhaul on the *Duck*.

"C'mon, hoss," Gil Carlisle said, his voice as silky as a Texas waltz, "you got nothin' to lose. What do you say?"

I said, "I'll see you around eleven-thirty."

I rolled out of bed early the next morning and straight into my patented, ten-minute exercise routine. Push-ups, reverse push-ups, crunches, lower back spasms, quit. Endorphin rush is a cruel hoax. Anyone who's ever played contact sports at the collegiate level can attest to that in later life. Aerobic exertion is nothing more than pain heaped atop pain. The only relief comes when you're finally done with abusing your musculoskeletal for the day. Which I more than was.

I stood up and stretched my aching lumbar. A lizard skittered past me and disappeared under the deco pink Frigidaire that came with the apartment. Kiddiot liked bringing in lizards to play with them. The only problem was, after awhile, he'd get bored and go back outside to take a nap or a sunbath, while his reptilian friends invariably found their way under the refrigerator. I used to pull the fridge out from the wall to set them free. But they didn't want freedom. They would go scurrying from under the refrigerator to under the matching pink stove to die there. Or under the bed to die there. Or under my pressboard, ready-to-assemble Ikea nightstand or dresser. Or under the purple Naugahyde couch that Mrs. Schmulowitz picked up at a police auction ("Nobody else bid on it! Can you believe that?"). Sometimes, the lizards Kiddiot invited in even managed to die behind the molded, one-piece plastic shower stall in my "bathroom," which was really nothing more than a corner of the garage cordoned off by two flimsy stud walls covered with sheetrock. To make the garage feel bigger, Mrs. Schmulowitz had the entire place painted hospital ship white. To make it feel more homey, she'd put down braided rugs. Over the apartment's lone window, which afforded a picturesque view of the alley, she'd hung frilly gingham curtains, more suited to a little girl's room. The cumulative effect did little to obscure the fact that the place was still a garage. But what the hell. It kept the rain off my head on those rare occasions when it rained in Rancho Bonita. Plus, at $750 a month, including utilities and high-speed internet service for my laptop, it was a relative steal by local standards. Throw in the free brisket dinner every Monday night during football season, and I had no complaints.

After showering and shaving, I pulled on a pair of Levi's and laced up my good Nikes. Hanging next to the stove in the freestanding metal locker that served as my closet were a half-dozen clean shirts. I picked a short-sleeve blue polo. Silk-screened on the breast was the "Above the Clouds Flight Academy" logo, and the silhouette of a high-wing Cessna. Some people said the plane looked like it was flying toward the sunset. Others said it was flying toward a sunrise. It all depended on whether you were a glass half-full or half-empty kind of person, I suppose. Stitched in cursive script below the airplane logo was the self-anointed title, "Chief Flight Instructor." Talk about delusions of grandeur.

My review of job listings on Craigslist the night before had yielded no viable prospects. I walked through the backyard, down along the left side of Mrs. Schmulowitz's house, through the gate of her picket fence, and fetched the morning paper from her lawn to review what few help wanted ads there were—a last-ditch attempt to hopefully find a job opportunity that would give me the legitimate excuse not to fly up to El Molino and accept a handout from my former father-in-law.

City of Rancho Bonita seeks Animal Control Officer. Hell, I can't even control an intellectually challenged cat. How could I possibly be expected to arm wrestle possums?

Grassroots Environmental group looking for organizers to help save endangered forests. Yeah, right. Let's cut down a bunch of trees and grind them into newsprint so we can get the word out about saving the ecosystem.

Couple seeking private chef to prepare fresh, organic meals 3 to 5 nights per week. Forget it. I'm a cook whose idea of an oven timer is a smoke detector.

After three minutes of scanning the want ads, I concluded that there were no jobs to be found in the greater Rancho Bonita area that required my skills, such as they were. I refolded the newspaper, quietly propped it against Mrs. Schmulowitz's door, and walked back to the garage.

Kiddiot was lounging out on top of the pink refrigerator like the Great Sphinx of Giza. The tip of his tail swayed back and forth, over the edge of the freezer. His eyes were closed, but I knew he was only pretending to be asleep, the way cats do.

I washed the day-old "Savory Turkey Platter" out of his bowl, of which he hadn't eaten a bite, and replaced it with a fresh can of "Tender Ocean Whitefish and Tuna in Delectable Juices." I set the food bowl down on the floor near the kitchen sink and waited for him to make his move. He got up, took his time stretching, and hopped onto the sink, then down, onto the floor. He approached his food bowl warily, like it was hiding an improvised explosive device. He sniffed the bowl from a foot away, flicked his tail a couple of times, leaped back on top of the counter, then up onto the refrigerator.

A wise man said once that the purpose of cats is to remind man that not everything in life has a purpose. He was wrong, at least so far as Kiddiot was concerned. Kiddiot's purpose was to remind me that friends and wives may come and go, but furry, antisocial mooches never leave.

"Anybody ever tell you you're less than worthless?"

Kiddiot bathed himself with his tongue and ignored me like some sort of lesser life form. I turned on the TV and dialed in *Animal Planet* so he could watch his favorite shows, grabbed my blue, sweat-stained Air Force Academy ball cap off a hook on the back of the door, and drove to the airport.

El Molino is up the coast and inland from Rancho Bonita. As the crow flies, it's about 115 miles. As a Cessna 172 flies, depending on winds aloft, the trip normally takes about an hour—the operative word being "normally." That morning, the winds came screaming out of the north, bucking my little airplane all over the sky, while reducing my ground speed at times to less than fifty knots. On Highway 101, 6,500 feet beneath the *Duck*'s wings, I watched cars passing me like I was standing still.

Bumpy air and pathetic ground speed aside, the extra time gave me an opportunity to think. I'd had a restless night, what with the heat and Savannah's unexpected intrusion in my life. The wee hours had been spent sweating atop the sheets and staring up at the ceiling, with memories of her coursing through my head, the soundtrack of my insomnia, an old Bob Dylan tune about switching off your emotions to cope with the loss of that special someone forever embedded on your brain.

The Buddha teaches that suffering is the essence of life, that desire is the root cause of that suffering. Get rid of that which you desire and you get rid of the suffering. Easy. And yet, as I fought the wind on my way toward El Molino that morning, I realized my desire for Savannah had never left me. I'd just learned to turn it off.

The coastal mountains north of Rancho Bonita gave way to the Agua Caliente Valley, a loose patchwork of gentle hills studded with stands of oaks and vineyards. After about fifteen minutes, Rancho Bonita Departure handed me off to Oakland Center, followed by several minutes of silence on the airwaves. I checked in to make sure the *Duck's* radios were still working.

"Oakland Center, Cessna Four Charlie Lima, how do you hear?"

"Loud and clear."

All was quiet because nobody else was stupid enough to be out flying. The high winds had grounded every other private pilot in the region. Half an hour later, I radioed Oakland to report that I had the El Molino airport in sight, fifteen miles off the nose of the plane.

"Four Charlie Lima, roger. El Molino altimeter two niner niner seven. Radar service terminated. Squawk VFR. Frequency change approved."

"Thanks for the help. Four Charlie Lima."

I switched over to the number-one radio to listen to the automated weather recording at the El Molino airport. The winds were 330 degrees at twenty-eight knots, gusting to thirty-five. On my number-two radio, I dialed in the airport's common traffic area frequency to listen for other airplanes coming or going. There were none. At seven miles out, I keyed the push-to-talk mic button on my yoke.

"El Molino traffic, Skyhawk Four Charlie Lima, seven miles south of the field at 4,500 feet descending, landing Runway Thirty-One, El Molino."

I eased back on the throttle and thumbed in a little forward trim to set up a 700 feet-per-minute descent, keeping Runway Thirty-One centered on the *Duck's* nose. Off my left wingtip, about five miles away, was the tourist-friendly burg of El Molino, population 29,000, whose founding fathers made their fortunes selling tourists on the medicinal virtues of soaking in El Molino's many hot springs and mud baths. More than a century later, with nearly 170 mostly ridiculously overpriced wineries and tasting rooms, the tourists were still being soaked.

The turbulence was severe enough that I twice smacked the top of my head on the cabin roof as I made my approach into the airport. Descending through 2,000 feet, I nearly collided with a seagull. He flashed below the *Duck's* left wing close enough that I could make out the red dot at the end of his beak.

By the time I dropped down to pattern altitude, the air had tamed somewhat. The orange wind sock was standing straight out, angled off the runway by about twenty degrees. Turning final, I held my right wingtip into the wind and touched down on my upwind wheel first. A textbook crosswind landing if I do say so myself. I glanced at the clock on the instrument panel as I rolled out. It was almost twelve-thirty—nearly an hour late to my meeting with Gilbert Carlisle, thanks to Mother Nature. Nothing I could do about it now. He'd either be there or he wouldn't.

There were abundant parking spaces across from the main terminal where the restaurant was located. The *Duck*, in fact, was the only plane on the ramp. I slid the gust lock into the control column on the pilot's side, secured the nose wheel with the aluminum travel chocks I keep in the baggage compartment, and secured the tie-down chains on the underside of both wings as tight as they would go. I made sure the door was good and locked, then made for the terminal.

The tarmac was like a wind tunnel. I leaned into the blow, head down, holding onto my ball cap. My eyes burned from the gale-force winds. My shirtsleeves flapped hard against my arms. As I got closer to the terminal, I could see a man in Wrangler jeans, a blue-checked cowboy shirt with pearl snaps, and ostrich skin cowboy boots holding open the door for me.

"Get on in here before you get blowed into another area code," Gil Carlisle said with a broad grin.

We shook hands as I slid past him into the terminal.

"I was starting to get a little worried," he said.

"Wind held me up. Sorry for the inconvenience."

"Hell, I'm just glad you could make it."

Standing protectively close beside him was a tall, muscular Latino in his mid-thirties. Gray slacks, white shirt, the frigid scowl of an on-duty Secret Service agent. The grip of what looked like a .40-caliber Glock pistol dangled from a shoulder holster under his left arm.

"This is Frank," Carlisle said.

"Since when did you start needing a bodyguard, Gil?"

"World's an increasingly dangerous place, hoss. A little precaution never hurt anybody."

Frank started to pat me down. Carlisle told him it wasn't necessary.

"This is my former son-in-law," he said. "I trust him implicitly."

My former father-in-law was a stocky man with thick lips. He was all but bald the last time I saw him. But where there was once shiny pate was now a forest of luxuriant curls the color of milk chocolate, with nary a trace of gray. Carlisle noticed me noticing.

"Four bucks a graft," he said proudly. "Hell, I could've damn near bought another island in the Caribbean for what the new hair ended up setting me back. I didn't want to get 'em, but the new honey, she insisted, bless her heart. That's the risk you take, datin' a showgirl young enough to be your grandbaby."

"Another risk is dying of a massive coronary."

Gil Carlisle laughed and bear-hugged me. "It's just damn good to see you, son. Been way too long. Hope you came hungry."

Frank the bodyguard took up his station at the entrance of the restaurant while Carlisle led me inside. The aromas were mouthwatering. Not a whiff of burning grease like most rural airport cafés, where the menus feature dishes like "Takeoff Tacos" and "The Barnstormer" burger. The restaurant at the El Molino airport caters to gourmands regardless of their interest in aviation. The kind of place that serves up lamb noisette in a blackberry reduction sauce and Peking duck breast seared rare at thirty bucks a plate. Small and intimate, with its tablecloths and pumpkin-colored walls, the restaurant looks like it belongs on Union Square in San Francisco or overlooking Rodeo Drive, not beside some windswept runway in the middle of farm fields.

"Truth be told," Carlisle said over his shoulder as I followed him, "it's good you showed up a little late. We were just wrapping up our meeting." He led me to a large round table where three men were eating lunch. "Gentlemen, I want y'all to say howdy to Mr. Cordell Logan. Used to be hitched to my daughter."

Carlisle introduced the man nearest me as Miles Zambelli, his executive assistant and chief financial advisor. Zambelli was in his early thirties. Mediterranean handsome, he wore fancy jeans and a black-striped, untucked dress shirt, tasseled loafers, rimless eyeglasses and a vague air of entitlement. He remained seated as introductions were made, eating and taking notes on a yellow legal pad, while shaking my outstretched hand with all the enthusiasm of a teenager forced to wash the dishes. His gold class ring bore the Harvard coat of arms, which explained a lot.

The others at the table stood respectfully to greet me as I approached. The taller of the two was decked out in beige golf pants and a pale yellow golf shirt, one of those fair-skinned, angularly athletic, mixed-race chaps who look good wearing anything. He was about thirty.

"Say hello to Lamont Royale," Carlisle said. "Mr. Royale's my right-hand man. Does my driving, helps me with my golf game and handles the cooking. Hell, if he didn't have a damn dick, I'd marry the son of a bitch."

"Call me Lamont, please," Royale said, shaking my hand.

"Lamont it is."

The other man Carlisle introduced as Pavel Tarasov, "oil broker extraordinaire."

"Cordell Logan," I said, "oil consumer."

He parted his jaws, displaying a set of teeth so white against his tanned face that my eyes hurt just looking at them. I wasn't sure if he was smiling or planning to bite me.

"I like this guy," Tarasov said, gripping my hand firmly and a little too long, his accent faintly Russian. He had dark, intelligent eyes and black, well-barbered hair. His grooming, tailored business suit, and the $20,000 Rolex lashed to his left wrist advertised a man of assets and taste. Only his hands, meaty and speckled with scar tissue, seemed out of character with the rest of him. The kind of hands more familiar with physical labor than laboring behind a desk. Hands that had no business protruding from the starched sleeves of a white dress shirt with French cuffs and blue garnet cuff links.

An attentive waiter whose name-tag identified him as "Steve" slid a chair over for me from another table without being asked and waited for us to settle.

"Gentlemen," Carlisle said, gesturing.

We sat.

Steve the waiter handed me a menu and asked if I'd like something to drink. The others were sharing a bottle of red wine. I myself was in a vodka martini mood. Chilled. With two fat Spanish olives. Then I remembered that I still had to fly myself home. Then I remembered that I don't drink. I hadn't touched a drop of liquor in seven years, ever since I'd quit working for the government.

"I'll take an Arnie."

"One Arnold Palmer, coming up," Steve said, and left to go fetch my drink.

"Mr. Carlisle tells me you are crackerjack instructor pilot," Tarasov said pleasantly.

"It keeps me off the streets."

"When I was boy, I dreamed to fly fighter jets. The MiG, yes? But my marks in school, they were, how do you say, shit? My father, he makes with his hands the chairs, tables. Anything you want, he can make. He teaches me how to use the tools, cutting the wood. Rich people, they *love* my furniture. I sell to Princess Diana armoire. Chest of drawers to king of Saudi Arabia."

"Not to brag, but I'm somewhat the fine furniture maker myself."

"Truly?"

"Let's just say they know me on a first-name basis at a certain Swedish furniture warehouse where, by the way, the meatballs and lingonberries are delicious."

Lamonte Royale laughed. No one else got the joke.

"So," I said to Tarasov, "what brings you to California?"

"Grapes," Tarasov said, refilling his wine glass.

"Mr. Tarasov is thinking about acquiring a few vineyards," Carlisle said. "He flew in to look over some properties. We decided El Molino would be mutually convenient for us to get together and hash out strategy on another little venture we're considering partnering up on." Carlisle leaned in close to me, his elbows on the table, his voice decidedly lower. "You ever hear of the Kashagan oil field?"

I hadn't.

"In Kazakhstan, the Caspian Sea," he said. "Supposed to be the biggest find in fifty years."

"A *hundred* years," Zambelli said.

"The biggest find in history," Tarasov said. "All we need are a few more investors, and the controlling share will be ours."

Steve the waiter ferried my lemonade-iced tea to the table and set it down on a paper coaster. "Have you had a chance to decide?"

I pointed to what Zambelli was eating. "I'll try some of that."

"Pistachio-encrusted halibut," Steve said. "Excellent choice."

Carlisle waited until he moved off, then leaned in once more and said, "If that field comes in the way our geologists think it will, even the smallest fractional owner'll be a billionaire. It'll make Bill Gates look like a hobo."

"I'm obviously in the wrong line of work," I said, only half-kidding.

"Hell, that's what I told my daughter when she married you," Carlisle said, chuckling.

"What did you tell her when she married Echevarria?"

Carlisle's smile melted. "I like you, Cordell. Always have. The day you and Savannah parted ways, I'll tell you what, the two of us cried our eyes out like babies."

I sipped my drink. If my former father-in-law was ill at ease revealing such personal intimacies in front of a potential business partner, he didn't show it. Nor did they. It was Zambelli who seemed most uncomfortable with his boss's candor.

"Mr. Carlisle," he said, clearing his throat, "I suggest such matters might be better discussed between you and Mr. Logan in a more private setting."

"I got nothing to hide from this man," Carlisle said, gesturing to Tarasov. "If we're gonna be in business together, he needs to know who I am and where I'm coming from. What you see is what you get. No more, no less."

"Honesty in all endeavors," Tarasov said.

Carlisle told him how the second husband of his daughter Savannah had died tragically in Los Angeles at the hands of a killer unknown. The case remained unsolved. He said he hoped to persuade Savannah's first husband, namely me, to pass along any relevant information about Echevarria to the police, given that I had once worked for Echevarria in marketing. Carlisle said he was confident my help could make all the difference in the police solving the case.

"To truth and justice," Tarasov said, hoisting his wine goblet.

"And the American way," Lamont Royale added with a smile.

"Like Superman," Tarasov said, impressed with himself that he actually got the joke.

They all clinked goblets.

"Truth, justice, and the American way," I said, tepidly raising my glass.

I glanced over at Zambelli. His eyes never left his plate.

FIVE

I lifted off from El Molino that afternoon with a bellyful of halibut and $25,000 in my pocket, drawn on Gilbert Carlisle's personal account at the Bank of Bimini. The money had come with one stipulation: Savannah was never to know that her father had paid me to talk to the police. I was to tell her only that I'd had a change of heart and decided to cooperate with the authorities because I realized it was the right thing to do. Or some such nonsense. Carlisle was so confident I would take his money that he'd had the cashier's check drafted the day before we met, according to the bank time stamp on the stub.

If the LAPD knew that I'd been paid to enlighten them about what Echevarria once did for a living, they would likely dismiss my information as less than objective. Carlisle didn't want that. Neither did I. Much as I hated to admit it, I was becoming increasingly curious about who might've murdered my former co-worker and romantic rival.

The list of suspects would've easily stretched around the block. War criminals. Cocaine kingpins. Serial killers. Traitors. Terrorists. The ones who got away. Survivors of the ones who didn't. All would've had good reason to kill Echevarria, or any other former go-to guy. The problem was, they would've had to know his real name to find him. We always used aliases in the field for that very reason. My gut told me that Echevarria's death had nothing to do with his having once worked for the government. But I wasn't being paid to play Sam Spade. I was being paid to make my ex-wife and her father happy. For $25,000, considering the delicate state of my personal finances, I'd make sure both were ecstatic.

The headwinds I fought flying north to see Carlisle shifted south and turned to quartering headwinds by the time I flew home. Typical. I climbed to 7,500 feet, then 9,500, then 11,500. There was little difference in the quality of the ride, nor in my ground speed. The air was churned up like white water on a river. I struggled to keep the *Duck* level and on course. By the time I landed back in Rancho Bonita, my arms felt heavy. The fingers of my left hand ached where I had gripped the yoke. I decided that whoever it was at Cessna who ruled out wing-leveling autopilots as standard equipment on 172's should come back in the next life as a fruit fly. Not a very Zen-like thought, I realized, but if the Buddha held a pilot's certificate, I knew he'd feel the same way.

I tied down the airplane, got in my truck and hit the freeway, driving south toward Rancho Bonita. Twelve minutes later, I was sitting in the Bank of America parking lot downtown, staring at a $25,000 cashier's check and wrestling anew with my conscience, wondering what I was doing even *thinking* about depositing Carlisle's bribe money. My phone rang. It was Savannah.

"I wanted to apologize for my behavior yesterday," she said. "Showing up unannounced. Some of the things I said. I guess I just wasn't thinking."

"Heat of the moment."

"Still no excuse."

I was quiet.

"Well, anyway," Savannah said, "I just wanted to say how sorry I was, barging into your life like that. I won't ever bother you again."

"Is that a promise or a threat?"

"It's whatever you want it to be."

I pondered the check in my hand, tapping it against the steering wheel.

"I always thought we had something, Logan," Savannah said, "but after awhile, you were never around to appreciate it. You were always gone. You don't water a flower, it dies. You stopped being there for me. Arlo was."

"I stopped being there because Arlo sent me off on business assignments while he took care of business at home. You ever stop to think about that?"

She was quiet.

"Did you love him?"

"I suppose you could call it that."

"Like you loved me?"

There was silence for what seemed like a long time. Then she said, "No. Not like I loved you."

A sea green Buick Skylark pulled in beside me. An ancient old man wearing one of those white Navy "skipper" caps with gold scrambled eggs on the bill, the kind of hats sailboat owners put on when they want to look especially goofy, got out and hobbled around to open the door for his passenger, an old lady wearing an identical hat. She kissed his hand while he tenderly helped her out of the Buick. Who says there's no such thing as eternal domestic bliss? I couldn't help it; I sighed like a schoolgirl.

"You'll be watching movies on Lifetime before long," I mumbled to myself.

"Did you say something?"

"Yeah. I said I need my head examined."

Any man with an ounce of self-respect would've ripped the check in half, hung up, and moved on with his life. But no man with an ounce of brains would've ever surrendered Savannah Carlisle as easily as I did. Maybe this was a way back to her. Even if it wasn't, it was still twenty-five large.

"I need the number for the detectives handling the case," I said.

"You'll call them? Really?"

"You said you wanted me to talk to them. I'll talk to them."

"Oh, Logan, that's fantastic!" The delight in Savannah's voice was genuine. "What made you change your mind?"

I watched Methuselah and his bride hobble arm-in-arm into the bank. She was leaning her head on his shoulder.

"Just give me the number," I said, "before I start heaving."

⊂━━◆━━⊃

The lead investigator in Echevarria's homicide answered his phone at the Los Angeles Police Department's Devonshire station on the first ring.

"Detective Czarnek."

Gravelly baritone. Smoker. He sounded world-weary and bad-ass. Somebody in the background was singing "Girl Watcher" by the O'Kaysions. I could hear others laughing. I identified myself and explained why I was calling. It took him a second to connect the dots.

"Which case was it again?"

"Arlo Echevarria."

"Echevarria, Echevarria." I heard a drawer slide open and the sound of files being gone through. "Echevarria, Echevarria. Oh, yeah, right. Echevarria, Arlo. And you say you're who again?"

I repeated my name. I told him that I was calling from Rancho Bonita, but that I'd be happy to drive to Los Angeles to meet with him at his convenience, to provide whatever information I could.

"You say you're up in Rancho Bonita?"

"That's what I said."

"Nice town if you can afford it."

"Tell me about it."

"Well, I tell you what, Mr.—what'd you say your name was again?"

"Logan."

"Mr. Logan, I wouldn't mind taking a little drive up the coast and come see you. Give my partner and me an excuse to breathe some air we can't actually see for a change."

"OK by me."

"There's a little Mexican place up your way I've eaten at— El Grande's," Czarnek said. "Best tortas this side of Ensenada. I believe the city of Los Angeles can afford to spring for lunch. What's tomorrow looking like for you?"

El Grande Taqueria is an anonymous, green and white taco shack on the working class, lower east side of Rancho Bonita, an eatery with undersized, overpriced servings and no atmosphere— unless you count the beer trucks and lowriders rumbling past out-side. You order your food at one window and pick it up at another. Hardly haute cuisine, but more than a few aficionados swear by the place. Half a dozen Mexican joints on Verde Street offered tastier chow in larger portions and at lower prices. But if the good tax-payers of Los Angeles were willing to spring for lunch, who was I to play enchilada snob? Two free meals in two days. An underem-ployed flight instructor could get used to that kind of treatment.

"Tomorrow's good," I said.

"Eleven o'clock?"

"A little early for Mexican food, isn't it?"

"We like to start early around here," Czarnek said. "Beat the traffic that way."

Whoever it was who was singing in the background was now joined by what sounded like at least two other male voices. The tune had changed. It was now Paul Anka's "(You're) Having My Baby." A man singing about the wonderment of pregnancy. Listening to it felt like the lyrical equivalent of being water-boarded. I told Czarnek I'd see him at eleven and signed off.

After that, I went inside the bank and deposited Gil Carlisle's check.

<hr />

LAPD homicide Detective Keith Czarnek was not what I imag-ined over the phone. He was about fifty and built like a pear. Pink cheeks. Pudgy hands. Receding blonde hair and a high forehead that was beaded with sweat and precancerous skin lesions. Except for the faded Marine Corps eagle, globe and anchor tattooed on his left forearm, and the requisite push-broom cop moustache insu-lating his top lip, there was nothing badass about the man.

"I'd mainline this stuff if I could," Czarnek said as he spooned salsa onto his torta.

"Face it," said Czarnek's partner, Detective John Windhauser, working on his fourth fish taco, "you're a beaner food addict."

We were sitting on molded white plastic chairs, around a molded plastic table. El Grande Taqueria was mobbed as usual. It was approximately 140 degrees in the shade of the restaurant's cor-rugated plastic awning. I picked at a cheese enchilada that had coagulated on my plate into a formless red and yellow blob.

"So," Windhauser said, low enough so the diners around us couldn't hear, "Mr. Echevarria was shot almost a month ago. How is it you decide to contact us only now?"

"I only heard about it a few days ago," I said.

Windhauser nodded a little too empathetically. He had a snowy crew cut and a cleft chin, and his face looked like Verdun, pock-marked and ravaged by the acne he'd evidently suffered as a teen-ager some five decades earlier. He wore pleated Dockers khakis and soft-soled black walking shoes and, like Czarnek, a short-sleeved, light-blue dress shirt. Windhauser's tie was red paisley. Czarnek's tie was one of those brown knit jobs with a square bottom, the kind popular back when Eisenhower was in the White House. Czarnek's gold tie bar said "187"—California penal code for homicide. Wind-hauser's tie tack was a set of tiny dangling handcuffs. Both detec-tives had removed their winter-weight wool sport coats and slung them over their seat backs as a concession to the merciless autumn heat. Other diners tried not to stare at the badge and Kimber .45-caliber pistol clipped to each of their belts.

"You can't find food like this in LA. This stuff's *authentico*," Czarnek said, mopping up chili sauce with a piece of tortilla. Drops of sweat fell from his face onto his plate.

"Got some salsa on your tie," Windhauser advised his partner.

"Look who's talking."

Windhauser looked down and held up his own tie for closer inspection. "Fuck." He dipped his paper napkin in his water glass and scrubbed the stain clean.

Neither cop seemed particularly eager to discuss Echevarria's murder. I didn't push it. We ate and talked mostly about flying. Windhauser boasted of having served two tours as a door gunner on a Huey in Vietnam. Czarnek confided that he got airsick riding the flying Dumbos at Disneyland. Their approach was straight from the Big Book of Standard Police Interrogation Techniques. Take your time. Build rapport. Put the interview subject at ease before you start jamming him. They smiled openly, their torsos and feet pointed toward me. Their rate of speech, vocal tone, the size and number of their gestures, all mirrored mine. The subliminal message they were trying to send was, "We like you. You should trust us." Both detectives were playing good cop. I wondered how long and which one would turn bad first. My money was on Windhauser. He had a tough time not narrowing his eyes when he looked at me.

"Must be nice, having your own airplane," Czarnek said, sipping iced *horchata* through a straw.

"The *Ruptured Duck*'s a good bird—aside from the fact that something's always breaking. That's what happens when you get old and crotchety."

"The *Ruptured Duck*. What kind of name is that?'" Windhauser asked.

"Everybody getting out of the service at the end of World War Two was supposed to wear a temporary insignia on their uniforms to let the military police know they'd been honorably discharged and weren't AWOL. The insignia was intended to look like an eagle inside a wreath. Only everybody decided that the eagle looked more like a duck. Some wiseacre said it looked like a 'ruptured duck.' The name stuck."

"So you went with it," Czarnek said.

"I would've gone with Tweetie, but it was already taken."

Czarnek smiled. Windhauser wiped his mouth, wadded his paper napkin, and tossed it on his plate. Then he sucked down some Diet Pepsi. Czarnek sniffed audibly and cleared his throat. The prearranged signal. Time to get down to police business.

"So, Mr. Logan," Windhauser said, "you say you knew Mr. Echevarria how?"

"We hunted terrorists together and usually killed them."

The two LAPD detectives glanced at each other, then at me.

"You wanna run that one by us again?" Czarnek said.

I told them how Echevarria and I had been assigned to a top-secret team of government assassins tasked in the wake of September 11th with terminating individuals across the globe who had been deemed threats to the homeland. I even used the term, "extreme prejudice." I explained how our rules of engagement dictated that there were no rules of engagement. I told them how we operated with clear understanding that if any of us were ever captured by hostile forces, the Secretary truly would disavow any knowledge of our activities. I explained that there was no shortage of evil people around the globe who would've loved to murder Echevarria, but that they were all on the run, or hunkered down overseas in remote rat holes like the tribal belt between Pakistan and Afghanistan, pursued relentlessly by counterterrorist forces and unable to take a decent dump in peace, let alone locate and murder a retired go-to guy living in anonymous obscurity in the San Fernando Valley. Yes, I told the two LAPD detectives, I knew it all sounded like so much made-up Hollywood, Mission Impossible guano, but there it was. The straight poop on Arlo Echevarria. They could do with the information as they wished, I said. I didn't care one way or the other.

Czarnek and Windhauser studied me. They looked at each other. Then they both started laughing.

"Oh, man," Czarnek said, dabbing at the corners of his eyes, "that is some wicked good shit."

"Extreme prejudice," Windhauser said, mimicking me between spasms. "Christ."

They had responded in the very manner I had anticipated, with disbelief. Everybody lies to the police. Cops hear crazy crap all the time from people they're sworn to protect as well as those they get paid to arrest: the CIA planted a chip in my head and is controlling my thoughts; Martians are living in my attic; the devil made me do it. But the "I Was a Paid Assassin for the Government" spiel, that was a new one.

Windhauser's laughter tapered to a cold smile. He fixed me with an iron stare meant to intimidate. "Some little hottie down at the beach you're trying to hit on, she might fall for that crock of shit. But you're not talking to *her* now, are you?"

"Could be little hotties down at the beach aren't necessarily my cup of tea if you get my drift, Detective, and I think you do." I winked at him provocatively.

Windhauser's smile departed altogether.

"If you think I'm gay," he said, "you're mistaken."

"Nothing wrong with being gay," I said. "Plenty of people are gay. They come out of the closet all the time. Even homicide cops."

Windhauser gripped the arms of his chair, his blood pressure twenty points higher than it was a minute before. He looked over at his partner and said, "Who the fuck does this asshole think he is?"

Czarnek unwrapped a piece of Nicorette White Ice Mint gum, watching me.

"We just want the truth, Mr. Logan," he said.

"I told you the truth."

Windhauser said, "I can't fucking believe we drove all the way up here to talk to this lying lump of shit."

"Be honest, Detective," I said, "you drove all the way up here for the tacos."

Windhauser glowered. A V-shaped vein rose in the middle of his forehead and throbbed noticeably.

"We talked to Mr. Echevarria's wife," Czarnek said. "She told us he worked for the federal government. But we can't find any record of that."

"You won't. Our operations were classified."

Windhauser got to his feet suddenly, like he wanted to lay hands on me. His plastic chair clattered onto its side. Other diners paused and looked over to see what the commotion was about. The restaurant fell silent.

"C'mon, partner, let's get out of here," Windhauser said, grabbing his jacket off the floor. "This guy's fucking nuts."

Czarnek stayed put, eyeing me. "Mrs. Echevarria told us she used to be your wife."

"She was. I never knew what true happiness was until we got married. Then it was too late."

"Why'd you break up, you don't mind me asking?"

"She dumped me."

"Why?" Windhauser demanded

"Because she fell in love with Echevarria."

Czarnek stopped chewing his gum. The detectives traded another look. Windhauser righted his chair and lowered himself into it.

"How exactly would you describe your relationship with your ex-wife?" Windhauser said.

"Strained."

"What about with Mr. Echevarria?" Czarnek said. "What kind of relationship did you have with him?"

"We had no relationship. Not after what he did to me."

"So, what you're saying is, the two of you stopped being friends after your wife left you for him. Is that what you're saying?"

I didn't say anything. I could see where this was going.

Czarnek reached into the breast pocket of his sport coat and got out a reporter's notebook. He flipped through the narrow pages to find where he'd jotted down the date of Echevarria's murder— October 24th. He asked me if I remembered what I was doing that night.

"It was a Monday," Czarnek added.

"I would've been watching football."

"By yourself?"

"With my landlady."

"How can you be so sure?"

"She makes me dinner every Monday night during football season. We always watch the game together."

"You two ever get it on?" Windhauser said. "Maybe at halftime?"

Another tactic from the Big Book of Standard Police Interrogation Techniques: Bad Cop periodically lets fly an outrageous accusation intended to infuriate the suspect who comes unglued and, in his unbridled anger, blurts the truth of his crime.

"My landlady is in her eighties," I said. "She only goes for old guys, Detective Windhauser. Like you."

Windhauser glared. His partner stifled a smile.

"You pretty sure she can vouch for your whereabouts that evening?" Czarnek asked.

"You'll have to ask her that."

"We intend to," Windhauser said.

The detectives were staring at me in a new light, a light that told me even though I was the one who'd called them, I was now suspect *numero uno* in the homicide of Arlo Echevarria.

Six

Inside the walled fortress that is America's intelligence community, analysts are trained to scientifically consider all possible explanations when trying to determine who bombed the jetliner or blew up the office tower. Unfortunately, intelligence analysts are human. Like all humans, they quickly form opinions as to guilt or innocence, then instinctively pursue the evidence that will buttress their preconceived beliefs. Evidence that conflicts with those preconceptions is commonly disregarded. Which is why we sometimes end up invading the wrong country.

Professionals in other occupations are no different. A patient complains of a stomachache. His doctor concludes that the patient must have indigestion or an ulcer because the last five patients he treated with similar symptoms had indigestion or an ulcer. The patient is sent home with antibiotics or a bottle of Tums and dies that night from a burst appendix. Two LAPD homicide detectives conclude that an ex-husband murdered the man his wife left him for because the detectives have investigated dozens of murders over the years and it is *always* the ex-husband or former boyfriend who did it.

Still, I walked out of El Grande Taqueria that day a free man. No handcuffs. No threats of, "We're going to have to take you down to the station for further questioning." Czarnek thanked me for agreeing to meet with them. He asked me if I would be willing to take a polygraph test at some point in the near future. I said I wouldn't mind at all. He said they'd be in touch and urged me to have a nice day, while Windhauser said nothing. I could tell by the way they watched me as I got in my truck, parked two spaces down from their unmarked Crown Vic, that it wouldn't matter whether I passed a lie-detector test or not. They'd already made up their minds about who murdered Arlo Echevarria. Like intelligence analysts, now all they had to do was make the pieces fit their puzzle.

I waited for a break in the traffic, then burned an illegal U-turn across three lanes of traffic while my new friends from the LAPD watched. I tossed them a casual wave and motored south on Verde Street, feeling a sense of relief. I'd done what my ex-wife wanted me to do, done what my ex-father-in-law had paid me to do. I'd told the police what I knew about the real Arlo Echevarria. If they didn't want to hear it, that was their problem. As far as I was concerned, I had fulfilled my end of the deal. I may still have been curious about who murdered Echevarria, but not so curious that I was willing to become more involved than I already was. Goddamn Savannah. I couldn't decide which I regretted more, cashing her father's check or not having been born rich.

She's nothing to you anymore, I told myself.

I almost believed it.

The light turned red at Federal Avenue, across the street from the old post office that was now a carpet showroom. A homeless guy was on the sidewalk out front, smoking a joint. Curled asleep beside him was a long, fat dog that looked like it had been assembled by committee. A hand-lettered cardboard sign was propped against the man's legs. It said, "Ninjas kidnapped my family. Need money for Kung Fu lessons." I tossed him a buck. Fair pay for a good laugh.

The light turned green. I hooked a right at the traffic circle and merged onto the freeway northbound, heading for the airport.

○══╪══○

Larry was sitting at a weathered picnic table in the shade behind his hangar, listening to Rush Limbaugh on a portable radio and eating his lunch—bologna and cheese sandwich, bag-o-chips and a Dr. Pepper. Larry had the same thing for lunch every day. Once, I heard him complain to his wife about the way she'd made his sandwich. "How many times I gotta tell ya," he seethed low into the phone, "you put the fuckin' cheese *between* the fuckin' slices of bologna." I believe it was the last sandwich she ever made him.

"I got your money," I said out the window as I pulled in and climbed out of my truck. "All of it."

"Call CNN," Larry said. "They're gonna definitely wanna break into regular programming for this."

"You know, Larry, for a comedian, you make a pretty piss-poor airplane mechanic."

I sat down opposite him at the picnic table and wrote out a check.

Larry picked crumbs out of his arm fur, watching me. "What'd you do, rob a bank or something?"

"Ex-father-in-law."

"You robbed your ex-father-in-law?"

"More or less."

I gave him the check. Larry folded it without looking at it and put it in his wallet.

"You been subleasing from me for, what, two years? That's the first time I've heard you say word one about family."

"He's not family."

"Used to be, though, right?" Larry said.

"How 'bout them Dodgers?" I said.

Larry grunted and finished his soda. My phone rang. The caller was male and foreign. His inflection was Spanish or Romanian, possibly Moldovan. Sort of like Dracula, only younger and hipper.

He said his name was Eugen Dragomir, and that he was a student at Cal State Rancho Bonita, whose campus was just up the road from the airport. The kid had seen my listing on Craigslist, he said, and was interested in learning to fly. Every other flight school between Camarillo and San Luis Obispo advertised online. Splashy, colorful web sites with animated graphics and streaming video testimonials from their many satisfied students. The fact that Dragomir could find no such web site for Above the Clouds Aviation, let alone any mention of it on Google, impressed him.

"Definitely old school," Dragomir said. "I want to learn from the best. Someone who knows what they're doing, who has been flying a long time."

"Well, as the old saying goes, there are old pilots and bold pilots," I said, trotting out the dustiest aphorism in the history of manned flight, "but there are no old, bold pilots."

He wanted to get started right away and said he could be by within the hour. I said my airplane and I would be ready.

Twenty minutes later, Eugen Dragomir rolled into Larry's hangar on a skateboard with a "Sex Wax" sticker on it. Gangly didn't begin to describe him. He was built like a 3-iron with a backpack and dark, Eastern European dreadlocks. He was wearing black Chuck Taylor high-tops, laces dragging on the ground, surfer shorts that came down below his knobby knees and a T-shirt with a visage of Bob Marley on his chest. A shark's tooth dangled from a leather strand looped around his pencil neck. He bobbed, swinging his spaghetti arms, as we strode out to the flight line. He was from Chisinau, the capital of Moldova, a fifth-year senior studying petrochemical engineering because that's what his petrochemical engineer father wanted.

"But I'm thinking of switching majors."

"To what?"

"Astronaut. I want to boldly go where no man has gone before."

"You mean, 'To boldly go where no *person* has gone before.' Space is a very politically correct place these days, Eugen."

He nodded like I was Confucius. He was all business, there to learn. I liked that.

I walked him through the preflight inspection, showing him how to check the *Duck's* control surfaces for loose rivets, climbing up on the wings to make sure there was adequate gas in the tanks, checking the oil, looking inside the engine compartment for anything that didn't look right, undoing the tie-down lines. He shadowed my every move, cocking his head as he listened, soaking it all in. When the walk-around was complete, I opened the left side door for him.

"Hop in."

"You want *me* to fly?"

"That's generally what pilots do."

"This is *sick!*"

After we got in and locked the doors, I explained engine-start procedures and let him do the starting. I demonstrated how to dial in the ATIS frequency for current conditions on the field, including winds, dew point and altimeter setting.

I changed frequencies to Clearance Delivery and let the controllers know who we were and where we wanted to fly.

"Good afternoon, Clearance," I said, "Skyhawk Four Charlie Lima."

"Skyhawk Four Charlie Lima, Rancho Bonita Clearance, good afternoon."

"Four Charlie Lima is a 172 slant uniform, northwest departure with information Yankee, 4,500 feet. We'll be doing some maneuvering outside the class delta. Request traffic advisories."

"Skyhawk Four Charlie Lima, on request."

We waited.

"Dude, this is, like, the baddest thing I've ever done in my life," Eugen said. "I mean, once I took my girlfriend to bungee jumping and she was all, 'I'm freaked,' and I was all—"

"Skyhawk Four Charlie Lima"—I held up my finger for Eugen to be quiet while the controller came back on the radio with our clearance—"expect Runway One-Seven left. Fly runway heading after departure. Maintain VFR at or below 1,500 feet. Expect own navigation within three minutes. Departure frequency, 125.4. Squawk 4621."

I jotted down a shorthand version of the instructions in a small notebook I keep in the plane for such purposes and read them back to the controller.

"Skyhawk Four Charlie Lima, read back correct. Contact ground, 121.6. Have a good flight."

I explained how next we contacted ground control to receive taxiing instructions.

"Tell them, 'Ground, Skyhawk Four Charlie Lima, ready to taxi from Premier with Yankee.'"

Eugen keyed the radio and repeated what I'd said.

"Skyhawk, Four Charlie Lima, roger. Taxi to One-Seven left via Bravo, hold short 2-6."

The kid was totally jazzed. I let him steer the plane. We nearly ran off the taxiway, but only once. Not bad for a beginner. At the run-up area next to the runway, with the airplane's parking brake set, I showed him how we revved the engine to 1700 RPMs, to make sure everything worked properly. Then we taxied to the hold-short line of the assigned runway. I switched radio frequencies to the tower.

"Rancho Bonita tower, Skyhawk Four Charlie Lima, ready One-Seven left."

"Four Charlie Lima, Rancho Bonita Tower, traffic on two-mile base. Runway One-Seven left, cleared for immediate takeoff."

"OK," I said, folding my hands placidly in my lap, "you've got the airplane."

I've watched fighter jocks with 5,000 hours take off with less elegance. The kid took to flying like a starving man at an all-you-can-eat buffet. We flew for an hour. Steep turns. Turns around a point. Climbs. Dives. Standard stuff for a fifty dollar introductory lesson. Just enough to make it all look effortless. Eugen Dragomir was a natural. I almost let him land.

"You sure you've never done this before?" I said as we were walking back toward my office.

"Maybe, like, in a previous life or something." He dug a damp, crumpled fifty dollar bill out of his board shorts. "If my father wrote a check for five thousand, would that be OK to start?"

"Sounds *mucho bueno* to me."

Another five grand. My day was looking better and better. I found a fresh logbook in my desk. I filled in the particulars of Eugen Dragomir's maiden flight, signed my name, and gave it to him. He held the book in his hand like it was a precious thing.

"Fortunately for you," I said, "my schedule's pretty flexible at present. Lemme know when the funds arrive. You'll be soloing in no time, guaranteed."

"Can't wait."

We bumped fists, then he retrieved his skateboard where he'd left it, against the wall of Larry's hangar. As he coasted toward the security gate, he smiled and waved with his thumb and pinkie extended, one of those Hawaiian "hang loose" signs.

I returned the gesture, feeling rather foolish.

California State University, Rancho Bonita, with its 18,500 undergrads and architectural hodgepodge of a campus nestled on a picturesque bluff overlooking the Pacific, is known perennially as a top-ten party school. Few students who ventured off campus and wanted me to teach them how to fly ever came close to mastering that goal. Surfing, boozing, blazing, and getting laid invariably took precedence. Eugen Dragomir seemed different. A studious kid. A great potential pilot.

Working with Alpha had compelled me to be distrustful of my fellow man. It was liberating, watching him roll away on his skateboard, to realize that you don't always have to question the motives and hidden agendas of everybody you meet. You can't go around being suspicious of everybody you cross paths with, I told myself. Not everybody's out to kill you.

<hr/>

Driving home that afternoon, somebody tried to kill me.

A car was following me. I first noticed it in my side-view mirror as I merged from the airport onto the southbound freeway, just past the Orchard Avenue exit. It was a white, two-door Honda Accord coupe, fifty meters in trail. No front license plate. Rear spoiler. Fat rims. Lowered suspension. Windshield tinted impenetrably black. A ride for dweebs convinced that tricking out a Japanese economy car will somehow improve their odds with the ladies.

I drifted casually into the fast lane. The Honda followed. I angled back into the center lane. The Honda did likewise, its driver careful to keep at least five car-lengths between us. My speedometer showed seventy. I bumped it up to seventy-five. The Honda driver pulled out into the fast lane and passed the cars separating us to settle in behind me once more, still keeping his distance. I knew I couldn't outrun him, not in an aging Tacoma with nearly as many miles on it as the space shuttle. What I could do, though, was fall back on my training and evade him.

I mashed down on the accelerator. It was like stepping on a dead frog. The speedometer crept slowly past eighty, then eighty-five. The front end began to wobble like Ronnie Reagan's head. The Honda driver knew he'd been made. He abandoned any pretense of a covert tail, floored it, and rapidly closed the gap between us.

The exit off the freeway at Valley View was a quarter-mile ahead. I waited until the Honda was about twenty feet behind me, then veered violently across traffic, cutting off a housewife in a silver minivan who made her displeasure known with an angry toot from her horn. Sorry, lady. I fishtailed onto the exit ramp, hoping my pursuer would overshoot the turnoff.

When I looked back, he was drafting my rear bumper.

We rocketed onto Valley View, the two of us, down a steep hill past San Roberto High School on the left and the Wisteria Shopping Center on the right. The light turned red just as I shot across the intersection at Hendricks Boulevard. The Honda never slowed down.

A quarter-mile straight ahead, Valley View came to a dead end. I could see it. So could the Honda driver behind his black tinted windows. I figured he was going to try to ram me and drive my truck into the wooden barrier at the end of the road. Why, I have no idea, but I wasn't about to wait and let him prove my theory correct.

I slammed the gearshift into second and flicked my steering wheel to the right a little, increasing the load transfer to the outer tires, then yanked hard on the emergency brake and spun left. The tires smoked and screamed as I skidded 180 degrees, coming to an abrupt stop in the opposite direction—your standard bootlegger's turn. Caught off-guard, the Honda driver overshot, skidded left and crashed broadside into the wooden barrier. He backed up, tires smoking, and reversed course to come at me again, but by then I'd already put 100 yards between us, turning down Zink Street and out of his sight line.

Zink gave way to a maze of residential streets with names like Cinderella Lane and Del Monaco Drive. There was a depressing sameness to all of the houses that no variance in landscaping or paint schemes could mute. I was glad I didn't live there.

By the time I found my way back out onto Hendricks, the main drag, my pursuer was nowhere around. I was angry at myself for not having had the presence of mind to read the Honda's rear license plate before bolting, but there was no use worrying about that now. I turned left onto Hendricks and drove back to the airport, checking my mirrors frequently.

Inside the hangar, I unlocked my desk, put the photo of Echevarria and me in the belly drawer and closed it. I opened the bottom drawer. Inside was a two-inch .357 Colt Python revolver. The little snub-nose had been my primary backup weapon during my time with Alpha. The only souvenir I kept from those days.

I was beginning to think it might come in handy.

Seven

Being the wondering type, I couldn't help but wonder whether my pursuer in the Honda was associated with Arlo Echevarria's murder. Echevarria and I had brought to justice any number of rabid animals who'd passed themselves off as human. Was there any truth to Savannah's assertion that maybe an embittered relative of one of those animals had hunted Echevarria down and now, maybe, was tracking me? I needed to lie low for awhile, get out of Dodge, until I could sort things out. Unless you're NORAD, it's a lot trickier to track a single-engine airplane than an imported pickup truck. So I flew.

From above on a clear day, when the freeways are moving and the smog is on hiatus, the Los Angeles Basin can look like the most peaceful place on the planet. Stretching east from the Pacific, the aerial view is an amorphous pastiche of business districts, each with its own high-rise nucleus, and of verdant hills and blue reservoirs and tree-lined neighborhoods where aquamarine swimming pools dot every other backyard. Such are the delusions of tranquility derived from on-high. Only at ground level does hard reality emerge: that of an impersonal, often unforgiving megalopolis where people like Arlo Echevarria are butchered every day.

Half an hour after departing Rancho Bonita, I landed at Van Nuys, the busiest general aviation airport in the nation. I taxied to transient parking on the north side of the field, to a secluded spot as far away from the street as I could find, shut down the *Duck's* engine, and called the number on the business card Savannah had given me. There was no answer. I told her answering machine that I was in town for a couple of days and needed a place to stay, somewhere quiet, where I could think things through without distraction. She called back less than a minute later.

"What happened? Did something happen? I know something happened." She was breathless. I could practically hear her pulse pounding through the phone.

"Nothing happened, Savannah. I just decided to get away for a couple of days, that's all."

"Logan, I *know* you. You've never done a spontaneous thing in your life. You're not the type to just 'get away' on the spur of the moment. It's about Arlo, isn't it?"

I told her about the Honda trying to run me off the road. Probably just some kid looking for a cheap thrill, I said. Nothing to be alarmed about.

"Like hell," Savannah said.

Fifteen minutes later, she rolled up in a platinum-colored Jaguar convertible. She was wearing a broad-brimmed floppy hat made from burgundy felt, and oversized Gucci sunglasses.

"Who're you supposed to be, Mata Hari?"

"Get in."

I tossed my beat-up leather flight bag onto the backseat. Stuffed inside were aerial charts, a razor, a toothbrush, a comb, two changes of clothes, and my revolver. I had barely lowered myself into her Jag when Savannah stomped on the gas, thundering out onto Hayvenhurst Avenue like Ricky Bobby at Talladega. We streaked through a red light and bombed a left on Sherman Way, making for the Santa Monica Freeway at thirty miles an hour over the posted limit.

"Slow down, Savannah."

"You were the one who said somebody's trying to kill you."

"I said somebody tried to run me off the road. A simple case of road rage. Now, slow down."

"Logan, do the math. Arlo's dead. You could be next."

I did the math. Based on Savannah's nominal driving skills, I calculated my chances at that moment of being killed in a vehicular accident were substantially greater than any threat posed by assassins unknown. I reached down and slid the Jaguar's gearshift into neutral. Disengaged from the automatic transmission, with Savannah's foot still on the gas, the engine screamed—nearly as loudly as she did.

"What are you doing?"

"Either slow it down or I'm punching out, right here and now."

I reached for the door handle.

"OK, OK." She eased up on the accelerator. "There, you happy now?"

"Happy comes when your work and words benefit yourself and others."

"What the hell's that supposed to mean?"

"Ask the Buddha. I'll let you know when I figure it out myself."

I slipped the gearshift back into drive. We merged onto the freeway heading south—straight into bumper-to-bumper congestion. A traffic jam in the City of Angels. What a surprise.

Savannah looked over at me expectantly. "You said you were going to talk to the police."

"I did."

"And you told them about Arlo? The truth?"

"I told them what I knew."

"Which was what?"

I gazed out the window and said nothing.

"Why can't you tell me?"

"Let it go, Savannah."

She exhaled.

I asked where we were going.

"My place. Unless you have a problem with that."

"Why? You mean because you used to live there with Echevarria?"

She pursed her lips. "I just don't want you to be uncomfortable, that's all."

"I passed uncomfortable on my way to numb about six years ago."

We drove in silence the rest of the way.

⊙━✦━⊙

Savannah's place was a two-story Tudor estate fronting a sweeping, tree-lined motor court hidden from the street behind tall hedges and an electronically controlled security gate of solid teakwood. The house was set on nearly an acre of rose gardens and rolling lawns a half-mile above Sunset Boulevard. Out back was a man-made waterfall that cascaded into a black-bottom swimming lagoon. I stooped to stir the water. It was warm as a baby's bath.

"Daddy must've been in a generous mood," I said.

Inside were antique English furnishings, hickory plank floors, cathedral ceilings, and a kitchen twice the size of my garage apartment. I tailed her upstairs and down a long hallway, to the guest suite. Handwoven tapestry panels of royal blue hung floor-to-ceiling from ten-foot-high walls. At one end of the room was a king-sized four-poster bed hewn from massive, ancient logs and covered by a purple velvet spread. The spread was embroidered with some sort of royal crest that matched the wall hangings and tasseled pillow shams piled against the headboard. At the other end of the room, beneath a pair of lace-covered windows that opened out onto the lagoon and surrounding gardens below, was an honest-to-goodness fainting couch. I couldn't decide if I'd arrived on the set of *Camelot* or *Gone with the Wind*.

"This is where you sleep," Savannah said.

"Where do you sleep?"

She looked at me with something approaching disgust.

"Those days are long gone, Logan."

I tossed my flight bag onto King Arthur's bed. "For your information, Savannah, I'm not interested in sleeping with you. You're a grieving widow. I respect that, even if I didn't respect the worthless piece of crap you're grieving for. So you can just chill."

She let go a small laugh like we both knew I couldn't possibly be serious about not wanting to bed her. Then she realized that my disinterest seemed genuine. A glint of disappointment flickered in her eyes.

"My apologies if I presumed things incorrectly," she said.

"I need to make a few calls."

"I'll fix us some dinner. I have some nice salmon I can grill. You do eat salmon, don't you?"

"You're telling me you don't have a chef? Place like this always has a chef. Butler, too. And a masseuse—at least one on call. I mean, what's the point of conspicuous wealth if you can't enjoy a few slaves, right?"

Savannah's eyes narrowed. "Forget the salmon. We'll be having mac 'n' cheese." She turned on her heel and left.

I shut the door and called Mrs. Schmulowitz. Would she mind feeding Kiddiot while I was away?

"How long you gone for, Bubeleh?"

"A few days at most."

"What do I feed him?"

"On the shelf above my bed. There are some cans of cat food, all different flavors."

"Which ones does he prefer?"

"It doesn't matter, Mrs. Schmulowitz. He won't eat any of them."

"He won't eat them but you keep feeding them to him? That's the most *meshuggeneh* thing I ever heard, because, I mean, let's face it, my God, he's positively portly. He's the William Shatner of cats— who, by the way, is a member of my tribe. He must be eating *something,* this cat of yours."

"If I knew the answer to that, Mrs. Schmulowitz, I'd know the answer to life itself."

"I'll make him a nice brisket. Nobody turns their nose up at my brisket, not even persnickety cats."

"You're a saint, Mrs. Schmulowitz."

"Wrong religion, kiddo." She hung up.

My next call was to an old friend I'll refer to as "Buzz" who works counterterrorism at the Defense Intelligence Agency.

The DIA is the American military's very own in-house CIA. Most Americans have never heard of it. DIA employees would have it no other way. Headquartered at both the Pentagon and across the Potomac River in a sprawling, highly secure building that resembles a giant silver aircraft carrier, it is the DIA that gathers and analyzes classified information to produce the actionable intelligence that the military's door-kickers rely on to bring terrorists to justice. Few DIA analysts look like what Hollywood would have you believe such spooks look like. They resemble librarians and community college professors, a decidedly academic bunch given to thick glasses and trousers that are too short, who toil at encrypted computers in secure, windowless offices, sipping coffee from mugs adorned with the Liberty Bell and patriotic idioms like, "These colors don't run." Buzz favored a mug that said "What SUV Would Jesus Drive?" On it was a drawing of the Messiah cruising the freeway in a Hummer, elbow crooked out the window like some long-haul trucker, holy hair billowing in the wind. When a particularly pious co-worker took exception to Buzz's blasphemy, their mutual supervisor, an avid golfer, urged Buzz to find himself another, less sacrilegious vessel for his coffee. So Buzz did. His new mug said, "Golfers have tiny balls."

"*Allahu akbar*," Buzz grunted when I called. "How's your scrotum?"

"I wouldn't know. It's been awhile since I used it."

"Join the club. When're you coming back to the dark side? Our little G-WOT just isn't the same without you."

"I suspect the global war on terror is doing just fine without me," I said. "Besides, you're the one who's indispensable."

"And if you believe that, I got some swamp land I wanna sell you. Hell, I envy your shit, Logan. I'd pull the pin, too, if I could. Go sit on a beach somewhere, chugging Coronas and making fun of the *touristas* all day. But my kid's got this crazy notion I'm supposed to pay his way through law school. So here I sit, saving the planet from tyranny, not to mention invasion from outer space. I haven't had a fucking day off in six weeks."

"Invasion from outer space?"

"Need-to-know basis. I'd tell you, but then, well, you know . . ."

"Oldest line in the book, Buzz."

"Cut me some slack, Logan. I'm a burned-out, underpaid civil servant."

We went way back, Buzz and I. One of the original go-to guys, he'd been there and done that a hundredfold by the time I clocked in at Alpha. Twice he'd been wounded on missions, the last time in Libya. Bleeding from just about everywhere from a rocket-propelled grenade that had exploded five feet away, Buzz ran down the terrorist who'd fired it at him and blew off the back of his head with a short-barreled, pistol-grip shotgun that Buzz called "The Bitch." Only afterward did he realize that the terrorist was an eleven-year-old boy. Fragments from the RPG eventually claimed Buzz's right eye, while recurrent nightmares of having killed a child robbed him of the desire to pull the trigger on anyone else ever again. He was assigned desk duty. By the time I arrived at Alpha, Buzz had built a network of personal contacts within the spook community so comprehensive, it had acquired its own acronym, BIA—the Buzz Intelligence Agency.

I asked him if he'd heard about what had happened to Echevarria, knowing that he undoubtedly possessed far more details than I did.

"I heard," Buzz said, "poor bastard."

"Anything you can enlighten me with?"

"Stand by one."

I could hear him get up from his desk to go close his office door. Then he was back.

"He was doing contract work for folks across the river," Buzz said. "Job apps, backgrounders, non-class shit is what I heard."

"You think what happened to him was job-related?"

"That's been knocked down. At least in this shop. I can't speak for the shop he was freelancing for. They've still got an open file on him. I know that much. He and your old lady split. You heard that, right?"

"She told me. Actually, I've gotten sort of peripherally involved in the case, asking around, talking to a few people."

"About what happened to Arlo, you mean?"

"Roger that."

"Jesus, Logan, the broad dumps you like a hot rock and now you're holding her fuckin' hand? Is that what happens? You move out there to the People's Republic of California, next thing you know, you're joining some masochist cult."

"I needed the cash."

"I guess you gotta do what you gotta do, eh?" Buzz said. "Look, I'm not saying what happened to Echevarria made my day, but I can't say I wasn't all that broke up when I heard about it, either. The guy was a dirtbag, going after that gal of yours. Last time I had anything halfway good to say about him, you and her were still together. I always thought that was a pretty shitty thing he did."

I thanked Buzz for his loyalty and asked him to keep me posted on anything else he might pick up through the grapevine on Echevarria's death. He assured me he'd call, but only if I agreed to buy him a six-pack the next time we crossed paths. I promised him a case.

That Echevarria was contracting for the CIA—"folks across the river," as Buzz put it—wasn't surprising. A lot of pensioners double dip as independent contractors after retiring from any number of federal intelligence organizations. What was surprising was that the CIA was actively investigating the murder. Typically, the agency let sleeping dogs lie. Probing the suspicious death of a covert operative can make it easier for foreign intelligence agents to confirm that the operative did, in fact, have ties to Langley. Other operators could be compromised as a result, along with the methods they used to carry out their clandestine missions. Whole spy networks have been unraveled virtually overnight in such fashion, their members rounded up and summarily shot.

Buzz had indicated that Echevarria was doing routine work for the CIA when he died, performing non-classified background checks on job applicants. Hardly cloak and dagger stuff. Why, then, would the agency continue probing his death when the LAPD's investigation remained ongoing? There had to be something else to it.

I considered calling some of my other former colleagues from Alpha to see what they might know. But even if they knew anything, I knew they wouldn't tell me. I'd jumped ship, left them in my wake. As far as they were all concerned, I was just another civilian puke.

⊶✦⊷

"What's the deal with place mats?"

"They keep food off the table. Plus, they look nice."

"Why do they always have to match the napkins?"

"Because they just do," Savannah said. "Now eat."

She set a steaming plate of macaroni and cheese down on the plum-colored place mat in front of me, which matched the plum-colored linen napkin on my lap. Along with the mac 'n' cheese came tomato wedges on the side, artfully arranged, topped with fresh-ground pepper.

I was sitting in a corner nook of Savannah's kitchen. The table and benches were made of wormwood. There was a bay window. The view was of the black-bottom pool and the green Hollywood hills beyond.

"Nice crib."

"Remember that little condo near Golden Gate Park, right after we got married? I always did like that place," Savannah said.

I remembered. Best time of my life.

"Macaroni needs salt," I said.

She grabbed a salt mill from the cooktop and a plate for herself. On the table were two crystal wine stems and an uncorked bottle of eight-year-old Petite Sirah from some vineyard in the Napa Valley that I probably would've been impressed by had I known the first thing about vino. She took a seat and poured me a glass without asking.

"Forgot the salad."

She slid out from the bench and crossed the twenty feet to the refrigerator, a massive, industrial-looking monster with stainless-steel doors that seemed out of place with the plank floors and antique-white cabinets. She got out a large blue ceramic bowl and brought it back to the table along with a set of silver tongs. The salad was spinach leaves topped with crescent moons of fresh avocado slices and finished with a raspberry vinaigrette. A salad for girls.

"Why would Arlo willingly move out of a palace like this?"

"Give me your plate."

"The question still stands, Savannah. Why did he leave you?"

She paused, my plate in one hand, the salad tongs in the other. I waited.

"Arlo, he, um, he found out that I had . . ." She cleared her throat and avoided my eyes. "That I had slept with someone else."

"You cheated on him?"

"It was a mistake."

I felt a sudden surge of moral righteousness, even if I had no right to.

"Was he a flight attendant?"

"Go to hell, Logan."

She dumped the tongs in the salad bowl and strode to the sink, her back turned to me, leaning on the polished granite countertop with both hands. Her shoulders shuddered almost imperceptibly. I could tell she was crying.

"Did you tell the police about this *mistake* of yours?"

"It had nothing to do with what happened to Arlo."

"How do you know that?"

She turned back toward me, her cheeks wet with tears. "It was a stupid thing to do. It meant nothing, OK?—*nothing.*"

"Obviously, it meant something to Arlo."

Savannah sighed and swiped at her eyes with both hands. "I suppose I deserved that," she said.

She seemed almost eager to tell me about how the "mistake" happened, as if by describing the spontaneous nature of it, she could explain away the guilt she obviously still carried as a result of it. Her father, she said, had invited Arlo and her out for the weekend to Palm Springs where he was attending a meeting with some potential investors. She and Arlo had been arguing.

"What were you arguing about?"

"He wanted to stay home and watch a baseball game or something. I don't really remember."

"So you went to Palm Springs alone."

Savannah shrugged. "There was this guy at dinner. I had a little too much to drink. We ended up in his room. I told him the next day never to call me and he never did. That was all it was. One night. End of story."

"Who was the guy?"

"It doesn't matter. Some guy, that's all."

"You had a fling. You ended it. Maybe the guy gets jealous. Decides he wants you all to himself. Next thing you know, Arlo's in an urn on your mantle."

"It wasn't like that, Logan. It wasn't anything other than what it was. Which was nothing."

"Who was he, Savannah?"

"I told you! Some guy. It had *nothing* to do with what happened to Arlo."

"Since when did you become a homicide detective?"

Savannah's mouth parted as she looked at me, like she'd finally figured something out.

"You want to know who I slept with because deep down, it bothers you, knowing the train left the station and you weren't the last stop. Admit it, Logan. You're getting some sort of perverse pleasure out of this."

Perverse pleasure? More like masochistic torture. I dabbed my mouth with my napkin that matched my place mat.

"Thanks for the chow," I said. "I'm going for a swim."

Eight

I hadn't thought to bring trunks, so I swam in my boxers. The water in Savannah's lagoon was wet, warm sunshine. I could see her watching me through the kitchen window.

Some people swim because they like the exercise. Me? I swim, on those rare occasions when I *do* swim, because it makes me feel like Flipper. Granted, nobody really knows how a dolphin genuinely feels except, perhaps, another dolphin. But I never saw Flipper when he wasn't smiling. Jumping through flaming hoops, head-butting SCUBA-diving criminals. Saving Ranger Ricks from peril. Always with a smile. We should all be so perpetually cheery. At some point, as I worked on my porpoise kick, Savannah left a couple of plush white bath towels on a chaise lounge poolside.

I was taking a hot shower an hour later when she came storming into the guest bathroom.

"You want to know who he was? Miles Zambelli. That was his name. The guy I slept with. Like it really matters. There. You satisfied now? You expect me to act like I have something to be ashamed of, and I don't."

The shower doors were fogged with steam. I said, "Try knocking next time."

"He didn't mean anything to me, Logan. And I didn't mean anything to him. And I resent the hell out of you demanding that I somehow have to account to you for my personal life!"

"Your father's legal advisor. *That* Miles Zambelli? That's who your 'mistake' was?"

Savannah blinked, stunned that I would know.

"Thirty. Dark hair. John Lennon glasses. Reeks of Ivy League." I slid open the shower door wide enough as modesty would allow—no sense in showing her all the splendor she'd been missing—and grabbed a towel off a wall hook. "The age difference there is what, fifteen years? Rather cougar-ish, wouldn't you say, Savannah?"

"How do you know Zambelli?"

"I met him yesterday."

"You met him *yesterday*? You want to tell me how *that* happened?"

"Not especially, no."

I wrapped the towel around my waist and crossed to the vanity, a converted antique sideboard, French mahogany, with double porcelain sinks and a beveled mirror. I wiped the steam off the glass and combed my hair. Savannah stood behind me, her expression one of incredulity.

"My father came to see you. That's why you talked to the police, isn't it?"

I should have said that it's a small world, and that I just happened to have met Zambelli on the street, or in some restaurant somewhere. Better yet, I should've just kept my mouth shut. But I didn't.

"Your father didn't come to see me, Savannah. I went to see him."

She planted her hands on her hips and glared. "I don't believe this! I ask you to talk to the police and you tell me to kiss off. But my father asks and it's, 'Yessir, Mr. Carlisle. Whatever I can do for you, sir!'"

"He wants to know who killed Arlo as much as you do. He asked me to talk briefly to the police. I did."

I walked into the guest bedroom. She stormed after me.

"He paid you, didn't he?"

"I'm getting dressed now, Savannah. You have two options: Do a one-eighty or enjoy the show."

She turned her back to me, arms folded indignantly. I dropped my towel and dug a clean pair of boxer briefs out of my flight bag.

"How much, Logan?"

"That's between your father and me." I stepped into my underwear, then put on a fresh polo shirt. I retrieved my semi-dirty jeans from the bed where I'd left them to go swimming and pulled them on. "Show's over," I said, cinching my belt. "You can turn around now."

"Miles Zambelli couldn't have killed Arlo," Savannah said, turning to face me. "He would've had no reason to. There was absolutely nothing between us. Just the one night. Like I said."

"How long before Echevarria was killed did you sleep with Zambelli?"

"I don't know. Three weeks. A month. I really don't remember."

"Did you tell the police this?"

"Why would I tell the police? I told you. It had nothing to do with what happened to Arlo."

"Does your father know?"

"He knows. Zambelli's the son my father never had. He wasn't exactly thrilled, but he understood. Things happen. God only knows my father has made his share of mistakes, too."

I sat down on the edge of the bed and tied my shoes. The thought of somebody like Zambelli having had his way with Savannah, however briefly, made my stomach raw.

"Anybody else you did I should know about?"

"Jesus, you're really something, you know that?" She turned and started to walk out.

"I need to borrow your car," I said.

"Seriously? You treat me like shit, then expect me to let you borrow my car? Just like that?"

"I need to go see where Arlo died."

<hr/>

Savannah's Jaguar had a dash-mounted GPS with one of those automated voices that remind you when to turn and when to "stay on the motorway." The voice was male and upper-crust British and irritating as hell. I couldn't figure out how to turn it off without turning off the whole navigational system.

"Please . . . return . . . to . . . route."

"Please shut the hell up."

Whoever programmed The Voice never factored in normal counter-surveillance methods. Descending the Hollywood Hills to the flats below, I negotiated several quick turns onto twisty side streets, checking my mirrors, pulling over and killing my lights, trying to spot any tails, the little revolver tucked under my left thigh for easy access. Each deviation from my designated route prompted a rebuke from The Voice.

"Please . . . return . . . to . . . route."

With the possible exception of the Invisible Man, no one was following me. I merged onto the Hollywood Freeway and headed westbound into the San Fernando Valley, toward Northridge and 5442 Williston Drive, the address Savannah had given me, where Arlo had lived out his final days.

It was nine-thirty on a Friday night, long past rush hour, but traffic remained at a crawl. Brake lights sparkled ahead of me, an endless ribbon of rubies, while to my left, four lanes of head-lights gleamed like rhinestones from the southbound procession of cars inching along in the opposite direction. Nobody honked their horn. Being trapped in your vehicle at any given time surrounded by thousands of other similarly imprisoned Los Angelinos is an accepted part of life in Southern California. A land going nowhere fast. It took me more than an hour to travel less than ten miles.

"Exit right in . . . one-half mile."

I got off the freeway on Reseda Boulevard and turned north. It was a five-minute drive to the working class suburb of Northridge. The Voice told me to make a hard right onto Roscoe Boulevard, then a left, another left, then a right. In the darkness, every street looked the same, every home the same as the one before it. The houses were tired and small, cracker boxes that once trumpeted the embodiment of postwar, middle-class privilege, but were now the domain of low-income renters, immigrants mostly, struggling to hang on in a weak economy.

The Voice announced that I had arrived at my destination. It was a good thing, too. I would've otherwise cruised right past 5442 Williston Drive.

I parked the Jag at the curb, behind a primer-gray Pontiac Bonneville. Bolted to the Bonneville's left front wheel was a yellow Denver boot for unpaid parking citations. On the back bumper was a sticker that said, "How's My Driving? Dial 1-800-EAT SHIT." Somewhere down the street, a small dog yapped incessantly. I untucked my shirt, slipped the revolver into my belt, and got out.

A real estate broker's sign was planted in the tiny patch of coarse, yellowed grass that had passed for Echevarria's front yard. On the wooden post below the sign was a clear plastic box with one-page color flyers inside. I took out a flyer and read it under the fluorescent mantle of a street light. The house boasted two bedrooms and one bath, fresh carpet, new paint, a self-defrosting refrigerator, and a "private and secure" backyard. It was, according to the flyer, "freeway convenient" and close to shopping—the "perfect, affordable home for the young professional or a small family just starting out." What it didn't say was that 5442 Williston Drive was a dump at any price. Nor did it say that a man had been shot to death just inside the front door. The wonders of creative marketing.

I folded the flyer and put it in my back pocket. Then I tried the door. Locked. Likewise the front window. I rubbed the back of my neck. I didn't know what I hoped to discover inside, only that on some vague level I couldn't define, I felt the need to find *something* that might help explain why Echevarria had been killed. I thought about the chase with the Honda, and about what Savannah had said, her concern that I might be next. I needed to rule out that possibility before I could return with any sense of security to my regular scheduled programming. For the moment, anyway, whether I liked it or not, I realized my future and Echevarria's past were linked.

I stood there on the front step where his killer had stood, a rectangle of cracked concrete no bigger than a four-by-eight sheet of plywood, and waited for divine inspiration to strike, but none came. I decided to force the lock. I slid my ATM card out of my wallet and was working it into the doorjamb when, from behind, a deep voice intoned, "The fuck you doing, man?"

I glanced back over my shoulder as casually as surprise would allow. Standing there was a light-skinned African-American fellow in a black sweat suit. He was staring at me down the barrel of a sawed-off, pump-action, 12-gauge shotgun.

"House hunting," I said.

"*House hunting?* What kind of crazy-ass motherfucker goes house hunting at eleven o'clock in the middle of the motherfuckin' night? Get them hands up, fool."

I raised my hands.

He was billiard-ball bald, probably close to sixty, but still formidable enough to be a threat even without the shotgun. A gold hoop glinted from his left earlobe in the street light. He resembled what I imagined Mr. Clean might look like someday when he's eligible for the senior discount at IHOP.

"Now," Mr. Clean said, "y'all wanna tell me what you're *really* doing out here?"

"I used to know the man who lived here. We were . . ." I swallowed hard and forced the word, ". . . friends. I'm trying to find out where he went."

"Where he went? He's dead, that's where he went. Somebody capped his ass. Maybe you, for all I know. Now, put them hands down and start walking across the lawn, normal-like—and nice and slow."

"Normal-like?"

"Walk! To the sidewalk—and don't be thinking about running, neither, cuz I *will* put a fuckin' hole in you. Now, walk."

I stepped off the porch and walked across the weeds toward the sidewalk. Mr. Clean stayed put, pivoting, tracking me with the barrel of his gun.

"Now turn around and walk back to me."

"And the point of these calisthenics would be . . . ?"

"This ain't Twenty Questions, motherfucker. Do it."

I turned and walked back toward him slowly. He kept the 12-gauge trained on me the entire way. Whatever he was hoping to discern by me strutting my stuff, I had no idea. The Buddha said that the greatest prayer is patience, but my patience with Mr. Clean was waning rapidly. I noticed that his trigger finger was extended, resting on the trigger guard, not curled around the trigger itself.

This told me that he was schooled in the use of firearms. Or watched a lot of war movies. It also told me that it would take him an extra split second to move that finger off the guard and onto the trigger when I moved to take the shotgun away from him.

"Always a good idea to slide your weapon off safe when you're planning to put a hole in somebody," I said, nodding toward the safety button forward of the gun's trigger guard.

He looked instinctively, checking to see if the safety was on. I sidestepped the barrel as he glanced down, grabbed the shotgun, twisted it out of his grasp, flipped it around, and leveled it at him.

A smile came to his face. "Ain't that a bitch. You Special Forces, ain't you? Some sort of Chuck Norris Ranger Delta motherfucker. I can tell by the way you move. Like a goddamn cat."

"Not my cat."

"Yeah, I was a SEAL myself," he said with a nonchalant sniff. "Saw some shit in the 'Nam, man, you wouldn't believe. 'Course, that was back in the day. I must be pretty goddamn rusty, letting you get the jump on me like that."

I asked him what SEAL team he'd been with.

"Which team? Team Six. Best of the best, baby." The same team that greased Osama bin Laden. Mr. Clean rubbed his nose with his thumb and index finger. When people feel anxious, their blood pressure rises, prompting soft tissue to swell, which makes their skin tingle, which causes them to scratch or rub. People feel anxious when they lie. His rubbing and hesitation in answering my question were easy giveaways.

I asked him why he made me walk back and forth across the lawn.

"Wanted to see if you was him."

"Him who?"

"The dude who capped the fella who used to live here. But you ain't."

"How do you know?"

"Ever watch Gomer Pyle?"

"A bit before my time. Caught a few reruns, though. An intellectually challenged Marine. Now, *there's* a novel concept."

"You know Big Foot?"

"Not personally. But I hear his feet are, like, huge."

"Shooter, he walked like Big Foot, or Gomer Pyle. Big rangy motherfucker, hunched over, like this." Mr. Clean demonstrated how the killer moved, stooped at the waist, arms swinging loosely. "I seen him gettin' away. With my own eyes. You walk different from him. More white boy. All stiff and shit. Like you got starch in your armpits."

I pumped out six shells, then tossed him back the empty 12-gauge.

"I lied," I said. "The weapon was off safety."

Mr. Clean grinned. "You bad as hell."

He told me he couldn't remember ever having had a conversation with Echevarria. They might've nodded to each other once or twice getting in or out of their cars, he said, or getting the mail, but that was about it.

"People around here, they ain't too neighborly cuz they be coming around, asking to borrow a couple eggs. Pretty soon it's ten bucks for baby milk or diapers. Then a C-note for the rent, just until next pay day, some shit like that. Then the moving van shows, motherfucker splits in the middle of the night and you ain't never gonna see one nickel of that money back."

Mr. Clean said he had no clue who might've murdered Echevarria or why, but expressed no surprise about the shooting. The neighborhood, he said, had been going to hell for as long as he'd been living there.

"The week before Arlo got it, there was some retired schoolteacher got shot one block over. I know two women been raped in the last six months, walking down Ventura Boulevard in broad fuckin' daylight. I mean, damn, the whole city's going to hell, you know what I'm sayin'?"

"Where's the Lone Ranger when you need him?"

"Or Batman," Mr. Clean said.

I gave him my card and told him to call if he came up with any superhero crime-fighting ideas.

I awoke early the next morning, made coffee, took a quick dip in my ex-wife's lagoon, an even quicker shower, and called the listing agent on Echevarria's house. We made arrangements to meet there at nine-thirty A.M. I was out the door by nine A.M. Savannah was still asleep.

A few deviations onto side streets assured me there was still no one tailing me. I got on the freeway. The westbound 101 was moving at a respectable fifty miles an hour. A raven-haired hottie in a convertible Saab glanced my way and smiled as she passed on the left. I decided I was in a good mood. The mood lasted all of five seconds.

"Prepare to exit," the GPS announced.

"That'll be enough out of you."

I didn't need The Voice harshing my mellow. Good pilots have innate navigational skills. I knew where I was going. I'd been there the night before. I turned off the GPS.

I was northbound on Reseda when my phone rang. Caller ID showed a private number.

"This is Logan."

"This conversation never happened," Buzz said.

"What conversation?" I said.

My DIA buddy had done some snooping. Made a few back-channel calls "across the river" to Langley, he said, where he learned that the CIA had concluded its investigation of Echevarria's murder. The agency's Counterterrorism Center could find no connection between the interests of their directorate and Echevarria's untimely demise.

"They could give a giant shit about him," Buzz said. "As far as Christians in Action are concerned, the guy never existed."

"A lot of help you are."

"Did I say I was done, dickweed?"

Buzz had logged into ALIEN, the DIA's super secret squirrel computer system, and queried whether Echevarria's name had appeared in any recent requests for intelligence information. The computer spit back a hit.

"Some dumbass at CENTCOM stiffed in an RFI for him about three months ago and was dumb enough to input Echevarria's name as the requester," Buzz said. "Echevarria doesn't show up on any cleared active TS-SCI registers so, boom, the request automatically gets dumped out of the system. The RFI never went through."

"He never got the information he wanted?"

"I believe I just said that."

A two-man LAPD cruiser proceeding southbound on Reseda Boulevard whipped a quick U-turn and settled in behind me. I could see the cop in the right seat typing on his Mobile Data Terminal—no doubt the Jaguar's license plate number, to see if the car was stolen.

"I need the name Echevarria wanted on that request for information."

"What's in it for me?"

"My eternal admiration."

"What about a gift certificate to Dave and Buster's?"

"I'll see what I can do."

The subject Echevarria sought to research in official files, Buzz said, was none other than Pavel Tarasov, the independent oil broker I'd met in El Molino—the same guy my former father-in-law hoped to do business with in Kazakhstan. Buzz started to spell out Tarasov's name for me phonetically. I stopped him.

"I know who he is," I said.

"Wait. Lemme guess. Gay lover?"

"You're my only gay lover, Buzz."

"Eat me, Logan."

"In your dreams, old friend."

He laughed. According to Buzz, Tarasov's name turned up in a handful of intelligence cables ranging as far back as the late 1990's. The man from Minsk had been identified variously as a self-made tycoon, an international playboy with a taste for large-breasted Scandinavian teenagers, and a suspected asset with peripheral ties to Russia's Foreign Intelligence Service.

"Could be Echevarria was freelancing a counter-intel op," Buzz speculated. "Drops his guard one night and this guy Tarasov fucks him up."

"Doesn't wash. I broke bread with Tarasov. He didn't strike me as a killer."

"When do they ever?"

Buzz had a point. The best killers rarely look the part, especially state-sponsored ones. Certainly, Tarasov would have been no exception to that rule. But Buzz knew as well as I did that "peripheral ties" to an intelligence operation did not a full-blown hit man make. Intelligence officers, theirs and ours, routinely debrief thousands of civilian business people every year whose travels take them to countries with perceived strategic importance. Tarasov, I suspected, was likely such an asset. Low grade. Hardly Boris Badenov. I told Buzz I appreciated his help, regardless.

"Just don't say I never gave you anything," he said.

"OK. I won't."

I signed off as the cops hit their candy bar lights and pulled me over.

A beefy black cop and his vertically challenged white partner climbed out of their patrol car and cautiously approached the Jaguar from either side, hands resting on the grips of their holstered pistols. I kept both hands on top of the steering wheel where they could see them.

"License, registration, and proof of insurance," the little cop said.

No, "Good morning, sir." No, "May I *please* see your license?" I don't care for imperiousness and I have serious problems with authority—a potentially bad combination at any traffic stop—but even more so in the city of Los Angeles, where a rookie was once rumored to have asked his sergeant, "We collared a guy who was beating the hell out of some poor slob for no reason at all. What do we charge him with?" The sergeant was alleged to have responded, "Impersonating a police officer."

I held my tongue, handed over my driver's license and insurance card, then reached into Savannah's glove box for the current registration that I assumed would be there. I could've just as easily been looking for a flamethrower given the way both officers tensed, waiting.

"You were clocked at twelve miles an hour over the posted limit," the little cop said. "It's also illegal to operate a motor vehicle in the state of California using a cellular telephone without a hands-free device." He was shaking his head at me like any dummy knew better.

I couldn't resist. "Well," I said, "at least you're short and to the point."

He smiled wanly, then got out his ticket book and began writing.

⊙━━◆━━⊙

After I autographed the citation, I continued north on Reseda, made a left, another left, then a hard right, just as I had the night before. The addresses on Williston Drive ticked down until I came to the house with "5442" stenciled in faded black paint on the curb out front. I noticed that the Pontiac with the Denver boot and the "How's My Driving?" bumper sticker was gone. So was the "For Sale" sign I'd seen planted in Echevarria's front yard. Then there was the yard itself. In less than twelve hours, the patch of parched weeds had been miraculously transformed into a lawn as lush and manicured as the infield at Dodger Stadium. Thriving clumps of red and white impatiens bordered the front walk. I thought for an instant that I was having some kind of acid flashback. Only I'd never dropped acid.

The neighborhood looked exactly as it did the night before, but Echevarria's former residence and the grounds surrounding it were definitely different. I double-checked the address against the one Savannah had jotted down for me: "5442" painted on the curb; "5442" in black numbers nailed up diagonally beside the front door.

The right address. Only I was on the wrong street.

Somehow, I'd turned one block before I was supposed to. Instead of making a left onto Williston Drive, I'd turned onto Radcliff Avenue. So much for innate navigational skills. I turned The

Voice back on. Two minutes later, I parked in front of Echevarria's house.

The real estate agent was waiting out front, pecking on an iPhone. She was squeezed into a white cotton blouse with a collar that spread over the lapels of her sunflower-yellow blazer, and a black skirt that Mr. Blackwell might've suggested was a tad too skimpy for a woman of such ample girth and mileage. The vanity plate on her pearl white Lexus read, "ISELL4U."

I turned off the ignition and got out.

"You must be Mr. Logan."

"If I must."

"Hi, Julie Roberts, Century 21." She shook my hand enthusiastically. "And, yes, I know it sounds like *Julia* Roberts, but we're not related, though the family resemblance *is* undeniable. I like to tell everybody we're sisters from other misters."

She waited with an expectant smile for me to respond to her over-rehearsed little quip. I tittered and apologized for being late. She handed me her business card as we walked to the front door.

I noticed that she'd stationed a couple of potted palms on the porch to make the house look less like the hovel it was. She asked me if I was pre-qualified loan-wise. I said I was. This seemed to please her. She asked me if I was working with any other agents. I said I wasn't. This seemed to please her even more. She put on a pair of frameless reading glasses, stooped to squint at the digital lockbox hanging from the knob, and punched in the combination. She removed a key from the box and turned the dead bolt. As she opened the front door, she looked back at me as if we were about to enter the Magic Kingdom and said, "Prepare to be ab-so-lutely amazed."

"Can't wait," I said.

The walls were freshly whitewashed. The carpeting in the living room was camel color and new. The kitchen appliances were old but serviceable. The cabinets were knotty pine, with strap-iron pulls and matching hinges, better suited to a cabin in Yogi and Boo-Boo's Jellystone Park than some downscale tract house in the San

Fernando Valley; but who was I to play interior designer? I lived in a converted garage.

"Isn't the light in here just *won*derful? And how about all this counter space," the real estate agent gushed, rapping on the counter with her knuckles. "FYI, this is *real* Formica, not the fake stuff."

"Wow."

Nothing about the house whispered murder scene. Any trace of blood had long since been scrubbed clean. I wondered if Echevarria's ghost roamed the place. I listened for it, but all I heard was a loud grinding sound.

"A full one horsepower," Julie Roberts said, turning off the garbage disposal. "Anything you want—chicken bones, peach pits. Gone. They don't make 'em like these anymore."

"Remind me not to put any fingers down there."

She led me into the bathroom. The tile top on the vanity was mint green with a darker green bull-nose trim. The grout had gone gray with age and was streaked with rust stains. Somebody had hung a new vinyl shower curtain with lime green polka dots. The bathroom reeked of Lysol.

"The seller, by the way, is highly motivated. He'll entertain any reasonable offer."

"Why's he selling?"

"He owns several rentals. He's just tired of the whole scene. Bad tenants, late payments, cats going pee-pee on everything, pardon my French—though not in this property, thank heavens, because you can *never* get that smell out, believe-you-me. He and his wife are retiring to Arizona. They want to be closer to the grandkids."

California law requires that a homeowner disclose any known problems associated with the history of the property they're selling. A leaky roof, barking dogs, people shot to death in the entryway— all must be revealed to the prospective buyer. The owner of the house had to have known about Echevarria's murder. Whether or not Julie Roberts did was another story. If she did, she covered it well.

"Let me show you the backyard," she said. "It has *loads* of potential."

The backyard was a mirror image of the front. A small patch of parched earth, only populated with vastly more dandelions. There was a chain-link fence and a gate that led to an alley. Piled against the gate were three rolls of stained carpeting and a half-dozen black Hefty bags filled with trash.

"You could build a fantastic deck out here," Julie Roberts said. "Put in a grill, hot tub, a privacy fence. Your own little Shangri-la. You ask me, the possibilities are ab-so-lutely endless."

"Ab-so-lutely."

I knelt, ripped open a trash bag and began sifting through the contents, much to Julie Roberts' bewilderment.

"May I ask what you're doing?"

"Recycling."

"Excuse me?"

"Ten cents a bottle. It's like found money."

The agent cleared her throat and smiled nervously. "I'm all for going green, but I, uh, really don't believe that rummaging through the trash like you're doing is, um, permissible."

"Our little secret," I said, scavenging an empty Snapple bottle like I'd just unearthed the treasure of Sierra Madre. "I won't tell if you don't."

That's when it occurred to her that she was alone, in a sketchy neighborhood, with a strange man who quite possibly was a few tacos short of a combo plate.

"Listen, not to be rude," she said with an anxious little chuckle, backing up toward the house, "but I really should be running along. I've got some, um, uh, you know, other pressing appointments. So, ah, um, feel free to, ah, you know, just look around, and uh . . . You've got my number. Call with any questions. Just do me a favor and lock up when you leave, OK?"

"Will do. By the way, I loved your sister in *Pretty Woman*."

Julie Roberts didn't hear me. She was already out of there.

The trash bag was mostly filled with used cleaning supplies. Mop heads. Rags. An empty bleach jug. I opened the second bag. Inside were empty paint cans, plastic tray liners stiff with dried white paint, and wads of used blue masking tape. The third bag held mounds of machine-shredded paper and unopened junk mail addressed to "Current Occupant." There were also several mail order catalogs. One was from the "Harry and David" company. Purveyors of fruits and nuts, soliciting business in the land of fruits and nuts. I had to smile.

The catalog was sticky with what looked and smelled like maple syrup. I was about to toss it back with the rest of the garbage and move onto the next bag when I noticed a shred of paper stuck to the back page. I peeled it free: it was a ticket stub from Turkish Airlines, a seat assignment, ripped in half. A partial name, "—mas Magnum" was printed on the remnant half—Thomas Magnum, Echevarria's *nom de guerre.* All of us in Alpha used such aliases in the field—usually the names of television characters we identified with. The reasoning was, were the bad guys to know our true identities, they might just come looking for us. And so we were Matt Dillon and Maynard G. Krebs and Jim Rockford and Gomez Addams and myriad others. Buzz's handle was Andy Sipowicz. I favored Napoleon Solo or Steve Urkel, depending on my mood.

The date printed on the ticket stub indicated that Echevarria had flown less than a week before he died. There was a flight number: 3183.

I called directory assistance and got a reservations number for Turkish Airlines.

"Please listen carefully as our prompts have changed." I punched "0." Fifteen seconds later, I was speaking with a real live Turk.

"Thank you for calling Turkish Airlines, a proud member of the Star Alliance. My name is Bedia. How may I assist you today?"

"This is Thomas Magnum. I flew your airline a couple months ago. Unfortunately, United says they have no record of my having been on the flight. Unless I send them proof, they won't credit my Mileage Plus account. Can't you help me?"

"I would be pleased to assist you with that, Mr. Magnum. What was the date and number of the flight?"

I gave her the particulars. She asked me how to spell Magnum. I could hear computer keys clicking over the phone.

"Here we are," she said after a few seconds. "Flight 3183, originating Ataturk, Istanbul, to New York's JFK, continuing on to Los Angeles International. I can email you a copy of the original ticket if you'd like, as well as ticket copies for any other flights you took that day."

"If you could check my other flights that would be great."

"Certainly." More computer keys clicking. "Yes, sir. It looks like you made an earlier connection from Atyrau to Istanbul."

I could feel my pulse surge. "Did you say Atyrau?"

"Yes, sir. Atyrau."

I told her emailed copies would not be necessary and thanked her for her time.

After I slipped the ticket stub in my pocket, I tossed the trash bag in which I'd found it into the trunk of Savannah's Jaguar along with another bag I'd yet to go through.

NINE

Savannah was sitting cross-legged on the lawn in front of her house, reading the Style section of *The New York Times*. She was barefoot, wearing a broad-brimmed straw sun hat, a black, form-fitting leotard top, and Daisy Duke-style cutoff jeans, short enough to reveal the bottoms of her front pockets. I tried to imagine that she weighed 400 pounds, but it didn't work.

I popped open the trunk and hauled out the two Hefty bags I'd taken from Echevarria's backyard.

"What are those?"

"What do they look like?"

"You're driving around with garbage bags in my Jaguar?"

"They're from your late husband's house."

"You found something," Savannah said, her voice rising with excitement.

I debated telling her about the Turkish Airlines ticket, about how Echevarria had apparently visited the port city of Atyrau in Kazakhstan days before he died. Having flown in and out of Atyrau more than a few times myself on various assignments, I knew that it was the commercial airport nearest the burgeoning Kashagan oil fields, where Savannah's father had prospective business interests with the men I'd lunched with in El Molino. It had to have been more than happenstance, Echevarria traveling through Atyrau just before he was murdered. Could be Buzz was correct. Could be Echevarria had gotten too close to Tarasov, uncovered something he shouldn't have, and paid for it with his life. I didn't know where the truth lay. I did, however, know that sharing what little of it I knew at that point with my ex-wife would only make it more difficult for me to explain to her the covert nature of how Echevarria and I once earned a living. I wasn't prepared to tell her that. I wasn't sure I'd ever be.

"What did you find?" Savannah demanded.

I closed the trunk lid.

"You've never told me anything, anyway, so why start now, right?" she said, smoldering.

"I need somewhere to spread this stuff out," I said.

She huffed a sigh as if to say, "I can't believe I'm accommodating this jerk," then led me inside.

<hr/>

The centerpiece of Savannah's den was a massive walnut desk, ornately hand-carved, of German origin, was my guess. The oak plank floor played host to a room-size, antique Persian rug worth more than my airplane. Above the moss rock fireplace was a stuffed moose head, its mouth curled in a taxidermy grin, its dark, glassy eyes staring down at us dully. I nodded toward it.

"You bag that yourself?"

"Came with the house," Savannah said, still steamed at me.

Old newspapers were stacked in a brass rack beside the desk. She spread some on the rug. I dumped out both trash bags on them.

"It's probably pointless to ask what you're looking for," she said.

"Probably."

She snatched up a copy of the *Wall Street Journal* from a mahogany side table and plopped down in an overstuffed armchair near the window, facing away from me, her naked thighs draped over the arm of the chair. I tried not to stare.

I got down on my knees and sifted through the garbage. Cans. Bottles. Newspapers. Junk mail. Used coffee filters filled with wet grounds. Used tissues filled with who-knows-what. There was nothing to be mined in the way of potential intelligence.

"I need to go see your father again," I said, tossing trash back in the bags.

Savannah put down her magazine. "This is starting to really piss me off. You tell him, but not me? My father wasn't married to Arlo, Logan, I was."

"Thanks for reminding me. I'd completely forgotten."

She gazed up at Bullwinkle as if for divine guidance. Maybe it was the way the sunlight filtered in through the windows, but she looked different. Sadder. Definitely older.

"I have a right to know who killed my husband."

"There's nothing I can tell you, Savannah."

"You can, but you won't. That's what you mean, isn't it?"

"I need a ride to my plane. You don't want to take me, I can catch a cab."

Savannah rubbed the back of her neck and sighed again. More than a little grudgingly, she said, "I'll get my shoes."

I called Carlisle's office in Nevada after she left the room. Lamont Royale answered the phone. I said I had some news for his boss that I needed to deliver in person. I told him I'd be at the North Las Vegas Airport in approximately three hours. Royale put me on hold. A minute later, he was back. He said he'd be waiting for me curbside when I arrived.

"Mr. Carlisle says to tell you he's looking forward to seeing you again, and asked that you please fly safe."

"I'll try not to crash."

Savannah drove me to the Van Nuys Airport without a word. We pulled in outside the executive terminal. She put the car in park, then turned to face me.

"I resent the fact you're willing to share information with my father, but not with me."

"He's paying for my services. You're not."

"How can you be so cruel? We shared a bed once."

"It's been a long time since we shared a bed, Savannah."

I grabbed my flight bag out of the backseat and got out. She looked like she was wiping her eyes as she drove away. I doubted it was the smog.

⊙═╬═⊙

Even at 9,500 feet, the air above the high desert northeast of Los Angeles was hot and uncomfortably bumpy. The *Duck* bucked the convective currents like an unbroken appaloosa. I eased the throttle back, readjusted the mixture, and rode out the thermals.

A fly had somehow found its way inside the cockpit. It buzzed around, strafing instruments, ricocheting off the windows. I tried to feel pity for the little bastard—he'd probably been a telemarketer in a previous life—but somewhere over Hesperia, after his twentieth attempted touch-and-go on my face, I rolled up a sectional map from my flight bag and whacked him into his next plane of existence. The Buddha, who values all life, including flies and telemarketers, would not have been pleased.

Just then, a shadow streaked across the windscreen, followed by a tremendous jolt that made the *Duck* pitch violently down and to the right—wake turbulence from another aircraft. Instinctively, I leveled the wings and raised the nose, my heart hammering in my ears. *I should've never killed that fly.* Forgive me, Buddha.

"Cessna Four Charlie Lima, Joshua Center," the controller said over my headphones, "traffic, ten o'clock, northwest bound, Predator UAV, 12,600 feet, descending."

Now you tell me. "Four Charlie Lima has the traffic," I said, keying the mic.

Ahead and to my left was a drone—an "unmanned aerial vehicle" in Air Force parlance—designed to fire laser-guided missiles at troublemakers like the late Osama bin Laden. It was twice as big as a Cessna 172, painted Air Force gray, with a bulbous nose, thin stubby wings, and an upside-down, V-shaped empennage. At that moment, in some bunker or trailer somewhere, some pilot with his hand on a joystick and his ass planted in a comfortable swivel chair, was watching a monitor and flying the UAV, sipping coffee. He probably never even saw me.

Las Vegas Approach cleared me into the restricted Class B airspace surrounding their city, vectoring me across the airport at Henderson, then over the east end of the main runways at McCarran International, where I watched two jumbo jets on parallel approaches float toward touchdown, 500 feet below me. From there, I banked left on an assigned heading of 280 degrees, flying directly over the casinos on the Strip. Approach handed me off to the tower at North Las Vegas and the controller instructed me to enter the pattern downwind for Runway One-Two right.

"Four Charlie Lima, winds, one-six-zero at seven, cleared to land, Runway One-Two right."

"Four Charlie Lima, cleared to land, one-two right."

My touchdown was a thing of beauty, all modesty aside. I painted it on, cleared the active runway, came to a stop on the taxiway and contacted ground control.

"Ground, Four Charlie Lima requests taxi to transit parking."

"Four Charlie Lima, roger. If you follow that white airport van that's just rolling up to your two o'clock, he'll get you where you need to go."

"Roger."

On the back of the van was a large sign that said, "Follow me." Who was I to argue?

The driver was a clean-cut kid of about twenty who said his name was Jeremiah. As we drew near the parking area, he jumped out of the van and guided me with hand signals into an open parking spot. I shut down the engine. Jeremiah quickly tied down the *Duck* for me, then drove me to the passenger terminal. I tried to tip him a couple of bucks, but he refused them.

"Just doing my job," Jeremiah said cheerfully.

"You should be cloned," I said.

A black Lincoln Town Car with tinted windows was waiting in the no-parking zone as I emerged from the terminal's main entrance. Lamont Royale got out from the driver's side.

"How was your flight?"

"Bumpy."

"Glad I wasn't with you. I don't handle turbulence too well."

"Turbulence is organic to the human experience. We learn from the bumps to appreciate the smooth."

"Man, that's heavy," Royale said. "You should think about starting your own cult."

"Only if there are tax exemptions and groupies."

He grinned, took my bag and deposited it in the trunk. I opened the rear passenger door. Sitting on the other side of the bench seat was Miles Zambelli.

"Welcome to Las Vegas," he said without looking up from his smartphone.

Royale shut my door, then climbed in behind the wheel. We pulled away from the airport and out onto Rancho Drive.

"Perhaps you'd care to tell me what it is you plan to discuss with Mr. Carlisle," Zambelli said, pecking away on his phone. "That way, he'll know what to expect and can prepare accordingly."

"I'd prefer it be a surprise."

"Mr. Carlisle doesn't care for surprises."

"I suspect he doesn't care for personal secretaries sticking their noses in places they don't belong, either."

Zambelli slowly looked up at me over the top of his John Lennon glasses with the kind of smug condescension those of the upper crust reserve for any lesser life form that dares to question their superiority.

"I'm his *executive* assistant," Zambelli said. "And, just so you're aware, there are no secrets between Mr. Carlisle and myself."

"Well, like the Buddha said, 'There's a first time for everything.'"

I decided I disliked Miles Zambelli. Not because he'd somehow managed to bed my ex-wife, nor because of the possibility, however remote, that he might've had something to do with the death of Arlo Echevarria. Even his ingrained superior smirk didn't do it. No, what chapped my ass about Miles Zambelli as we motored south onto the Strip was the fact that he broke wind like a dairy cow, silent and deadly, while pretending all the while that it wasn't him baking the brownies. The limo stunk like a Chicago stockyard. I could see Royale in the rearview mirror, squinting and trying not to gag. It was 110 degrees outside. I opened my window anyway.

Flanking Las Vegas Boulevard, the sidewalks outside the casinos were a milieu of protuberant bellies and cottage-cheese thighs, of sunburned Midwestern tourists sloshing margaritas out of plastic cups and snapping digital photos of themselves in front of fake Roman statues and laughing way too hard, as if to convince themselves of all the crazy fun they were having. Everybody seemed to be talking on cell phones except the homeless people, who talked to themselves. There were young guys with tattoos of skulls and dragonflies, young women with bare midriffs and pierced belly buttons, corpulent old ladies in electric scooter chairs with unfiltered cigarettes dangling from their lips, couples in matching casino souvenir T-shirts towing matching rolling luggage. There were attractive young Asian women in black pantsuits offering free tickets to come watch C-list comedians perform in exchange for interminable time-share presentations, while sad-eyed Latino laborers patrolled seemingly every street corner, handing out pornographic color flyers to every passerby, including prepubescent children walking with their parents.

To hell with the stink inside the limo. I rolled my window back up before I could catch some disease.

Zambelli took out a square of felt from his trouser pocket, unfolded it, and carefully polished his glasses.

"I have my own theories as to what may have happened to Mr. Echevarria," he said.

"Really? Do tell."

"I'd urge you to check out his first wife. My understanding is that she had more than enough reason to hurt him."

"And you know this how?"

"Let's just say I have my sources."

Zambelli let loose another silent stink torpedo. My eyes were stinging. We were about to have a little chat about proper etiquette and how he was either going to have to stop with the ass rumblings or I was going to have to put my foot up his rectum, when we rear-ended a black Cadillac SUV with tinted windows and chrome rims.

The noise of the crash was worse than the crash itself—the screech of brakes followed a half-second later by a jolting explosion of metal-on-metal and the tinkling cascade of broken glass. The limo bucked a couple of feet into the air like a Brahma Bull, then fell back down, bouncing on its suspension.

Zambelli stared straight ahead, blinking. He looked like he was in shock but appeared otherwise unhurt. The same could be said for Royale. The steering wheel airbag had deployed. Steam spewed from the limo's crumpled hood.

"Everybody OK?"

"I'm fine," Zambelli said.

"It wasn't my fault." Royale said. "The guy stopped short."

I undid my seatbelt and got out.

The other driver was already surveying the damage. The rear end of his SUV was stove in like an empty Budweiser can. Pieces of bumper and other debris littered the street. He circled and paced and kept shouting, "Look at my ride!"

He was about five-nine, solid and wide. Shaved skull. Baggy shorts. No shirt. No neck. Pumped pecs and grossly oversized arms— the kind you build juicing steroids. A tattooed German cross took up the whole of his upper back. Over his heart, in six-inch gothic script and surrounded by a daisy chain of intertwined ivy and little swastikas, were the letters "AB"—for Aryan Brotherhood. The dude was either an avowed white supremacist or he played one on TV.

"So," I said, "how's your day going otherwise?"

"What kind of stupid fucking question is that? Jesus Christ! Look at my fucking ride!" He was in a 'roid rage. His topaz eyes looked like they were about to explode out of his bullet head.

"Relax, cowboy. Insurance'll cover it."

"I got no insurance, fuckhead!"

"We do. Trust me, your pimpmobile will be back in shape before you know it. Better'n new. And you won't be out a penny. The important thing is, nobody got hurt, right?"

He drew a deep breath and let it out, trying to dial down his temper. "I want a rental car while mine's in the shop—and none of them little fuckin' Hello Kitty Jap rides, neither."

"I'm sure that can be arranged."

Other cars maneuvered around us through the intersection. Two drivers rolled down their windows to holler that they'd called 911. I could hear an emergency siren in the distance.

Royale climbed out of the limo and strode over. "Why'd you stop?" he demanded of the Aryan.

"Why did I stop? I stopped because the light was yellow, asshole!"

"You stop at a red light, not yellow."

"Maybe in Africa."

"I'm not African, motherfucker. I'm American!"

"Who you calling a motherfucker, you little spade faggot!"

They grappled. The skinhead grabbed a handful of Lamont Royale's shirt and was about to slam him face-first into the side of the SUV, when I hooked his arm and flipped him over my left thigh, judo-style. He landed on his face, scraping his forehead bloody. Bits of gravel stuck to the wound. He bounced to his feet and flicked open a switchblade.

"You just made the worst mistake of your life," he snarled.

"If you only knew how many mistakes I've made in life, Adolf, I'm confident you'd retract that statement."

"Fuck you."

He lunged. I sidestepped the blade, snatched his hand, then twisted it back and away from his body, splintering the joint with an audible snap. *A deceptively benign sound*, I thought. *Like Mrs. Schmulowitz clicking her tongue.* He dropped the knife and rolled around on the street, clutching his broken wrist and writhing in agony.

"You'll pay for this! I'm suing your ass! You hear me?"

I picked up the knife, retracted the blade, and put it in my pocket. I could have lectured him on the notion that suffering is really payback for our own bad deeds, and that I would probably be repaid with excellent karma for putting down a racist puke like him. But I didn't. It probably wouldn't have done any good anyway.

"Thanks, man," Lamont Royale said. "I owe you one."

"My good deed for the day," I said.

A fire engine and paramedic unit rolled up. Zambelli walked over, looking like some NASCAR fan who'd just witnessed a spectacular crash, his expression one of horror and rapture.

"You totally *owned* that guy," he said.

"I'm just glad you had my back."

I doubted my sarcasm was lost on him. The man went to Harvard.

TEN

Gil Carlisle's 14,000-square foot penthouse occupied the top three floors of a fifty-four-story high-rise one block off the Las Vegas strip and a thousand light years from the tumblin' tumbleweeds of west Texas where he'd grown up. Cut-crystal chandeliers hung from twenty-three-foot ceilings. There were fragrantly fresh gardenias in Waterford vases, and a circular stairway hewn from solid French limestone. There was Frank the bodyguard, standing watch near the private elevator where my ex-father-in-law greeted me.

"Seven bathrooms, seven bidets," Carlisle observed proudly with a sweep of his hand as he walked me into the living room. "Hell, I didn't even know what a bidet was before I bought the place. Y'all want something to drink? An Arnold Palmer, some lemonade or something? Mr. Royale can whip you up anything you want."

"Mango nectar," I said, for the hell of it.

"On the rocks?" Royale said.

"Rocks are for cavemen."

"Blended it is."

He strode across the living room to a fully stocked bar that looked like it had been salvaged from the saloon scene of some Old Western movie.

"Never knew you to be a mango man," Carlisle said.

"The Buddha was big into mangos. Tons of vitamins."

"Makes sense."

I had no idea whether the Buddha liked or loathed mango juice. I only asked for a glass of the stuff because the still-bitter former son-in-law in me wanted to let my still-controlling ex-father-in-law know that I wasn't quite as predictable as that guy who'd been only too willing a few days earlier to pocket his $25,000 check like some junkie scoring a fix.

"Yeah, Mr. Royale's one of a kind," Carlisle said, loud enough for Lamont to hear. "Came to work for me about six months ago. I don't know how I ever lived without him. Cooks like a damn French chef and hits a drive 300 yards, straight as a Comanche's arrow. He keeps giving me lessons out on the course, I'm gonna be joining the tour. Me and Tiger."

"Luckiest day of my life, the day I went to work for Mr. Carlisle," Royale said, slicing a fresh mango from behind the bar.

Carlisle and I sat down on a long couch covered in steer hide. He asked me if I intended to press charges against the knife-wielding skinhead whose wrist I'd broken on the way in from the airport. I said I had better things to do.

Zambelli entered. "Sir, excuse my interruption. Mr. Tarasov just faxed in the draft memorandum of agreement on the Kashagan limited partnership. Everything appears to be in order." He handed Carlisle a sheaf of documents and gave me a sideways look while Carlisle took a gold Mont Blanc fountain pen from his shirt pocket and unscrewed the cap.

I waited as Carlisle skimmed the documents and edited the partnership agreement.

"Mr. Logan was reluctant to share information with me," Zambelli said, more to me than his boss. "He said he was concerned about confidentiality."

"My young assistant here is chompin' at the bit to know what you've learned with respect to Mr. Echevarria since we last spoke," Carlisle said. "I'd have to say he's not alone."

"I'd prefer that we talk alone."

"Whatever you have to say to me, you can say in front of Mr. Zambelli."

Zambelli's lips curled in a gloating smile.

Carlisle handed Zambelli the documents, returned the gold pen to his shirt pocket, crossed his arms and waited for me to dish.

I asked him when was the last time he'd spoken with Echevarria.

Carlisle looked away, thinking. "You know," he said after a few seconds, "I don't rightly remember. About a week before he passed, as best I can recall."

"Echevarria flew to Kazakhstan a week before he died. I assume you knew that."

Zambelli cleared his throat and pretended to sift through the signed documents, while Carlisle gazed at me a little too dispassionately. "What's that got to do with the price of eggs?"

"You're planning to do business in Kazakhstan, Echevarria goes to Kazakhstan. A week later, he's murdered."

Carlisle got up and looked out at the view. Through his eighty-foot expanse of greenhouse-style windows, he could take in all of downtown Las Vegas and the sunbaked wastelands of Nevada beyond.

"It's important to know the lay of the land, who your friends and enemies are, before you start writing big checks," he said, watching traffic crawl along on the boulevard below. "I had Arlo do some digging for me. Just to be on the safe side."

"When you say 'friends,' you mean Tarasov?"

"Among others."

"Did Echevarria turn up anything?"

"Nothing to suggest that Tarasov would do him any harm."

"Unless, of course, Arlo *did* find something, and somebody took him out before he got a chance to tell you."

"If Arlo had anything to say, I'm sure he would've called me."

"You don't call with sensitive information," I said. "You deliver it in person."

"Sounds to me like you've been watching too many spy movies, Mr. Logan," Zambelli said.

"Who has time for movies? I'm too busy watching *Dancing with the Stars*."

Carlisle turned somberly from the window. "I know that you and Arlo worked for the government in some kind of sensitive job, tracking people, whatever it was the two of you did. We had some beers once. He started telling me things he probably shouldn't have. I hushed him up before he got too far. Never told Savannah a word of it. The point is, I hired him because he was married to my daughter and needed the work. But I can tell you one thing, beyond question: the job he did for me had nothing to do with who killed him or why."

"Are you aware that Pavel Tarasov has been linked to Russian intelligence?"

Carlisle rubbed his eyes and ran his hand across his mouth. "Look, I have every confidence that had Arlo found out anything significant, anything at all, he would've let me know. Pavel Tarasov's a good man. I've seen his heart. I'll consider myself fortunate indeed to be in business with him."

"If he's such a good man," I said, "why did you have Echevarria investigate him?"

"Like I said. Better safe than sorry." Carlisle crossed to the bar and poured himself a scotch.

"Why didn't you tell me your daughter and your assistant, Mr. Zambelli, slept together?"

"That's none of your goddamn business!" Zambelli said. He took an angry step toward me with clenched fists, then thought better of it.

"Maybe not my business," I said, "but it *is* the LAPD's business."

"How the hell's it their business?" Carlisle said.

"Wife has fling, husband leaves, husband turns up dead. I'm no homicide investigator, but I do believe that when they get to the 'who done it' list, the whole jealous lover scenario is usually right up there, no?"

"If you're insinuating that I was somehow jealous of Mr. Echevarria, or that I had anything to do in any way with his death," Zambelli said, "you're sadly mistaken."

Carlisle surveyed me coldly. "You have no right to come into my house, making bullshit insinuations like that."

"You're right, Gil. I probably should've made them at the police station."

Carlisle's eyes were flat hard stones. Gone was the velvet twang from his voice. "Did you tell the police what happened between Savannah and Mr. Zambelli?"

"You asked me to tell them what I knew about Echevarria. That's what I did. Nothing more, nothing less."

"Very good," he said, heading for the door. "I suggest you keep it that way."

"Why don't you want the police to know about Savannah's affair, Gil?"

"Mr. Royale will see you back to your airplane," Carlisle said.

He disappeared down a long hallway. The forcefulness of his stride conveyed barely bridled anger. Zambelli shot me a contemptuous look and followed after him, nearly colliding with Lamont, who swerved like a running back and somehow managed to hang on to the highball glass of mango juice he'd prepared without spilling a drop. A pink hibiscus floated on top.

"The hibiscus is edible," he said, as if he hadn't heard a word of my exchange with Carlisle and Zambelli.

"Bonus," I said.

⊙━━◆━━⊙

Lamont Royale chauffeured me back to the North Las Vegas airport in Carlisle's four-seat Rolls-Royce Phantom Drophead convertible. The car had teakwood paneling and the initials "GC" stitched into its leather headrests. I rode shotgun.

"Don't be too upset with him," Lamont said. "Mr. Carlisle's a fine man."

"I'll take your word for it."

Royale told me how he was originally from Florida. He'd had a few minor scrapes with the law growing up, he said, and was grateful to Carlisle for having taken a chance on him. He told me how much he missed his girlfriend, a dental hygienist named Laura who lived with her widowed father in Los Angeles. They saw each other on weekends, taking turns driving across the desert.

"They're real tight, Laura and her dad; she doesn't want to be too far away from him," Lamont said, glancing over his shoulder as he changed lanes. "I'd move to LA, but then I'd have to quit working for Mr. Carlisle. I just can't see doing that. Best job I ever had."

"Stuck between the rock and hard place."

"Exactly."

He asked me how long Savannah and I had been married.

Long enough to know better, I said.

We stopped at a red light. A van pulled up in the next lane over, hauling a rolling billboard—a toll-free number and the words, "Fresh Hot Girls Delivered To Your Door In 20 Minutes or Less!!!" superimposed over the picture of a huge naked breast.

"I feel terrible for Savannah. She's such a class act," Royale said. "I hope they catch whoever killed Mr. Echevarria. I never had the pleasure of meeting him, but I'm sure he was a real good guy."

"I'm sorry, did you say something?" I said, distracted by the giant breast.

"You don't really think Miles Zambelli had anything to do with it, do you?" Royale said.

"I think that low-wing airplanes are easier to taxi in a cross-wind than high-wing planes. I think that the national championship in college football should be decided in single-elimination tournament play, like basketball. I also happen to think my landlady makes the best brisket this side of the Wailing Wall. Beyond that, I don't know what I really think anymore."

"I just don't think Miles is capable of murder," Royale said.

"You push somebody hard enough," I said, "they're capable of anything."

〇━━◆━━〇

Traffic on Interstate 15 was stop-and-go from Baker south to Victorville as a legion of Southern Californians, their weekend debaucheries in Sin City come to an end, inched their way down Cajon Pass and into the eastern fringes of the Los Angeles Basin. Driving would've taken seven hours given all the congestion. I made it back to Rancho Bonita via air in a little more than two.

Leonardo da Vinci is purported to have said that once a person has tasted flight, "You will walk the earth with your eyes turned skywards, for there you have been and there you will long to return." Old Leo nailed it—at least on days when the vagaries of Mother Nature aren't factored into the mix, as was the case that afternoon. The weather had improved radically in time for my flight back to Rancho Bonita. No clouds. No turbulence. So silky was the air that it felt like the *Duck* was fixed in time and place, dangling there on some invisible thread while the earth glided silently by beneath us. I tried to think profound thoughts. Like how privileged I was to be unshackled from the wingless masses two miles below me, and how grateful I should've felt simply to be alive on such a glorious day. But all I could think about was how that little weenie, Miles Zambelli, had slept with my ex-wife. Which didn't even begin to compare with the venom I harbored for Echevarria. Even now, after all the years, I despised him for having stolen Savannah. I hated myself even more for my inability to let go of it. We'd been brothers-in-arms. Spilled blood together. Gotten stinking blind-eyed drunk together. The Buddha believed that to understand everything was to forgive everything. I had a long way to go, I realized, before I could forgive Arlo Echevarria for *anything*, let alone everything. But I told myself that I would try harder. To find who killed him would be a big first step. Given our shared history, I suppose I owed him that much.

"Cessna Four Charlie Lima, Joshua Approach, turn right thirty degrees for traffic, Boeing 737, four miles southbound, descending out of 11,000 feet into Burbank. Caution wake turbulence."

"Four Charlie Lima is coming right thirty degrees, looking for traffic."

The jetliner was approaching from above and to my right. I tipped my starboard wing, nudged the right rudder pedal and eased into a standard rate turn. My new course would take me well behind the jet. The trick would be to avoid flying through the vortexes of violent air corkscrewing down and away from his wingtips—invisible mini-tornadoes that could easily flip the *Duck* like a flapjack and definitely ruin my day. I turned another twenty degrees and widened the angle between us until our opposing paths were roughly parallel. By the time I turned back on my original heading, we'd be far behind him.

The 737 passed off my left wingtip at a distance of less than two miles. I could see an Eskimo's face painted on the vertical stabilizer. Alaska Airlines. I wondered how many Eskimos were on board. My guess was zero.

⊂━━┼━━⊃

I checked the answering machine in my office at the airport after landing. There were no messages. Not that I expected any. OK, that's a lie. I had hoped that maybe Savannah would've called to offer a truce. But I suppose she could have just as easily called me on my cell phone. She hadn't done that, either.

Kiddiot was asleep in the oak tree when I got home. I told him that I'd missed him and encouraged him to come down and share some quality time. He raised his head, yawned, and went back to sleep. My punishment for having abandoned him.

"He wouldn't touch his food," Mrs. Schmulowitz said, dragging a trash bag out her back door. "I'm telling you, that is one persnickety cat."

I took the bag from her despite her insistence that she was perfectly capable of taking out her own garbage and deposited it in a can out in the alley.

"By the way, somebody else came by looking for you," she said when I walked back into the yard through the gate. "Not the hunky bill collector, either."

"Who was it?"

"I didn't ask. But I'll tell you one thing: whoever he was, he was no fan of yours. Some piece of work, this *schmuck*. He wanted to know where you were. Tells me he's your friend. So I say to him, 'If you're his friend, you must know where he is. You don't gotta ask me.' Then he gives me this look, like Paul Muni in *Scarface*, you know, the original, before the remake, the one with—what the blazes is his name?"

"Al Pacino?"

"Al Pacino—always screaming! Every movie like a human steam whistle, this man. OK, Mr. Top of Your Lungs, we know your vocal cords work. What else did you get for Hanukkah? Paul Muni never had to raise his voice. Not once. Now, *there* was an actor. And I'll let you in on a little secret: his name wasn't Muni. It was Meier—Meshilem Meier Weisenfreund. And I don't have to tell you what kind of name *that* is. That's right. Paul Muni was Hebrew! Lauren Bacall, too, *and* Kirk Douglas. *And* William Shatner! Not to mention Mr. Spock."

"Not to change the subject, Mrs. Schmulowitz, but could we please go back to the *schmuck* who came to see me?"

"The *schmuck*. Right. So anyway, again he asks me, 'Where is he?' Meaning you. So I tell him, 'Listen, buster brown, if you don't get off my porch in the next five seconds, I'm calling the cops.' He gives me that look again, like I'm supposed to be afraid, then turns around and leaves. A real *shtik fleish mit tzvei eigen*, that one."

The man she described was dusky, five-foot-ten, maybe taller, 180 pounds or so.

"Built like a wide receiver," Mrs. Schmulowitz said.

He wore sunglasses, blue jeans, a plain white T-shirt, untucked, and a yellow ball cap with the logo of a cow on it.

"You sure it was a cow?"

Mrs. Schmulowitz smirked. "I may not come from a long line of farmers, Bubeleh, but I do know what a cow looks like."

"What about his car? What did that look like?"

"Small. White. With fancy schmancy wheels, and one of *those things* on the back."

"Things?"

"Like a race car."

"A spoiler?"

"Spoiler, schmoiler. One of those *things*. Like a *wing*."

I asked her if the car could've been a Honda.

"What do I know from a Honda?" Mrs. Schmulowitz said. "All these cars today. A New Yorker. A Buick Regal. Now, *those* were cars!"

White. Small. With fancy schmancy wheels. And one of those *things* on the back. It sounded suspiciously like the car that had pursued me from the airport before I left for Los Angeles.

Kiddiot climbed down from the tree with slow caution, one paw after the other, and jumped the last couple of feet to the ground. He rubbed up against Mrs. Schmulowitz's legs, making little chirping noises. When he was finished showing my landlady how much he was into her, he sauntered toward me—and trotted past without stopping, straight into the garage. I made a note to self: no more cat toys for Kiddiot from the clearance bin at Petco. No more Taco Bell leftovers, either. Not until he showed me some love, too.

"Some nerve," Mrs. Schmulowitz observed. "After all you've done for him."

⸺⬦⸺

You don't need an appointment at Primo's on Cortez Avenue in downtown Rancho Bonita. You walk in and climb into Primo's ancient barber chair, assuming it's otherwise unoccupied. Primo hands you a well-worn *Playboy* without asking and pins a sanitary neck strip around your neck. He takes a cutting smock and flaps it high into the air, the way matadors flap capes, then lets it settle gently around your shoulders while you thumb through the magazine. He raises the chair with a few pumps of the pneumatic lift, pivots you so you're facing the mirror, and then, standing beside you, comb and scissors at the ready, asks, "So, how would you like your hair cut today?" Then he proceeds to ignore your detailed instructions and cuts your hair the way *he* thinks it should be cut, which is usually not half-bad. For fifteen bucks, including a beard trim and a five-minute neck rub, you can't go wrong.

Business was slow that morning. Primo was sitting in the chair, his own jet-black hair pomaded and perfectly combed as usual, wearing his usual spotless sky-blue Mexican wedding shirt. The bell jingled over the door. Primo looked up from the latest issue of *Boxing Monthly*.

"*Que pasa*, Logan?"

"How've you been, champ?"

"It's all good, boss."

Primo got up out of his barber chair, a little stiff, befitting a sixty-one-year-old former fighter. I settled into the chair. The comfortable brown leather seat was warm and bowed like an old swayback horse. He handed me a *Playboy*.

After the sanitary strip had been pinned in place and the smock settled down around me, he said, "And how would we like our haircut today?"

"In silence," I said, perusing Miss February. "Need to catch up on my reading."

"In silence it shall be," Primo said.

Our little joke.

Primo and I rarely talked while he worked his magic on my tresses. We liked it that way, content in each other's company. No need to humor or impress. He'd been a pretty good welterweight in his prime, I gleaned from what little of his career he'd shared with me. His nose was bent like the blade of a hockey stick—a souvenir from a summer night forty years earlier when he'd gone twelve rounds with Pipino Cuevas at the Fabulous Forum. The crowd cheered, "Primo! Primo! Primo!" over and over as he stood toe-to-toe with the younger, stronger Cuevas, giving as good as he got, only to loose on a split decision. Every writer sitting ringside that night said it was a con job. But it didn't matter to Primo. He'd gone the distance with the champion when every bookie from Reno to Tijuana swore the match wouldn't last two minutes.

He got out barber shears and a clean comb from a drawer while I read all about Miss February. I was old enough to be her father. Snip-snip-snip. Primo circled me like he was still in the ring, clipping and combing. The shop was redolent of bay rum and Aqua Velva. My scalp tingled pleasurably. I closed my eyes and let my mind drift. Fifteen minutes later, we were done.

He handed me a mirror to check the back of my head. I nodded my approval and gave him twenty bucks. He deposited the bill in an old cigar box and took out a five spot.

"Keep the change."

Primo forced the bill into my hand. "No way, boss."

"It's called a tip, Primo."

"You ain't been in for a cut in three months, Logan. That tells me you gotta be more hard up than me. So you keep it. Spend it on your lady. Buy her some flowers or something."

I made a joke about him not realizing how much flowers cost these days.

"Don't matter how much they cost. Just get 'em. It'll make her feel good," Primo said. "The thing you always gotta remember about women is this: at any given moment, they are what they feel."

Primo's version of a fortune cookie. Every customer got one on their way out the door, whether they wanted it or not.

"I have no idea what that means, champ."

"Go buy yourself a copy of *Cosmo*," Primo said. "Probably do you some good."

He was right. It probably would've helped, if I'd actually had a woman in my life. One particular woman, anyway.

ELEVEN

They say meditation is an adventure in self-discovery. It's supposed to bring one a sense of fullness, of completion. It is, according to those who swear by its power, the eternal essence of nature taking on the order of the universe within the mortal human frame. Whatever the hell that means.

I've tried sitting and meditating. The sit-stand method of meditation. The recliner-chair method. I've tried mirror gazing. All with no joy. While I wait for the indescribable bliss that the earth is supposed to unleash upon those who meditate with sincerity and patience, my head is filled with questions like, "Who do the Broncos play Sunday?" or "Does anyone *really* know what Jell-O is made of?" or "I wonder what Savannah is doing right now?"

Savannah. It always seemed to come back to Savannah.

I was sitting lotus-like on the sand at Jenkins Beach, trying to become one with the universe and failing miserably. In the haze, the oil platforms two miles offshore resembled aircraft carriers. A jogger ran past me, her path paralleling the retreating tide line. She was petite, mid-twenties, with sinewy legs and a strong, determined face more handsome than pretty. Her chestnut hair was pulled back in a severely tight ponytail that flapped side-to-side like a metronome, the way Savannah's hair did, when we used to go running together.

I shut my eyes and tried to focus on my inner self. "I am not this library of memories. I have no history. I have no biography." I repeated it over and over, my self-inquiry incantation. "I am the space. I have always been the space, and I crush these bonds of attachment *now*."

But it was no use. The universe and I definitely were not one.

My phone rang. The caller ID said Savannah Echevarria. She was angry with me. What else was new?

"First, you tell my father you think his business partner killed Arlo—"

"—I never said that."

"Then, you have the audacity to tell him that Miles Zambelli did it?"

"I never said that, Savannah."

"Well, you certainly insinuated it!"

"You asked me to help. I'm trying to."

"I asked you to go to the police. I didn't ask you to piss off everybody. You need to stop asking all these questions."

"Why? Because you're afraid of what I'll find out?"

The anxiety in her voice was undeniable. "Just stop. Please. Before it's too late."

She hung up.

I sat on the beach the rest of the afternoon, staring at the waves, trying to comprehend her words. *Before it's too late.* Why did Savannah want me to back off when she'd been so adamant that I get involved to begin with? I thought of Primo's advice: *At any given moment, a woman is what she feels.* Savannah's fear was palpable. But why? What had happened in the interim between her begging me to tell the police what I knew about Echevarria, and her insisting that I stop asking questions about who may have killed him? The answer had to be in the kind of questions I was asking. Or the people I was asking them to.

I called Buzz. Dangling the promise of a gift certificate to Dave and Buster's, I asked him to check the records for me on Miles Zambelli. Buzz said he'd get back to me.

I drove a circuitous route to the airport, checking my mirrors frequently, my gun tucked between my legs. Nobody followed me.

○═⟨═○

Larry's hangar was empty. He'd gone for the night. There were two messages on my answering machine. The first was from Eugen

Dragomir, my one and only prospective student pilot. His father was rushing him a check made out in my name for $5,000. Eugen would be by with the money as soon as it arrived. I allowed myself a smile. Another five grand on top of the twenty-five large from Carlisle. I vowed not to tell Kiddiot. Knowing him, he would definitely demand I buy him more cat toys.

The second message was from Lamont Royale. He said he needed to speak with me urgently. I called him at the number he left. It took him several rings to answer.

"I'm in the middle of something," he said in a hoarse whisper. "Let me get back to you."

"I'll be here."

I sat down at my desk and reread the paid death notice Savannah placed in the *Times* after Echevarria died.

He was born in Oakland in 1961. Bullshit. The Arlo Echevarria I knew was born in Guatemala and emigrated at age five, crossing the border at Calexico with his mother, both hidden behind the driver's seat of a tractor-trailer truck hauling cantaloupes up from Zacatecas. They'd settled in San Diego and later Oceanside, where Echevarria's mother found work cleaning the bachelor officers' quarters at Camp Pendleton. The Marines made a lasting impression on Echevarria. He would enlist in the Corps on his seventeenth birthday.

He earned a business degree from San Francisco State. Like hell. The only college Echevarria ever graduated from was what we in Alpha jokingly referred to as the "University of Direct Action." Like the rest of us, he'd earned a bachelor's in close quarters battle and a PhD in "Look at Me so Much as Sideways and I Will Fucking Blow Your Shit Away."

He'd built a successful international trading company. The trading company was little more than a mail drop in a three-story Art Deco office building on Geary Street with gilded styling and a terra cotta exterior, a half-mile west of downtown San Francisco. An outsourced answering service in New Delhi fielded incoming telephone traffic. The operators were instructed to say that Mr. Echevarria was "in a sales meeting" and to take a message whenever anyone called.

"He is survived by his loving and devoted wife and soul mate, Savannah . . . Spare me. To have a soul mate, one first needs a soul. Arlo Echevarria had no soul as far as I was concerned, not after wrecking my marriage. There were times, sure, when I stepped on my own meat in the course of the marriage, but that didn't give him the right to leave his wife and take mine, even if mine ultimately chose to go willingly. As a fellow operator, Echevarria should've kept his hands off my wife in the same way I kept my hands off his. Not that I was even for a moment attracted to his wife. The Janice Echevarria I remembered from the few times I'd met her was a foul-mouth she-devil with too much mascara and too little regard for her husband's welfare beyond how much money he brought home. Under the circumstances, I suppose I couldn't much blame Echevarria for having made a play for Savannah. Then again, maybe I could.

I folded Echevarria's death notice and returned it to the belly drawer of my desk. I thought about what Miles Zambelli had told me in the limo driving in from North Vegas, how Janice Echevarria, Arlo's first wife, had abundant reasons for wanting him dead. The planet is thick with divorced people who secretly wish such ill on their former spouses. Very few, fortunately, ever attempt to carry out those fantasies.

My office phone rang. It was Lamont Royale, calling from a very loud casino. He said he had hoped to talk to me in confidence while I was still in Las Vegas, but that would've been impossible. Carlisle, he said, planted listening devices everywhere, including all of his automobiles.

"I have some . . . on . . . Mr.—" Lamont said.

I could barely hear him above the din of carnival music and the metallic clink-clink-clink of slot machines paying out.

"Say again?"

He repeated himself, only louder and slower. "I have some information on Mr. Echevarria's murder."

Something thudded heavily just then against the concrete floor to my left, caromed off my trash can, and came to rest near my feet. I looked down: the object resembled the kind of cardboard roll toilet paper comes on, only metal and painted olive drab, with a big metal cap on each end. A stun grenade.

"*Five-banger,*" I thought to myself.

BANG! BANG! BANG! BANG! BANG!

A succession of deafening but otherwise harmless explosions meant to shock, not kill, rocked the hangar, as helmeted SWAT officers in green Nomex flight suits from the Rancho Bonita PD came swarming in with short-barrel shotguns and MP-9 submachine guns. They were yelling "On the ground!" and "Get on the ground!" and "Lemme see your hands!" and it looked like they couldn't wait to put a bullet in somebody, anybody. I sat with my hands folded placidly on my desk so that somebody wouldn't be me. Two seconds later, I was kissing the concrete, gun barrels jammed against my head, knees against my back, while my arms were yanked painfully behind me and my wrists handcuffed. I noticed there were many dust bunnies under my desk and a ballpoint pen I'd been hunting for more than a month. I remember thinking to myself, *I really do need to do some cleaning around here.*

The police yelled, "Clear!" and two SWAT officers hoisted me up off the floor by my armpits. A third frisked me, a big, jarhead-looking dude with freckles.

"I'd offer you coffee," I said to the lawmen, "but, one, I don't have any, and, two, you guys look like you're already way over-caffeinated."

It wasn't hard to find the two-inch revolver stuck in my belt. Freckles handed the weapon to his sergeant, then finished patting me down.

"He's clean," Freckles said. The officers who'd hoisted me off the floor slammed me back down into my desk chair.

Czarnek and Windhauser strolled in as if on cue.

"Five-banger," I said to the detectives. "A little overkill, don't you think?"

Windhauser propped his ass on the corner of my desk, planted a cowboy-booted foot up on my chair, and squinted hard at me, arms folded, while Czarnek read me my Miranda rights from a little laminated card. I told them I understood my rights. I was happy to talk. The entertainment value alone would make the conversation more than worthwhile.

Windhauser smoothed the ends of his Wyatt Earp moustache with his thumb and index finger and said, "We know you killed him, Logan."

"Killed who?"

"You *know* who."

"You play games with us, Mr. Logan," Czarnek said, working his Nicorette, "and I guarantee you, it's gonna go a lot harder on you than you can ever possibly imagine."

They had on the same winter-weight wool sport coats they wore the last time I'd seen them. Same color shirts. Same ties.

"*Dragnet* called," I said. "They'd like their wardrobe back."

Windhauser grunted.

"We spoke to your ex-wife," Czarnek said. "She confirmed you were quite upset with Mr. Echevarria as far as the two of them getting, you know, romantically involved."

"Guilty as charged."

The two detectives looked at each other. This was starting out better than they'd planned.

"So, you're saying you *did* do him?" Windhauser said.

"I'm saying I was upset. I didn't say I killed him—not that I didn't frequently consider it."

Another look between them.

"Lemme spell it out for you," Windhauser said. "We got a warrant to search for the murder weapon. So we're gonna toss this place—I mean, *rip it the fuck up*. We don't find the weapon here, we're gonna toss your apartment cuz we got a warrant for it, too, OK? And if we don't find it there, we're gonna rip up your airplane. Then we're gonna rip up your truck. We don't find the gun by then, we're gonna come back and start all over again. So why don't you just do yourself and everybody else a favor and tell us where it's at."

"You guys need some new threads," I said. "I mean, tweed is so three years ago."

Windhauser exhaled. He got up, took a couple of steps toward the door, then turned and pointed a finger at me. "You think you're so fucking smart. Lemme tell you something, chuck wagon, this is gonna go south on you in a hurry unless you start singing another tune."

"Did you just call me *chuck wagon?*"

The SWAT sergeant stepped in. "We found this on him," he said, showing Windhauser my little revolver. "Bad boy was fully loaded."

Freckles and his sergeant shared a celebratory fist bump. The murder weapon had been recovered. Case closed.

"It's Miller time," Freckles said.

Windhauser stared up at the ceiling and rubbed the vein in his forehead.

"Maybe if you morons had bothered to *read* the warrant, you'd know the weapon is a .40-cal semi-auto, not some fucking wheel gun! I don't even know why we even bothered calling you people in to assist. I mean, Jesus Christ!" He shouldered past Freckles and out of the hangar.

The Rancho Bonita sergeant looked forlorn enough at having been put in his place by the big city detective that for a moment I thought he might start crying. He handed my revolver to Czarnek who tucked it in his sport coat, dug a fresh toothpick out of the breast pocket of his shirt and began picking his teeth.

"We checked with your landlady," he said. "She confirmed you and her have dinner Monday nights during football season. Only she has no specific recollection of the night Echevarria was killed."

"We had pot roast with carrots and potatoes. The gravy was excellent. No lumps."

"Yeah, well, I'm sure it was delicious but, see, here's the deal: if the old lady can't remember eating with you that night, and you got no other alibi, then we got no choice but to start looking for that semi-auto. Unless you want to tell us where it is."

"Look in the desk."

Czarnek cocked his head and his eyebrow, intrigued. "It can't be that easy." He pulled open a side drawer and started tearing through it like a kid opening a present on Christmas Day.

"Belly drawer," I said.

He shut the drawer he was rummaging through and opened the one I'd told him to check. Inside were mostly aircraft maintenance records and FAA paperwork. Czarnek found the photo of Echevarria and me, posing with the dead Arab.

"Your ex-wife showed us this picture," he said. "You Photoshop this?"

"Photoshop. Right. I'm still trying to figure out how to retrieve email."

Czarnek set the picture aside and dug deeper through the drawer.

"No gun," he said when he was finished.

"Never said there was a gun."

"Then what the hell was I just looking for?"

"Receipt."

"A receipt?"

"One pint of vanilla ice cream, one frozen apple pie, and, if I recall correctly, six cans of Fancy Feast cat food."

Czarnek spit his gum into my trash can. "OK," he said. "I'll bite."

"Mrs. Schmulowitz forgot dessert that night," I said. "She sent me out at halftime—which, according to your records, would've been just about when Echevarria got shot. I walked over to the Portola Street Market, a couple blocks from my apartment. Owner's name is Kang. Good guy, except he's an Oakland Raider fan. Kang'll remember me being there that night. He remembers everything."

Czarnek looked at me questioningly, then went back through the belly drawer to find the computerized cash register receipt. The date and time stamp confirmed that I'd made my purchase within five minutes of when Echevarria's neighbors began calling 911 to report gunshots.

"Without traffic, Echevarria's house is a good hour and a half drive from Rancho Bonita," I said. "Even if I'd flown there that night, I would've had to land at Van Nuys, then rent a car or take a taxi. There's no way I could've been there and at Kang's market within a span of five minutes. Unless, of course, I was Carlos Castaneda."

"Who's Carlos Castaneda?"

"The whole Mesoamerican, shamanism thing, being in two places at once?"

Czarnek gazed at me blankly.

"Forget it," I said.

He conceded that there was no way any prosecutor would ever file murder charges against me, not with the receipt he had in his hand, and not after Kang, the owner of the market, vouched for my whereabouts that night.

"I do find it a little strange, you keeping receipts from the corner grocery store," Czarnek said.

"My landlady's thinking of taking flying lessons. As a prospective student, the pie and ice cream are legitimate business expenses."

Czarnek glanced at the receipt. "What about the cat food?"

"Cat's narcoleptic, not to mention the fact he has the IQ of a houseplant. I'm fairly confident the FAA would never issue him a pilot's license."

Czarnek probably would've laughed if the LAPD didn't have an image to maintain. He tucked the receipt back in the belly drawer of my desk. Then he unhooked the cuffs.

<hr>

Windhauser wasn't happy about his partner wanting to cut me loose. He theorized that I could've cooked up a cover story by having somebody go to Kang's market and get a time-stamped receipt for me, while I was really down in LA, murdering Echevarria. Windhauser even insisted that Czarnek drive us over to the Portola Street Market so that he could personally question Kang. I waited unobserved in the backseat of the detectives' Crown Vic, the windows rolled down, and enjoyed the show.

Kang stood behind his cash register, arms folded, answering Windhauser's questions while watching a strung-out speed freak in a hooded sweatshirt prowling the bread and donut aisle. Kang was a stout hardhead with shifting slits for eyes that missed nothing. He'd been a martial arts instructor in the South Korean Army. No would-be shoplifter ever made it out the door at Kang's market on Portola Street in one piece. Ever.

He told Windhauser he was "100 percent positive" he'd seen me the night of the murder.

"Logan give me crap at halftime for being Raider fan. He funny dude. Good customer."

"How can you be so sure it was halftime when he came in," Windhauser said.

"Halftime, we talk. Game, I watch. No talking."

"How do I know you're not covering for him?"

Kang's eye slits shifted from the meth head to Windhauser like the detective's question was delivered in a foreign language.

"Maybe he calls in," Windhauser speculated. "Maybe he says, 'Hey, Kang, old buddy, do me a favor and ring me up some pie and whatnot and I'll be by in a couple hours to pick it up.' You figure the request is a little weird, but what the hell? The guy's a good customer. Isn't that what you just told me?"

"He buy ice cream and want me to put it under counter? Ice cream melt under counter."

"The freezer. Whatever. I'm just saying."

Kang shifted his eye slits back to the druggie, who was getting a little too intimate with a twelve-pack of Ding Dongs.

"You gonna buy those or have-a-sex with them?"

The tweaker looked over at the no-nonsense Korean shopkeeper and the no-nonsense bulge under Windhauser's sport coat, and wisely returned the Ding Dongs to the shelf.

"Ice cream in a bag, under a-da counter," Kang said to Windhauser, still watching the crank head. "You fuckin' crazy, man."

"Look," Windhauser said, "you need to understand something here, chief. We're conducting a homicide investigation. Let me repeat that: a *homicide* investigation, OK? I find out you're providing false and misleading information, you're on the first sampan back to Peking."

Kang slowly shifted both eye slits back toward Windhauser like the battleship Missouri bringing all guns to bear.

"I'm *Korean*-American," he said. "Now get the fuck out of my store, *chief.*"

The detectives drove me the two blocks home. Windhauser said he still harbored suspicions, but conceded that there was no evidence to keep me in custody. Czarnek said he hoped there were no hard feelings and shook my hand. I offered to take them both sightseeing in my airplane. Forgive and forget, I always say. Well, maybe not always. Czarnek said he'd definitely think about it and gave me my gun back. Windhauser said nothing.

○══╾══○

I returned Lamont Royale's call the next morning and got his voice mail. If he had any insights as to who killed Echevarria, I told him, I was all ears. My next call was to Detective Czarnek. I asked him to fax me a copy of Echevarria's autopsy report.

"I can't do that," Czarnek said.

"Sure you can. All you do is put some paper in the machine and hit send."

"I'd have to clear it with my supervisor, and I don't think he'd go for it."

"I'm trying to help you, Detective."

Czarnek exhaled. "I know."

Kiddiot sat in front of his cat door and looked at it like he'd never seen it before, yowling mournfully to be let out. No use arguing with an animal that dumb. I opened the people door. He sauntered past my feet and into the backyard like he was the one doing me a big favor.

I asked Czarnek if the LAPD had any other suspects in the case. He cleared his throat and lowered his voice.

"You were it," he said.

I could hear Windhauser's voice in the background. He was bitching to someone about how much he'd been ripped off for termite repairs on his house.

"How many other homicides you guys working?" I asked Czarnek.

"I don't even fucking know at this point," the detective said. "Gangs are keeping us crazy busy right now. Big turf war going on. Pacoima Flats and Paxton Street Locos. Little punks. I'd like to take a bazooka to all of 'em."

"I know a couple of places where you could pick one up cheap."

"That story you rattled off at lunch the other day," Czarnek said, "about you and Echevarria doing the Lord's work. That true?"

"Well, if it wasn't, it ought to be."

There was a pause like he was thinking about it. Then he said, "Gimme your fax number."

I had no fax number. Mainly because I had no fax machine. Couldn't afford one. I gave Czarnek the number to Larry's machine in the hangar instead.

Larry's fax machine was broken. Something about the feeder mechanism. Every incoming page looked like it had gone through an accordion, then splotched black. Larry said he'd been intending to get the piece of crap fixed but lacked the necessary funds. Now that I'd finally paid him what I owed him in back rent, he could send it out for repair.

"I'll get to it next week," he said, bent over his workbench, tinkering with a troublesome magneto.

I called Czarnek back, told him my machine was on the fritz, and gave him the number for my "other fax." I didn't tell him I happened to share it with Kinko's.

<hr/>

The seven-page report was waiting for me by the time I drove downtown to the copy shop a half-hour later. Czarnek had also faxed a copy of the LAPD's preliminary investigation of Echevarria's homicide, including witness statements.

"Interesting reading," the clerk said.

"Only if you like blood and gore," I said.

She was maybe twenty-two, not unattractive in an underfed, nose ring, urban grunge kind of way. "I'm totally into blood and gore," she said. "Seriously, I would *kill* to work for CSI." She slid the faxed pages into a flat paper bag. "You know where else I'd like to work? Caltrans. Picking up road kill. Would that be a *great* job or what?"

"'Enjoys scraping dead animals off the freeway.' I've heard that's one of eHarmony's twenty-nine dimensions of compatibility."

She smiled. "With tax, it comes to nineteen dollars and thirty-one cents."

I gave her a twenty and she handed me my change, accidentally dropping a quarter on the floor.

"Oops. Sorry about that." Her Kinko's polo shirt hiked a few inches above her waistline as she stooped to pick up the coin, exposing what looked like a bowl of fruit inked across the small of her back.

They must've passed some new law. Every woman in California under the age of twenty-five is now required to visit her local tattoo parlor so that some sleazoid can etch a permanent reminder of a temporary feeling just north of her butt crack and call it art.

Like a bumper sticker on a Bentley, I thought, trying not to stare.

She handed me the quarter and my receipt. I said I'd let her know if I heard about any vacancies in the field of dead animal retrieval. She thanked me like she meant it.

A block down the street was a coffee shop. The barista working the counter was all pimples and puka necklace. I ordered a cup of black coffee to go. Not a grande Chai Creme Frappuccino. Not a skinny Caramel Macchiato with soy milk. A cup of coffee. Black. To go. The extraordinarily unusual nature of my order seemed to throw him.

"That's a first," he said. "Could I get a name?"

"Lord Emilio Fishbinder, member of Parliament."

He scrawled something with a Sharpie on a wax paper cup and said, "Next in line."

I waited. The place featured the usual collection of office workers reluctant to return to their desks, college girls commiserating about their loser boyfriends, and a paunchy Hemingway wannabe pecking away on his laptop, trying hard to appear deep in creative thought.

"Order ready for Lord Emilio."

I fetched my coffee, sat down at a table outside and read Arlo Echevarria's autopsy report.

If it's true what your mother says, that it's all about what a person is inside, then Arlo Echevarria was a human garbage disposal. Among the approximately 500 milliliters of partially digested contents found in his stomach, the coroner identified tortillas chips, a hot dog, peanuts, barbequed chicken, bamboo shoots, penne pasta with spinach, white rice, and what appeared to be either a Milky Way or Snickers candy bar. His blood-alcohol content registered .07 percent. No narcotics were found in his system. The autopsy also revealed that Echevarria had gone through life with an undescended testicle. Who knew?

The bullet that most likely killed him entered his body slightly above his nipples, fifteen inches below the top of his head and left of his midline. It ripped through the second intercostal space, shredded the lateral edge of his sternum, perforated the arch of his aorta, deflected one and a half inches at the junction of his left subclavian and left common carotid arteries, then punched through the upper lobe of his left lung and fractured the left aspect of his third thoracic vertebra before exiting the middle of his upper back. There was abundant gunpowder stippling around the entry wound, as well as stippling around the other two wounds to Echevarria's torso. This meant that all three shots had been fired at a distance close enough to singe his skin through his T-shirt. Bullet fragments recovered during the autopsy were consistent with a Smith & Wesson .40-caliber, 165-grain, copper-jacketed round.

What the autopsy report told me was that whoever killed Echevarria wanted him *seriously* dead. It also confirmed that the killer was no pro. The oversized caliber of the murder weapon was proof alone of that. Professionals typically prefer .22-caliber pistols.

A .22 is quieter, smaller, more easily concealed. Granted, a .22 slug is roughly half that of a .40-caliber round and offers considerably less stopping power, but a .22 often causes greater damage than larger bullets, with just enough power to ricochet off bones and through vital tissue, bouncing around inside the body like a ping-pong ball. The professional also knows that a .22 bullet is made of soft, unjacketed lead. It deforms easily. That and the fact that it is the most common round made in America makes it virtually impossible to trace. But that wasn't how I knew definitively that Echevarria's murder was the work of a non-pro.

It was the location of the wounds themselves.

Firearms rarely kill instantly. Unless it's a clean head shot, victims often are able to fight on for several seconds before succumbing to shock caused by their catastrophic loss of blood. A dying shooter can squeeze off a lot of rounds in that amount of time. The trick, then, is to place your shots in such a way that your adversary has little chance of returning fire. The technique we used in Alpha, the same technique taught to virtually all trained killers, goes by many titles—the "Mozambique Drill," the "Rhodesian Drill," the "Failure Drill," "Body Armor Defeat," the "2+1 Drill"—but it's all essentially the same concept: two quick shots fired at the target's center mass, or chest, followed by a deliberate third shot to the head.

I learned the method from an alcoholic, chain-smoking former Spetsnaz commando, Laz Kizlyak, who served as Alpha's senior weapons instructor. Laz had honed his craft kidnapping and executing dissidents in Chechnya and Afghanistan before defecting to the West.

"Trauma of impact and wound channel from two shots to center mass cause reflexive nervous system to collapse ninety-six percent of time," I remember him saying in his thick accent my first day on the range. "In other four percent, adrenaline or stimulant drugs will override reflex. This, my lovelies, is why you put third bullet in motherfucker's brain."

I don't know where he got his numbers, but the man knew guns like Hef knows the female form. The only time I ever saw Laz's hand not trembling was when it was holding a loaded weapon.

He taught us to double-tap our first two shots, aiming at the target's center, pausing a millisecond to reassess, then squeezing off the head shot, ideally between the eyes. Any higher, the bullet could deflect off skull bone. Any lower, and it was unlikely to produce the kind of catastrophic damage to the nervous system that Laz liked to call, "The gift that keeps on giving."

We practiced shooting until the process became reflexive muscle memory. Then we practiced more. I would eventually put Laz's lessons to good use in the field more times than I care to remember. Two quick shots to the chest, reassess, then one to the head. The industry standard.

I got good at it. Arlo Echevarria got even better.

I sipped some coffee and watched a scruffy panhandler shake down a couple of Japanese tourists too frightened to tell him no. Then I read the LAPD's report. Every witness said they had heard a single gunshot that night, a pause, then two more shots in quick succession. All three bullets had been delivered to the torso. None to the head. Poor technique. Too much gun.

And then there was Echevarria's own perplexing lack of defensive countermeasures. The nine-millimeter Beretta that the LAPD found wedged in the small of his back, though fully loaded, was effectively worthless. He would've first had to draw and chamber a round before using the weapon against his assailant—a split-second response that in a tactical environment could mean the difference between death and life. A trained hunter-killer doesn't open his front door with such complacency to a stranger late at night in a shitty neighborhood if they legitimately fear someone is out to harm them. You come to the door with pistol in hand, ready to rock. Either Echevarria felt he had nothing to fear, or he'd simply grown complacent in his retirement. Or maybe the whiskey he'd drunk that night had dulled his instincts. I pondered the irony of it: the master caught flat-footed by some bush leaguer. It happens sometimes, I suppose.

I got up to toss my empty coffee cup when Lamont Royale called. He said he was outside the pro shop of the Las Vegas Country

Club and couldn't talk long; Carlisle was inside, testing out new putters. Their tee time was in five minutes.

"I tried calling you back last night," Royale said. "I heard explosions, then the line went dead."

"I was gearing up for the Fourth of July."

"But it's November."

"When you're a true patriot, it's never too early to celebrate the birth of our illustrious nation."

"OK, whatever," Royale said.

"You said last night you had some information about Echevarria?"

"Actually, it's more about his first wife."

Royale told me he'd overheard a heated phone conversation between Savannah and Echevarria less than a week before he died. Savannah was out visiting her father in Las Vegas. According to Royale, Echevarria's ex-wife, Janice, had discovered a diamond ring missing from a safe deposit box. Echevarria, cheapskate that he was, had given Savannah the ring for their engagement without revealing how he'd acquired it. Janice had demanded the ring back.

"He admitted to Savannah where he got the ring, and that if his ex-wife didn't get it back, she was going to put a contract out on him—and she had the resources to do it, too," Royale said. "Savannah was so mad about him giving her some other woman's ring in the first place, she threw it down the garbage disposal."

"Did you tell the LAPD this?"

"I didn't think it was my place, considering I was listening in on a private conversation. I don't know whether it means anything or not. But I thought I should mention it to somebody. Whatever you do, I'd really appreciate you keeping my name out of it. I don't want to upset Mr. Carlisle more than he already is."

"Heaven forbid," I said.

⊙─────⊙

Savannah agreed to meet me that afternoon at a little café across the street from the Santa Monica Airport. The walls were decorated with pictures of classic airplanes and posters advertising old barnstorming movies, the kind of films in which rock-jawed fly-boys in leather helmets and silk scarves always get the girl. My kind of place.

I tied down the *Duck* and made the three-minute walk to the restaurant.

Savannah was parked in a corner booth, behind her big designer shades.

"They make a mean mushroom burger here," I said, sliding in.

"What's so important, you had to see me right away?" she said.

I asked her about the diamond engagement ring.

"You flew all the way down here to ask me that?"

"You know me. Any excuse to fly."

Savannah picked nervously at her lower lip. The busboy brought over menus and glasses of water. She waited until he moved off.

"Did Arlo tell you his ex-wife threatened to kill him?"

"He said it like it was a joke—'She's gonna put a contract out on me if I don't give it back.' I'm sure she was angry with him, just like I was. I probably said I was going to kill him, too. Heat of the moment, Logan. People say things. Arlo didn't take any of it seriously. He knew it was just talk. Hell, I was afraid he might put a contract out on me for throwing the ring away after he told me where he got it."

"Did you tell the police about any of this?"

"And waste their time? What for? Arlo wasn't murdered because I threw away his ex-wife's ring, Logan. He was murdered because of who he was, what he did. He was killed by a professional."

I told her about reading Echevarria's autopsy report and about the decidedly unprofessional way in which he was murdered. I said there was always a possibility the shooter had tried to look amateurish on purpose, to throw investigators off his trail, but that I doubted it.

"The killer didn't conform to modern shooting doctrine," I said.

"You worked in marketing. What would you know about 'modern shooting doctrine'?"

"I read a lot."

Savannah gazed scornfully at me with her sunglasses still on. She knew better.

The waitress was about fifty or so, a bottle blonde sausaged into blue jeans that housed a pair of hips nearly wide enough to land my airplane on. Savannah said she wasn't hungry. My aspiring Buddhist impulses urged me to go with a salad, but my nihilistic past insisted otherwise. I ordered steak fries and a mushroom cheeseburger.

"I love a man who loves his meat," the waitress said, jotting down the order. "Name's Honey. Lemme know if you need *any*thing."

Savannah watched her move off. "Honey my ass."

"She knows a big tipper when she sees one."

"You said you were a vegetarian."

"I prefer to think of myself as more of a work in progress."

"There's this thing now, Logan, in case you haven't heard. It's called cholesterol."

"I didn't know you still cared."

"Yeah? Well, maybe I do. Which is why I want you to stop."

"We're not married anymore, Savannah. If I want a mushroom cheeseburger, I'll order a mushroom cheeseburger."

"That's not what I meant." A helicopter flew low overhead, its engine rattling the restaurant like a minor temblor. Savannah waited. Then she said quietly, "I think my father may know something about Arlo's murder."

"What makes you think that?"

She shook her head, done talking about it. She took off her sunglasses and rubbed her eyes. They were rimmed red from crying.

"What's wrong, Savannah?"

She sipped some water and put her sunglasses back on. "Had I known what I was getting you into, I never would've asked you," she said. "Whatever my father paid you, I'll double it. I just want you to go home. Forget about Arlo. Forget all about this."

"I can't do that."

"Yes, you can. It's easy. Just get back in your airplane and go."

I couldn't think of anything to tell her but the truth.

"Arlo saved my life once. I owe him at least this much."

We were on Mindanao, the southern part facing the Sulu archipelago arching toward Malaysia. Negotiations between the

Moros and the government had broken down the week before. The Islamic Liberation Front was attacking government forces. Our mission was to kill every senior Moro leader we encountered. Through the palms fronting the shoreline outside Zamboanga City, I watched just after sundown as native fishermen in outrigger canoes cast their nets into a placid sea for sardines and eel, as they had done for hundreds of years. I was standing on a low bluff, the view reminding me of some South Pacific landscape Gauguin might've painted, when the first RPG came whooshing in. The warhead would've struck me square had Echevarria not tackled me a half-second before it hit. But I couldn't tell that to his widow, my ex-wife. I'd sworn an oath. Some bonds are stronger than those between a man and a woman. That's just how it is.

"How did Arlo save your life?"

I lied. "We were walking to lunch one day, crossing Mason. There was a cable car coming. I looked the wrong way and didn't see it. He pulled me back right before I got run over."

"Why didn't you ever tell me this before?"

"Must've slipped my mind."

She gazed at me for a long moment, her lips pursed. Then she said, "Next time, tell a better lie," then left to go to the restroom. She never came back.

"Where'd your friend go?" Honey asked with more than passing curiosity when she brought me my burger a few minutes later. "She looked like she had a lot on her mind."

"Her husband was shot to death. She wanted me to talk to the police about what I knew. Now she thinks her father might know something. She's afraid I might be next. But I'm not worried. Wanna know why? Because the Buddha said that if you transcend love, you transcend worry, and if you transcend worry, you transcend fear."

Honey laughed nervously. "Makes sense," she said, like she suddenly realized she was waiting on a crazy person. "Catsup, mustard?"

"I'm good, thanks."

She never came back either.

TWELVE

The wife Arlo Echevarria abandoned to marry mine was herself remarried. Janice Echevarria's second husband, Manila-born Harry Ramos, was a venture capitalist and liaison for several foreign-based energy companies doing business in North America. He was also nearly twenty years Janice's junior. They lived atop Nob Hill in a Greek revival mansion with Italianate colonnades, surrounded by rolling lawns, a priceless collection of marble statuary and an enviably unobstructed view of San Francisco Bay. Janice showed me into her sun-splashed parlor. She wore an off-white pleated skirt that came midway down her calves, maroon spike pumps, a maroon cashmere turtleneck, and a sapphire brooch fat enough to choke my cat.

"How was your drive?"

"I flew up. Landed at San Carlos and rented a car." I gave her my business card.

"That's right. You're a pilot."

She gestured toward a matching pair of richly upholstered wing-back chairs. We sat. On the lamp table between us was a sterling silver coffee service with two bone china cups and a plate of chocolate-dipped biscotti.

"Cream and sugar?"

"Black, please." I glanced around the room while she poured. "I remember when you and Arlo used to live in Oakland, up in the hills."

Janice Ramos handed me a cup and saucer. "I'm glad he's dead," she said without a trace of remorse.

She had short dark hair and dark, deep-set Mediterranean eyes that flashed fire when she was angry, which was her default mode. Her narrow lips were perpetually downturned in what some men might describe as a sexy pout. Take away the mansion and fancy jewels, and she was still every inch the same shrew Echevarria traded up for my wife.

"Arlo never had any feelings for anybody other than himself," she said, dipping a wedge of biscotti in her coffee. "You of all people should appreciate that fact. I mean, be honest, Logan. In all the time the two of you worked together, did he ever *once* mention me, or his son?"

"I'm sure on some level he cared for you both."

"You obviously didn't know him very well then."

I've never understood how two people who once vowed to spend eternity together could grow so far apart that one or both of them would be glad to see the other planted six feet under. I asked her if she had anything to do with his death.

"I only wish," she said. "I couldn't imagine ever enjoying anything more."

"I understand he stole a ring from you."

"Not just a ring. My grandmother's wedding ring."

"You get divorced and six years later, you discover the ring missing? How does that work?"

"I didn't realize he'd taken it until a couple of months ago. I was inventorying all my jewelry to update the insurance. We had a small safe deposit box I'd forgotten all about. The bank records showed that Arlo was the only person who had accessed the box."

"Did you threaten to put a contract out on him?"

She stared at me hard. "Arlo Echevarria was a piece of filth. He lied to me. He lied to everyone he ever met. He was a worthless, conniving husband and a worthless, disengaged father. I mean, it tells you something when your own son hates you. I would've killed him myself, believe me, with my own hands, if I could've gotten away with it."

"So you had somebody else do it for you."

Janice laughed. "If I knew people like that, Logan, I'd take out half of Congress," she said with a blunt candor that told me she was likely telling the truth, "and I wouldn't stop there."

She told me that she and her husband were visiting his family in the Philippines when they got the news. Someone from the LAPD telephoned in the middle of the night, a lady police officer—she didn't catch the name—who apologized for calling so late and said it was her sad duty to inform Janice that her former spouse had met with apparent foul play. She told Janice she was sorry for her loss, to which Janice said she replied, "What loss?"

"She asked me if I had any idea of who might've shot him," Janice said, licking chocolate from her little finger. "I told her I didn't know and I didn't care. Arlo was already dead to me, a long time before that."

The officer asked as a matter of routine if Janice could vouch for her whereabouts in the days leading up to Echevarria's death. She said she provided the names of each of her chauffeurs, cooks, gardeners, maids, corporate pilots and masseuse. All of them, she said, confirmed that she'd been abroad when Echevarria was gunned down. She even volunteered to take a polygraph some weeks later, which she said she aced. The same, she acknowledged, could not be said for their son, Micah.

"They gave him a lie-detector test and it came back 'inconclusive.' He was just nervous. The police knew that. Micah would never hurt anybody."

"Not even the father he despised?"

"He had no use for his father, just like his father had no use for him. Quite frankly, Micah has no interest in how Arlo died, and neither do I."

"Then why'd you agree to see me?"

She set her cup down on the coffee table and smoothed her skirt. "My husband's away on a business trip for three weeks. I'm fucking bored." The come-hither quality of her smile was the very definition of transparent.

"Where'd he go, your husband, if you don't mind me asking?"

"Kazakhstan. Looking at oil properties."

"It's all the rage," I said. "Everybody used to go to Disneyworld. Now they go to Kazakhstan."

"What's that supposed to mean?"

"It means I should be going." I stood.

Disappointed by my apparent lack of carnal interest in her, she turned with sagged shoulders and watched a freighter heading out to sea under the Golden Gate, its deck stacked five deep with multicolored cargo containers.

"I'd like to talk to your son," I said.

"What for?"

"To see what, if anything, he might know about the circumstances of Arlo's death."

"I don't know his current address. He was living somewhere in the East Bay last I heard. He moves around a lot."

"You wouldn't happen to have his cell phone number?"

She sighed, jotted the number on a slip of paper and handed it to me.

"I don't approve of my son's lifestyle," Janice said, "but if you do see him, tell him I still love him."

⊙━✦━⊙

I called Micah Echevarria later that morning. Before hanging up on me, he said he didn't want to talk to me about his father or anything else. When I called him back to say I thought we'd been cut off, he told me to kiss off and hung up again. Whatever happened to telephone etiquette?

I drove across the Bay Bridge into Oakland and stopped for a late breakfast at the Full House Café on MacArthur Boulevard. I'd discovered the Full House years before while tailing an agent from a Middle Eastern country who'd gone there to meet with two Hezbollah operatives interested in acquiring stolen Army anti-tank missiles. I'd grabbed a seat at the counter—an electro-acoustic listening bud planted in my ear—and feasted on red hash made from beets and pork sausage while the Arabs negotiated a price for the missiles at a table near the window. After breakfast, I followed them to a self-storage yard across from the San Mateo County Fairgrounds where the rockets were stashed, then on toward Reno, where they intended to celebrate their deal by touring the local whorehouses. They never made it to Nevada. All three died when their rental car spun off an icy Donner Pass. The CHP called it brake failure. My supervisors called it a job well done.

The Full House had changed little over the years since I'd been there. I ordered my eggs over easy, called Buzz and asked for another favor.

"I'm still waiting on that gift certificate," he said.

"It's in the mail."

"Like I've never heard that before."

I gave him Micah Echevarria's cell phone number. I needed a corresponding address, I said, and any other readily available information that might offer me relevant insights as to what made the kid tick. I also wanted to know if there was anything in any intelligence files implicating Harry Ramos, Janice Echevarria's second husband, whose interests in Kazakhstan oil seemed to coincide with those of my former father-in-law and his prospective Russian business partner, Pavel Tarasov. Buzz said he'd have to call me back.

I was finished with breakfast and working on my third cup of coffee when he did.

There were abundant references to Ramos on file, Buzz said, mostly having to do with his many overseas investments, but nothing to suggest that he, either personally or by corporate DBA, had ever been associated with any known intelligence operations, foreign or domestic. Nor had he ever been implicated in any criminal investigations. Computerized link analysis failed to connect him even remotely to Tarasov or, for the matter, Gil Carlisle.

Echevarria's son came out clean, too, Buzz said, at least as far as intelligence activities were concerned. The kid's arrest record was another matter. Buzz had run his name through the FBI's NCIC database. Micah Echevarria and California's penal codes were hardly strangers: two citations for a minor in possession of alcohol, one misdemeanor shoplifting charge reduced to an infraction, and one third-degree assault charge as a result of a street fight for which he'd spent a month in the San Jose County Jail. In the three years since being issued a driver's license, he'd chalked up three moving violations, all for speeding. He rode a Harley.

I thanked Buzz yet again for his help, and told him I owed him big-time.

"Yeah, yeah," he said, "the check's in the mail. Spare me."

Some say the West Oakland neighborhood known as Ghost Town derived its moniker from the two casket companies that once competed for business there. Others say it's because of the killings that have plagued the area for decades. One thing beyond debate is that Ghost Town is the kind of place where even the police don't go at night unless they're obligated to—and only then with overwhelming backup. Just my luck that Arlo Echevarria's son resided in the heart of Ghost Town.

The address Buzz provided was off of 30th and Union streets in the shadow of the 580 Freeway, a bedraggled duplex sandwiched between two small warehouses. There were steel burglar bars bolted to the windows and gang graffiti splashed on the clapboard walls. A Chevy Caprice Classic, its hood and trunk open to the sky, sat rusting on the dirt amid a sea of calcified dog poop that passed for a front yard.

I observed no motorcycle as I cruised past. I drove around the block, parked my rental subcompact four houses up the street, and waited for Micah Echevarria to come home.

The first gangster, a lookout, showed up within five minutes of my arrival. He was pedaling a tricked-out bicycle absurdly small for his lanky, sixteen-year-old frame, checking me out as he rolled past—ridiculously oversized blue jeans bagging, boxer shorts showing, wearing a black, oversized Raiders hoodie with the hood up, and sucking on a Tootsie Pop. He coasted down the street, glanced at me over his shoulder once more and veered around the corner, out of sight.

Another ten minutes passed and there he was again, still on his bike, this time escorted by five other homeboys on foot. They strode all big and bad toward my car with their hands shoved menacingly in their pockets. I rolled down the window.

"What's up, gents?"

The oldest among them was also the biggest. He was about twenty. He looked like a cross between Tupac and the left side of the Raider defensive line.

"Where you from, man?" Tupac demanded.

"A better question might be, 'Where am I going?' Or, 'How can I change myself to become a happier and more compassionate human being?' Or, 'How can I find common ground between my spiritual self and my ever-growing understanding of the natural world?'"

The homeboys looked at each other.

"No, man," Tupac repeated, "I mean, like, where you *from*?"

"Oh, you mean, like, where am I *from*? Like, am I from county probation and am I here to violate every one of your sorry asses for carrying concealed weapons and associating with known felons? Or am I, like, a decoy cop, sitting here waiting for some little shitheads to try and jack me, so that my SWAT backups, who are all camped out right around the corner and just dying to kick your sorry asses, can come flying in here and make it on to the next episode of *Cops*? Is that, like, what you mean?"

A couple of the 'bangers glanced over their shoulders, looking for the Oakland SWAT team, wiping their mouths anxiously, blinking a little faster.

"He ain't nothin'," the kid on the bike said to Tupac.

Tupac grunted contemptuously and spit sideways, eyeing me the entire time. "Ain't no thing but a chicken wing," he said, and walked on, a kiss-my-ass, Snoop Dog hitch in his get-along. The others followed after him like he was the Pied Piper.

I uncocked the revolver in my hand and stuffed it back in my belt. Nobody bothered me after that.

⊶———⊷

Micah Echevarria thundered home on his Harley hog around eight P.M. wearing a crash helmet reminiscent of Hitler's Wehrmacht, and a Marlon Brando leather jacket with a "California Mongols" patch stitched across the back. He rumbled into the front yard and up the porch steps, unstrapped his helmet, and lashed the bike to the railing with a padlocked chain looped through the front forks. Then he unlocked the door and started inside. I went in right behind him.

"Welcome home, Micah."

He tried to fend me off, but I already had a solid arm bar on him. He was face down on the living room floor before he knew it, his wrist twisted behind him, my knee in his back.

"What the fuck!"

"Relax, buddy. I'm Logan. We spoke earlier. I just want to talk."

"I told you! I got nothing to say to you! Now, get the fuck outta my house before I fuckin' call the cops!"

I patted him down. He had a Rambo-style hunting knife in his right boot. I tossed it on the carpet, out of his reach.

"I'm going to let you up now, OK? Nice and easy. Just talk, that's all."

Slowly I eased my grip on his arm and backed off. He laid there on the carpet trying to catch his breath. I'd last seen him when he was in elementary school. Arlo was hosting a Super Bowl party and had rented an ocean-view suite at Miami's Fontainebleau hotel on the government's dime. Select members of Alpha were invited with their significant others. Savannah and I went. It was the only time I ever saw Echevarria interact with his son—if you can call giving an insecure kid twenty bucks and telling him to go hang out at the pool by himself interaction. I didn't pay much attention to Micah Echevarria that day, either, I'm ashamed to say. Nor did I pay much attention to the moves Echevarria was putting on my wife. I was too busy watching the game and slamming down free liquor. Micah was a gawky fledgling back then. He'd grown into a slender, handsome young man, with a face predominated by his mother's sharp features and his father's dark-hued skin tone. His hair was straggly and clung to his face in long, sweaty strands. He had a wispy Fu Manchu moustache.

"You don't remember me, do you?"

He sat up, rubbing his wrist. "Go fuck yourself," he said.

"I'm trying to find out what happened to your father, who killed him."

"I don't give a shit what happened to my father."

I went to help him up. He pushed my hand angrily aside, stood and walked into the kitchen. The place was a pit. Filthy pots and dishes piled in the sink. The trash overflowing with empty beer bottles. Motorcycle parts strewn about the greasy linoleum floor. A bong shaped like a skull resting on the counter. Micah opened the refrigerator and uncapped a Corona.

I asked him what he was doing when he got the news that his father had been killed.

He took a long swallow of beer. "I don't fucking remember."

"How did you find out he was dead?"

"My mother called. Look, there's nothin' I can tell you, OK? I didn't know the dude. I can't remember the last time I even fucking saw him. So why don't you just fucking leave."

He walked past me and back into the living room. Posters of Hendrix and Che Guevara were tacked to the wall. He plopped down on the futon, jammed his knife back inside his boot, grabbed the TV remote and started watching Animal Planet. A bunch of meerkats were running around. I sat down beside him.

"My cat loves this show," I said. "What he really loves, though, is Sponge Bob."

Micah wouldn't look at me. "Look, I don't know who shot my old man," he said. "If you're thinking it was me, it wasn't, OK? I was in school when it happened."

"Your old man was killed a couple of hours before midnight. Must be night school."

The kid changed channels. A professional wrestler dressed like Zorro was bashing his opponent across the back with an acoustic guitar.

I persisted. "What kind of school meets that late at night?"

Annoyed, Micah dug through a jumble of junk mail heaped atop an overturned cardboard box that doubled as a lamp table. He found what he was looking for and tossed it in my lap: a brochure for something called Oaksterdam University. I glanced through it while wrestlers beat the pretend tar out of each other on TV.

Oaksterdam University was a trade school that gave new meaning to the expression, "higher education." The school prepared its students for positions in California's booming medical marijuana industry. For $200 tuition, you could learn all about how to grow your own weed, which strains work best on which ailments, and how to open your own pot dispensary. You could also learn ways to minimize the chances of the DEA raiding your dispensary and sending you to prison for violating federal narcotics regulations.

"Must be a total trip," I said, "going to Oaksterdam home football games."

The front door opened. A young woman walked in toting a twelve-pack of Coronas. She was Asian. Petite. Pretty. Doc Martens boots, camo cargo pants, tight-fitting black tank top. There was a small silver hoop in her lower lip and matching rings in each nostril. Both eyebrows were similarly pierced, as was the cartilage up and down both ears. She paused, surprised, with her hand on the knob, like she was interrupting something important.

"Come on in," I said, standing. "We were just finishing up, weren't we, Mr. Echevarria?"

"He knows my old man," he said to the girl, then corrected himself, "or did."

"Cool."

She shut the door, walked into the kitchen and stashed the beer in the refrigerator.

I left my card on the TV and walked to the front door. The girl sat down close beside Micah on the futon and fired up a Marlboro light. I told him I was sorry about what happened to his father. I wished they'd enjoyed a closer relationship, I said, but that sometimes, that's how it goes between fathers and sons. I quoted William Penn, about how a child taught to live on little owes more to his old man's wisdom than the kid whose old man gives him everything.

"Who's William Penn?" the girl said.

"A lot of people think he's the guy on the Quaker Oats box, but Quaker Oats says the resemblance is merely coincidental. By the way, Micah, before I forget, your mother said to tell you she still loves you."

He stared at the TV and pretended not to hear me.

I left.

Two pit bulls were playing tug-of-war in the yard across the street with what was left of a lime-green bra. They forgot the bra and started barking and snarling at me through the chain-link fence as I walked to my car.

"Hey."

I turned. Micah's girlfriend bounded out the front door, down the steps after me.

"He's really a very sweet guy," she said. "Sweetest guy I've ever known. He's just a little freaked out right now."

"Aren't we all?"

"He wants everybody to think he hated his dad. But when his mom told him what happened, he started crying. I mean, he was really broke up about it. Couldn't sleep for days. Couldn't eat. I think he was maybe hoping they could get together some day, but now . . ." She exhaled. "I just thought you should know, being how you used to work with him."

I thanked her for letting me know.

"He wrote a poem about his dad, if you're interested," Micah's girlfriend said.

"I'm definitely interested."

"Go to YouTube and type in his name—you do know You-Tube, right?"

"On the Internets. I understand it's a series of tubes."

She tilted her head down and away, exposing the side of her neck, while softly stroking her suprasternal notch, the dimple between her collarbones—subconscious gestures usually meant to convey sexual attraction.

"You're different," she said. "And I definitely dig different."

"You better head on back inside before your boyfriend starts wondering what you're doing out here with an old man."

"Not so old," she said coyly.

I watched her walk back inside. I wondered if she set off airport metal detectors with her face.

The street lights had come on, the ones that hadn't been shot out, anyway. In their harsh vapor glare, I noticed that somebody had keyed my rental car. One long bumper-to-bumper scratch along the driver's side. My money was on the gangster I'd seen sucking the Tootsie Pop. Oh, the many entertaining things I would do to him if only he'd ride by once more. I realized that my vengeful thoughts were contrary to the Buddha's teachings. The essence of Buddhism is harmlessness. Hatred and revenge are the twin evils of mankind. But that didn't stop me from wanting to snatch the little punk off his dumb little bicycle and mess his shit up good.

Thirteen

Flight service was advertising low ceilings and poor visibility from San Francisco all the way south to Monterey. High pressure was breaking down. A cold front was moving in. I filed IFR, picked up my clearance from Norcal Departure, and took off from the San Carlos Airport a few minutes before midnight. Climbing through 500 feet, the headlights from the nearby 101 freeway disappeared. I was in the soup.

There's something uniquely calming about flying a small plane alone on instruments at night without an autopilot. Everything fades away that might otherwise distract you from the tasks of piloting. You're in a cocoon. In the soft red luminescence of the cockpit, you check and cross-check your instruments incessantly, scanning to make sure each is working properly, that one doesn't contradict another. You check your gauges, your GPS, your floating compass, never taking your eyes off the instruments, trusting them to keep you upright and on course. If the clouds demand it, you do this for hours, cross-checking, working the radios, holding your assigned course, maintaining your assigned altitude, staying focused. Do it long enough and it becomes automatic. Only then do you have time to think.

I replayed the tapes in my head of my meetings with Echevarria's ex-wife and son. Both obviously remained embittered by how Echevarria had treated them, but their respective body language suggested strongly that neither was involved in his death. If lingering resentments over interpersonal relationships were motives for murder, half the earth's population would be dead and the other half in prison. Somebody murdered Arlo Echevarria, but it wasn't his former spouse or estranged offspring. Of that I was fairly certain. I was less certain about Janice Echevarria's second husband,

Harry Ramos. Was he involved in the same oil deal as Carlisle and Tarasov? Was he a competitor? Did any of it have anything to do with how Arlo Echevarria met his end? I wondered.

"Cessna Four Charlie Lima, Oakland Center," a voice intoned over my headset, interrupting my reverie, "cleared direct Jarrett, maintain 9,000 feet."

I repeated the instructions from air traffic control. Seconds later, the clouds gave way and I was cruising above the moonlit overcast in smooth clear air. Off my left wing, the peaks of the Western Sierra floated above the milky blanket like islands on a sea of white. Ahead of me and to the south, the city of San Luis Obispo glowed beneath the creamy, translucent deck: a modern day Atlantis. Another forty-five minutes and I'd be home.

Center handed me off to Rancho Bonita Approach. The controller cleared me for the ILS approach into Runway Eight. I nailed the localizer dead-nuts center, squared the glide-slope indicator, slowed my airspeed and rode the needles all the way down at a steady ninety knots, breaking out of the clouds at 400 feet, feeling fine about what a damn gifted pilot I was—until I bounced it on. As Wilbur or Orville once said, every landing's an adventure.

I taxied in and shut down. The airport was quiet. No grumbling whine of jet turbines. No piston-driven engines. Only the whisper of the wind intruded upon the darkness—a tranquility so perfect, a man could almost forget his troubles.

Almost.

<hr/>

My ex-wife's Jaguar was parked in Mrs. Schmulowitz's driveway. There was a light on in my garage apartment. I didn't know whether to be enraged by the intrusion or aroused. As I unlocked the door and entered, I found Savannah in my bed, under the sheets, a nickel-plated revolver with an eight-inch barrel and plenty of scrollwork pointed at me. My cat was perched atop her chest, purring, his paws tucked contentedly underneath him.

"Your landlady let me in," she said, lowering the gun as I locked the door behind me. "I told her I was your sister. I hope you don't mind."

"Once again I find myself asking, 'What're you doing here, Savannah?'"

"I'm scared."

"You told me in Santa Monica that you thought your father might know something about what happened to Arlo. Is that why you're afraid?"

"I asked him if he knew anything and he said no. But he's acting very weird. Ever since you went to go see him. He thinks people are out to get him. Even you. He says he doesn't know who to trust anymore."

"Welcome to the club."

"I'm sorry I got you into all this, Logan. I just don't want to see anything bad happen to you, that's all."

I nodded with my chin toward her gun. "Where'd you get the fancy shootin' iron? Roy Rogers?"

The revolver was a gift from her father, she said, given to her after Arlo moved out. A woman without a man needs protection, Carlisle had told her. He'd even paid for shooting lessons. I asked her how she got my address.

"Online."

You can find just about anything online. Edible movie props. The most shocking items ever recovered from a dog's stomach. The secret history of the mullet. Anything and everything but a surefire way to purge yourself of those roiling emotions you feel deep inside for that one woman you wish you could forget and hope like hell you never will.

I tossed my wallet and keys on the wooden orange crate that served as my nightstand and dropped my loose change in an empty coffee can on top of the pink Frigidaire.

"You feed the cat?"

"I tried. He didn't seem very hungry."

Kiddiot looked as happy as I'd ever seen him, sitting there on my ex-wife all nice and cozy, purring his feline ass off.

"What's his name?"

"His name is mud," I said.

My last meal had been breakfast in Oakland. I grabbed a tortilla and a slice of yellow cheese out of the refrigerator. I flicked some mold off the cheese, and rolled what was left of the slice inside the tortilla.

"I would've made you something," Savannah said, "but I didn't know when you'd be back. Plus, I checked the 'frig. You don't really have anything to make."

"I think you'd better leave," I said, wolfing down the tortilla.

"Logan, didn't you hear what I said? I'm scared."

"You've got plenty of money. Hire a bodyguard. Hell, hire ten bodyguards, for all I care."

She was slack-jawed. How could I be so callous?

"Don't make me go, Logan. Please. Not tonight."

"I'm tired, Savannah. I need to get some sleep. Now, if it's not too inconvenient, take that six-shooter of yours and get out of my bed."

She exhaled resignedly, picked up Kiddiot who meowed in complaint, and set him aside, then slid out from under my sheets. She was wearing a sheer blue satin robe that came midway down her thighs and what appeared to be nothing underneath. Not that I would've ever looked, mind you.

"It's one-thirty in the morning," she said, lashing the robe tightly around her. "Where do you expect me to go?"

"Lots of hotels in town."

"You don't think I tried that first? There are no vacancies. There's some big festival going on."

There was always some big festival going on in Rancho Bonita. If it wasn't the Sand Castle Building Festival, it was the Guacamole Eating Festival, or the International Film Watching Festival, or the Greek Salad Festival. There was even a festival, replete with a giant parade of half-naked, fully inebriated people, commemorating Summer Solstice. Every week, another festival, another excuse for local hoteliers to jack up room rates and sock it to the out-of-towners.

"Logan, please. Just for the night."

I was too tired to fight her and too conflicted. I wadded up my upper sheet, lobbed it to her and pointed to my purple Naugahyde couch.

"Thank you." She lay down on the couch and tucked the sheet in around her. Kiddiot jumped up and snuggled in once more on top of her.

I pulled my shirt over my head, tossed it on the floor and turned off the light, got out of my jeans and swung into bed. The wool cover was scratchy without a top sheet, but the bottom sheet was warm where Savannah had been seconds earlier. I tried not to think about how good it felt. My life had been perfectly tolerable before she reappeared unannounced and uninvited—OK, maybe not *perfectly* tolerable, but tolerable enough. I wanted her to leave. I wanted to make love to her. Hell, I didn't know what I wanted. Except maybe a little loyalty from my cat. I could hear him purring clear across the garage.

"Someone keeps calling me," Savannah said, "a private number. They call and hang up. Last night, there was a car outside my house. Just sitting there. For over two hours. I called the police. They never came."

"What kind of car?"

"Small. White. With tinted windows."

"And a spoiler on the back."

"A spoiler?"

"A wing."

I could see Savannah prop herself up on one elbow in the darkness. "How'd you know that?"

The same car that chased me. The same car Mrs. Schmulowitz saw outside her house.

"Lucky guess," I said.

Savannah tried to get comfortable on the couch. The Naugahyde squeaked every time she shifted her weight. With every squeak, I felt like a bigger jerk. Real Buddhists are supposed to demonstrate compassion toward all beings, including ex-wives. Yet, here I was, making mine spend the night sticking to fake leather. I exhaled and threw off my covers.

"Get in. I'll take the couch."

"I'm fine right here."

"Get in the goddamn bed, Savannah."

"I said I'm fine."

We would've been there another hour arguing about it had I not proposed a compromise.

"OK, look. How about this: we both take the bed? Your side, my side. Berlin Wall down the middle. No monkey business. Just sleep."

She thought about it a minute. Then she said, "Deal."

We remade the bed with the top sheet under the blanket and climbed in like two prize fighters, each on our respective side of the squared circle.

"I really appreciate this, Logan."

She was asleep within five minutes.

I lay there for more than an hour, listening to her breathing softly, afraid to move, afraid I might touch her. According to Mrs. Schmulowitz, Dr. Phil says the best thing to do when you can't sleep is not try. So I didn't. I got out of bed as quietly as I could, careful not to disturb her, sat down at the card table that doubled as my home office, fired up my laptop, turned the sound down low, and signed on to YouTube, that video repository of all topics inane and amazing. Ten seconds later, there was Micah Echevarria, sitting on his living room sofa, staring out at me. His face, captured in low light on what I assumed was his girlfriend's camera phone, was fuzzy and handheld shaky, but I could still make out the tendrils of marijuana smoke wafting behind him.

"My father fucking sucked at the job," he began, "but he was still my father. So I suppose I owe him something. This poem's for him."

I'm on firm literary footing when I say Micah Echevarria was no Alfred Lord Tennyson. His poem, recited from a spiral notebook, was vitriolic and peppered with forced, clunky rhymes like "deserted and perverted" and "hate and berate." It was all about how his father had abandoned him as a child.

"And now you are dead and dead means forever," he intoned, "and more than a few would say, well, better late than never. But there are days when I feel that you being killed is really nothing more than a nightmare fulfilled. Because now I will wonder for the rest of my life if we couldn't have been friends without anger or strife. So, goodbye, old man, wherever you are. In purgatory or hell, or on some shining star. If you'll still be my dad, I'll still be your son, and maybe someday, we can still have some fun."

The last line caught in Micah's throat. He nodded off-camera and the screen went blank. Bad meter aside, it was a poignant reading.

Kids murder their parents. Ride little Timmy about taking out the trash and, instead of calling Child Protective Services to complain about how abused he is, Timmy takes matters into his own tiny hands and smokes you with the Luger that Gramps brought back from the war; the one you told him never to touch, the one you kept "hidden" in your nightstand with one round in the chamber because it's every American's inalienable right to keep a fully loaded, semi-automatic weapon within easy reach at bedtime, because you never know when the Krauts might decide to start another war. Or maybe Daddy walks out on little Timmy and Timmy's mom. Resentments fester over the years. Little Timmy grows up. One night, he decides it's finally time for a little payback, and puts three slugs in Daddy's chest. It happens. But I doubted Micah Echevarria was little Timmy. If I'd learned anything in too many years hunting sociopaths in bad places, it's that the culpable don't usually post poems about their victims on YouTube.

I turned off the laptop and got back in bed. Savannah never stirred. Somewhere around four A.M., I drifted off. I don't remember what I dreamed about.

⚬══✠══⚬

There was a cocktail lounge in West Hollywood called the Wet Spot I remembered from my operational days, a sultry, intimate haunt with red-leather booths, where former apparatchiks mixed indistinguishably with Russian organized crime and Israeli mafia types, blowhards all with unbuttoned silk shirts and bulging crotches, who eagerly ordered $100 shots of Stoli if it meant impressing the Eurotrash starlet they were hoping to bang that night. The bar's owner was a charming, heavyset thug named Gennady Bondarenko who, before seeking asylum at the U.S. embassy in Madrid, worked diplomatic cover for the main intelligence directorate of the Russian Armed Forces General Staff. He also happened to be related by marriage to Laz, my old shooting instructor from Alpha, which is how I first met him. Bondarenko was seemingly on a first-name basis with just about every disaffected former Soviet citizen living on the West Coast. I decided to drive down that afternoon from Rancho Bonita to see what, if anything, he could tell me of Pavel Tarasov.

Mrs. Schmulowitz insisted first on serving us breakfast at her kitchen table in honor of my "sister's" visit. There were scrambled eggs cooked with onion and smoked salmon, and bagels from the only bakery in Rancho Bonita that made them fresh daily. I tried to explain that Savannah wasn't really my sister, but Mrs. Schmulowitz was too intent explaining why California bagels were such *schlect* compared to their New York counterparts.

"I'm telling you, it's the water," Mrs. Schmulowitz said, a small glob of cream cheese clinging to the corner of her mouth. "People make jokes about New York water. Go ahead. Laugh. But they don't know what the hell they're talking about. The United Nations took a vote. New York water is the best—the BEST, period. End of story. You can look it up but why bother? I'm telling you!"

Savannah said she couldn't remember ever having eaten more delicious eggs. Mrs. Schmulowitz said she couldn't remember my ever having mentioned a sister—then observed that Savannah and I bore absolutely no familial resemblance.

"Could be your mother knew the milkman," Mrs. Schmulowitz said with a wink. "It's very possible she didn't have enough money to pay the bill for the milk. Maybe the milkman gave her a little break if you know what I mean and I think you do. Hey,

I give you some milk, you give me some 'sugar.' I'm not saying it occurred, yes or no, but it wouldn't be the first time."

Savannah put down her coffee cup. "Well, actually, Mrs. Schmulowitz—"

"I myself enjoyed such an arrangement during my second marriage," Mrs. Schmulowitz confided, cutting her off. "He should've been a movie star, this milkman. Talk about biceps. Carrying all those milk bottles up and down all the stairs all day? We took one look at each other and all of our clothes suddenly disappeared. It was off the charts. Sometimes, these things happen. What can I say?"

Savannah nodded and tried not to smile. I started to say that we really needed to be going, when Mrs. Schmulowitz's chest began ringing. She reached into her sports bra, got out her cell phone, and answered it.

"Hello? . . . Who? . . . Arnie! Hello, my love, one minute." Her eyes lit up and she cupped her hand over the phone. "It's my son, the doctor—well, he's not really a *doctor* doctor. Not the kind that does hysterectomies. He's a teacher, a professor of history. The greatest. Will you excuse me, dears?"

"Of course," Savannah said.

"Arnie," Mrs. Schmulowitz said into the phone. "How are you, doll? Is everything OK?"

I cleared the table and Savannah washed the dishes while Mrs. Schmulowitz lost herself in happy conversation with her only child.

They were still chatting and laughing by the time we left.

Fourteen

"I always wanted kids," Savannah said. "Probably too late now."

"You never said anything about wanting kids when we were together."

"You just weren't listening, Logan. Six years, I never heard *you* say a word about wanting a family."

I checked my side view mirror again. Nobody on our tail. We were on the 101, heading toward Los Angeles, the Pacific to our right. Savannah was driving. Traffic was light. The Jag was pushing eighty. I leaned my power leather seat back and watched a pod of at least twenty dolphins swimming parallel to the shoreline.

"Arlo didn't want more kids," she said. "He said one was enough for him."

The thought of Savannah having a baby with Arlo Echevarria, or anyone else for that matter, made my stomach cramp. She was right about one thing, though: I was no family man. The instincts just weren't there. Maybe it was because of how I grew up, the lack of role models, shunted among foster parents after the oncologist told my mother that there was nothing more he could do for her. My father was long gone by then. For years, I'd kept a photo of him in an old cigar box, a Polaroid snapshot of a young, unsmiling soldier on border duty in West Germany that came with the one and only birthday greeting he ever sent me. "Money's tight," it said, "times are hard, here's your stupid birthday card." I was eight. Not that I'm making excuses for myself. I just didn't care to be a father. I didn't know how to be one. And, apparently, given how his own son turned out, neither did Arlo Echevarria.

"You should be grateful you didn't have a kid with that guy," I said. "He was an abysmal failure at fatherhood."

"And I suppose you wouldn't have been?"

The blood was pulsing in my neck. "What makes you think *you'd* make such a great mother? All you cared about was your career. Now that the phone's no longer ringing off the hook, you think it might be fun to go shopping at Gymboree and learn all about potty training? Gimme a break."

Savannah's eyes were wet with tears. Once again, I'd gone too far.

"I didn't mean that," I said.

"Yes, you did. Every word."

A stylist needs 1,600 hours of formal training before he or she can legally trim a single head of hair in the state of California, but you don't need five minutes of instruction to bring another human being into the world. Nobody knows whether they'll be worth anything as a parent until they're already on the job, and by then, it's usually too late. I thought about sharing my observations with Savannah on the subject, but I knew she didn't want to hear them.

⚬══╪══⚬

The intimate West Hollywood lounge I remembered as the Wet Spot was no more. It was now a discothèque called Propaganda. Gone were the leather banquettes and piano bar, replaced by a throbbing dance club done up all in red, with mirror disco balls hanging from the ceiling, and Bolshevik-chic posters of Lenin on the walls. The cocktail waitresses wore glossy jackboots and red leather, form-fitting Commie uniforms that showed plenty of thigh. The only element that apparently hadn't changed, aside from the name over the door, was the clientele. There was still plenty of chest hair and Eurotrash. Techno tunes pounded from the speakers, loud enough that I could feel the bass throbbing in the pit of my throat. Propaganda was mobbed. It wasn't even happy hour.

"They make a mean apple martini here," Savannah shouted over the music.

"You've been here?"

"Once or twice." She headed off toward the bar, through throngs of gyrating dancers.

A bouncer dressed like a Soviet infantryman stood guard near the door. I walked over and asked if Gennady Bondarenko was still the owner. He leaned closer and touched his ear like he couldn't hear me. I repeated myself, only louder.

"You want to see Mr. Bondarenko?"

I nodded. His accent was working-class British. A Sig Sauer pistol rode his right hip in a pancake holster.

"And what, if I may ask, is the purpose of your visit?"

"I'm from Publisher's Clearing House," I yelled into his ear. "I'm here to give Mr. Bondarenko his million dollar grand prize. I left the balloons in the van."

The bouncer leaned his head back and laughed. He had no fillings. He asked me to turn around with my hands on the wall, and gave me a quick pat down. I'd left my revolver in Savannah's car. Along with the balloons.

"Who shall I say is here to see him?"

"Tell him a friend of Laz."

The bouncer typed a text message on his iPhone. Two brunettes in hip-huggers and spandex tops strutted past us to go have a smoke outside. One of them smiled at me. I smiled back despite my better self.

The bouncer's phone beeped. He read the response to his text message. Then he yelled in my ear. "Straight back, up the stairs. There's a door marked, 'Private.' Off you go."

I nodded my thanks and started working my way through the club. The dance floor was packed with young women and stylishly unshaven young men all trying desperately to look their sexy best, gyrating and toasting each other with shouts of, "*Za vas!*"—"To you!"—when "Staying Alive" by the Bee Gees began playing and everybody started cheering wildly like they'd all just won the lotto. A gym rat with too much gel in his hair started to rock out and backed straight into me.

"Watch the fuck where you're going, gramps," he said.

We both knew he was in the wrong. We both knew he was trying to impress the young lady he was dancing with. We both knew that the situation would quickly escalate were I to let it.

"My mistake," I said with a smile and kept walking.

I couldn't decide if it was the Buddha's influence or me mellowing with age. Either way, I had to admit, it felt kind of good, not forcing the issue.

I reached the stairway the bouncer directed me to. I looked back for Savannah but couldn't see her through the crowd. I climbed the stairs and walked down a short hallway to a door marked, "Private." I knocked.

"You are the one who is friend of Laz?" The voice on the other side of the door was Russian, female, older.

"We used to work together," I said, "for the same company."

"You have photo ID?"

I got out my driver's license and slid it under the door. A few seconds went by, then the door bolt turned, followed by a second lock. A hand slid the security chain from its track. The door opened a crack, revealing a thick, low-slung, middle-aged woman in a pink velour warm-up suit. Her hair was the color of carrot juice. She was puffing on a Virginia Slim.

"I am Anya," she said, handing me back my license, "sister of Laz."

"Cordell Logan. I'm a friend of Laz. I'm looking for Gennady Bondarenko. Is he around?"

"Gennady is my husband." She glanced furtively behind me to make sure no one else was coming up the stairs, then gestured. "You will please to come in."

Anya Bondarenko locked the door behind me and slid the safety chain back in place. Inside the office was an executive desk made of burl wood with a matching filing cabinet, a freestanding bank safe, and a foldout couch. A sixty-one-inch plasma television hung from the far wall. A big, square-jawed twenty-year-old in camouflage fatigue pants and a sky-blue UCLA T-shirt lounged on the couch, nursing a Heineken and watching Jerry Springer. He had close-cropped hair the color of night and three days' worth of facial stubble black enough to be blue.

"This is Marko. My nephew. He is here to visit from Omsk."

The kid didn't respond, transfixed as he was by the TV.

"His English is no good," Anya said, eyeing me through a tobacco haze. "You look familiar to me."

"I used to come in once in awhile. Years ago."

"Would you care for cocktail?"

"Alas, those days are behind me."

"Too bad for you." She inhaled what was left of her cigarette, blew the smoke out her nose, and dropped the butt into a Diet Pepsi can, which hissed, then poured three fingers of Absolut into a crystal tumbler.

"So," she said, "I call Laz, but he has heard nothing."

"Nothing about what?"

She looked at me like I was a slow learner. "Laz. I call him. 'Have you heard from Gennady?' He tells me no. He says, 'I will make calls.' This is yesterday. Now, you come. So, you tell me, where is my husband?"

I explained that her brother Laz and I hadn't spoken in a few years. My visit and Gennady's apparent disappearance, I said, were mere coincidence.

Anya Bondarenko slumped into the chair behind the desk and looked down at her glass mournfully. "I thought my brother sends you. Now I am thinking my husband has left me for another woman."

"You don't know where he is?"

"I have not seen Gennady for five days." She lit another Virginia Slim, drawing the smoke deep into her lungs. "You have business with him?"

"In a manner of speaking."

"You work for government?"

"Used to."

She shrugged. "What is it you do now, your job?"

I gave her my business card.

She squinted at it through the smoke. "Cordell Logan, CFI. What is this, CFI? You are on TV?"

"Not CSI," I said, correcting her. "CFI. It means I'm a certified flight instructor."

"You are pilot?"

"According to the FAA."

"What is FAA?"

"The sorriest excuse for a bureaucracy on this or any other planet. Listen, Mrs. Bondarenko, if you see your husband, tell him I need to speak with him. It's important."

"If I see him," said, "the first thing I will do is give him the back of my hand for scaring me this way. Then I will tell him."

"*Spasiba.*"

"*Puzhalsta.*"

She walked me to the door.

"*Dasvidaniya*, Marko."

Anya Bondarenko's nephew fired a chilly glance over his shoulder at me, conveying his displeasure at my interrupting his TV-watching. I understood his annoyance. That Jerry Springer is quality entertainment.

⊙━━◆━━⊙

Savannah was sipping an apple martini at the bar. The same gym rat who'd backed into me on the dance floor was putting the moves on her. She was doing her best to ignore him, but he would not be ignored.

"One drink. It's not like I'm asking you to blow me or something." He was leaning into her, shirt unbuttoned, giving his pheromone musk a chance to work its seductive magic.

"Having fun?" I said as I walked over to her.

"Thank God," Savannah yelled at me over the music. "Where've you been?"

"Playing Kojak."

The trip was a bust, I told her. The man I'd come to see wasn't in.

"So what do you want to do?" she said.

"Go back to your place and regroup."

"She's with *you*?" the gym rat said, like he couldn't believe it.

"For the moment, anyway," I said.

Savannah shot me a disdainful look as I followed her out.

The gym rat grabbed my arm. "The chick's into me, man. I can *feel* it. If she's really not with you, why don't you just be cool and step off." His cologne smelled like something a wolverine might excrete in the middle of mating season.

"Trust me, my friend," I said, "on your best day, you couldn't handle it." I tried to go around him, but he wouldn't let me.

"Dude, nobody walks away from me. We're talking here." He was suddenly in my face, shaking out his arms, like we were about to go three rounds. His glowering eyes and cold, Mike Tyson-like smile were meant to convey the potential for unbridled mayhem. I noticed he was wearing braces on his teeth. Difficult to sell the stone cold-killer persona when your mouth looks like Radio Shack.

"Nice grillwork," I said, unable to hold back. "What kind of reception do you get with those bad boys?"

"You come in here and make jokes about me? Dude, you got no fucking idea who you're dealing with."

"Oh, I think I have a pretty good idea, actually. Have a nice day."

I tried to go around him once more. He grabbed my shoulder and turned me toward him, looping a sloppy roundhouse punch that I slipped easily. I rotated left and fired a shovel hook to his left ear that sent him crashing back into the bar, knocking another guy and his date off their stools like they were bowling pins. The pulsing techno music suddenly stopped. The gym rat was out cold on the floor.

The bouncer came sprinting over. "Everybody cool it!"

Savannah was incensed. "We're here twenty minutes and you get in a fist fight?"

"The term 'fight' conveys fighting. This was more self-defense."

She didn't buy it. Neither did the two people I'd knocked from their barstools.

The guy wore glasses and a rayon aloha shirt with little woody wagons on it. A CPA's version of Sunset Boulevard chic.

"What is your fucking problem, buddy?" he wailed at me, struggling to help his woman off the floor.

His date was a powerfully built woman with stringy brown hair who outweighed him by a good fifty pounds. In her right hand was a nine-millimeter pistol, which she pointed in my face. In her left hand was a six-pointed gold star that said, "Deputy Sheriff, Los Angeles County."

"Turn around," she said, her lower lip bleeding, "and put your filthy hands on your head."

⊙━━╪━━⊙

Compared to military MREs, dining at the West Hollywood jail is *haute cuisine*. My fellow inmates and I enjoyed well-seasoned, perfectly breaded fish sticks for supper and scrambled eggs for breakfast with Tater Tots cooked just right. Even my amiable cell mates, the outlaw bikers Bad Dawg and his brother, Mad Dawg, both agreed that when it came to in-custody meals, West Hollywood rated four stars.

"LAPD, you get powdered eggs," Bad said.

"That's cruel and unusual punishment, right there, Dawg," Mad said.

"No, Dawg. Cruel and unusual are them mystery meat sandwiches LAPD feeds you for lunch."

For habitual recidivists who looked like charter members of the ZZ Top fan club, the Dawg brothers could not have been more hospitable. That I'd been booked into their cell on suspicion of assaulting a peace officer only upped my personal stock as far as they were concerned.

I asked them what they were in for. Their tag-team explanation took nearly an hour to tell, a rambling tale about an abusive father and a drug-addled mother, dirt-bag running buddies, cheating women, evil cops, crooked attorneys, corrupt judges, and how never to rob a Wells Fargo bank located across the street from an FBI field office.

"Especially on FBI payday," Bad added.

"Good to know," I said.

We spent the night debating why Johnny Cash always wore black and dozed on stainless-steel cots under fluorescent lights, while some guy two cells down kept screaming that Dick Cheney was trying to kill him. Shortly after breakfast, one of our jailers appeared and informed me that I was to be released forthwith without bail. The Dawgs called me a lucky sumbitch and told me to keep in touch. I promised them I wouldn't.

The jailer escorted me to the booking cage just inside the rear door of the sheriff's station where I signed for my belt, cell phone, keys and wallet. I was made to count my money to make sure it equaled the amount I'd been booked in with, and then escorted to the station's main entrance.

Savannah was waiting for me in the lobby. She was with Detective Czarnek.

"I called him," Savannah said, "like you asked."

I thanked them both for coming.

"You lucked out," Czarnek said, chewing nicotine gum. "My captain and the under-sheriff played basketball together in high school. Got him to drop your case as a favor. That lounge lizard you decked? He had a warrant outstanding out of Long Beach. Failure to appear on a moving violation. Long as we make that go away, he never saw you."

"And the deputy who took a tumble, she's cool with that?"

"Aside from you fucking up her love life. The guy she was out with didn't know she was a cop."

"What did he think she was—a Romanian weightlifter?"

Czarnek grinned. "Tell you what, I certainly wouldn't mess with that chick. She could kick *my* ass in a heartbeat."

"You guys are awful," Savannah said.

We walked out of the sheriff's station and onto San Vicente Boulevard. The morning air felt heavy and smelled of rain. A rare treat in Los Angeles. Czarnek's plain-wrap Crown Vic was parked in a red zone at the curb. He'd looped the microphone cord of his police radio over the rearview mirror to let the meter maid know the car belonged to a detective, but either the meter maid didn't see it or didn't care. A parking ticket was wedged under the left wiper blade.

"Fuck."

Czarnek snatched the ticket off the windshield and stuffed it in his sport coat. He was wearing a different coat than when I saw him last. This one was brown.

I asked him why he was so willing to help me get out of jail. "Quid pro quo," Czarnek said. "I need you to take a ride with me." He got in his car and cranked the ignition.

I told Savannah I was sorry for my behavior the night before. She made a remark about me not being a very good Buddhist. I agreed.

A city bus roared past, racing to make the light at Santa Monica Boulevard. The slipstream mussed her hair a little. I reached out impulsively and tamed a wild strand. She didn't stop me.

Czarnek lowered the passenger window and said, "Take your time. What the hell. I got nothing else to do."

Savannah was looking at me. She was too beautiful and I was a damn fool for feeling what I was feeling at that moment. I told her to go home and lock her doors. I'd be there when I could.

She said, "Is that a promise or a threat?"

I smiled.

○══▸══○

We turned at the light and drove east on Santa Monica Boulevard. It started raining. Big, greasy drops smeared the windshield, just enough to leave a blurry film whenever Czarnek worked his wipers.

"That's the problem with Los Angeles," Czarnek said. "Either it rains too much or not enough."

"LA can be accused of many things," I said, "but moderation is not one of them."

We passed a bus stop where two elderly African-American women sat with plastic grocery bags over their heads. Impromptu foul weather gear. I asked Czarnek if he'd seen the poem Micah Echevarria had posted on YouTube about his father. Czarnek hadn't. He said he'd check it out when he got a chance.

"Maybe it's just me," I said, "but who drives 400 miles on their motorcycle to shoot their father, then turns around, drives back and waxes poetic in cyberspace about how much they'll miss not having the chance to know him better?"

"People do all kinds of crazy shit," Czarnek said. "I had a lady once stabbed her husband twenty-two times with a steak knife—I mean, sliced and diced this guy—then rents a billboard on San Vicente with their wedding picture on it that says, 'Beloved Marvin, the best of the best.'"

The detective reached into the ashtray without taking his eyes off the road and pried a fresh square of nicotine-laced gum from its plastic wrapper. I asked him where we were going.

"Coroner's office," he said, popping the gum in his mouth. "There's a body I'm hoping you can help us ID."

"Who's the lucky stiff?"

"That Russian friend of yours you went to go see. At least we think it's him."

"How'd you know I was going to see Bondarenko?"

"Your ex. She told me when she called to say you'd been taken into custody. Said you'd gone to this club in West Hollywood looking for some guy named Baskin Robbins who possibly had information on Echevarria."

"Bondarenko, you mean."

"Close enough."

Czarnek said he'd never heard of Bondarenko—not that he necessarily would've, working garden-variety homicides in the Valley. He ran the name through the LAPD's Detective Case Tracking System as well as the California Department of Justice's missing persons database. He found that Bondarenko showed up not only on a recently filed missing persons report, but was also the focus of long-standing interest among members of the LAPD's Counterterrorism and Criminal Intelligence Bureau. On a hunch, Czarnek said he called the coroner's office to see if anyone fitting Bondarenko's description had been brought in. Among the seven unclaimed John Does in the medical examiner's current inventory, one matched Bondarenko in approximate weight, height and age.

"There was other identifying evidence," Czarnek said.

"What kind of *other* evidence?"

"That's what I'm hoping you can tell us."

He sprayed the windshield, smearing raindrops across the glass.

"Fucking LA," he said.

FIFTEEN

The Winnebago was stolen out of West Covina, set ablaze, then rolled down into an arroyo less than a mile from the Rose Bowl. By the time the trucks got there, it was burning like a funeral pyre. Firefighters quickly foamed down the motor home and checked inside for possible victims. The charred corpse of a man was found, its hands missing. Marks on the wrists suggested that a power saw with a serrated, reciprocating blade had been used to remove them.

"They wanted to hide the decedent's identity," pathologist Doug Roth said as he led Czarnek and me into the elevator at the LA County Coroner's Office. "No fingerprints. A total CSI. I love my work."

Czarnek looked down at his rubber-soled oxfords and tried not to roll his eyes. Dr. Roth was in his late thirties, autopsy-ready in turquoise scrubs. His sideburns flared below his earlobes. A bushy cookie duster flourished below his lower lip. He punched the down button.

"Detective Czarnek tells me you have an interesting work history," Roth said.

"Detective Czarnek wouldn't know the truth if it ran over him with a semi."

"A regular Seinfeld, this guy," Czarnek said, chewing his gum.

The elevator doors opened. Dr. Roth led us down a hallway and into a dressing room. There were shelves stocked with scrubs, caps, gloves, and protective booties.

"You know the drill. I'll be right back," Roth said to Czarnek, and left.

We put on surgical smocks and fabric booties over our shoes. "I never knew death could be so contagious," I said.

"They don't want you getting anything on your street clothes," Czarnek said. "Lawyers, they'll sue for anything. Which reminds me. If you drop a child molester and an attorney off the Empire State Building, you know which one hits first?"

"Who cares."

"Exactly."

Roth returned and handed us each a respirator equipped with an N-100 hepa filter. "Standard procedure, strictly precautionary," he said. "Nothing to get freaked about."

"I promise I won't sue," I said.

Czarnek tossed his gum in a receptacle for toxic waste. We pulled on our surgical gloves, masked up and followed Roth to a windowless stainless-steel door marked, "Security Floor, Authorized Personnel Only." Scotch-taped to the wall beside the door was a sheet of green construction paper announcing the coroner's office's upcoming annual holiday potluck: A-through-I, bring meat; J-through-R, a side dish; S-through-Z, soft drinks or dessert. The announcement was adorned with stickers of Christmas trees and Stars of David. Roth tapped an entry code on a computerized keypad. The electronic lock clicked. Roth held the door for us.

"Welcome to the show," he said.

○══╪══○

The dead are not conveniently stored in stainless-steel pull-out drawers at the LA County Coroner's Office, as they are in Hollywood's version of reality. There are too many cadavers for such cushy accommodations. Most bodies don't even rate body bags. A decent quality bag can cost upwards of sixty bucks apiece these days. In the cash-strapped City of Angels, corpses are instead packaged like 7-Eleven burritos in opaque plastic sheeting—Saran wrap, only beefier—then stacked floor-to-ceiling in an oversized walk-in cooler. When room runs out in the cooler, the human burritos are stacked in the corridors.

Business was brisk that day at the coroner's office. The newly departed lay all around. One body in particular caught my eye.

It was on a gurney. Brown. Slender. Young. It was shirtless and wearing oversized chinos, the kind favored by Latino gangbangers. Its hair was buzzed short, close enough that I could read the letters "VNE" tattooed on the scalp in Old English script. There was a symmetrical bullet wound the size of a dime in the back of the skull. There was another hole the size of a fist where the nose used to be. The left eye dangled from its socket by the optic nerve like a handset on an old wall phone. A coroner's technician in scrubs and a mask was fingerprinting the dead boy. The boy's hand was still supple. No rigor. Not yet autopsied.

"Hey, Doc," the tech said to Roth as we strode past, rolling the tip of the boy's left thumb on an electronic, handheld scanning device, "why don't blind people skydive?"

"Because it scares the crap out of the dog."

"You heard it already, huh?"

We walked past three autopsy rooms where postmortem examinations were in full swing—pathologists sawing skulls and weighing internal organs on hanging scales like so many tomatoes at the grocery store. In one room, a doctor was stitching up the gaping, Y-shaped incision he'd made in the chest of a young girl, tugging on the catgut with both fists as though he were lacing up a hiking boot. The cadaver flopped limply on the stainless-steel table like a rag doll.

"This way, gentlemen," Dr. Roth said.

He led us into what looked to be a converted meeting room. The conference table and chairs were pushed to one side, replaced by a flat metal table on wheels. On the table was the charred body of a man laying on its back. Its hands were missing.

"He was shot, then torched postmortem," Roth said. "They obviously burned him and sawed off his hands to make it harder to ID him."

The bullet had left a perfectly neat hole just above the dead man's left ear. The pathologist had removed the skull cap to retrieve the fatal round and examine the victim's brain. The man's head had been sawed in half, like an orange.

"Single GSW to the left temporal lobe, .40-cal, copper jacket," Czarnek said. "The round matched the ones we pulled out of your friend, Arlo Echevarria."

"The plot thickens," I said.

Czarnek unwrapped a fresh square of gum. "You recognize this guy?"

"His own mother wouldn't recognize him," I said. A patch of blackened skin had been scraped clean from the body's right shoulder during the pathologist's examination, revealing a tattoo—a miniature martini glass bearing what looked to be the initials, "WS."

"The missing persons report his wife filed indicated he had a 'WS' tattooed on his left shoulder," Czarnek said. "I checked corporate DBA's. Baskin Robbins owned a lounge called the Wet Spot. The tattoo's on his right shoulder, so, obviously, Mrs. Baskin Robbins got that part wrong, but, I mean, what are the odds?"

"It just goes to show," I said, "how well do we truly know the people we're married to?"

The tattoo was confirmation enough as far as I was concerned that the otherwise unrecognizable crispy critter I was standing over was Bondarenko. Poor Gennady. I always kind of liked the guy, even if he was an old school Commie. Always good for a free drink and the occasional tidbit of actionable intelligence. Looking down at what was left of him, I couldn't say I was surprised by the terrible violence that had marked his end of days. His arena had been one of sketchy characters, a landscape of ever-shifting loyalties bought and sold. The crowd he'd catered to and curried favor with embodied the very definition of dangerously unpredictable. Sometimes, when you run with the bulls, you get gored.

"If you already knew it was Bondarenko," I said, "why'd you bring me here to ID him?"

"Show him," Czarnek said to the pathologist.

Roth picked up the surgically removed chest plate like the lid from a garbage can and set it aside. Bits of blackened skin flaked off like burnt bread crumbs.

"I was dissecting the soft tissue adherent to the posterior plate," Roth said, "when I first noticed it." He flipped the breastplate over and set it on the table beside the body. Rib bones branched outward from the exposed sternum like the truncated legs of a scorpion. "At first, I thought it was some sort of new pacemaker or insulin pump, but it's different from any medical device I've ever seen. Plus, its placement is substantially lower than normal implantation sites. That's it, right there." He pointed. "Very unusual. Never seen anything like it before."

I leaned in for a better look: a metallic object the approximate size and shape of a matchbox, with a two-inch-long wire lead protruding from it, was affixed between the lower ribs, held in place by titanium surgical screws.

Czarnek said, "What the hell is that?"

"It's a remotely triggered explosive device."

"A *bomb*?"

"Give that man a cookie."

"Jesus." Dr. Roth backed away fearfully from the autopsy table. So did Czarnek.

"Not to worry," I said, "it's most likely inert."

"You sure about that?" Czarnek said warily.

"It's got a thermal safety to prevent accidental detonation. If the core temperature of the host body drops below a certain point—say, upon death, for example—the weapon automatically disarms itself. Plus, the battery's probably already dead if it's been in for any length of time."

I'd seen an identical device in postmortem photos of another man, a well-known contract killer. NSA had intercepted communications indicating that a certain North African despot intended to assassinate a professor at American University in Cairo whose writings, the dictator felt, blasphemed the teachings of Mohammed, peace be upon Him. Arrangements were made through a network of cutouts working for German intelligence to have the killer check into a luxurious boutique hotel on the banks of the river Nile the night before the hit. There, he was told, two runners-up from the Miss World pageant would be waiting in bed for him—an all-expenses-paid pre-assassination assignation, courtesy of the appreciative dictator. Alpha's orders were to take the would-be assassin alive so our interrogators could identify and roll up his handlers. The plan didn't quite work out that way. He smelled a trap in the hotel parking lot and went for his gun. Echevarria shot him dead. The body was stashed in a rental car and flown to Dover Air Force Base, where the bomb was discovered during autopsy, removed and analyzed extensively.

We learned later that the Russians had implanted such weapons in perhaps as many as a dozen intelligence assets without their knowledge during appendectomies, hernia repairs and other routine surgical procedures requiring general anesthesia. The theory was that these assets could then be maneuvered within lethal range of targeted foreign enemies while arousing little suspicion because they appeared otherwise unarmed. Packed with highly explosive G2ZT, a nitrogen-based tetrazole refined in the laboratories of a Stuttgart-based chemical weapons conglomerate Deiter-Becker-Deutsche, the explosive could then be detonated by radio signal from as far away as a half-mile. The bomb itself was said to have a killing radius of ten meters.

"Suicide bombers who don't know they're suicide bombers," Czarnek marveled. "What will they think of next?"

"Back in the day, nobody in their right mind wanted the job," I said. "Now, they grow on trees. Amazing what seventy-two virgins'll buy."

⊙━━◆━━⊙

Morning overcast had given way to wispy cirrostratus and anemic sunshine by the time we left the coroner's office. An afternoon storm was moving in. Maybe this one would bring real rain.

Czarnek said he wanted to interview Bondarenko's widow and wanted me to go with him.

"She knows you," the detective said. "She might be more willing to talk with you there."

I didn't relish the idea of having to be there when he informed her that her husband was dead, and told him as much. Czarnek offered to buy me lunch in exchange. The best Italian food in Los Angeles, he said. Who was I to say no?

We took surface streets skirting the Golden State Freeway up to the working class enclave of Lincoln Heights on the eastern fringes of Chinatown, a five-minute drive. To the north, the undulating peaks of the San Gabriels wore a fresh dusting of white. The snow line ran in precise parallel to the dun-colored elevations below, as if some giant artist had drawn it with a straight edge across the south face of the mountains. Czarnek wheeled across opposing traffic lanes and into a small lot next to an Italian deli made of cinder blocks. Two unmarked detective cars and four LAPD black and whites were already parked there.

An Italian lady who looked to be about as old as Mrs. Schmulowitz sat on a stool behind the cash register. She smiled at Czarnek as we walked by like she knew him. The tables were covered with red and white checkered plastic cloths and occupied by cops hunched over sausage sandwiches and plates heaped high with steaming pasta primavera, all talking and laughing. A few glanced at us as we walked in, nodding politely to Czarnek, then sizing me up as if to say, "Who's the perp?"

We waited inside the door for a spot to open up.

"Popular place," I said.

"We get a discount, half off," Czarnek said. "Used to be, a cop couldn't pay for a meal in this town, but those days are long gone."

Two bellied detectives vacated a table in the rear near the kitchen and ambled past, toward the cash register. The one who wasn't paying the check rolled a toothpick out of a dispenser on the counter.

"Where's that crazy partner of yours?" he said to Czarnek.

"Mental health day."

"How're things up in Valley Bureau?"

"Can't complain," Czarnek said.

"Beats working for a living."

"Does most days."

"Keep your powder dry, Keith," the detective said as he pushed open the door.

"You do the same, Manny," Czarnek said.

The old lady behind the cash register handed us each a plastic laminated menu and gestured toward the open table. There was a plastic potted geranium on it and a candle in an old Chianti bottle, its sides caked with dried candle wax like frozen, multicolored waterfalls. We waited until the busboy finished wiping down the tablecloth, then sat.

Czarnek spat his gum in a paper napkin. The waitress waddled over with two green plastic water glasses and a red plastic basket lined with a green paper and piled with warm garlic bread. I ordered the eggplant. Czarnek went with chicken piccata and a side of fried mozzarella sticks.

"Those things'll kill you," I said of his choice in appetizers.

"Hey, I quit cigarettes. You gotta croak of something." He got out a pen and a thin reporter's notebook. "I need to know what you know about this Russian connection to Echevarria," he said.

I told him what I knew of Bondarenko's ties to the Russian Foreign Intelligence Service, of Carlisle's plans in Kazakhstan with Tarasov, the Russian oilman, and Tarasov's own purported ties to Russian intelligence. I told him about Janice Echevarria's husband, Harry Ramos, and the possible interest Ramos shared with Tarasov and Carlisle in the Kashagan oil field. I described the nonchalant way in which Carlisle had reacted when I told him I knew that Echevarria had been to Kazakhstan a week before his death, and Carlisle's flip-flop, how he'd first paid me to brief the LAPD on Echevarria's true work history, then demanded I stop asking questions.

Czarnek looked up from his notepad.

"How much did he pay you?"

"Twenty-five large."

The detective sat back in his chair like I'd just informed him the Tooth Fairy wasn't real. "Jesus," he said, "if *that* were to ever make it into open court . . ."

I ate some garlic bread and licked the olive oil off my fingers.

"Why do you think Carlisle wants you to back off?" Czarnek said.

"Theory one: He's afraid my digging around might blow his chances of scoring big in Kazakhstan. Theory two: He's somehow involved with Tarasov in Echevarria's murder."

"What about Baskin Robbins' murder?"

"That's theory number three."

I didn't volunteer my theory number four: that Carlisle feared I might incriminate his daughter and assistant, Miles Zambelli, in an ongoing murder investigation. While I doubted that Savannah's one-night stand prompted Zambelli to kill Echevarria in some kind of jealous rage, I couldn't very well tell Czarnek about their tryst without implicating them both. I may have been bitter over what my ex-wife had done to me years before, but I wasn't that vindictive. I let it go.

"Carlisle's personal assistant banged your ex-wife," Czarnek said matter-of-factly. "That's why Echevarria walked out on her. But I assume you knew that already, right?"

"Savannah must've told you."

"She told me about her father paying you to talk to us, too." Czarnek reached for the bread basket. "I don't see Zambelli capping Echevarria. Not the type, not on paper, anyway. Now, this Russian, that's a different story. Echevarria's son, too. We got multiple witnesses that put the kid at Echevarria's apartment the night before. They were arguing, him and his old man."

"The kid was in Oakland the night of the murder," I said.

"So he says," Czarnek said.

The waitress brought our meals. Czarnek insisted it was the best chicken piccata he'd ever eaten. My eggplant tasted like something Jeffrey Dahmer might've kept in a Tupperware bowl in his freezer.

SIXTEEN

Anya Bondarenko took the news of her husband's death stoically, like a spouse who understood intuitively that the man she'd married years before was not destined to share with her the journey into old age. "At least," she said, pouring herself more vodka, "he was not found fucking other woman."

Czarnek asked if she or her late husband knew or had ever heard of Pavel Tarasov. The name rang no bell, she said, nor did Arlo Echevarria, or Gil Carlisle.

"What about Harry Ramos?" I said.

"Who?"

"Harry Ramos."

"Harry Ramos . . . Harry Ramos." Gennady Bondarenko's widow lit a Virginia Slim and let the smoke settle in her lungs, giving her time to run the name through the Rolodex in her head. "I know this name," she said.

She crossed from behind her late husband's desk to the office safe from which she extracted a file folder with what looked to be various business-related correspondence. She licked her thumb and carefully perused each document before finding the one she was looking for, then handed it to me without comment.

It was a month-old letter thanking Gennady Bondarenko for his interest and possible investment in a limited partnership that was acquiring drilling rights in the "exciting" Kashagan oil field of Kazakhstan. The letter was cosigned by the partnership's legal counsel, Miles Zambelli, and its resident business agent, Harry Ramos. I gave it to Czarnek to read.

Anya Bondarenko took another drag from her cigarette. "This Harry Ramos, he comes to see Gennady. Very fancy. Big song and dance. 'We will make millions in this oil. Buy big house next to

J.Lo,' he tells Gennady. Gennady says we will invest our savings in this oil. I say, 'No, this is very, very bad idea.' We should buy Quiznos franchise in Tarzana. We fight. Back and forth. All night. Gennady will not listen. Then, he tells me he must go to see somebody on Fairfax. One hour later, he is back, his face white, the blood gone. He tells me, 'Forget the oil. We will buy the Quiznos.' But now . . ." Tears filled her eyes.

I asked her who her husband went to see that night. She shrugged.

"Gennady never said."

∘═╾═∘

The Hollywood Freeway was anything but free. Czarnek tuned his car radio to a news station with traffic reports every ten minutes. The radio let us know all about road conditions in south Orange County and east to the Inland Empire, but not word one on why the 101 was a parking lot. Gridlock in central Los Angeles at any given hour of the day apparently had stopped being news long ago.

"Might as well be in goddamn prison," the detective said, chewing the hell out of his gum, fingers strumming the top of his steering wheel impatiently.

Fed up, he switched on the car's flashing police lights and spun the wheel hard, wedging his unmarked Crown Vic between the stationary traffic to our left and the barrier wall to our right, its segmented concrete dividers streaked with scrape marks left by other, lesser drivers who'd tried the same maneuver and failed. We drove the shoulder that way for nearly a mile, exited onto Beverly Boulevard, and took surface streets into the hills, up to Savannah's house.

Czarnek dropped me off outside the gate. He said he and his partner would be taking a hard look at Harry Ramos, Zambelli and Tarasov as suspects in the homicides of Echevarria and Bondarenko.

"I still don't see it," Czarnek said as I got out of the car.

"See what?"

"All that spook shit you told my partner and me about when we were up having lunch in Rancho Bonita. Government agent. Taking out high-value targets. Doing the Lord's work. I mean, I'm looking at you and there's a disconnect there. You don't look the part, you or Echevarria. James Bond, now *he* looked the part."

"James Bond wouldn't have lasted five minutes."

Czarnek smiled. "Behave yourself, Logan."

"Fair skies, Detective."

He drove on. I pressed the intercom button on the speaker box beside the gate.

"Yes?" The voice sounded young and Latina.

"Cordell Logan to see Ms. Echevarria."

The gate buzzed and swung open. I walked up the drive. There was a metallic silver S-Class Mercedes parked in front of the house. The woman whose voice I heard on the box was waiting for me on the front steps. She said her name was Alameda Guzman, Savannah's housekeeper. Mid-twenties. Big horsy smile. Size 00 jeans. Glossy black hair down to the small of her back.

"Mrs. Echevarria has told me much about you," she said.

"All lies."

"She's with a patient right now. Would you like to come in and wait?"

"A patient. Right."

"Actually, we were just finishing up," Savannah said, emerging from the house.

You would've never guessed from her ebullient mood that her life at that moment was anything but perfect. With her was a baggy-eyed, olive-skinned man in his mid-forties who looked like a walking billboard for Brooks Brothers Friday Casual. His yellow, monogrammed, button-down shirt was tucked into a pair of indigo, dry clean-only jeans with knife-edge creases. He was toting an eel skin briefcase in his left hand.

"Cordell Logan," Savannah said, making introductions, "Danny Katz."

Katz's grip wasn't a handshake; it was a Herculean test of wills. His eyes held steady on mine as he tried to crush my fingers.

"Nice to meet you, Mr. Logan." The accent was South African.

"Mr. Katz," I said, squeezing harder.

He gritted his teeth, smiling through the pain, and finally let go, hoping Savannah didn't notice him rubbing the circulation back into his hand.

"Danny's a new client," Savannah said proudly. "He needed help with some time-management issues, to get his priorities squared away and his life back on track. So I told him, 'Sounds to me like what you need is a life coach.'"

"That or a nagging ex-wife," I said.

Savannah smiled but it looked more like a death threat.

I asked how they met.

"We were at the Beverly Center," Danny said. "I was backing out of a space and accidentally scraped her bumper. I left a note apologizing, with my number. I felt so terrible."

"He not only covered the repairs to my car," Savannah said, "he insisted on giving me free dry cleaning for a year. Danny owns a dry-cleaning shop."

"Seven actually," he said, correcting her.

"Seven? Wow. How do you stand that kind of excitement?"

Katz didn't appreciate my humor. "And what is it that you do, Mr. Logan?"

"Me? As little as possible."

He smiled thinly, turned to Savannah and shook her hand. "A most productive meeting. I trust we can do it again soon."

"Anytime. Call me."

He nodded curtly to me, eased himself into his Mercedes and drove away. Alameda went back inside. Savannah's hands were on her hips. She was pissed at me. So what else is new?

"Why do you have to be such an overbearing dick all the time?"

"How long have you known this guy?"

"I don't know. A couple weeks. So what?"

"He just *happens* to run into your car and leaves you a note? You don't know what his story is, Savannah. He could be anybody. Who else are you planning to let just waltz in here—Jack the Ripper?"

Buddhists don't believe they're punished for their anger. They believe they're punished *by* their anger. At that moment, I was being punished by both. I unloaded on my former wife like a drill instructor addicted to Red Bulls. Wasn't she the one who said she was getting strange phone calls and afraid someone was shadowing her? Wasn't she the one who said she feared for her safety and mine?

"You have no situational awareness," I said, "and that can get you killed."

"You're being irrational."

"*I'm* being irrational? Who showed up unannounced at my apartment armed like Annie Oakley because they were so goddamn scared? You act like it was all a bad dream. Everything's peachy once more in the fairy-tale land of Savannah Carlisle Echevarria."

"Danny Katz is a dry cleaner. Let me repeat that: a *dry cleaner*. Not a murderer."

"Did I or did I not instruct you to lock your doors?"

"You're not my boss, Logan! We're divorced, remember?" She stormed inside her sumptuous house, slamming the door behind her.

I paced the front lawn, trying to chill out. She was right about one thing: I *was* irrational. All that morning, when I wasn't staring inside charred human remains at the coroner's office and helping the LAPD with investigative leads, I'd been thinking about Savannah. She said she'd be waiting for me when we parted company outside the West Hollywood jail. In my anticipation and excitement, I had somehow gotten it into my horny schoolboy head that "waiting for me" meant more than it apparently did. Not that I ever expected her to meet me at the door naked. Then again, maybe I did. Hey, I'm male. But the one thing I definitely hadn't expected was being greeted by an alleged dry cleaning magnate who resembled any number of Mossad and South African field agents of questionable loyalty who I used to cross paths with all the time. Maybe that's what set me off, the way Katz looked. Hell, he probably was who he claimed to be—a nice, hardworking dry cleaner. Took pride in his work. Got the tough stains out.

I could've told her that I was sorry, but I knew that would be a giant time-waster. The Savannah I'd been married to was the kind of woman who took her time forgiving and forgetting—time being measured in weeks and sometimes months, depending on the perceived degree of transgression. Nothing in her behavior suggested to me that she had changed since our divorce. I was in for the cold shoulder, the silent treatment. I didn't need any more of that. I got more than my share from Kiddiot.

Alameda emerged from the house to ask if I wanted a cold drink. What I wanted was a lift back to Rancho Bonita. She said she'd convey my request and went back inside. I could hear Alameda's singsong words, muffled through the walls of Savannah's *nouveau riche* villa paid for with her daddy's money.

"You want to go back to Rancho Bonita?" Savannah said as she flung open the front door moments later and charged down the steps toward me. "Go on! Leave! Get out of my sight."

She hurled her car keys at me, turned and marched back up the steps. The front windows rattled from the concussion of her slamming the door behind her.

I wished in that moment there was a way to rewind time. If only I'd checked the "Sorry, Can't Make It!" box on the RSVP to the wedding of my old academy roommate instead of the box that said, "We/I'd Love To Come!!!" If only I had ducked out of the cathedral before the reception, before the buffet line, before divine providence compelled me to glance up from the sushi rolls I was piling on my plate and across the crowded catering hall—clichéd, I admit—there to meet the gaze of the most beautiful woman I'd ever seen. If only I had gone and sat down and enjoyed my post-nuptials nosh, or chatted up the minister or the bride's mother. But by that point, I was on autopilot. Savannah Carlisle was engaged in conversation with some nerdy civil engineer doing his best to impress her with all the thrilling details of his latest highway drainage project. She was sipping a Manhattan and trying not to look bored as he blathered on.

"I came over here to ask you if you wanted a drink," I said to her, ignoring the engineer, "but I have to tell you something right up front: I'm a little concerned."

"Concerned about what?" she said, like I was about to ask her to donate one of her kidneys to me.

"Hey, buddy, we're talking here," the engineer said.

"We were just wrapping things up," Savannah said to him with a polite smile.

The guy got the hint and retreated to the buffet table. She turned back to me.

"Concerned about what?" she repeated.

"Where all this is headed."

She gave me a sideways glance. Intrigued but trying not to look like it. "Excuse me?"

"We talk, have a couple of drinks. You give me your number after I get up the nerve to ask for it. I wait the requisite number of days, then call. We go catch a flick, maybe grab a burger afterwards, get past all those pre-game sexual jitters, jump in the rack, and quickly develop one of those deeply satisfying emotional relationships that transcends the mere physical. We realize in short order that this thing has soul mate written all over it, so we decide to cohabitate. Next thing you know, we're shopping for rings and swapping 'I do's.' We buy us a little house in the 'burbs. Picket fence, gardenias, the whole nine yards. You want a family, I want my own airplane, but, hey, what I want more than anything is to make you, the love of my life, happy. So we get pregnant. Now I'm resentful as hell of all the time you're devoting to little Cordell junior. The romance fizzles. We knock out another kid or two, hoping to save the union, only now I'm putting in sixty hours a week to pay for all the violin and karate lessons, and the new minivan, and the snazzy granite countertops you just *had* to have. You're so busy arranging play dates for the kids and playing chauffeur—when you're not whipping out gourmet dinners that I'm too exhausted to eat after work because I'm slaving like a dog—that you start to let yourself go. Pretty soon, you're wearing muumuus which, as everybody knows, are a big turn-off for any male who isn't native Hawaiian. So, to cope with our nonexistent sex life and my male ego that requires constant reinforcement, I bed my buxom personal assistant which, of course, you find out about because I completely suck at lying.

Now we have to explain to our children the definition of 'community property' and why Thanksgiving at Daddy's and Christmas at Mommy's is really super-fun. It's just so goddamn tragic. So here's the deal: if you *do* decide to talk to me, let's just keep the whole thing strictly carnal, OK?"

Savannah's lips curled in a sly smile.

"Roses," she said, "not gardenias. Preferably yellow."

We talked until dawn. Two months later, we were hitched.

If only . . .

I bent down and picked up the car keys she'd thrown at me. A breeze had kicked up out of the west. What few clouds there were in the sky were high and gossamer thin. I would have preferred flying home. My ex-wife's luxury sedan would have to do.

<hr>

The sign said forty miles to Oxnard. The Jag was on cruise control. Traffic was sparse. I sang along to Bachman-Turner Overdrive's "Let It Ride" turned up as loud as it would go. Nothing like a kickass road song and an unclogged stretch of highway to forget what ails you. I belted it out, not giving a damn whether any of my fellow motorists saw me or not.

My phone buzzed. I turned down the radio. Lamont Royale, Gil Carlisle's right hand man, was on the line. He was curious to know whether the tip he'd passed along, about Janice Echevarria's engagement ring and the death threat she'd allegedly made against Arlo, had borne fruit.

Janice may have been upset that Arlo Echevarria stole her ring, but she didn't have him killed for it. Of that I was fairly confident. I was less certain about what role, if any, Janice's second husband, Harry Ramos, had played in Echevarria's death—and in that of Gennady Bondarenko. It was Ramos, after all, who had pitched Bondarenko on the merits of an oil venture in Kazakhstan in the weeks before Bondarenko's death—the very same venture that my former father-in-law, his legal advisor, Miles Zambelli, and Russian business partner, Pavel Tarasov, were now pursuing. The murders of

Echevarria and Bondarenko were unquestionably linked—forensics had shown they'd been shot to death with the same gun. But I wasn't about to get into all of that with the right hand man of the guy who, quite possibly, had orchestrated both slayings.

"Are you asking out of personal interest, Lamont, or on behalf of your boss?"

"Mr. Carlisle has no idea I'm even talking to you, Mr. Logan. I consider him and his daughter family. I'm just trying to help."

"The police are looking into it," is all I said.

"Would you know whether they've ruled out Mr. Carlisle or Mr. Zambelli as a suspect?"

"They haven't ruled out anyone at this point, so far as I know."

"OK, well, whatever. I just thought I'd ask. Like I said, I'm just trying to help, that's all."

My phone chirped—a text message from Micah Echevarria. It said, "kneed too talk ASAP." Proper grammar. The first casualty of the Digital Revolution.

Royale promised to let me know if he came up with any other information. He started to tell me how generous Carlisle had been to him, how he'd saved him from a life on the streets, when we were disconnected. Unreliable cell phone reception. The second casualty of the Digital Revolution.

I returned Micah Echevarria's text message with a phone call.

"The fucking LAPD's saying I shot my own father!" he shouted over the phone. "Some detective named Czarnek. I already told them I was in school that night, but he says everybody they've talked to was too wasted to remember me being there. It's fucking bullshit, man!"

"Why tell me all this? I'm the guy you told to go perform a particular carnal act on himself, which, by the way, I'm fairly sure is impossible."

"Look, I'm sorry, OK? I was pissed. You jumped me and choked me out. What was I supposed to say?"

Micah Echevarria said he'd had time to reflect. We'd watched meerkats on TV together. He liked meerkats. I seemed to as well.

Perhaps it was possible that I wasn't the complete turd he thought I was upon first impression.

"Anybody who likes animal shows can't be all bad," he said.

"My cat loves animal shows and he's beyond bad."

"Yeah, but he's just a cat."

"Good luck telling him that. He thinks it's his world; we all just live in it."

"I need you to talk to the cops. Get 'em off my fuckin' back."

"They say they have witnesses who saw you at your dad's place the night before he was shot."

The kid cleared his throat. "So what? Don't mean I fucking shot him."

"You said you hadn't seen him in a long time. You lied to me."

"I lied because you came fucking busting into my house! Plus, you said you and my old man were friends. What was I supposed to do? Give you a fucking hug? He abandoned us, OK? He abandoned my mom."

I told him that I'd seen the clip he'd posted on YouTube. His poem about Echevarria struck me as heartfelt, I said.

"So you'll tell the cops I didn't do it?"

"You drove all the way down from Oakland to LA to see your father the night before he died. I need to know why."

"I wanted to talk to him about a business proposition."

"What kind of proposition?"

"Are you gonna help me or not?"

"What kind of business proposition?"

He blew some air. I waited.

"A weed dispensary," Micah said.

"You wanted your father to bankroll a pot shop?"

"For medical purposes. Dude, it's perfectly legal. Prime location, low overhead. You can make serious bank. He was good for it. He had the coin. That fine bitch he hooked up with after he dumped my mom, she was fucking rich, man. But he wouldn't listen to me. He said it was a stupid idea."

I toyed with the notion of setting the kid straight—that "fine bitch" who married his father used to be married to me—but what would've been the point?

"So you argued with your father," I said.

"Yeah, we argued. But that don't mean I capped him. He told me go talk to my mother if I wanted money. I told him I already did. She thought it was a stupid idea, too. For once, they agreed on something. He tells me I need to get a job, go work for a living for once in my life. Same thing she said. I told him he could go eat his fuckin' money and rode back up to Oakland. Couple days later, my mother calls and tells me he got shot. I fucking partied all night, man."

I could hear a diesel engine behind him, revving, and the hiss of air brakes. He was outside a truck stop somewhere. I asked where he was calling from. He said Nevada.

I glanced up in my rearview mirror. A small white car was coming up fast in the left lane. A Honda. With a rear spoiler.

"If you're innocent, why are you running?"

"I ain't running," he said. "I just don't want to be trying to clear my name from inside a jail cell, that's all."

"No such word as *ain't*," I said. "Stay put. I'll be right back."

I set the phone down on the center console and watched the Honda converge. Adrenaline sluiced through my veins, a metallic taste on the edges of my tongue. I reached under the driver's seat where I'd stashed my revolver and wedged it for quick access between my right thigh and the seat cushion. I needn't have bothered. The white car whizzed past me—a Honda with a yellow Lab riding right seat. The dog yawned as he motored by. I grabbed up the phone. By what manner, I asked Micah Echevarria, did he propose that I get the police off his back?

"My old man said something that night I went to see him," Arlo's son said, "something I didn't tell the cops."

I waited.

"He said a friend of his got killed. Some guy he used to work with."

"I need a name, Micah."

"He didn't say a name. The guy was from Arizona somewhere. That's all he said."

"Did your father mention anybody named Bondarenko?"

"No."

"What about a guy named Pavel Tarasov?"

"He didn't talk names, OK? Just that some friend got killed. He said he couldn't give me any money because he had to pay for a plane ticket to the funeral. But, see, what I'm saying is, if his friend gets killed, then he gets killed, it ain't me doing 'em both, you know what I'm saying? It's more like a, you know, one of those things. What do you call it?"

"A conspiracy."

"A conspiracy. Exactly."

I told him I'd talk to the police and see what I could do.

It was hard for Micah Echevarria to say thank you. He did anyway.

SEVENTEEN

I washed out the petrified Tuna Feast in gravy that Kiddiot refused to eat while I was away and refilled his dish with Chicken Feast in gravy, the last can of cat food I had in the house. I knew he wouldn't eat that, either. I wish I could say that his refusing to eat, like other cats, was his way of punishing me for my having left him alone, but I knew him better than that. I was barely a blip on Kiddiot's feline radar. He watched me refill his water bowl, flicked his tail a couple of times, and left.

Buzz was working on a plate of lasagna when I phoned him at his home in suburban Maryland. He excused himself from the dinner table and took the call outside.

"This better be important," he said. "I'm freezing my ass off out here. My goddamn testicles have shrunk up so much, they're now ovaries."

I asked him if he'd heard of any other former members of Alpha aside from Echevarria who had died in recent months under mysterious circumstances. I told him what Micah Echevarria had said about his father planning to attend the funeral in Arizona. Buzz drew a blank.

"Could've been the funeral of somebody he knew before he went to Alpha," Buzz said.

"Possibly."

Buzz said he'd call around and see what he could find out. His teeth were chattering audibly. I urged him to go back inside before he froze to death. He asked me what the weather was like in California. I told him he didn't want to know.

"It's, like, fifty below zero out here," Buzz said. "My next door neighbor's a vice cop. He said the hookers downtown are charging twenty bucks just to blow on your hands."

I needed cat food and craved a cold beer. Not drinking anymore totally sucked.

Kang was on duty behind the register at his grocery store, as he always was, arms folded, as they always were. "Some cop came in the other day," he said. "He ask a lot of questions. Says you bad mo'fo'. I tell him get lost. Logan good guy."

"You're the man, Kang."

I pulled a bottle of cream soda from the freezer, set it on the counter, and fetched a half-dozen cans of cat food off a shelf in the back, not bothering to check which flavors. Kang uncapped my soda with an opener tethered to the counter by a shoestring and loaded the cat food in a plastic bag.

"So what you do, anyhow," he said, "kill somebody?"

"If I did, they deserved it."

I handed him twenty bucks and sipped my soda while he rang up the purchase. He handed me my change.

"LA cop right. You one bad mo'fo'," Kang said, then slipped a Slim Jim into the bag, on the house, "but you still Kang number one customer."

"Rock on."

We slapped a high-five. I grabbed my bag. As I turned to go, a good-looking blonde who wasn't watching where she was going ran into me. I bear-hugged her to break her fall.

"Any landing you can walk away from," I said.

A smile of recognition replaced Charise MacInerny's startled expression.

"Cordell Logan, what are you doing here?" She looped her arms around my waist and hugged me back. She was wearing tan cargo shorts and a pink tank top and smelled like lilacs.

"I live right around the corner," I said. "What's your excuse?"

She said she and her fiancé, Louis, were going on a picnic when Louis realized he'd run out of smokes. "I'm trying to get him to stop," Charise said, "but you know how pig-headed lawyers can be. So I said I'd buy him a pack of cigarettes—low tar. Better than nothing, right?"

"Next best thing to quitting."

Louis was slouched in his Lamborghini parked across the street, stereo bass thumping to some rap tune, watching us from behind his Ray-Bans. Mr. Cool. The same guy I'd seen waiting outside the airport for her the week before. I waved howdy. Louis just stared. I wondered how long their relationship would last.

"Been flying lately?" Charise said.

"Every chance I get. My soul is in the sky."

Charise cocked her head like a poodle trying to comprehend what you said to it.

"Shakespeare," I said, "*Midsummer Night's Dream*."

"Right. Of course. Shakespeare." Charise nodded like she got it. "I *love* Shakespeare. Especially in that one movie he was in with Gwyneth Paltrow."

I nearly said something caustic but didn't. Call it maturity.

"Me, too, Charise."

I asked her if she'd found any new recreational activities in lieu of flying that sparked her passion. She said she was getting a tummy tuck.

"I wouldn't have the stomach for that," I said.

Charise smiled. "Well, anyway, it was just so great seeing you again, Cordell."

"Take care, Charise."

A goodbye hug and I was out the door, heading home. When I looked back, her boyfriend was engaged in a heated conversation on his cell phone, no doubt negotiating some outrageously exorbitant fee—more money than I'll probably ever earn in my life.

With apologies to the Buddha, I wanted to slap his lawyerly ass.

<hr/>

I was in bed that night, on my stomach, trying to sleep—hard to do with a tomcat on your back giving himself a bath—when the phone rang and startled us both. I rolled one way. Kiddiot, who'd dug his claws reflexively into my skin at the sound of the phone, rolled the other.

"You malicious pelt. What did I ever do to you?"

He hopped off the bed onto the floor and stretched like he couldn't have cared less, head down, butt high, flexing his front paws. Blood trickled down my back. I could've sworn in the darkness that he was laughing at me. The phone was still ringing. The digital clock on the nightstand read 3:02 A.M.

"Hello?"

"I can't sleep," Savannah said.

"You and my stupid cat." I wondered how early the Humane Society drop-off window opened in the morning.

"I just wanted to say I was sorry," she said. "I know you were only concerned about my safety. You weren't trying to be a control freak. I overreacted."

I was tired and bleeding and in no mood to placate my former wife at three in the morning.

"Anything else?"

It was hardly the magnanimous response she had anticipated.

"Yeah, there's something else. I need my car back."

"I'll see what I can do."

"What do you mean, you'll see what you can do? What kind of crap is that? I let you borrow my car, you self-centered jerk, and now you refuse to give it back?"

"I said I'd see what I could do."

"I want it back, Logan. Today. This afternoon. Or I'm calling the police and reporting it stolen."

"Gee, I'm glad we could have this little chat, Savannah. Thanks for calling. Always a pleasure talking to you."

The line went dead.

I got up, switched on the light over my bathroom sink and angled my back facing the mirror. There were three, two inch-long gouges on my left shoulder where Kiddiot had nailed me. I unrolled eight inches of toilet paper, wiped off the wounds as best I could, killed the light, and laid back down on my stomach so the blood wouldn't stain the sheet. I was still awake three hours later when the first gauzy rays of morning sun came stealing through the gingham curtain shading the garage door window.

I showered, inspected Kiddiot's food bowl to make sure he still had plenty not to eat, then drove to the airport to check on the welfare of my airplane. Planes are like boats. As many bad things can happen to them standing still as moving. Not this time. Except for several large birds that had used the *Duck* as an outhouse, all was well. I fired up the engine, contacted ground control without having to smack the audio panel to get the radios to work, and received clearance to taxi to the wash rack on the other side of the field.

After I hosed off all the guano, I taxied back to Larry's hangar. Larry was sitting cross-legged on the tarmac outside, fixing the nose gear on a Glasair III. He was flashing an inordinate amount of butt crack, even for Larry. The back of his T-shirt said, "My life is a very complicated drinking game."

I shut down the *Duck's* engine and got out.

"Nice ride," Larry said, nodding toward Savannah's Jaguar parked in the lot. "Nice ride."

"A loaner. Ex-wife's car."

"Your ex drives a Jag? Brother, you screwed the pooch. Sugar mama with that kind of bread, you don't throw back."

"Wasn't me that bid *adieu*."

I cinched the *Duck's* tie-down ropes.

"FYI, some guy came by looking for you this morning," Larry said. "A real dick. Starts yelling at me from the other side of the security fence, 'Where's Logan?' I tell him, 'What do I look like, his babysitter?' He tells me to eat shit and stalks off."

"Was he driving a Honda?"

"Didn't see his car."

"What'd he look like?"

"Dark hair, dark skin. Thirty. Jeans. Sunglasses. Could've been Mexican. Hard to tell."

"You just described more than half the male population of California, Larry."

"What you want me to do, Logan, take a picture next time I see him?"

"Might help."

"The guy looked pissed, that's what I remember."

"Probably one of my many satisfied former students."

"Not this guy. I'd watch my back, Logan. He didn't seem quite right in the head. Just my gut."

"Of which you do happen to have a generous supply, Larry."

Larry flipped me off. I took it as a loving gesture.

The red light was blinking on my office answering machine. Six new messages. Four were hang-ups from a "private caller" with a blocked number. The fifth message was from Buzz asking me to call him back on his cell. The last call, less than an hour old, was from Eugen Dragomir. The five grand from his father had arrived. The kid said he wanted to drop off the money and start flying as soon as possible. Given his obvious eagerness to get in the air and monopolize my oh-so-busy schedule, I decided it might be prudent to take care of ancillary matters first. I called Buzz. He was in his basement, he said, enjoying the warmth of a new space heater. The spy who'd come in from the cold. Literally.

"The Amish make 'em—the cabinets, not the heaters. The heaters, the gooks make," Buzz said. "Anyway, the fucking thing cranks out about a billion BTU's. It's like goddamn Miami Beach down here."

"Nobody says gooks anymore, Buzz, unless they're wearing robes and burning crosses."

"Hey, I don't need you schooling me on political correctness, Logan. I get all I need from the wife. She's so liberal, she wears progressive lenses. That thing you asked me about, former co-workers checking out prematurely? You want the skinny or not?"

"Ready to copy."

"I checked open-source databases on every name I could think of," Buzz said. "You remember a guy named Rob Emerson, joined the group in early 2003?"

"Who?"

"Robbie Emerson. Went by 'Herman Munster.' Looked like he free-fell out of the ugly tree and hit every branch on the way down."

Robbie Emerson. Herman Munster. A face floated faintly up from the swampy reaches of my prefrontal lobes. He'd left Alpha less than a month after I rotated in. The story I remembered was that he'd been cashiered for flunking a polygraph.

"He was a Ranger. Got the Silver Star in Mogadishu."

"Not bad, Logan. At least we know you don't got the Alzheimer's. Anyway, the weekend before Echevarria gets it, Emerson drives into the desert outside Phoenix and eats his gun. That's according to local law enforcement. His wife told some newspaper out there he had no reason to kill himself."

His fall from grace, according to Buzz, began after Emerson and some Navy SEALs he'd been training with in Little Creek, Virginia, stopped off after work at a dive bar popular among the frogmen. He'd had a few beers and gotten cozy with a woman who worked as a receptionist in the Washington office of a European trade group that brokered international arms deals. The SEALs suspected that the woman, a Bulgarian, was a "floater," someone used sporadically for intelligence gathering. Emerson had failed to report this contact during a later polygraph exam (those of us in Alpha were routinely polygraphed every six months). Echevarria, who'd been instrumental in bringing him into the group, defended Emerson, arguing that he was being railroaded—Emerson claimed he'd simply forgotten having met the woman. Moreover, there was no evidence he'd passed along any sensitive information of any kind to her—but the command staff didn't want to hear it. He was stripped of his security clearance, relieved of duty and ultimately forced to retire. He'd bounced between civilian jobs, construction mostly, boasting to acquaintances that he didn't have to work because he was secretly wealthy, before landing a part-time gig at a Home Depot in the Phoenix suburb of Glendale.

"Maybe it wasn't suicide, like his wife says, but you sure as hell gotta wonder about his timing," Buzz said. "Let's say Robbie Emerson did get whacked. Then Echevarria gets whacked. Maybe we all should be watching our asses. I mean, it's true what Gold-finger said: Once is happenstance, twice is coincidence. The third time is enemy action."

"It's a sad day when lazy, butt-ugly, over-paid civil servants start quoting lines from movies and calling it operational doctrine, Buzz."

"Who you calling over-paid?"

I told him about the murder of Gennady Bondarenko, and about being chased by the white Honda. I told him about the repeated hang-ups on my answering machine, and about the angry, dark-complected man who, according to Larry, had come looking for me at the airport.

"If it was me and I was dealing with all that shit, I'd be packing heavy," Buzz said. "One primary weapon, one backup, some frags, and an AT-4, because nothing says I love you like a man-portable missile."

"You should be writing your own advice column, Buzz. Call it, 'Dear Miss Armed to the Teeth.'"

"Probably make more money than I'm making now."

He'd already emailed me two news stories on the death of Robbie Emerson by the time we hung up.

Both stories had run in the online edition of the *Arizona Republic*. Neither mentioned Emerson's record of military service. The first article described how police were investigating the dis-covery of an unidentified body found shot to death in the desert outside Scottsdale. The second article, posted two days later, offered more detail: A utility crew stringing digital cable line on a dirt road had discovered Emerson's body slumped behind the wheel of his Chevy Silverado. Authorities believed he'd been dead less than twenty-four hours. A brief suicide note was recovered from the scene. The manager at the Home Depot where Emerson worked said he'd seemed upset the day before his death. Yet his widow insisted that he hadn't killed himself. "He was about to be a grand-father," Emma Emerson was quoted as saying.

Maybe Robbie Emerson died at his own hand, or not. Maybe his death had nothing to do with the murders of Echevarria and Bondarenko, or maybe it had everything to do with them. Yogi

Berra once said that some things in life are too coincidental to be coincidence. Perhaps Robbie Emerson's demise was one of those things. Or perhaps not. All I knew was that my afternoon, as usual, was free—plenty of time to make a few calls and play connect the dots.

I was about to contact Detective Czarnek and tell him what I'd learned when Eugen Dragomir showed up on his skateboard with a $5,000 check and said, "Let's go flying."

The check was drawn on an account from Zurich-based Massio Trust, Ltd. Among banks catering to the international uber-wealthy, Massio's impeccable reputation for asset security and client confidentiality was nonpareil. Which, as any intelligence analyst worth his or her salt will tell you, made Massio Trust a financial institution of choice among certain organized crime operations, including several Russian mafia subsets. But I didn't think much about it at that moment. Only rich men and fools look a gift horse in the mouth. I left my revolver in my desk.

After walking Eugin through our preflight inspection, we climbed into the *Duck*, got the engine going, and listened to the ATIS. The recording indicated that there was a TFR in effect with a thirty-mile radius just north of Rancho Bonita. I told the controller that we would be conducting training maneuvers well to the west, out over the ocean.

"What's a TFR?" Eugin said.

"Temporary no-fly zone. It means the Vice President's in town for the weekend."

The veep and his wife were regulars to the Rancho Bonita area. An old friend of his from graduate school days who'd made good as a hedge fund manager owned a ranch up the coast with horses and a stocked bass pond, and the Second Family visited there often, accompanied by the press, Secret Service, and fully armed Air Force fighter jets that maintained a round-the-clock combat air patrol high overhead, ready to vaporize anything man-made that penetrated the restricted, thirty-mile zone accidentally or otherwise.

I had him taxi to the run-up area, then do an engine run-up to make sure everything was working properly. The tower cleared us for takeoff and we launched. Three minutes later, the controller said, "Resume own navigation, maintain appropriate VFR altitude."

"Own nav, own altitude," I radioed.

We were headed out to sea. Once we got up to 3,000 feet, I leveled off and showed Dragomir how to induce a stall, pulling the nose up, bleeding off the airspeed, until the *Duck* buffeted, pitched over and plummeted toward the waves below. I showed him how to push the yoke forward to break the stall while leveling the wings and adding power, then how to raise the nose to recover lost altitude. We climbed back up to 3,000 feet and did a couple of clearing turns. I said to Dragomir, "Your turn."

Most students tense up when practicing how to recover from stalls. As the warning horn moans in their ears and the plane suddenly drops out from under them, many grit their teeth and close their eyes in terror. Some even barf. Not this kid. He was Right Stuff incarnate. Perfect recovery every time. We practiced slow flight and standard-rate turns. Again, his technique was perfect. I couldn't help but be impressed.

"Cessna Four Charlie Lima, traffic, three moving to your four o'clock, three miles northwest bound, altitude indicates 3,000 feet unverified, type unknown. I'm not talking to him."

Off the *Duck*'s starboard wingtip, I caught the glint of sunlight reflecting from the twin propellers of what looked to be a Beech Baron, far enough away that there seemed little chance of the two of us scraping paint.

"Four Charlie Lima has the traffic in sight, no factor," I said.

"Four Charlie Lima, thank you. Maintain visual separation from that traffic."

"Roger."

Just to be on the safe side, I had Dragomir turn left twenty degrees. The Baron appeared to parallel our turn. I told Dragomir to turn twenty degrees more. The Baron turned as well. He was now less than two miles away and closing.

"You'll need to schedule a flight physical with an FAA examiner before you can solo," I said, keeping one eye on the twin. "Every licensed private pilot has to pass a medical exam at least every two years."

Dragomir said he disliked physicians. "I had my appendix out two months ago. It still hurts," he said, lifting his T-shirt to show me the scar. "Sometimes, I swear, it feels like there's something still in there."

I'm not paranoid. But let's say for the sake of argument that you're an ex-government operative and that your former co-worker, a fellow operative, has been savagely murdered. Let's say individuals unknown are leaving hang-up calls on your answering machine and, by all indications, stalking you. Let's say that your former contact in Russian intelligence has turned up on the coroner's slab, implanted with a radio-controlled explosive device that can be detonated from as far away as a half-mile. And let's say that some college kid who hails from a former Soviet republic shows up out of seemingly nowhere with oddly innate piloting skills, and hands you a check issued by a financial institution that caters to the very individuals you once hunted. Let's say he discloses that he was recently operated on, and that, sometimes, *it feels like there's something still in there.* Let's also say that a twin-engine aircraft easily fifty knots an hour faster than your plane is angling directly toward you, and that you've suddenly convinced yourself that the kid sitting beside you with the surgical scar on his belly has been unwittingly implanted with a bomb identical to the one they found inside your Russian friend, and that if that other airplane gets within a half-mile of you, that bomb will detonate.

Under similar circumstances, any prudent pilot would've done exactly what I did: initiate air combat maneuvers.

"I have the plane," I said.

"You don't want me to fly?"

"Eugen, take your hands off the fucking yoke!"

Eugen Dragomir relinquished the control wheel like it was diseased.

In a Cessna 172, a roll is ordinarily something you eat, not do. But this was no ordinary situation. I rolled the *Duck* inverted and executed a descending half-loop, reversing course before rolling out wings level on a 180-degree divergent bearing. Your standard split-S Dog Fighting 101. The Baron pilot was having none of it. When I looked back over my right shoulder, he was banking steeply, still a couple of miles off, angling once more toward the *Duck's* tail.

I dialed up the emergency frequency, 121.5, on my number-one radio and called air traffic control.

"Mayday, Mayday, Mayday. Cessna Four Charlie Lima is under attack."

The only response was static. I smacked the audio panel and tried it again. This time, there was no static. There was no nothing. The radio was dead.

Dragomir was looking over at me wide-eyed, like it was all way more than he'd bargained for.

"*Under attack?* What the fuck, dude!"

I was too preoccupied to offer any immediate explanations.

We were never going to outrun a twin-engine Baron. That much I knew. The *Duck* literally was a sitting duck. There was only one way out: threaten the safety of the Vice President of the United States.

By the time the two F-16's intercepted us and ordered me to land via the rocking of their missile-laden wings, the Baron had vanished. Secret Service agents in suits and armed with Belgium-made submachine-pistols were waiting on the tarmac at the Rancho Bonita Airport as we touched down. They handcuffed Dragomir and me, searched the *Duck* for weapons, then drove us in a black Chevy Suburban with darkly tinted windows past a burgeoning phalanx of news crews to the airport's security office. The agents seemed little interested in hearing how I had no choice but to violate the Vice President's temporary no-fly zone or risk getting blown out of the sky by the mysterious Beech Baron. I was accused of having imagined the threat. They laughed when I shared with them my fanciful work history, just as Czarnek and his partner had done.

Radar tracks confirmed that, in fact, there had been another private plane flying in my vicinity, but at no time had it posed a hazard significant enough to warrant my intentionally busting a TFR, the agents insisted. The Baron was traced to a Camarillo-based cardiologist who'd become distracted while trying to familiarize himself with a state-of-the-art GPS navigation system newly installed on his airplane, which explained his erratic flying.

It was well past sundown before the lead agent, an energetic African-American woman named Rachel Fargas, grew weary of grilling me and let me go—but only after I surrendered my pilot's license to her. She told me that officials from the FAA and U.S. Attorney's office would be in touch to discuss possible criminal actions. The good news, Fargas said, was that the Secret Service would not divulge my name to the press as a matter of fairness until such time as any actual charges were filed.

"What about my student?"

"You were pilot in command. As far as we're concerned, the student was just along for the ride," Fargas said. "We released him two hours ago."

The news media was gone by the time I was let go. I walked to Larry's hangar, unlocked the door, and dropped off my flight bag inside my office, suddenly feeling very exhausted. The light was flashing on my answering machine. There were three messages: one from some attorney representing Savannah's father who asked that I return his call at my earliest convenience; one from Eugen Dragomir saying he still wanted to go flying with me, assuming neither one of us went to prison; and one from my landlady.

"I just wanted to let you know," Mrs. Schmulowitz said, "that somebody threw a bomb in your apartment. But don't worry, Bubeleh. We're still having brisket Monday night."

EIGHTEEN

My first thoughts when notified that my apartment had been torched were of Kiddiot's welfare. OK, that's not entirely correct.

In truth, my first thoughts were, "Gee, I hope all my stuff didn't burn up because I really can't afford to buy all new stuff right now," followed by, "Gee, I wonder who did it?" Not that I didn't concern myself with the safety of my ungrateful, indifferent feline roommate. But I figured that if anybody could survive a firebombing, like a cockroach, it was him. He'd probably slept through the whole thing up in his tree.

I pulled up and parked Savannah's Jaguar in front of Mrs. Schmulowitz's house. "Your kitty's A-OK," she said as she met me outside. "I made some tuna noodle casserole for him. Does he eat any of it? Not a bite. He's on the divan, taking a nap. He was exhausted."

"You'd be exhausted, too, Mrs. Schmulowitz, if you slept twenty-two hours a day."

I asked Mrs. Schmulowitz if she was A-OK. She assured me she was. She'd been down at the beach, going for a run, she said, when the fire apparently broke out. An eighty-nine-year-old woman jogging along the sand in Lycra shorts and a sports bra. I wondered how many tourists took pictures.

I followed her through the side gate and into her backyard. Yellow "Do Not Cross" police tape encircled what little was left of the garage Kiddiot and I once called home. All four walls, though scorched, were still standing. The roof was caved in. What was left of the rafters jutted skyward at crazy angles like spars from some giant broken umbrella. Fortunately, the firefighters had kept the flames from spreading to Mrs. Schmulowitz's house.

"A *feier zol im trefen,*" Mrs. Schmulowitz said. "He should burn up, whoever did this, the Nazi *gonif.*"

From the alley, I looked in through the shattered window of the garage door, through which a makeshift bomb had obviously been tossed. There was nothing I could see inside that the fire hadn't blackened. The stench of burnt wet wood crawled into my head and for a moment I was transported back to a dank Central American jungle. In a monsoonal rain, we'd chased a high-level cocaine kingpin into a small village. He'd taken refuge in the village church and refused to come out. Echevarria pumped in an incendiary rifle grenade, hoping to get him to rethink his position. The church went up like a tiki torch and the kingpin came out firing. I shot him in the neck. He was the first man I ever killed close enough to see his face.

Mrs. Schmulowitz handed me the business card of a Detective Ostrow from the Rancho Bonita PD.

"He wanted you to call him as soon as you came home," she said. "They think it was arson."

"You haven't asked me who I think did it," I said.

Mrs. Schmulowitz shrugged. "If I thought it was any of my business, Bubeleh, I would've asked. What's important is, nobody got hurt."

I put my arm around her bony shoulder. I told her I was sorry for bringing trouble into her life. Not to worry, she said. Insurance would replace the garage. My personal possessions were another matter.

"Please tell me you didn't have anything valuable in there."

"It's only stuff, Mrs. Schmulowitz." I gave her a wink to let her know that stuff really didn't matter.

If you're a Buddhist, you believe greed and dependence on material possessions are the basis for most human suffering. The more simply you live, the more enlightened you become. I felt very enlightened at that moment. My home was gone along with all my clothes except those I was wearing. What few sentimental touchstones I'd kept over the years—a photo of my biological parents, my degree from the Air Force Academy, the first pilot wings I ever pinned on my uniform, my marriage certificate to Savannah—were all gone. All I had left was the *Duck*, a truck with 176,000 miles on it, and a cat that showed me about as much loyalty as a hooker at a Shriners' convention. Mrs. Schmulowitz offered to let me stay rent-free in her house for as long as I wanted, but the thought of spending even one night on her mohair sofa gave me hives. I thanked her for her kindness and said I'd make other arrangements.

A news van from one of the local TV stations turned down the alley as we were talking and stopped in front of us. An on-air reporter less than half my age hopped out in a suit coat and tie, cargo shorts and running shoes. The top half of him looked like he was on Wall Street; the bottom half, like he was heading off to play beach volleyball. He spewed his words like a high-velocity assault weapon.

"What's up folks Chip Pfeiffer Action News can you tell us what happened do you live here we're doing a story for the five o'clock broadcast we heard it might be arson do you know why anybody would want to burn down this garage you mind if we get a few shots Heather do me a favor and start us off over there with a two-shot of me interviewing these people."

Chip's videographer, Heather, was already roaming the back-yard like she owned the place. She had close-cropped brown hair and thighs like a short-track speed skater. The firefighters had somehow managed to avoid Mrs. Schmulowitz's precious geraniums while dousing her burning garage; peering through her viewfinder, Heather seemed to trample every one of them. Mrs. Schmulowitz seemed not to notice or care, dazzled as she was by the sudden presence of the news media.

I was less than dazzled.

"You're on private property," I said.

"We're just doing our job trying to report the news, sir," Chip said.

"What you're doing is invading this nice lady's privacy. And I'm about to invade your rectum with my foot because a) I don't care for your attitude and b) you presume that microphone gives you the right to do whatever you want. I've got news for you. This just in: it doesn't."

"It's OK, Cordell," Mrs. Schmulowitz said, making goo-goo eyes at Chip. "These sweet young people can film all they want."

"The first thing these sweet young people are going to do is apologize for nuking your flowers," I said. "Then they're going to courteously ask your permission to access your property."

Heather looked at me indignantly. Chip tried to stare me down, then realized I wasn't screwing around. He swallowed down the lump in his throat, sufficiently cowed, and said deferentially to Mrs. Schmulowitz, "We're very sorry for messing up your flowers, ma'am. My station will be happy to replace them. Would it be possible for us to get a few shots of your garage from inside your yard? We'd also like to interview you on-camera—if that's OK with you."

"You want to put *me* on television?"

Mrs. Schmulowitz beamed like Mr. DeMille had just called for her close-up. She said she needed to go put on something more appropriate if she was going to appear on camera, and breathlessly hurried inside.

I waited in the hallway outside her bedroom while she changed out of her sports bra. She told me how she long ago dreamed of a career as a stage actress, but shelved her budding Broadway ambitions when she married and became a mother. Now, seven decades later, here she was again, standing at the precipice of fame.

"I'm sorry all your stuff got charbroiled," Mrs. Schmulowitz said, "but that cockamamie garage burning down could be the best thing that's happened to me in years. It just goes to show you, Bubeleh, there's a reason for everything."

The number of rungs on the ladder of celebrity between the Great White Way and an appearance on Rancho Bonita's local five o'clock news could be measured in light-years, but who was I to burst an old lady's bubble? I asked her for a favor. The reporter, I said, would likely inquire as to why anyone would've wanted to burn down the garage. Did it have something to do with her tenant? What did he do for a living? Who did he know who might've done such a horrible thing? It was the reporter's job to ask questions. The best thing to do, I suggested, was to be polite in response but vague, to tell Action News that she wasn't really at liberty to discuss specifics, and to refer the reporter instead to the police.

Mrs. Schmulowitz emerged from her closet in shiny white boots and a sparkly red leotard with a matching sparkly skirt, like something a baton twirler might've worn during halftime at the Rose Bowl, circa 1950.

"There's something you're not telling me, Bubeleh," she said, admiring herself in a full-length mirror hanging from the back of her bedroom door, "but don't you worry, your secret, whatever it is, is safe with me. Loose lips sink ships. You sure you don't want to sleep on my sofa until you can find somewhere else?"

"That's Plan B. I'll let you know if Plan A doesn't fly. But thanks, in any case, Mrs. Schmulowitz."

A sad thought came to her. She turned slowly from the mirror to face me. "If you go, who will I watch football with on Monday nights? Who will I cook brisket for?"

"You're not getting rid of me that easy. You'll still see me on Mondays. Giants, baby, all the way."

Mrs. Schmulowitz patted me on the cheek, relieved, then turned back to the mirror.

"Well, what do you think?"

"I think your star on the Walk of Fame awaits."

She blew me a kiss and strode outside in her baton twirler outfit to meet her adoring public.

I called the number on the business card she'd given me from Detective Ostrow of the Rancho Bonita Police Department. Ostrow's machine answered.

"Hi, this is Kyle Ostrow. I can't take your call right now. Please leave a message. If this is an emergency, hang up and dial 9-1-1."

He sounded like he was in his twenties. Laid-back California surfer-dude inflection. I said why I was calling and left my cell number. My next call was to Savannah. She didn't answer, either. After the beep, I said, "It's me. I'm returning your car."

Nobody followed me down to LA.

○━━┿━━○

Savannah wasn't home. Her housekeeper, Alameda, informed me through the speaker box at the security gate that the lady of the house had taken a taxi to go counsel a client. Alameda wasn't sure when she'd be home. I told her I'd be back.

The "Find Shopping" feature on the Jaguar's dash-mounted GPS guided me out of the Hollywood Hills, past the CBS studios, and down to the flats of Los Angeles' Fairfax District, to a Kmart on 3rd Street. Into my shopping cart I tossed a six-pack of boxer shorts made in China, a twelve-pack of crew socks made in Costa Rica, three short-sleeve polo shirts made in Vietnam, two pairs of cargo pants and a pair of jeans made in Malaysia, a gray pullover fleece, also from Malaysia, about a month's supply of toothpaste, mouthwash, a comb, deodorant and razors, and a medium-size Little Caesars vegetarian pizza from the kiosk near the store's entrance. As I was loading my toiletries and new wardrobe into the trunk of Savannah's Jaguar, I realized I'd forgotten a toothbrush.

I went back inside, picked out a blue toothbrush with one of those rubber gum massagers that I can never figure out how to use correctly, and walked to the check-out counter. My phone rang while I stood in line.

"Mr. Logan, hey, what's up? This is Detective Kyle Ostrow, Rancho Bonita Police Department. Got a sec?"

"What can I do for you, Detective?"

"Well, sir, as I'm sure you're aware by now, your apartment got burned pretty bad. We're looking at it as a possible arson."

"So I heard."

Forensics, Ostrow said, confirmed that someone had lobbed in a makeshift firebomb. Gasoline had been used as the accelerant. He asked if I knew of anyone who would've wanted to do me harm.

I suggested he contact Czarnek at the LAPD who could fill him in on the whole story.

"What story would that be?"

"The one I'd prefer not having to spend the next twenty minutes rehashing when Detective Czarnek can provide you all the pertinent details."

"I'm just trying to help, Mr. Logan. I'm on your side."

One must be nicer to his fellow human beings if one hopes to return in the next life as something other than a telemarketer or a snail. An earnest, hardworking cop like Ostrow didn't need another impertinent asshole giving him grief, I realized, so I offered him the Cliffs-Notes version of my resume. About doing things to bad people in the name of national security. About Echevarria's murder. About the bomb inside Bondarenko's chest. About being chased on the ground and, while I couldn't prove it, in the air.

"Wow," is all Detective Ostrow could say when I was finished.

I gave him Czarnek's number and signed off.

My fellow Kmart shoppers with whom I'd been waiting in the check-out line avoided eye contact with me. Even though I'd lowered my voice, they had all apparently overheard my conversation with Ostrow. And not only that. I could feel a breeze on the small of my back—my shirt had hiked up, probably when I'd stooped to load Savannah's trunk in the parking lot. The butt of my revolver was protruding from my waistband for all to see. I casually pulled down my shirt.

A biker chick in line directly behind me—waiting to buy a cartload of coloring books, bath towels, and a new George Foreman grill—glanced anxiously at the uniformed rent-a-cop standing guard near the entrance. The guard was scraping his fingernails with a penknife. He looked old enough to be Mrs. Schmulowitz's father.

"I'm auditioning for a part on *CSI Miami*," I explained. "I play a retired government hit man. Could be my big break."

You could tell by their lack of response and the way they avoided my eyes that they feared me. Some men like that feeling, the power of it. I never have. Even when I was with Alpha, when survival depended on exercising such power, I did so only because I had to, not because I wanted to. There's a difference.

I made some lame excuse about forgetting to buy floss and retreated from the check-out line, ditched the toothbrush, and walked past the security guard, out of the store. He never looked up from his fingernails.

"Somebody burned down your *apartment*? Logan, my God."

Savannah bit her lip. She said she hoped the fire had nothing to do with her having dragged me into the investigation of Echevarria's murder, but that she feared there was a correlation.

I was too busy devouring my Kmart pizza over her kitchen sink to offer details about the fire that I'm sure she wanted to hear. Nor did I much feel like cluing her in about how my pilot's license had been lifted by the feds. So I just ate.

"You're being uncouth," Savannah said.

"*Au contraire*. I'm being green. No washing of extraneous dishes. No wasting of water. Friend of the planet."

"That's right. You're Buddhist now. I forgot." She picked a mushroom off my pizza without asking my permission and ate it.

"Help yourself," I said with some sarcasm.

"Don't mind if I do."

She grabbed up a slice and ate over the sink with me. I wasn't going to make an issue of it. She was, after all, letting me stay at her house until I could find more permanent digs. I had accepted reluctantly. It was either that or Mrs. Schmulowitz's itchy sofa.

"I got a call today from your father's attorney," I said. "I didn't call him back. You wouldn't happen to know what's up with that, would you?"

"My father and I aren't speaking at the moment," Savannah said. "He's mad at me. He's convinced he made a major mistake, asking you to go to the police about Arlo."

"He wouldn't have asked me if you hadn't asked first."

Savannah was looking at me and I was looking at her, and what was not said between us in that moment could've filled an entire shelf of self-help books about longing and coping with loss and how to get laid. That was my take on it, anyway. Who knows what she was really thinking?

"I'm going to bed," Savannah said, wiping her mouth with a paper towel. "You can turn off the lights when you're done down here."

There was a small rip in the left seat of her Levi's through which I observed flawless skin. No panties. I tried not to stare.

"You got an extra toothbrush I can borrow?"

"Hallway closet. Bottom drawer."

"Thanks."

A week earlier, I'd been a humble flight instructor, content, for the most part, to put the past behind me and almost pay my bills. Now here I was, at my ex-wife's mercy, bunking in her guest room and having to ask her for a goddamn toothbrush because mine had burned up along with virtually everything else I owned. I swore that come morning, I would leave and never look back. Screw her. Screw Echevarria. Screw it all. Maybe I'd fly up to British Columbia, slap a couple of pontoons on the *Duck*, and make a good living shuttling salmon fishermen in and out of the bush. Or make my way down to the Caribbean and run air charters in and out of Barbados. Bikinis and margaritas. A pilot could get used to that. Yeah, come morning, I told myself, I'd be gone like a hawk on the wing. Then I remembered: I was officially grounded.

Some days you're the kitten, some days you're the lawnmower.

I turned off the kitchen lights and ate what was left of my pizza in the dark.

Nineteen

The sun was not quite up and neither was I when Czarnek called me the next morning to let me know that Detective Ostrow from Rancho Bonita PD had called, told him that my apartment had been bombed, and wanted to compare notes. Like Ostrow, Czarnek could barely contain his glee. Most of the killings he investigated, he said, were pathetically ordinary. Gang-related drive-bys, jealous control freaks strangling their girlfriends, scorned wives stabbing their cheating husbands with kitchen knives or running them over with the family wagon. Same old, same old. But this, he said, this was something gloriously different. Echevarria's murder was rapidly turning into the makings of a by-God international conspiracy.

"It's like eating cheeseburgers every day for lunch," he said. "Then one day, presto, it's *empanadas* with fresh *pico de gallo*."

Food analogies aside, Czarnek said he couldn't divulge what progress he'd made in the case since we'd spoken last, given the sensitive nature of the ongoing investigation, then proceeded to do just that. He was too pumped not to.

According to Czarnek, the late Gennady Bondarenko had been moonlighting as a consultant—a fixer, essentially—for an LA-based consortium of Russian expatriates eager to stake oil leases in Kazakhstan. The consortium would've found itself in direct competition with Gil Carlisle and Pavel Tarasov for the very same leases. The LAPD was working the theory that Bondarenko's consortium, aware that Echevarria was snooping around in Kazakhstan on behalf of Carlisle, had him killed to deter Carlisle's and Tarasov's business interests there. Bondarenko, in turn, had been murdered to derail the consortium's ambitions. A homicidal tit-for-tat.

The particularly brutal manner of Bondarenko's death, Czarnek said, suggested the handiwork of any number of Russian freelancers now living in Southern California. Many were trained killers who boasted of current or former ties to the Kremlin. Czarnek, his partner and a handful of Russian-speaking LAPD detectives who'd been brought in on the case as part of a task force had identified more than twenty viable culprits in Bondarenko's murder, though none specifically in Echevarria's.

"The same .40-caliber pistol was used in both homicides," Czarnek said. "All we have to do is find the weapon and it's two for the price of one."

"Here's a crazy thought: what if Carlisle hired Micah Echevarria to kill Bondarenko? After all, the kid blew away his own father. How hard could it be to shoot a total stranger in the head, saw off his hands and set him on fire?"

Czarnek knew I was yanking his chain.

"We're not barking up that tree right at present," he said.

"So, you're saying the kid's not a suspect?"

"Sometimes, when you try something on it fits, sometimes it doesn't," Czarnek said.

"I'll let him know he's out of the running for Miss Congeniality. What about Miles Zambelli?"

"Who?"

"Miles Zambelli. Carlisle's personal assistant."

"The assistant. Yeah, we took a look at him, too. We got multiple wits that put him at some conference in London the night Echevarria got hit. Guy's got a solid alibi and no rap sheet. Not so much as a parking ticket."

The same, Czarnek said, was true of Janet Echevarria's second husband, Henry Ramos. Why Ramos had paid Bondarenko a visit shortly before his death remained unknown. Detectives were planning to question him upon his return from the business trip to Kazakhstan.

I told Czarnek what Micah Echevarria had said about his father planning to attend the funeral of a friend in Arizona, and how I believed that friend to be former Alpha member Robbie Emerson whose wife was convinced that he hadn't killed himself, despite a gun and note having been recovered at the scene.

"If I had a dime for every sobbing widow convinced her husband didn't shoot himself and got whacked," Czarnek said, "I'd be living the good life up in Tahoe. I'm sure the local cops checked it out."

"You don't mind me double-checking? The guy served in my old unit."

"You wanna waste your time? Have at it. My dance card's full up right now."

"I'll let you know if I find out anything."

"Do that. Just do me a favor, Logan, OK?"

"Anything for you, Detective."

"Try to stay out of trouble? Please? My day's already exhausting enough as it is."

He said he'd let me know if anything broke in the case. I said I'd try not to hold my breath given the glacial pace at which he and the LAPD seemed to undertake murder investigations.

"You're a barrel of laughs, Logan. By the way, there's a rumor going around you won't be flying the friendly skies for awhile."

"You heard about that one, huh?"

"Violating the Vice President's airspace and freaking out his security detail? Everybody's heard about that one. It's all over the news. Good thing I didn't vote for the guy. I might be pissed at you, too. Nothing personal, Logan, but you do tend to piss off your fair share of people. I mean, when that detective from Rancho Bonita called me and asked who I thought might've bombed your apartment, I didn't even know where to start."

"Start at the beginning. My deprived childhood. Being raised by wolves in the forest. Being voted, 'Most Likely to Have Zero Friends on Facebook When Facebook Is Invented Someday.' A tragic tale, Detective, the story of my life. It makes *Phantom of the Opera* look like *Beach Blanket Bingo*. Who among us, under such circumstances, would not piss off their fair share of people?"

"You're fucking nuts," Czarnek said.

"When you've got it," I said, "flaunt it."

There was a telephone listing without an address for an "R. and E. Emerson" in Glendale, Arizona. I called. The woman who answered started to say hello but fumbled the phone, which clattered to the floor with a jarring clang. She picked it up and tried again.

"'Lo?"

"Emma Emerson?"

"Who's this?" Her words were slurred, like someone who'd been abruptly awakened from sleep after getting hammered the night before. It wasn't yet seven in the morning Arizona time.

I apologized for waking her up. I told her I'd served with her husband, and that I'd only recently heard about his death. I was calling, I said, to express my condolences.

"'Scuse me one second," she said. More clanging and clattering as she dropped the phone again. Her footsteps grew distant. I could hear coughing, a deep, tubercular hack. Then a labored groan. Then a toilet flushing. A few seconds later, she was back.

"Phone's not cordless," she said. "That way, they can't listen in."

"Who's *they*, Mrs. Emerson?"

"I can't talk about it over the phone."

"But you just said they can't listen in."

"I know what I said!" She popped open a can of something and took a long gulp. "My Robbie was with Alpha. Were you with Alpha?"

I balked. Any decent operator knows what to do when people start sniffing around for confirmation of his work on the dark side. He lies. He falls back on plausible, well-rehearsed cover stories—the ordinary desk job, the unremarkable home life. He bobs and weaves, redirecting the conversation: *Alpha? Never heard of it. Man, that was some kind of gully washer we had last night, wasn't it? This pasta salad is delicious. What did you put in it? You look great. Have you lost weight?* But how do you obfuscate when the person asking the questions was clearly privy, by whatever degree, to the same shadow world in which you once operated? The answer is, you don't.

"Yes, ma'am," I said. "I was with Alpha."

Emma Emerson gulped down more of whatever it was she was drinking. "Cops said it was suicide, but I know it wasn't. They just said that cuz they're all scared to death."

"Of what?"

"I just said, I can't talk about it over the phone."

She asked me where I was calling from. I told her California.

"My Robbie and me, we honeymooned in San Diego after he got back from Desert Storm. The first war. Ate lobster. I was pregnant." She started crying.

I rattled off something about how the death of a loved one is never easy, and asked if I could come talk to her about what had happened to her husband. I could drive out that afternoon, I said, if that worked for her.

"I don't know you," Emma Emerson said, sniffing back tears.

"No, ma'am, you don't, but I knew your husband. And I know that if there were unanswered questions regarding my death, and he was talking to my wife, he'd want to get to the bottom of it, too."

She wouldn't give me her home address because she didn't know whom to trust and whom not to, she said. We agreed to meet instead in the parking lot of a mini-mart on North Dysart Road, just off Interstate-10, in west Phoenix. If I checked out OK, she said, we'd drive to her house where she would show me "all the evidence" confirming her claim that her husband could not have killed himself. She'd be driving his truck, she said. His blood was still all over the inside of it when the police finally released it to her from the impound lot. She'd spent an entire day cleaning it up with rags and a half-gallon of bleach. It was, she said, the hardest thing she'd had to do in her life.

"And don't think about trying nothing funny, cuz I got a gun and I know how to use it," Emma Emerson said. "It's an Army gun. My Robbie kept it when he left the service. Just don't tell nobody."

"Mum's the word."

I showered, shaved, and brushed my teeth, courtesy of my ex-wife. After I combed my hair, I put on the clothes I'd bought the night before. The boxer shorts were too big in the waist and the pants too long, but they'd have to do. I was stuffing my dirty laundry in the Kmart bag when there was a soft knock at the door.

Savannah was in her blue robe. Her hair was mussed. She looked like she'd been up all night.

"You want some breakfast?"

She seemed surprised I'd say yes.

⊙━━✦━━⊙

I leaned against the refrigerator, sipping coffee from a ceramic mug, watching my ex-wife scramble eggs. I was pondering the concept of forgiveness. In Buddhism, to forgive is to prevent harmful thoughts from wreaking havoc on your mental well-being. I realized I was way beyond that. The havoc that had been wrought still ran deep. I wanted to forgive. I wanted to tell her that I'd messed up big-time, and that in retrospect, she'd had every right under the circumstances to do what she did with Echevarria. But the resentments that consumed me in the wake of our divorce remained in place six years later. They'd eased over time perhaps, but they were still there. A palpable presence, a sour taste in my mouth.

"Bacon?"

"No, thanks."

"That's right. You don't eat bacon."

"Only when the Buddha's not looking."

"Tomatoes?"

"Sure."

Savannah diced a tomato on a cutting board and ground sea salt into a bowl containing half-a-dozen raw eggs. She added some cream, forked the eggs to a froth, then poured the concoction into a stainless-steel skillet simmering on her center island cooktop.

"Sometimes," she said, slowly swishing the eggs back and forth, "I wish I'd never met Arlo."

"Kind of makes two of us."

The sun was beginning to peek over the ridgeline, fingers of light probing the lush green arroyos and the hills below. We sat in the corner nook of Savannah's kitchen, close but not too close, and ate breakfast—I did, anyway. Savannah's hands were clasped to her mouth as if in supplication, her down-turned eyes fixed on my plate. I noticed she was still wearing her wedding band.

"Good chow," I said.

"Glad you like it."

Couples reunite after tumultuous breakups. They've even been known occasionally to live happily ever after. *What if Savannah and I did?* The thought rumbled around inside my head as I ate. I was tempted to throw it out there for discussion. But what if she said no? I'd come off looking weak. Or, worse, what if she said yes, let's give it another go, one more shot? I'd be left wondering how long before she sautéed my heart once more and walked out on me again.

"The best thing I ever did," Savannah said, "was marrying you. And the worst."

"Boy howdy, do I know *that* feeling."

She searched my eyes. I'd like to think she was looking for a hint of reprieve, some small clue to affirm her unspoken desire to strip me naked and have mind-altering, three-alarm breakfast-nook sex with me, but her face was a cipher. Hell, I never could figure out the woman, anyhow.

I finished the last of my eggs. "I need to borrow your car again."

"Why? Where're you going?"

"Phoenix."

"You have an airplane."

An airplane, yes, but no license to legally fly it.

"Plane's in the shop," I said, lying. "I need to get to Phoenix this afternoon."

"What's so important you have to be there this afternoon?"

"Can I borrow your car, Savannah, yes or no?"

"Not unless you tell me what's so important in Phoenix that you have to be there today."

I didn't have time to deliver the whole truth and nothing but.

"Somebody died," I said.

"Somebody connected to Arlo?"

"Possibly."

"They were murdered, too, weren't they?"

"More like suicide."

"I asked you to stop all this, Logan."

"And I told you, I can't."

"Right. Because Arlo saved you from getting hit by a *streetcar*. And I'm supposed to actually believe that?"

"Little-known fact: More people are killed every year by streetcars than killer bees."

"You're so totally full of shit, you know that?"

"Look it up, you don't believe me."

Savannah shook her head. "Someday," she said, "you'll tell me the truth. Maybe."

Someday. Maybe. But not today.

I set my plate in the sink.

"I need a go or no-go on the car, Savannah."

Savannah sighed. "The keys are on the desk in the study," she said. "Just bring it back full."

⚬━━┿━━⚬

I eased the Jaguar to the end of the driveway and waited while the security gate swung slowly inward. I was thinking that the last thing I wanted to do was spend six hours driving across the desert to Phoenix to grill some woman I'd never met about whether her husband whom I barely knew did or didn't kill himself. I had the FAA to do battle with, my pilot's license to restore, a flight school to run into the ground. What did I care how Robbie Emerson died? I suppose the same could've been said about Arlo Echevarria. So what if I owed him my life? Had some dipstick in a Domino's shirt lit me up like a Christmas tree instead of him, there's no way that self-absorbed son of a bitch would've ever gone hunting *my* killer. Not after I stole *his* wife. I pondered the notion of giving Gil Carlisle back his money—what was left of it, anyway. But something stopped me. Not some lesson from the Buddha about fidelity to the memory of a friend—even if that friend turned out to be the opposite—and not some cheesy, ready-room pep talk about completing the mission regardless the cost. No, what kept me from putting the Jag in reverse and giving Savannah back her keys was the ill-formed notion that somehow, if I could just piece the puzzle

– 226 –

together and deliver her some closure, that she would be there, waiting for me in the end, and that we could resume life together as if Arlo Echevarria never existed. Improbable, I realized, but there it was. Whatever I owed Arlo Echevarria, I decided, would be paid in full by my making the trek to Arizona. My conscience would be assuaged, the ledger balanced.

Immersed as I was in such thoughts, it took me a second to notice the black van with tinted windows that turned sharply into the driveway and skidded to a loud, screeching stop directly in front of Savannah's car.

The driver was already out of the van and advancing toward me, reaching his right hand into a blue Dodger warm-up jacket like he was going for a weapon. He was about thirty and on the thin side, with a long loping stride, shaved head, milk chocolate skin, moon face, ballistic-shooter sunglasses. I drew my revolver, threw open the Jag's passenger door and, shielding myself behind it, squared his chest in my gun sights.

"Whoa! Whoa! Whoa!" He slammed on the brakes like some cartoon character. "Ain't no need for none of that, brother. C'mon now."

"Get your hands up where I can see 'em."

"No worries. Take it easy." He reached for the clouds.

"Now turn around with your fingers interlocked on the back of your head."

"Anything you want, brother. Be cool now. C'mon."

I advanced on him in a two-handed combat crouch and ordered him to spread his legs shoulder-width. When I got close enough, I patted him down from behind with one hand, my gun trained on him with the other. He was unarmed.

"What's under the jacket?"

"Legal papers." He turned his head and eyeballed me, his hands still in the air. "Are you Mr. Cordell Logan?"

"Only if you're from Publishers Clearing House."

"Publisher's *what*?" He realized I was messing with him. "No, man, I'm a—"

"Process server," I said, finishing his sentence for him and stuffing my revolver back in my belt. "No balloons. That should've been my first clue."

I apologized for nearly killing him. He professed no hard feelings.

"In my line of work, comes with the turf," he said, handing me a temporary protective order with my name printed on it. "You've been duly served."

"Duly noted."

He backed his van up and sped off down the hill in search of his next litigant.

The protective order, signed by one Ronald Jablonsky, district court judge from Clark County, Nevada, accused me of harassing my former father-in-law, his assistant, Miles Zambelli, and Savannah. It ordered me to cease and desist in the matter of Arlo Echevarria, warning that I would be prosecuted to the fullest extent of the law if I failed to do so. I wondered how big a bribe Carlisle had slipped the judge. I crumpled the paper, tossed it in the backseat, and headed east, out of the city, the sun in my eyes.

Savannah called.

"My housekeeper just told me there was some big commotion down on the street."

"Your father served me with a cease and desist. How'd he know I was at your house?"

"I told him."

"Thanks a bunch."

"Whatever you may think of him, Logan, he's still my father."

She'd called him after she'd gone to bed, she said, because she was confused about her feelings for me and needed to talk it through with someone. Her father, she said, had offered to buy her a first-class ticket and put her up at his flat in Paris for a month, all expenses paid—enough time for her to come to her senses and realize that she had no business ever giving me the time of day again.

"So what did you tell him?"

"I told him I'd have to think about it."

"Personally, I would've gone with the place in Paris."

"Of course you would've," Savannah said.

I promised I'd have her car back the next day, if not sooner.

TWENTY

As the objective observer motors across much of rural America, he is often struck by the thought, "How could anyone with half a brain ever live in a hell hole like this?" Certainly, the extreme eastern reaches of Southern California, where the desertscape turns more lunar-like with the passing of each bleak, interminable mile, embody the very definition of such godforsaken places. Places where the reception on one's car radio becomes limited to Mexican border blaster mega-stations, gospel-thumping fearmongers, and twangy country-western tunes like, "There Ain't Enough Room in My Fruit of the Looms to Hold All My Lovin' for You." Places better flown over than driven through.

I was listening to Johnny Cash's "I've Been Flushed from the Bathroom of Your Heart," pondering the profundity of the Man in Black's lyrics, when Miles Zambelli telephoned. Much as I disliked Zambelli, I was happy to talk to him. Given that I still had another two hours of boring, featureless desert ahead of me, I would've been happy to talk to just about anybody.

He said he was speaking on behalf of Carlisle, who was concerned that my making "unfounded and inflammatory" inquiries in Echevarria's death threatened to derail the oil deal with Tarasov in Kazakhstan.

"Neither Mr. Carlisle nor Mr. Tarasov appreciates you continuing to make these ridiculous inquiries," Zambelli said, "and, quite frankly, neither do I. You will cease and desist, or Mr. Carlisle will have no choice but to demand reimbursement in full of the monies he paid you which, if you'll recall, required you to do nothing more than very briefly apprise the police as to the nature of Mr. Echevarria's employment history."

"Please inform Mr. Carlisle I am in receipt of the court order issued by Judge Jablowme, and that I have filed it accordingly. Also please inform Mr. Carlisle that any and all monies paid me to date have already been expended on cheap wine and even cheaper women."

"If you think this is a joking matter, Mr. Logan, I would advise you to think again. As you continue to cast outrageous aspersions on wholly innocent individuals in the death of Mr. Echevarria, including Mr. Carlisle and myself, you're also interfering with an ongoing police investigation. And I can assure you, sir, we will not stand for it."

"That is some mighty fine speechifying, Miles. Did you learn that at Harvard Law or watching *Law and Order*?"

I wasn't sure if the connection was lost before or after he hung up on me.

⊂━━◆━━⊃

Emma Emerson arrived twenty minutes late for our rendezvous in the mini-mart parking lot on Phoenix's west side. She was driving her late husband's red Silverado. Though it was still daylight, I flashed my headlights three times to let her know it was me she was looking for, then got out and walked over.

She was an anorexic, fifty-something brunette in jeans and a goose-down vest, even though it was eighty degrees outside, and bulging, slightly misaligned green eyes that never quite met mine.

"Got any ID on you?"

I dug the driver's license out of my wallet and held it up for her inspection. Resting on her lap was a nine-millimeter Beretta. A vintage Winchester carbine rode in a gun rack mounted on the inside of the truck's rear window behind her, along with a .223-caliber Ruger survival rifle with a plastic laminate stock.

"I don't remember Robbie ever saying anything about serving with Cordell Logan, no middle name," she said, peering at my license photo. "Sounds like one of them made-up Hollywood names to me."

"The studios made me change it. My real name's Norma Jean Baker."

She eyed me suspiciously without so much as a rumor of a smile. Grabbing a pack of unfiltered Camels from the truck's center console, she eased one between her lips, fired it up with a match, and said, "I'm gonna ask you two questions. Get either one wrong, we're done. Got it?"

"I just hope they're true or false. I don't do well on multiple choice."

Tendrils of smoke shot out of her nose. "True or false: The standard-issue weapon of Alpha tactical teams was the MP-5 submachine gun."

"There was no standard-issue weapon. Every man carried whatever he qualified on, as long as it shot standard NATO ammunition."

If she was impressed, she didn't show it.

"Second question: What name did my Robbie use in the field?"

"Herman Munster."

She exhaled, openly relieved, and nodded approvingly. "Can't be too careful who you're dealing with these days." She glanced over at Savannah's Jaguar. "That your car?"

"Ex-wife's car."

"She must still love the hell outta you if she let you borrow a vehicle like that. You still love her?"

"All depends on how horny I am at the moment."

Emma Emerson grinned. She was missing an upper incisor.

"The last honest man on earth," she said. "Get in."

<hr/>

We merged from I-10 onto the Agua Fria Freeway, heading north past half-built subdivisions, tan stucco and faux-Spanish tile structures, most of them abandoned amid the nation's Great Recession. Emma rocked back in her seat to check her side view mirrors, then leaned forward over the steering wheel, scanning the skies above and ahead of us like she was looking for enemy aircraft.

"Want a beer?"

"Wish I could."

"Suit yourself."

She reached behind her seat without taking her eyes off the road and fished a Bud Light out of a red and white Igloo cooler. "Everything's over at the house," she said, "all the evidence of who killed my Robbie."

She popped open the can.

"Why do you think he was killed?"

"Cuz they wanted him killed."

"Who's *they*, Emma?"

She glanced over at me "Who do you think? The government."

Robbie Emerson had gleaned volumes about Alpha's tactics, techniques and procedures—much of which he'd appeared to have shared with his wife. Knowledge of even Alpha's name was classified TS/SCI back when the group was operational. So sensitive were its activities that even the Buddha would've required a full background investigation to be briefed. But that hadn't stopped Emma Emerson from apparently learning all about Alpha from her late husband. She droned on and on about all the many classified missions in which he'd participated, and what an outstanding covert operator he'd been.

I asked her if he'd ever talked about Arlo Echevarria.

"All the time. Robbie loved Arlo. The only one who ever stood up for him."

"Then you heard what happened to Echevarria."

Emma looked over at me. "What're you talking about?"

"Echevarria was killed. About a month and a half ago. Shot to death."

"Jesus." She gulped down half her beer. "Robbie called Arlo to tell him some Russians were out to get him. He called to warn Arlo."

"When was this?"

"The night before they found him out in the desert. Don't you see? They murdered Arlo to cover their tracks, just like they did my Robbie, just like they're gonna do you. They know you know."

"Know what, Emma?"

She didn't answer, scanning the skies and checking her mirrors. We were doing ninety in the slow lane, passing cars on the right.

"You said 'some Russians.'"

"Fuck the Russians! They're in on it, too! They all are! You know who it was!" She reached behind her, steering with her right hand, trying to wrestle the Winchester out of the gun rack and nearly sideswiping a big rig hauling a load of sheetrock. "Take the rifle. Take it!"

I grabbed the Winchester out of the rack before she shot herself with it. Or me. She was straining forward in her seat, peering intently upward, through the windshield.

"There!" she said, pointing, "Right there! You see it? There it is!"

I followed her sight line to a Bell Ranger cruising at our eleven o'clock position, about 1,500 feet AGL, paralleling the freeway. "Channel 11 Action News" was emblazoned on the side of the helicopter's fuselage.

"You mean the news chopper?"

"News chopper. Yeah, right."

She veered violently off the freeway, ignoring the red light at the bottom of the off-ramp, and fishtailing onto Union Hills Drive, racing eastward. I could see the TV helicopter through the truck's rear window. It continued to parallel the freeway, flying on a perpendicular course, away from us.

"Lost him." She lit another cigarette with trembling hands. "God, that was close."

I soon realized that the news helicopter wasn't the only thing Emma Emerson had lost.

⚓

She lived in a two-bedroom mobile home across the street from the clubhouse in a treeless, sun-blanched trailer park on Scottsdale's north side. Three deadbolt locks secured the corrugated aluminum front door. Robbie Emerson's widow quietly put her ear to the door and listened with the pistol in her right hand, hammer back. Satisfied we weren't walking into an ambush, she undid the deadbolts. I followed her inside.

Dozens of banker boxes filled with papers were heaped haphazardly atop each other almost to the ceiling, creating wobbly cardboard walls through which narrow passageways had been constructed like some sort of indoor corn maze. Newspapers and magazines and clothes and cartons of ammunition were piled on the furniture. There was nowhere to sit. The trailer reeked of tobacco and garlic.

"In here," Emma said, sidestepping between walls of boxes and into the trailer's cramped galley kitchen. She put the pistol on top of the refrigerator, snatched a half-gallon bottle of off-brand bourbon from a cupboard next to the stove and poured herself a glass. The kitchen table, barely big enough for two people, was crammed with boxes, files, and an old CRT-type computer monitor.

"You need to see this," she said, sitting down at the table and typing.

I stood over her shoulder and watched. Black and white video appeared on the computer screen: a broad V-formation of lights in the night sky. I remembered seeing the same footage on the news years earlier. The Air Force said the lights were nothing more than flares dropped by military aircraft on a training exercise outside Phoenix, but hundreds of eyewitnesses insisted otherwise. What they saw that night, they said, was an enormous UFO.

Emma lit a fresh Camel. "That's the alien mother spaceship," she said, gesturing with her chin to the computer screen. "Where everybody took all those pictures of it was right near where those utility workers found Robbie. Same location. That's why Robbie was killed. That's why Arlo was killed. To keep them quiet because they knew all about the arrangement."

"What arrangement would that be, Emma?"

"The reverse engineering stuff they're doing at Area 51! I thought you said you were with Alpha. Jesus."

Her late husband's top-secret security clearance, she said, had afforded him detailed knowledge of hush-hush research programs that allowed scientists working for the Defense Department to parlay technology gifted by ETs into the development of technological advances ranging from Stealth bombers to longer-lasting light bulbs.

"Robbie knew things he wasn't supposed to know, so they made it *look* like he killed himself," Emma said. "They're gonna kill you and everybody else who was ever with Alpha, just like they did him and Arlo Echevarria because they know you all know the truth."

"You're saying the aliens killed your husband?"

"Christ, do I have to spell it out for you? Not the aliens. They're too smart for that. They make these big defense contractors hire professional killers, Russians, because they don't want the public to know they're all in cahoots." She gulped some bourbon. "The CEOs of these companies, they're making trillions of dollars, cashing in on all the tech transfer! The police won't do nothing because they're afraid they'll get killed, too, just like my Robbie. So nobody says a word."

"Did Robbie tell you all this?"

"He didn't want to put me at risk. Far as he was concerned, the less I knew, the safer I'd be. But I figured it all out, believe me, the whole story. Mailed Arlo a book that lays it all out, the whole cover-up, to protect him, because I knew how much Robbie respected him. But Arlo must not have read it, cuz if he'd of had any sense at all, he would've run for the hills before they got him."

I asked her about the suicide note her husband had allegedly left behind.

"That wasn't him that wrote it. The grays forged his hand-writing to make it look like he'd killed himself." She removed a sheet of paper from a file. "The police would only give me a copy. Said the original was evidence."

She handed me the copy of her husband's suicide note. In steady block print it said, "I can't do it. I'm sorry."

"Robbie would've never shot himself, not in a million years," Emma said. "Our daughter's having a baby. She's due any day. Robbie was gonna be a grandpa. You should've seen him. He was so excited. Them aliens, the grays, they was the ones who made him do it. The police can deny it all they want, but I got the proof."

She handed me an envelope from the Arizona Motor Vehicle Division. Inside was Robbie Emerson's driver's license.

"This came in the mail the week after he died," she said.

The photo on Emerson's license made him look older than his fifty-seven years. He had thinning hair and a straggly beard flecked with gray and stared listlessly into the camera, like some shell-shocked veteran resigned to his fate. He looked to me like a man who could've easily put a pistol to his skull and squeezed one off.

"Look at the date on the license," Emma said. "He goes and renews his license two days before his birthday, then, five days later, you're telling me he drives into the desert and shoots himself? Who in their right mind renews their driver's license, then five days later does that?"

She showed me a prescription bottle with Emerson's name on it—Prozac, the same anti-depressant Savannah dropped like candy toward the end of our marriage. Savannah always said she needed happy pills because her career wasn't going well, but I always wondered if it was because of me.

"Look at the date on the bottle," Emma said. "He refills the prescription and three days later, he kills himself? Gimme a break. It makes no sense. None of it."

"I'm sorry, Emma."

She stared at the photo on his driver's license for a long time, caressing it with her thumb. Then she got up from the table and hurried unsteadily into the bathroom, slamming a hollow core door behind her that did little to mask the sounds of her retching into the toilet.

I leafed through one of the file jackets piled on the table. The folder was crammed with newspaper clippings detailing alien abductions. Other similar file jackets held clippings about cattle mutilations, crop circles, and, inexplicably, singer Wayne Newton. There were files for insurance claim forms, warranties and receipts, and annual tax returns. There was also a file thick with copies of cashier's checks made out to Emma Emerson, each in the $1,000–$5,000 range and dating as far back as 2003—the same year Robbie Emerson joined Alpha. All of the checks had been issued by Massio Trust, Ltd.—the same Massio Trust whose banking clients included members of the Russian mafia and the father of Eugen Dragomir, my one and only student pilot.

It's a small world, I thought, *but not that small.*

Emma emerged from the bathroom wiping her mouth with a washcloth. She looked wan.

"Who was Robbie working for when he died, Emma?"

"Home Depot. Part-time. Why do you wanna know that?"

I held up one of the cashier's checks. She tried to snatch it away.

"You got no right looking in my personal files! Who the hell do you think you are?"

"He parlayed his security clearance into a little income on the side, selling innocent tips here and there to certain interested foreign parties. What kinds of weapons we used. Basic tactics. He figured, 'Where's the harm in it? It's information they probably know already.' Only he couldn't deposit dirty money under his real name, so he had the checks made out to you. That way, if anybody ever asked him during a polygraph, 'Have you ever accepted illicit funds from any foreign parties?' he could say no and the needles wouldn't budge."

"My Robbie served his country. He was a hero. He would never do something like that. *Ever.*" Her carotids were pounding like jackhammers.

"You're lying, Emma. I can see it in your neck."

She covered her throat with her hand to cloak her throbbing arteries. Tears spilled down her cheeks.

"All I want is the truth, Emma. Same as you."

She winced almost imperceptibly and licked her lips. The truth, Emma conceded, was that she didn't know where all the money came from. Her husband never said. Checks would arrive every month or so—a thousand bucks here, two thousand there—and she would dutifully deposit them. She had her suspicions that perhaps he was involved in some peripheral way with the alien technology transfer cover-up, she said, but she was never certain.

"He came home very upset the day before he died. I asked him if something had happened at work. He said he'd got in an argument with somebody, but he wouldn't tell me who, or what it was about."

"You mentioned Russians."

Emma sat back down at the table and stared mournfully at her hands.

"Is that who came to see Robbie that day, Emma? A Russian?"

"I don't know. Maybe. I'm not sure."

"Robbie called Echevarria, to warn him about 'some Russians.' Isn't that what you said?"

"I don't know. I think so. I was cooking bacon. The TV was on. Robbie was on the phone."

"Did you tell the police this?"

"They said he was already depressed, taking pills, whatever. Robbie was never like that, arguing with people. He was never the same after they made him retire—all that crap about him being in that bar with that European woman and supposedly telling her things—but I know he didn't kill himself. And not you or anybody else on this earth can ever tell me otherwise."

She sat down once more at the table and keened mournfully.

You seem to have this effect on a lot of women, Logan, I thought to myself.

I rested my hand on her shoulder. "For the sake of the entire human race," I said, trying to make her feel better, "I only hope the grays were not involved."

Emma looked up at me appreciatively, her eyes glistening.

"I'm not off my rocker."

"No one said you were, Emma."

○══╬══○

After Robbie Emerson's widow dropped me back at Savannah's car, I drove to the Home Depot where he'd worked. The manager looked like Babe Ruth in an orange apron. He was at the service desk, on the phone, trying to placate an irate woman who'd accidentally dropped a ninety-pound bag of dry cement mix on her foot and was now threatening to sue. I waited until he hung up.

"Hell hath no fury," the manager said.

"You don't know the half of it," I said.

I told him my name, said I was looking into Emerson's death, and asked whether it might be possible to see store surveillance tape taken the day before Emerson died.

"You guys already went through all the tape. I thought you said there was nothing there."

"I'm not a detective. I just play one on TV."

The manager looked at me funny. "Come again?"

"Mr. Emerson and I served together in the same unit. I'm just trying to find out what happened to him."

"Look," the manager said, "I'm ex-infantry myself. Desert Storm. But unless you've got a court order, or you're the police, I can't help you. Corporate policy. I'm sorry."

"Desert Storm? I was over myself."

"Is that right? Who were you with?"

"Air Force. I flew A-10s."

"Hog driver, huh?"

"Shake and bake, baby."

"You guys saved our bacon more than once, that's for sure."

"Good times," I said.

The manager looked away wistfully as the trace of some distant memory crossed his face. He was quiet for a long moment. "You know," he said finally, "I never really got a chance to thank you guys properly." He stuck out his hand. "My name's Ted, by the way."

<hr />

The surveillance tape, shot by a video camera hanging from the corrugated aluminum ceiling, was grainy and without audio. Still, Robbie Emerson's likeness was unmistakable. No wonder he went by "Herman Munster" during field operations. Anybody that grody-looking, you can spot with a satellite. He was wearing his Home Depot apron, arguing animatedly in the plumbing department with a lanky customer who stood with his back to the camera. The customer wore jeans, a plain green T-shirt, a black or possibly blue baseball cap, and sunglasses. He carried in his right hand a red plastic case about two-and-a-half feet long. The word, "Milwaukee," was printed on the side of the case.

"Looks like a Sawzall," I said.

"Fifteen amp Super Sawzall," Ted said. "One of our better sellers. You can cut through a two-by-six like butter with one of those bad boys."

"Or cut off somebody's hands."

"You are one strange dude," the manager said.

"It's been said of me before."

Inside the Home Depot's darkened security office, the store's security director, a squat, bespectacled retired postal inspector named Skaggs, reclined in a well-worn swivel chair while monitoring a wall of eleven camera monitors, each of which shifted its view automatically every ten seconds, covering every aisle as well as the store's parking lot and loading docks.

The heated discussion between Emerson and the faceless customer played out silently on a twelfth monitor. Ten seconds of video on a repetitive loop. I moved in closer for a better look.

"Play it again."

Skaggs replayed the clip. And again. The man carrying the Sawzall case never showed his face to the camera.

"Nobody heard what they were arguing about?" I asked.

"None of our associates," Ted said. "We talked to everybody who was on-shift at the time."

"What about any customers?"

"Nobody heard anything so far as we were able to determine," Skaggs said.

"What about when the guy goes to pay for the saw?" I said. "You must've gotten a better shot of his face then."

Skaggs spooled up another video clip. "The camera covering those registers, unfortunately, was down that afternoon for maintenance. This was as good a picture as we could get."

The second clip, also shot from on high, captured the man with the Sawzall swiping a credit card at a self-service check-out stand, but the on-screen resolution was no better than the first clip. With his baseball cap pulled low and wraparound sunglasses, the man's face was impossible to make out.

"He paid with plastic," I said. "You can ID him that way."

Ted looked chagrined. "Yeah, well, unfortunately, we had a problem with that, too. American Express reported the card stolen out of California about an hour after we processed the transaction."

Scottsdale police, he said, had reviewed the videotape and concluded that the faceless crook who bought the Sawzall probably had little, if anything, to do with Emerson's decision to kill himself the following day.

"That guy might've set Robbie off for whatever reason," Ted said, "but Robbie was always wound up pretty tight anyway, always about two seconds from going off on somebody for something. I mean, if anybody was unhappy with his life and was gonna, you know, do himself in, it was him. The cops said that's what all the evidence pointed to and that's good enough for me. I don't want to sound cruel or anything but, really, the only reason I hired him was because he'd been a grunt, like me. I probably was gonna have to let him go anyway given his attitude."

"Mighty considerate, him saving you the trouble."

"That's not what I meant."

"I know what you meant. Robbie Emerson was far from perfect. He made his share of mistakes. But the man did earn a Silver Star defending his country. He deserved better than a six-word goodbye note and a bullet in his brain."

I stalked out of the security office, which was in the back of the store, and through the paint department, making for the main entrance. Ted hustled to catch up.

"Look, I'm sorry," he said. "I know he was your friend."

"Forget it."

"That crack you made," he said, "about cutting somebody's hands off. I'm just curious. What was that all about?"

"Me flapping my gums."

The image of Gennady Bondarenko's charred carcass flashed through my head. According to the coroner, Bondarenko's hands appeared to have been removed by a power tool equipped with a reciprocating blade. Like a Sawzall. Robbie Emerson had shot himself soon after arguing with a man who'd purchased such a saw. According to his widow, Emerson had called Arlo Echevarria the night before he died to warn him that someone was out to get him. Echevarria and Bondarenko had been murdered with the same handgun. I was never a whiz at higher math, but I needed no algebraic equation to figure a possible common denominator in the deaths of all three men:

The guy who bought the Sawzall.

All I needed to do was find him.

Twenty-one

Darkness had descended on the Valley of the Sun by the time I persuaded Ted the Home Depot manager to give me the name and account number of the guy whose stolen credit card had been used to purchase the power saw. Ted expressed concern about violating privacy laws and what his superiors at corporate headquarters might say if they knew that he was passing along confidential information to a non-cop like me. I'd like to think I won him over by my undeniably charismatic persona alone. But my having flown close air-support missions in the Gulf, helping clear the way for ground pounders like Ted, probably had more to do with it than anything else.

I hoped that the card's owner might have some inkling as to how it ended up in the hands of the man on the videotape who'd exchanged words with Robbie Emerson, but my hopes sagged after Ted gave me the cardholder's name: Richard Smith, with no middle initial. Ted said he didn't have Smith's address. I'd have to get that from American Express. The chances of Amex complying without a court order, I knew, were zero. The chances of locating someone with so common a name without an address of record, I also knew, were less than zero.

I was too tired to make the drive back to Los Angeles. I found a Best Western just off the freeway with free HBO and a complimentary continental breakfast for forty-nine bucks a night. Not bad. There was a Taco Bell conveniently situated across the parking lot. I enjoyed a Burrito Supreme value meal, stole a handful of napkins if only to keep in practice, then walked back to my room. Come morning, I'd return to California, pass along to the LAPD what I'd learned about Emerson and his possible connection to Echevarria's murder, and get back to being a failing flight instructor in serious shit with the FAA.

My room was spartan but clean. The motel's walls were thankfully stout enough that with the TV turned up, I almost couldn't hear the couple next door going at it like libidinous Sumo wrestlers. I took a long shower, toweled off, and stretched out on the bed to think.

Aliens-obsessed Emma Emerson may have been a few yards shy of a first down, but her micro-expressions—those involuntary, almost imperceptible facial movements we all make that can inadvertently reveal hidden emotions—told me she was telling the truth about not knowing who'd been issuing cashier's checks in her name all those years. It sounded like Kremlin standard operating procedure to me. "Palm oil," the Russians call it, relatively small amounts of money paid to a prospective intelligence asset for non-sensitive, often open-source information. The asset figures he's pulling a fast one over on his handlers. After all, he's trading on "secrets" that aren't really secrets. No harm, no foul. Then, one day, his handlers take him aside and give him a choice: Do exactly as we say from now on or we will let the FBI know that you've been on our payroll, and you will go to prison for a very long time.

I knew that Gil Carlisle's new prospective business partner, Pavel Tarasov, had reputed ties to Russian intelligence. I knew that Carlisle had hired Echevarria to check out Tarasov's background. Robbie Emerson, according to his widow, had purportedly warned Echevarria that Russians were after him. Now both Emerson and Echevarria were dead. Was it possible that the Russians had Emerson by his short hairs? Did they make demands on him that he couldn't meet? Is that why he wrote, "I can't do it, I'm sorry," before putting the gun to his head?

Nearly a week had elapsed since my meeting with Carlisle in Las Vegas, when he'd claimed that Echevarria's investigation of Tarasov's background had turned up nothing incriminating. But the manner in which he'd said it—rubbing his eyes, running his hand across his mouth—suggested deceit. What, if anything, was my former father-in-law hiding?

The couple next door was still banging around like walruses in heat. There was nothing on TV. I decided for lack of anything better to do to dial up Carlisle and find out what he really knew. Problem was, the battery on my phone was nearly dead, and I'd left my charger back at Savannah's house. I'd have to use the room phone. I might as well have been calling Saturn for all I knew about what the call was going to cost me. What the hell. It's only money. At that moment, anyway, thanks to Carlisle, I had plenty.

Lamont Royale answered the phone. Carlisle wasn't in. He and Pavel Tarasov, Royale said, were out having dinner and drinks, mapping business strategy.

"Is there something I can help you with, or a message you'd like to leave?"

"Just have him call me back if he gets in before midnight." I gave Royale the number and the extension to my room.

"Area code six-oh-two. That's what, Arizona?"

"I'm in Phoenix."

"I could never live there," Royale said. "Too hot in the summer."

"Right. Like Vegas is the North Pole."

He laughed politely. "I'll tell Mr. Carlisle you called. Have a wonderful evening."

The grunting and moaning emanating from the love fest next door sounded like Chewbacca from *Star Wars* times two. I turned off the lamp and tried to sleep.

The free continental breakfast was the usual assortment of stale donuts, soggy Danish, dry cereal in little boxes, mealy apples, over-ripe bananas, a machine dispensing watery fruit drinks, and coffee that tasted like you could strip antique furniture with it. My fellow travelers and I sat in the motel's dining area and ate in glum silence, avoiding eye contact.

I was polishing off a Styrofoam bowl of Raisin Bran when Pavel Tarasov walked in. With him were two knuckle draggers in black leather jackets, both working hard to look like the badasses they wanted everyone to think they were. I sat back a little, pressing into the seat back, making sure my revolver was still wedged under my shirt in the small of my back, just in case.

Tarasov muttered something to his bodyguards. They hovered in the lobby while he sat down in the chair across from me and surveyed my meal.

"Why do you Americans insist on calling it 'continental' breakfast? On which continent beside your own would people eat such garbage?"

"Americans invented the Oreo—and the *deep-fried* Oreo," I said. "We'll eat anything."

He smiled. "Mr. Carlisle said I might find you here. The number you called him from, the motel phone, I had my people look up the address and fly me down in my Gulfstream."

"Nice bird. I'm prepared to trade you straight across. Your jet for my Cessna. I'll even throw in the headsets. They're vintage."

Tarasov wasn't smiling anymore. "Mr. Carlisle tells me you've been quite a busy man."

"The same can be said for you, running around, killing people."

"I have no idea what you are talking about, Mr. Logan," Tarasov said, his voice pitching slightly higher.

Either he was lying or a possible alumnus of the Vienna Boys' Choir.

He said he didn't know Gennady Bondarenko or anything about Bondarenko's murder. Ditto Robbie Emerson. He denied any links to any Russian intelligence agencies.

Breaking eye contact when answering a question conveys possible deception. With each answer, Tarasov held my eyes unwaveringly, like someone who'd been trained in counter-interrogation techniques.

"I am an honest businessman, Mr. Logan, and you are ruining my business. You will stop or you will be dealt with accordingly."

"Are you threatening me, Mr. Tarasov?"

He stood and stared down at me coldly.

"As you cooked the porridge, so must you eat it."

"You Russians definitely have the market cornered on obscure proverbs, but I hate to break it to you: Americans don't eat porridge. We're all too busy eating deep-fried Oreos."

There's a condescending smirk people convey when they think you've made a grave mistake. Pursed lips. A subtle side-to-side shake of the head. These were Pavel Tarasov's gestures as he looked at me.

"A pleasure to see you again, Mr. Logan."

I watched him walk out of the hotel with his two body-guards, finished my Raisin Bran, and turned in my room key to the matronly clerk working the front desk.

Savannah's Jaguar was parked in the shade, around the corner from the motel's office. I spent the better part of an hour exam-ining the car for hidden explosives, then drove back to California, checking the mirrors frequently, my gun within easy reach.

⌖

Savannah was standing in her driveway in a black string bikini, wet from a swim. Her top begged to be untied. I fantasized about slowly undoing the towel wrapped about her hips. She was a vision. Goddamn her.

"How was traffic?"

I climbed out of her Jaguar and tossed her the keys. "You live in Southern California, Savannah. How do you think traffic was?"

A six-hour drive under normal conditions had taken nine, courtesy of a jackknifed big-rig that had shut down Interstate 10 in both directions east of Palm Springs.

"Find anything of interest in Phoenix?"

"Nothing worth mentioning."

"Nothing is ever worth mentioning with you, is it, Logan?"

"I need to borrow your bathroom."

She followed me inside. She would've followed me into the toilet had I not shut the door.

"I let you stay in my house. I cook for you, loan you my car. This is how you treat me?"

"Do you mind? I'm trying to concentrate in here."

She growled with exasperation on the other side of the door and stomped away.

After relieving myself, I made my way to the guest room, plugged in my phone recharger and checked my voice mail. There were two messages from some investigator named Bob Ayling at the FAA's Flight Standards District Office in Van Nuys, wanting to set up a meeting to discuss my incursion of the Vice President's airspace, and no less than twenty calls from television, radio, and newspaper reporters, all seeking to interview me for the same reason. My name, obviously, had been leaked. They could all take my fifteen minutes of infamy and shove it for all I cared.

I returned the FAA guy's call. He wasn't in. I left word on his machine. I called Czarnek. He wasn't in, either. My phone beeped with an incoming call. I hit the green button.

"Skeeter's Towing Service."

"Logan?"

"Who's this?"

"Marvis Woodley."

"I don't know any Marvis Woodley."

"You was by my house last week. Took my twelve-gauge away fro' me. Remember?"

Echevarria's nosy neighbor, Mr. Clean. He of the shotgun in my face.

"How could I forget. What can I do for you, Marvis?"

"He's here, man. Just down the block."

"Who's down the block?"

"The killer! The dude that capped Arlo."

A squatter had broken into a bank-owned foreclosure down the street from his house and was now encamped there full-time, Woodley said. When he ordered the squatter to leave, he ordered Woodley to fuck off, then shoved a pistol in his face.

"I know I seen this dude somewhere before, right? So I go home and I'm sitting there. All of a sudden—damn!—that's the fool that shot Echevarria! Same weird-ass walk, same arms. Same fuckin' dude! I'd swear it on a stack of Bibles."

"So call the LAPD."

"Fuck that. I didn't talk to them racist motherfuckers before they stomped Rodney King and I ain't talkin' to 'em now." No,

Woodley said, he was going to apprehend the killer of Arlo Echevarria himself. A citizen's arrest. With me backing him up.

"It's a dumb idea, Marvis. A dumb, dangerous idea."

"The hell you talking, dangerous? I seen the way you handled that shotgun, man. You got dangerous in your damn blood."

I told Woodley there was not one scintilla of evidence suggesting even the remote possibility that Echevarria's murderer had been a homeless squatter. What's more, I said, murderers typically do not move in down the street from the scenes of their crimes where they could easily draw attention from nosy neighbors of the Marvis Woodley variety.

"You can look it up," I said. "It's all in *Miss Manners' Crazy Mad Dog Killer Handbook: Socially Acceptable Ways to Murder People and Get Away with It for Fun and Profit.*"

There was a pause. Then Woodley said, not sure whether to believe me, "There's a fucking *book*?"

Savannah appeared in the doorway. She'd changed out of her swimsuit and into jeans and a madras blouse.

"I'm trying to make a point here, Marvis. Whoever you saw down the street, whoever you *think* you saw, it's not the guy who killed Arlo."

"Who're you talking to?" Savannah demanded.

I tuned her out.

"You said you and Arlo was buddies, ain't that what you told me?" Woodley said. "Arlo was military. I was military. You was military—I could see it on you, OK? Military don't leave a buddy behind. Ever. You know that, man."

"I know a detective. I'm happy to pass along your number to him."

"I just told you! I ain't talking to no fuckin' LAPD—and I won't tell him where the guy's at, neither. Now, the way I see it, you got two ways to go. You can get your ass over here and back me up, or you can leave a buddy behind and live with that. There it is. What'll it be, troop?"

Marvis Woodley's logic was as ill-formed as his ambitions to collar Echevarria's murderer independent of the police. This was no battlefield. We weren't at war. Whatever bonds Echevarria and I once forged in combat were broken long ago. And yet, on some level that defied logic, Woodley's sermon resonated. Much as I tried to deny it, part of me did feel like I was abandoning a former fellow go-to guy, however loathsome he may have turned out to be. I felt guilty for reasons I couldn't explain. If you're Buddhist, you know that there's no place for guilt. There's no place for even feeling guilty about feeling guilty. But that's how I felt. Guilty as sin.

"I'll get back to you," I told Woodley and hung up.

"Who was that?" Savannah asked again.

"Arlo's next door neighbor. Thinks whoever killed him moved in down the street."

"Are you serious?"

I shrugged. "He won't talk to the cops. Wants me to back him up so he can make the arrest himself."

"Why would he want *you* to back him up?"

"Because he's a fruitcake, Savannah."

"I want to go over there."

"No, you don't."

"What if it's the guy, Logan?"

"It's not the guy, Savannah."

"But what if it is?"

There was no use arguing with her. There never was.

"Even if it's not him, I want to see where Arlo died. I've never been there."

"You can see where Arlo died after you drop me off at the bus station."

I started gathering up my stuff. She looked at me disbelievingly.

"You're going home?"

"I did what you wanted me to do, Savannah. I did what your father wanted. More than I probably should have. I'm done with this."

"Fine. Do whatever you want." She curled up on the bed, her back to me, sulking.

Part of me wanted to lay down beside her, to press myself into her and hold her like I once did. Another part wanted to scream at her for messing with my head. Love and hate. Yin and yang. I closed my eyes and practiced calming breaths, striving in vain for the tranquility and humility of the Zen master I aspired to be. Accompanying Savannah to see where Echevarria died and convincing Marvis Woodley to call the cops would take an hour at most, I told myself. No biggie. Then I'd be gone, back to Rancho Bonita to resolve my issues with the FAA and back in the air, back to my life. Maybe someday that life would have a place in it for Savannah Echevarria. Agreeing to do what she wanted me to do in this one instance, I realized, couldn't hurt my chances of that happening. Brownie points, I believe the Buddha called them.

"If I agree to go over there with you, will you take me to the bus station?"

"I'll take you all the way to Rancho Bonita if you want."

"The bus'll be fine."

I called Marvis Woodley back and told him I was on my way over.

"Hooah. I knew you'd come around, motherfucker!"

"Hooah," I said tepidly and hung up.

"Thank you for doing this," Savannah said.

I wanted to put my fist through something but didn't.

Savannah stood on the sidewalk and quietly cried outside the place where Echevarria spent his last days. Why are people always drawn to places of violent death like murder scenes? Is it the quest for ultimate intimacy, the desire to share in that final awful moment when life ends, to perhaps glimpse whatever there may be waiting beyond? I don't know what Savannah was hoping to find or what she saw as she gazed at the dumpy little tract house where Echevarria's life came to an abrupt end. Whatever it was, she wasn't saying.

I asked if she wanted to have a look inside. She shook her head no.

Marvis Woodley spotted us and came over from next door. I made introductions. He told Savannah he was sorry for her loss.

"Best neighbor I ever had," he said.

"Logan says you have information on the man who shot him."

"Yes, ma'am." Marvis lowered his voice and said he'd mapped out a plan to capture the suspect. Did we want to go inside to discuss it?

"That would not be my first choice," I said.

Savannah shot me the stink eye and walked with Woodley to his house. I sighed and followed them.

The interior of Marvis Woodley's home was as orderly as a barracks. Everything in its place. Everything at right angles. There were plastic covers on the lampshades, plastic runners on the mauve-colored carpet, macramé coasters on the dustless coffee table. Savannah and I sat on the plastic slipcovered couch while Woodley paced the living room like Patton, hands clasped behind his back. He used terms like *dynamic entry* and *superior firepower* as he laid out his plan for capturing the transient that he was convinced had murdered Arlo Echevarria, while his little white yapper dog ricocheted off the walls and jumped up on the couch, trying to kiss me on the lips. Woodley would yell, "Rambo, get down!" and the mutt would do so, but only for a second or two, before jumping back up on the couch to get at my lips—when he wasn't trying to hump Savannah's leg.

"What kind of dog is he?" Savannah said, fending him off.

A dog I wanted to punt.

"Coton de Tuléar," Marvis said. "Bred for the kings of Madagascar, only this one thinks he *is* king. Thinks he don't have to take orders from nobody."

When Rambo tried to hump my leg, I scooped him up and locked him in the bathroom.

Woodley was too wrapped up in his pre-assault briefing to pay much attention. He'd already conducted two "surveillances" of the house that morning during walks with Rambo, he said, and confirmed the killer was inside. The man we were after drove a beat-to-shit El Camino, which he parked on the street. Woodley's plan called for me to knock on the killer's door and say that I'd accidentally sideswiped the El Camino. He would then emerge unsuspectingly from his redoubt to inspect the damage, at which point Woodley would jump him. Together we would subdue him with duct tape. Then Woodley would call the police to come cart the son of a bitch off to Folsom. Savannah would capture the citizen's arrest on Woodley's cell phone camera, then he would sell the footage to the major TV networks. He was hoping for his own reality series, or maybe a movie deal. We'd split millions.

"If this guy's the killer, I'm a theoretical physicist," I said. "I don't care whether you trust the LAPD or not. This is their gig, Marvis, not yours."

He glared, nostrils flaring, like he was about to lay hands on me—or try. "I already told you. Fuck the LAPD. Don't you get it? This is my ticket to ride, man."

Rambo was scratching at the bathroom door, whining and yapping like he was trapped in there with Freddy Krueger. Woodley yelled at him to shut up. Rambo whined only louder.

"My old lady's dog," he said apologetically. "Left him with me when she split for good."

He opened the bathroom door and released him. Rambo padded over to the front door and lay down, panting in relief at having been sprung from solitary.

"OK, here's the situation," Marvis said. He was looking at me not in anger this time, but with resignation. "The truth is . . ." He licked his lips nervously.

"SEAL Team Six didn't come along until after Vietnam," I said, finishing his words for him. "The truth is, you were never a SEAL, were you?"

He steepled his fingers prayerfully, rubbing his palms together slowly, ashamed to meet my eyes, and shook his head no.

Only a wannabe ever brags to a stranger about being a member of the Navy's premier counterterrorist unit. Those of us in Alpha, of course, knew who they were. The community wasn't that big. We referred to SEALs as the "junior varsity." Not that they were in any way deficient at what they did. They were quite good, actually. It's just that we were better.

Savannah eyed Woodley with a puzzled expression, then me. "Somebody want to tell me what this has to do with Arlo?"

Woodley sank into a blue velvet La-Z-Boy recliner, his favorite chair, given the well-worn cushions. "Me and Arlo was battle buddies," he said. "Maybe we never served together, but we was battle buddies just the same."

Marvis Woodley may never have been a Navy commando, but he was a Vietnam War-era veteran, he said. He'd toiled for a year below decks in the post office of an aircraft carrier patrolling Yankee Station in the Gulf of Tonkin, sorting the mail, rarely seeing the sun, both relieved and disappointed at having avoided combat. The life that followed had devolved into an unfulfilling career as a letter carrier and a series of failed, childless marriages. Many nights after work, he would pound down a forty-ounce bottle of Olde English and fantasize about running a garden hose from the tailpipe of his Monte Carlo, sliding in his favorite Aaron Neville CD, and going to sleep forever. But he never had the stones for that. Then Echevarria moved in next door and everything changed, Marvis said. The two men started hanging out. Sometimes, they'd order in Chinese food and watch baseball on Echevarria's big screen plasma. But mostly they just drank. The booze loosened Echevarria's tongue and he would let slip stories—incredible stories about a group of elite shadow warriors that no one had ever heard about.

"I couldn't sit there and bore the man about being some lame-ass clerk on some lame-ass ship, watching movies and eating ice cream and shit, not after all he done," Marvis said, "so I start telling my own stories. Being a SEAL, zapping gooks, all that. Arlo, he was just a kid when Vietnam was going down. The hell he gonna do, call me a liar? I ain't saying what I did was right, but . . ."

Savannah covered her mouth as she listened. Everything Marvis said confirmed what she'd long suspected but could never get Echevarria or me to admit. The lives we hid from her.

"Truth is," Marvis said, drawing a deep breath and letting it go, "I ain't never done anything my whole life. This is my one chance."

"Take down the bad guy *mano a mano*," I said, "be the hero you never were."

Marvis shrugged like a little kid caught in a lie. I pitied him.

"You're certain this guy's the shooter?"

"No doubt in my military mind."

"What's the address?"

Marvis recited it by memory. The house was four doors down and across the street, south toward the Ventura Freeway. I got out my phone and called Czarnek.

"Who you calling?" Marvis said.

"LAPD."

"You can't do that!" He sprang to his feet. Rambo, startled, began running around and yapping like the place was on fire. "You can't, man," Marvis pleaded. "Let me do this. For Arlo. For all the lies I told him. Please."

I glanced over at Savannah. Her eyes were filled with tears.

"If Arlo were here today," I said, "I know what he'd say: 'Never send a man where you can send a grenade.' You're a good man, Marvis, but you're no grenade. You did your job. It's time to let others do theirs."

He rubbed the back of his neck, staring up at the ceiling, then disappeared into his kitchen. His dog padded after him. The house was quiet.

"Detective Czarnek."

He apologized for not returning my earlier call. The turf war had escalated between the Paxton Street Locos and Pacoima Flats, he said, and was monopolizing his time.

I walked outside, far enough away from Savannah that she couldn't overhear my conversation, and briefed Czarnek on what I'd learned on my trip to Phoenix regarding Robbie Emerson and the possible Russian connection to the death of Echevarria. I told him about the mysterious man who'd bought a Sawzall from the Home Depot where Emerson worked, using a stolen American Express card issued to one Richard Smith, no middle initial, address unknown.

"A Sawzall?" Czarnek sounded distracted.

"Reciprocating saw," I reminded him, "like the kind that took off Bondarenko's hands?"

"A Sawzall. I remember. Right."

"If I was a big deal LAPD detective, I might stiff in a call to American Express, get the billing address, and go ring Richard Smith's doorbell. You never know. He might have some ideas as to who made off with his card."

"If you were a big deal LAPD detective," Czarnek said, "you'd be too busy dealing with little shitheads in the projects killing each other. I'll get to it when I can."

I told him about Marvis Woodley's claim that Echevarria's murderer had moved in down the street.

"That would be a first," Czarnek said. Then again, he conceded, he'd seen weirder occurrences in nearly thirty years protecting and serving the good citizens of Los Angeles. Way weirder.

I agreed that Woodley's tip defied plausibility. But under the circumstances, I said, the LAPD was compelled to check it out. "Somebody calls up to report they know where a murder suspect is holed up, the police department ignores it and he kills somebody else, that's not gonna go over too big with John Q. Public or city hall."

"Must be hard being right all the time," Czarnek said.

"You have no idea."

Twenty-two

If Buddhists are correct that less is more, then clearly there were no Buddhists among the LAPD tacticians who planned the raid that afternoon on the house where Marvis Woodley asserted that Arlo Echevarria's killer had taken refuge. Six uniformed officers in helmets and tactical vests covered two others who snuck through the alley and into the backyard. Glass shattered as the pair in back smashed windows to distract the suspect inside. This was followed immediately by more than a dozen other officers armed with pistols, shotguns and assault rifles who breeched the door with a handheld battering ram and rushed in shouting the usual cop stuff. At Alpha, we would've made entry with four operators, max. And without all the annoying yelling.

Savannah, Marvis Woodley, and I looked on with Czarnek and his partner, Windhauser, from behind the detectives' unmarked Crown Victoria, which was parked in front of Marvis's house. Others in the neighbors watched, too, people of color, mostly, standing on their porches with their arms folded.

Czarnek pressed his cell phone to his ear, waiting for word that the suspect had been taken in custody. His forehead and armpits were wet even though it wasn't hot outside and he was in shirtsleeves. He was giving his anti-smoking gum a workout. His partner gnawed on a toothpick.

"This better be the guy," Windhauser said. "I ain't got time for this bullshit."

"Trust me," Marvis said, "it's the guy."

The guy had been sitting on the toilet in a glazed euphoria, the syringe needle he'd stolen from his diabetic grandmother still stuck between his toes, when the men in blue came barging in.

Startled into something approaching lucidity by all the yelling and breaking of glass, he made what police call a "furtive move" toward a serrated steak knife that he'd used to cut the bottom off a Diet Pepsi can, which he'd then used to mix the heroin, on which he'd been orbiting the planet. For his trouble, he received two barbed electrodes to the neck and a 50,000-volt hello–how-do-you-do, courtesy of Taser International, Inc.

Two patrolmen dragged the dazed suspect, handcuffed and still naked, out of the house and into the back of a black and white.

"That's him, that's the dude!" Woodley said.

Czarnek and Windhauser strode toward the patrol unit. Savannah started to go with them.

"Where do you think you're going?" Windhauser said to her.

"I just want to look at him," she said.

"You're not looking at anybody. Get back behind the car."

"C'mon, John," Czarnek said, "if she was your wife . . ."

"I'm senior lead on this case and I say she stays put." Little angry globs of spittle shot from Windhauser's lips as he spoke. He turned toward Savannah. "Get back behind the vehicle. Now. Do you understand?"

"You're being a dick for no reason, Windhauser." I said. "All the lady wants to do is look the man in the face who may have shot her husband, though we both know that's highly unlikely."

"She's obstructing a police investigation. And so are you."

"Nobody's obstructing anything. What if, miracle of miracles, it is the guy? What if she's seen him before and can positively ID him? But you didn't think of that, did you, Joe Friday, because thinking requires a brain and the LAPD by all indications didn't issue you one of those."

The wishbone vein in Windhauser's forehead bulged like rope. Did he not know that hypertension is America's silent killer?

"Fuck you, Logan."

"That's all you got? *Fuck you, Logan*? C'mon, Detective, where's the creativity? How about, 'Fuck you, Logan, and everybody who looks like you.' Or, 'Click your heels together three times, Logan, and go fuck yourself.' Or—"

"Whatever!" Windhauser seethed. "She wants to eyeball him, I could give a shit. But you stay put, or I *will* arrest you for obstruction." He motioned impatiently for Savannah to follow him. "Let's go. I don't got all day."

She rewarded me with an appreciative smile and tagged after the detectives. The kind of smile that makes a man want to do handstands and sing Barry Manilow songs. If I were that kind of man.

"What about me?" Marvis said. "I was the one who saw him first."

"C'mon," Czarnek said.

Marvis jogged to catch up with the detectives. "It's him," he kept saying. "I *know* it is."

It wasn't, as it turned out. Not by a mile.

⊙══✦══⊙

A quick background check determined that the junkie Marvis Woodley identified as Arlo Echevarria's killer was a recidivist named Nicholas Sulak who'd racked up so many priors that clerks at the LAPD's Records and Identification Division had to install a new toner cartridge to print out all seventeen pages of his arrest record. None of Sulak's close encounters with Johnny Law factored much as far as Echevarria's murder was concerned, with one noteworthy exception: nine months before Echevarria was gunned down, Sulak was picked up in Riverside for lifting a pack of cotton balls and two cans of Hormel chili from a mom and pop bodega. He was two weeks out of prison. Rather than trifle with misdemeanor shoplifting charges, county prosecutors had kicked his case to state authorities, who promptly revoked Sulak's parole. On the night of Echevarria's death, Sulak was in his cell at medium-security Wasco State Prison, 125 miles away. He would not be released for another two weeks. There was no way he could've shot Echevarria.

Czarnek emerged from the house holding the pistol Sulak had allegedly pointed at Woodley. The weapon was found buried under a pile of filthy clothes. Closer inspection determined that it was a squirt gun.

"Our captain's gonna want to know why we committed half of Valley Bureau day watch to nab some fucking hype with a squirt gun."

"Tell him what Friedrich von Schiller once said: 'He that is overcautious will accomplish little.'"

"Who's Friedrich von Schiller?"

"German writer. Big *Sturm und Drang* guy. Invented potato pancakes."

"I thought it was the guy," Marvis kept saying.

"Fucking ridiculous," Windhauser said. He climbed in on the driver's side of the Crown Vic and slammed the door. "You coming or what?" he yelled at Czarnek.

"Gimme a minute."

There was no statute of limitations on homicide, Czarnek told Savannah. The LAPD still had leads to pursue and would continue to work the case vigorously until it was solved.

"That's a lie," Savannah said, "and you know it."

The other police cars were starting to pull out. "I'll let you know as soon as anything breaks," Czarnek said.

"I'm sure you will," she responded derisively.

Czarnek watched her walk with Marvis Woodley back to his house.

"Good lord," he said, "that is one gorgeous creature."

"So was Medusa."

Czarnek said he would continue to explore the Bondarenko connection, but conceded that the pace of the investigation might be even further slowed. With gang violence exploding in the San Fernando Valley, every detective was working overtime, juggling more cases than they could handle. It didn't help, he said, that normally knowledgeable street sources within Los Angeles' Russian émigré community professed to know nothing about the murder of either Bondarenko or Echevarria. I asked him if he'd looked into Harry Ramos' possible involvement in the case.

"Harry Ramos?"

"Janice Echevarria's second husband. He was on a business trip to Kazakhstan when I talked to her."

"Oh, yeah, him. Yeah, he's supposed to call us when he gets back to San Fran."

"Let's go already, for Chrissake," Windhauser said. "I gotta eat before I pass out."

"He's hypoglycemic," Czarnek explained.

Windhauser glared at me. "You get any other big leads, do us all a favor. Keep 'em to yourself."

"I assume this means we won't be taking any warm showers together anytime soon."

"You got a bad attitude, Logan, you know that?"

"Better a bad attitude than delusions of adequacy, Detective."

"What's that supposed to mean?"

I just smiled. Czarnek tried not to.

Windhauser grumbled something nasty under his breath and threw the car into gear. The two detectives sped off like they were late for the early bird special at T.G.I. Friday's.

Come to think of it, I was starting to get a little hungry myself.

⊙═══╬═══⊙

Savannah was sitting beside Marvis Woodley on his sofa. He shook his head side to side and kept looking down at his hands, rubbing them together.

"I could've sworn it was him."

The hype the LAPD hauled off looked exactly like the man who'd breezed past his window the night Echevarria was killed, Woodley said. All he'd ever wanted to do was square things with Arlo, make amends for all those lies he told him. And now this. Woodley looked like he was about to cry. Rambo rested his furry little head on his master's foot. Man's best friend. You can be Saddam Hussein and your dog will love you, regardless. Unlike certain cats.

"You did nothing wrong," Savannah assured him. "You were just trying to help. Arlo would've done the same for you."

"He told me he wanted to move out of Los Angeles," Marvis said. "That teacher who got shot the week before over on the next block was the last straw for him. He told me if he ever had the money, he was gonna buy himself his own island up in Washington or somewhere like that and live on it the rest of his life." Marvis wiped the wetness from his eyes. "I told him, I says, 'Fool, you can't live on no island all by yourself. No man can.' And you know what he says to me? He says, 'Marvis, I'd live there with my wife if she'd ever take me back.'"

Savannah's chin quivered. "Arlo really said that?"

"Every word."

I rolled my eyes.

He and Echevarria had eaten dinner together the night he died, Marvis said. Chinese food delivered from Johnny Wang's Golden Dragon Asian Bistro, the same joint on Sherman Way where they ordered in for dinner every week or so. Egg rolls, kung pao beef, twice-cooked pork, pork fried rice. They washed all the MSG down with a pint of Jameson and still had room for fortune cookies. Marvis's fortune that night had been worth saving, he said. He dug the slip of paper out of his wallet and handed it to Savannah. She read it aloud:

"You will meet a man named Wright. He is often wrong."

Marvis chuckled. "Wright and wrong. Can you believe that?" Then he began to blubber about how he was probably the last man to have seen Echevarria alive. Soon Savannah was blubbering, too.

I went outside and called Mrs. Schmulowitz to see how she and Kiddiot were doing. A "nice young man" from the insurance company had already been by, she said. He'd informed her that a big check would be mailed to her within two weeks so she could begin rebuilding the garage, Mrs. Schmulowitz said. She'd decided to bake a German chocolate cake in celebration. This brought us to Kiddiot who, she said, was doing more than fine in my absence.

"He got up on the counter and helped himself to a big slice of cake. What kind of crazy *meshuggener* cat likes German chocolate cake?"

"At least he's eating."

I told her I'd be back in Rancho Bonita that afternoon to take him off her hands. No rush, Mrs. Schmulowitz said. She and

Kiddiot were getting along fine. She repeated her offer to let me use her sofa, but I'd already inconvenienced her enough, I told her. Mrs. Schmulowitz, however, refused to take no for an answer. She launched into a long dissertation about how her first husband had met a bum on the subway in Brooklyn and insisted that they take him in for a few days until the bum could get on his feet, and how he turned out to be a thief who stole Mrs. Schmulowitz's silver. There was a beep on my phone. Another call coming in. Mrs. Schmulowitz kept droning on obliviously about how the bum refused to leave after taking one bite of her famous blintzes and my phone kept beeping and Mrs. Schmulowitz kept talking until finally I interjected and told her that I would be happy to finish listening to her story when I saw her in person—"OK, I gotta go, Mrs. Schmulowitz"—and signed off.

Detective Ostrow at Rancho Bonita PD was on the other line, coughing and apologizing for sounding like he was about to hack up a lung. He'd been out surfing that morning before work, he said, when a big roller broke the wrong way and he gulped a bellyful of seawater—a "Neptune cocktail" as he put it.

"Gnarly," I said.

He asked me if I knew anyone who drove a white Honda or possibly a Toyota of the same color, with tinted windows and a spoiler on the back. A couple of neighbors, he said, had seen a vehicle matching that description cruising the alley behind Mrs. Schmulowitz's garage an hour or so before the firebombing.

I told him about my various close encounters with the mysterious Honda. And, no, I said, anticipating his next question, I didn't catch the license plate number.

"Well, whoever he is, we'll find him eventually," Ostrow said. "That's the cool thing about being a cop in a community like Rancho Bonita where the crime rate isn't through the roof. We actually get to investigate stuff, unlike LAPD. Speaking of which, I called Detective Czarnek. He hasn't called me back."

"I'll yank his chain next time I talk to him, which may or may not be in this millennium." Ostrow urged me to have a great day. I told him to hang ten.

"You'd never know it to look at him," Savannah said, as she emerged from Marvis's house, "but that man is a very sensitive soul. He scheduled a session with me so I could teach him a few tools on grief-coping. Sometimes I think I could use some of those tools myself." She gazed wistfully at the house next door where Echevarria had lived.

"I can catch a cab to the bus station if you want to stand here all day and reminisce."

Savannah's eyes flashed. "Does being so insensitive come to you naturally, Logan, or do you work at it?"

An acrid something surged up from my gut and burned the back of my throat. The taste of shame. Instead of affording my ex-wife a modicum of empathy, as any compassionate human being would've done under similar circumstances, I'd reverted to the jilted and jealous ex-husband. I needed to work on my Chi or I was coming back as a snail in the next life for sure.

"I'm sorry for being a jerk, Savannah."

"I've come to expect nothing less. Get in. I'll drive you to the bus station."

"Look, I haven't had anything to eat since breakfast. How about I spring for dinner and we call it even? You can drive me to the bus station after that."

Savannah turned her head and looked through me with those eyes.

"I don't understand you," she said. "I never have."

Twenty-three

Savannah wanted to eat at the Chinese restaurant that had delivered Echevarria's last meal. No problem, I said. I wanted to show her how completely unfazed I was by her pining after the man for whom she'd left me. All modesty aside, my performance deserved an Oscar.

Johnny Wang's Golden Dragon Asian Bistro was sandwiched in a strip mall between a Vietnamese nail salon and a storefront for Madam Magdala, Fortune Teller to Hollywood Stars. A sign hung in the madam's window that said "Closed," next to another sign that said, "Walk-ins always welcomed."

"Why keep regular business hours," I said as we got out of Savannah's car, "if you know in advance when your next customer's coming in?"

Savannah didn't feel much like talking.

Seating inside Johnny Wang's was configured like a coach car on a passenger train. Ten booths, five along each wall, bisected by a broad aisle leading to a kitchen in the back. Every booth was empty. An elderly Chinese man who looked like he could be somebody named Johnny Wang was perched on a stool behind the door, reading a Mandarin-language newspaper. He smiled at us as we walked in and gestured.

"Anywhere you like."

I followed Savannah past an aquarium built into the wall. The glass was fuzzy green with algae. The koi inside had grown too large for the tank. The fish crowded together, barely moving, fan tails swaying anemically in the filthy, bubbling water. I felt bad for them. We took the last booth in the back on the right. I sat facing the door.

An aging waitress with a heavily creased face who looked like she could be somebody named Mrs. Johnny Wang ferried a dented tin teapot with a bamboo handle and two cloisonné cups to our table. She was wearing a white tuxedo shirt, black bow tie with a tuxedo vest, and black trousers.

"You very pretty," Mrs. Wang said.

"Why, thank you," I said.

"I mean her."

"You're very kind," Savannah said.

"You like something drink maybe? Beer? Wine?"

"I'm fine with water," Savannah said.

"Water's good for me, too—as long as it's not from the aquarium."

Mrs. Wang handed us menus. A young Asian man of about twenty with spiked hair and a Van Halen T-shirt emerged from the kitchen and asked her a question in Mandarin. She responded curtly. They began yelling at each other in their native tongue, arguing as if we were not present. Pretty soon Johnny Wang was yelling, too. They were all yelling.

"Knock it off!"

They stopped, startled by my outburst.

"The Buddha doesn't like arguing," I said. "It's not conducive to bliss."

"My grandson, Benjamin, he no like the hard work!" Mrs. Wang complained.

"I go to school full-time!"

"Ooohhh, Mr. Cal Tech. You think you so fancy! School no hard work. School easy! Restaurant, *that* hard work!" She started yelling at him in Mandarin again.

Benjamin rolled his eyes and pleaded his case to Savannah and me.

"I ask for one lousy day off a week and they have a meltdown. Three years I'm working here. For what—six bucks an hour? All the lo mein I can eat? Dude, I am *so* over lo mein."

"You make good tips," his grandmother countered.

"Good tips? The tips barely pay for my gas! And do you pay me for gas? No!"

The grandmother swore something angry and foreign under her breath and marched into the kitchen.

"You must be the delivery driver," I said.

"Until I graduate," Benjamin said, "then I'm outta here."

I asked him if the name Arlo Echevarria rang a bell. It didn't.

"He lived on Williston Drive," I said. "You used to deliver there."

Benjamin thought for a second. "5442. Dude got shot a couple months back."

"That's him."

The kid was pleased with himself. "I can't remember names, but street numbers, I got a head for those. That dude, man, I was there, like, an hour before he got killed, too. Could've been me, ya know? Like that guy OJ cut up. Goldberg, or whatever his name was."

"Always better to be lucky than good," I said.

"Was he a friend of yours or something, the dude on Williston?"

"He was my husband," Savannah said evenly.

"Shit. Really?"

She nodded.

Benjamin cleared his throat and dug his hands into his pockets. "I'm really sorry."

"It's OK."

Detectives questioned him about his whereabouts that night, Benjamin said, but quickly ruled him out as a suspect in Echevarria's murder. As the fatal shots were being fired, he was more than two miles away in Grenada Hills, delivering Szechwan scallops and orange peel shrimp to a lesbian music producer and her "like, totally hot" sixteen-year-old lover.

"I wished I could've helped the cops out," Benjamin said. "I mean, he always tipped pretty good, your husband, you know? But I didn't have anything to tell them. I didn't see anything weird or anything like that. Dude seemed normal. I gave him the food, he paid with cash. Just like always."

"What was his mood like?" Savannah wanted to know.

"His mood? OK, I guess. I don't really know." He fidgeted, running his hand back and forth across his mouth. "I didn't really know him, you know? I'm just the delivery guy. He was always real nice to me, though, your husband. Seemed like a nice dude."

Savannah smiled, however painfully, letting the kid know she appreciated his kindness.

Benjamin studied the fish swimming in the aquarium. "Nothing bad ever happened around here when I was a kid, except for maybe the 'quake back in '94, but I barely remember that. Now, people get killed all the time. My math teacher, Mr. Ortiz, he got shot over on Elmira Avenue, like a block away from your husband's house. 5442. I used to deliver there, too. A math teacher. Can you believe that?"

"It's a violent world," I said.

Eastbound traffic on Sherman Way was backed up a mile. A car accident? Malfunctioning stoplight? What did it matter? It was Los Angeles. Savannah said she was happy to drive me north to Rancho Bonita instead of south, to the Greyhound station downtown, but I declined.

She turned sharply down a residential street. Houses whizzed by. Block after block, all the same. It would be easy to get lost in such neighborhoods, the same way I'd gotten lost looking for Echevarria's house without benefit of the Jaguar's GPS. I wondered how many aerospace and automobile workers over the years—when there were still such industries in the San Fernando Valley—had inadvertently turned down the wrong streets and into the wrong driveways after stopping off for a few beers on their way home, while their wives waited to cuss them out for being late for supper yet again.

Some synapse in my brain suddenly sparked, a rare instant of complete lucidity. I could feel my heart surging to regain rhythm.

"Shit."

Savannah looked over at me. "What?"

I called directory assistance and got the number for the Chinese restaurant where we'd just eaten. The old man answered the phone.

"Johnny Wang."

"Is Benjamin there?"

"Who?"

"Your grandson."

"Who?"

"Your delivery driver."

"You want delivery? Okey-doke. What you like?"

"I need to speak with Benjamin."

"You like broccoli beef?"

"I . . . would . . . like . . . to . . . talk . . . to . . . Benjamin."

"Oh. You want talk to Benjamin?"

"Yes. Benjamin."

Johnny Wang cupped his hand over the phone and yelled something in Mandarin. I could hear Mrs. Wang yelling something back. Then Johnny Wang was back.

"Benjamin, he coming now."

Savannah was frowning, trying to watch the road and me.

"What is it, Logan?"

"Hello?" Benjamin sounded out of breath.

I gave him my name and reminded him that Savannah and I had been in a few minutes earlier.

"You said something about your math teacher, Mr. Ortiz, getting shot a couple weeks ago. What was Mr. Ortiz's address again?"

"Why do you want to know that?"

"All I need is the address, Ben."

"I'm not gonna get in trouble, am I?"

"Only if you don't give me the address."

There was a long pause. Then Benjamin said, "Elmira Avenue, 5442."

"How old was Mr. Ortiz?"

"I dunno. Pretty up there. Like, fifty. Why?"

I thanked him and hung up.

Savannah braked at a four-way stop. A man with a mestizo's leathery face and wishbone legs, who was probably younger than he looked, wheeled an ice cream pushcart across the intersection. He was wearing a white straw cowboy hat and silver rodeo belt buckle as big as a pie plate. I punched the address into the Jaguar's GPS:

Elmira Avenue paralleled Williston Drive.

One block over.

Jesus.

"A math teacher gets shot at 5442 Elmira Avenue. Less than a week later, Echevarria gets shot at 5442 Williston. The exact same address. One street away."

"It's a violent world, Logan. You said it yourself."

"What if the math teacher was a screw-up?"

"What're you talking about?"

"It's dark, the houses in that neighborhood all look the same. The shooter's after Arlo, but he confuses one street for another. Ends up at 5442 Elmira—only he thinks it's 5442 Williston. Same address, one block over. I made the same mistake. The teacher's the same approximate age as Arlo. Both Latino. Bang, bang, bang. The shooter splits, then realizes later, 'I killed the wrong guy.' He lays low for a few days, goes back to the right address when the heat's off and takes out Arlo."

"If there was any truth to your theory, I'm sure the police would've looked into it by now."

"We're not dealing with Scotland Yard here, Savannah. It's the LAPD."

I probably should've called Czarnek. But given his burgeoning case load and what a disaster Marvis Woodley's tip about the junkie with the squirt gun had turned out to be, I doubted he would ever talk to me again.

I told Savannah to turn around.

"Don't tell me what to do."

"I'm asking. Please turn around. Elmira Avenue. Maybe somebody there saw something."

"I thought you were in such a big hurry to get to the bus station," Savannah said.

"There's always the next bus," I said.

But for the black steel security grates covering the windows and front door, the retired teacher's house looked like Arlo Echevarria's. Same uninspired architecture. Same blighted lawn. Only the paint scheme was different: Green Bay Packers green with gold trim.

"Mr. Ortiz must've been a cheesehead," I said.

"What's a cheesehead?"

"How in the hell did I ever stay married to somebody for so long who knows absolutely nothing about football?"

"The sex," Savannah said.

No arguments there. I tried the doorbell. Broken. I knocked. No answer. No sound or sign of life inside. There were sooty smudges around the knob and up and down the frame. Finger-print powder.

Savannah followed me around back.

A kidney-shaped swimming pool drained of water took up most of the tiny backyard. There was a six-foot privacy fence of redwood slats, many of which were rotted and falling down. Through the gaps in the fence, across the alley and the street beyond, I could see the front of Echevarria's house. It looked tranquil, undisturbed.

Not so where Mr. Ortiz had died. The back door had been booted off its hinges, the jam splintered. Someone had tried to secure the opening after the fact by slapping up a thin sheet of plywood where the door had been, then tacking it into place with a few roofing nails. I peeled back the plywood and peeked inside:

The back door led into the kitchen. The unplugged refrig-erator was standing open, its shelves overgrown with moldy, unrec-ognizable lumps of fetid food and swarming with flies. A jumble of filthy cooking pots was heaped atop a harvest gold electric range. More dirty pans and dishes were piled in the sink. A rusty swath of dried blood trailed out from the green Astroturf covering the kitchen floor into the living room. From the way the blood had pooled at the base of the sink, it appeared as if Mr. Ortiz had been shot there, then dragged into the living room, or crawled.

"What do you see?" Savannah said.

"I see that *Better Homes and Gardens* won't be doing any photo shoots here anytime soon."

I pounded the plywood back into place with the palm of my hand.

Savannah followed me to the house next door, to the west. The front yard was littered with skateboards and a battered street hockey net. No one was home. We tried the house to the east. A large dog barked and snarled, pawing frantically from behind the door to get at us. No one was home there, either.

Of all the houses on the block, the one directly across the street was by far the most decrepit, which was saying a lot considering that preventative maintenance seemed to be an abstract concept among the late Mr. Ortiz's neighbors. Much of the roof was covered by rotting canvas tarps held in place using bricks and dead palm fronds. An untended maze of bougainvillea vines clung to the wood siding and covered what few windows still had glass left in them rather than cardboard. There was a pear tree not much bigger than a sapling out front. The tree was pruned so severely that it no longer resembled a plant so much as it did an amputee: the end of each severed limb had been bandaged with a tiny round Band-Aid.

The front door opened as Savannah and I made our way up the front walk. A thin old man was standing in the shadows behind a steel-reinforced screen door, naked but for a pair of baggy boxer shorts adorned with little smiley faces. He was unshorn and wild-eyed, like Howard Hughes in his recluse phase.

Savannah took refuge behind me.

"Are you Jesus Christ?" the man demanded.

"My ex-wife used to think so."

My ex-wife jabbed me in the kidney.

"I don't take *Newsweek*," the man said, "and I don't take the newspaper and I don't take Girl Scout cookies, so don't ask me cuz I ain't buying *nothing* from nobody."

"It's OK, sir. We're not selling anything. There was a shooting across the street several weeks ago. Your neighbor, Mr. Ortiz, a retired teacher, was murdered. Did you happen to see anything?"

"Hell, I seen *everything*."

He spied something over my shoulder, blurted out "God-dammit!" and flung open the screen door, pushing past Savannah and me into the front yard, his old-man balls swaying under his skivvies like a pair of drunken sailors. Some Band-Aids had fallen from the branches of his pear tree. He picked one off the ground and tenderly reattached it as if the tree's survival depended on it.

"They come along and do this just to torment me," he said. "Kids today. Got no respect for anything."

"Sir, can you tell me what you saw the night Mr. Ortiz was murdered?"

He peered suspiciously at Savannah, then leaned closer to me. "Who's the skirt?"

"She's with me."

"You from Langley?"

"You know we couldn't tell you that, even if we were."

He nodded like we were all in on some big secret and re-bandaged another tree limb.

"I'm inside reading my Bible," he said, "when I hear this *pop,* then *pop—pop.* Little faggot had it coming. Used to have sex parties over there. I always knew one of his playmates was gonna cap his ass someday. I look out. Here comes this guy running out of the house. Jumps in a car he's got parked the wrong way in front of my house, and takes off."

"What'd he look like, the shooter?"

"Six foot, 160 maybe. Jeans. Hooded sweatshirt. Young. Didn't see his face. No moon that night. Let there be light, God said, in the firmament of the heavens to divide the day from the night; and let them be for signs, and for seasons, and for days, and years."

"What kind of car was he driving?"

"White two-door Honda."

My pulse kicked into overdrive.

"You didn't, by any chance, catch the license plate, did you?"

"Three Mary King Lincoln three six eight. Got it all right up here in safe storage," the old man said, tapping his temple with a crooked finger. "Went out with my flashlight when I heard him pull up. Was gonna call it in to traffic enforcement for the way he was parked, only he didn't stick around long enough."

"Did you tell the police this?"

"Let them figure it out. They all think I'm nuts, anyway."

"I find that hard to believe," Savannah said condescendingly.

I shot her a disapproving glance. She looked at me as if to say, "I'm just trying to help."

"I used to be a cop," the man said, "before them geniuses at Parker Center said I wasn't fit to—" He pressed his left index finger to his ear, like he was on a long distance phone call with a bad connection. "But you just told me . . . Well, if they ain't from Langley, where the hell are they from?"

He looked up at me, his face suddenly contorted with fear.

"You're not from Langley at all," he said. "The sulfur, I can smell it on you!"

He slowly backed away from me, then turned and ran back into his house, slamming and locking the door behind him. "I am Gabriel, the archangel!" he yelled. "You hear me, Beelzebub? I invoke the power of the Holy Spirit, the power of the burning bush, and order you to return to the bowels of Abaddon! Now, get the fuck off my property!"

I heard the click-clack of a round being chambered. A rifle barrel poked through a broken window. It was aiming at me.

"Five seconds, devil! Then I'm blastin'!"

Buddhism has no devils. No demons or mythological beasts. Not even any flammable shrubbery. No special effects. If any religion is low-fat, it's Buddhism. The crazy old coot could've benefited from a teaching or two. But I wasn't about to start sermonizing. Not with a rifle barrel pointed in my direction by a man who thought I was El Diablo.

I grabbed Savannah by the arm and got off his property.

Twenty-four

"You're dreaming," Czarnek said. "Some lunatic gives you a plate number and you expect me to just drop everything and roll out the cavalry, especially after chasing your last tip? You can forget it, Logan. I'm already in enough trouble with my supervisor as it is."

"That lunatic's a former cop," I reminded Czarnek.

Savannah and I were parked down the street from the dead teacher's house. I put the phone on speaker so she could listen in.

"I know who he is," Czarnek said. "His name's Norman Buckhalter. Everybody calls him 'Abnorman.' Got tossed off the department for a bad shooting back in the eighties. Been in and out of the psych ward ever since. Calls us all the time with all kinds of crazy shit."

"Run the plate, get me an address, I'll do the legwork myself. It'll take you five minutes."

"I run that plate, I go to jail. It's called misuse of police resources."

"OK, then run the plate and *you* check it out."

"The cases aren't connected, Logan."

"Two murders, days apart, one block apart, same street number, both middle-age Latinos, and they're not connected? We have a saying where I come from, Czarnek: 'If it walks like a duck and talks like a duck, the goddamn murders are connected.'"

"There were two different weapons used. Echevarria got shot with a .40-cal. The teacher got it with a .45. Plus, every witness we talked to said Echevarria's shooter had brown skin. Two wits on Elmira said the guy who shot the teacher was Caucasian. And nobody except Abnorman Buckhalter said anything about seeing any white Honda."

I let Czarnek know about the white Honda that had been seen lurking near my garage apartment shortly before the place caught fire, and how Detective Ostrow from Rancho Bonita PD was eager to compare notes with him.

"There's a million white Hondas in the United States," Czarnek said. "It's probably just coincidence."

"This is hardly what I would describe as proactive law enforcement, Detective."

"I told you, I got gang case files piling up on my desk faster than I can read 'em. Look, I'll get to your Detective Ostrow when I can. And if it'll get you off my butt, I'll drop by Abnorman's place. Maybe next week, OK?"

"Joe Friday's rolling over in his grave," I said.

"I'm sure Joe Friday would find the situation less than ideal," Czarnek said, "as we all do."

"You know what I find, Detective Czarnek?" Savannah blurted into the phone. "I find it amazing that you're getting paid to be a detective, because from where I sit, it doesn't look like you could find your ass in the dark with both hands tied behind your back, let alone find the man who killed my husband."

She hung up on him.

"Well played," I said.

"You think that whacko knew what he was talking about, with the license plate?"

"Just because somebody's nuttier than a port-a-potty at an almond festival doesn't make them incapable of conveying the truth."

"You are one profoundly articulate guy, Logan," Savannah said, shaking her head in disgust.

"What can I say? It's a gift."

The sky was streaked brown. She sniffed the air. "There's a fire somewhere. You can smell it."

There was always a fire somewhere in Southern California this time of year, when the offshore winds turned the arroyos and hillsides to tinder. A spark from a weed wacker and entire neighborhoods went up in flames. Yet regardless of the risks, whether by fire or temblor or mudslide or murder, no true Angelino ever gave serious thought to living anywhere else. They were all too busy, I suppose, vying for their own reality shows.

"I'll take you to the bus station now," Savannah said.

I didn't protest.

She slid the Jag's polished walnut gear shifter into drive. We drove south on Elmira Avenue, toward the freeway.

Strange how random recollections can pop into your head at any given moment for every reason and no reason at all. At that moment, my mind's eye filled with the image of Ray Allen, my high school football coach, flinging a helmet at me in the locker room after a game for failing to catch a pass. We'd been down by three touchdowns with less than a minute to play, and the football had been thrown ten yards in front of me, but that didn't matter to Coach Allen. "If you don't believe in your heart you can win," he screamed, his cheeks florid with rage, "then there's no point in getting out of bed at the end of the day." No one dared to correct Coach Allen. Certainly not to his face.

"Never quit," was the message Coach Allen was selling that day. Back then, I took to heart every dumb sports cliché every coach ever trotted out—too much, probably. Now I was stuck with them. My overwhelming urge was to get on the bus and get the hell out of Dodge. The only problem is, quitters never win and winners never quit.

Screw it.

I called Buzz and asked him to run the license plate the crazy ex-cop had volunteered. Buzz gave me grief about the illegalities of accessing official government records for unofficial purposes, and how I already owed him big-time for all the many other favors he'd done for me, then said it would probably take a few minutes to get back with the information I wanted. He was in the doctor's office, he said.

"Nothing serious, I hope."

"Hemorrhoids are flaring up. Plus, I'm out of Viagra."

"Too much information, Buzz."

"You ever wonder why they call it an asteroid when it's outside the atmosphere, but they call it a hemorrhoid when it's inside your ass?"

"Gotta run, Buzz," I said and signed off.

"One of your *marketing* contacts," Savannah said sarcastically.

"A buddy."

"Why can't you just tell me the truth, Logan?"

"That is the truth."

She shook her head, aggravated with me per usual, and turned on news radio. The fire she'd smelled was burning in the mountains northwest of Los Angeles. Nearly twenty structures were already burned, and hundreds more threatened. Evacuations were being ordered. Water-bombing helicopters and a DC-10 carrying 12,000 gallons of retardant had been called in to stop the advancing flames. Much depended on the winds, and the winds weren't cooperating. I ached for those who'd lost their homes, and those who soon would. I knew the feeling.

"People just don't call up a 'buddy' and get confidential DMV records," Savannah said.

"It's a good buddy."

"It's the CIA. That's who you and Arlo used to work for, isn't it?"

"You know, Savannah, you could continue busting my *huevos*, or we could go get a drink and wait until my good buddy gets back to me with the information I requested."

Savannah thought about it for a minute. "I'd prefer busting your *huevos*."

"Why am I not surprised?"

○━━◆━━○

Jingle's Happy Place was anything but. Just another dive watering hole on Lankershim Boulevard, across the street from an empty used-car dealership gone bust. A big screen plasma was tuned to Sports Center. A hockey game was on. The Fun Room regulars, a handful of aging bikers and what looked to be blue collar retirees on fixed incomes, paid little attention to the television, preoccupied as they were with getting hammered on long-necked Buds and shots of tequila. They nudged each other and checked out Savannah as she walked in. We laid claim to two stools near the door.

The bartender was bald, with a wife beater T-shirt that afforded an unobstructed view of his heavily tattooed arms and neck—a multicolored kaleidoscope of hobbits, skulls and dragons. Five gold loops dangled from each of his earlobes. He tossed down a couple of cocktail napkins and stared in sullen silence at us, waiting. I ordered club soda with a lemon twist. Savannah went with a glass of Chardonnay.

"Something dry," she said.

The barkeep stalked off to get our drinks without a word.

"I just realized something," she said. "I don't even know what your favorite season is."

I looked over at her.

"I'm serious. We were married for how long? That's how private you were, Logan. Always distracted, rarely engaged—except when we were in bed. And every year, it just got worse."

"You should've said something."

"Are you kidding? I said everything I could think of. Over and over. You just never heard me."

A covert life is lived in boxes. Marriage and family are locked in one box; career in another. The arrangement isn't for everyone. Every member of Alpha had been divorced at least once. Perhaps if I'd had it to do all over again, I might have gone a different route. Left the Air Force and gone to work for the airlines. Moved Savannah to the suburbs and started a family. Shared a life together. A *real* life. But that was the past. A Buddhist doesn't dwell on the past. He concentrates on the present.

"Fall," I said.

She looked over at me.

"My favorite season."

"I would've guessed summer," Savannah said. She got up to go to the ladies room.

"You coming back this time?"

"There's a possibility."

I smiled.

The regulars ogled her as she walked.

Our drinks arrived. There was no lemon twist in my club soda, but I let it slide. You pick your battles. My phone rang. Caller ID indicated it was Buzz.

"That was quick."

"How long does it take to go rooting around somebody's anus and write a prescription?" Buzz said. "The guy tells me I need more fiber. *More* fiber? Talk to my wife. I'm already tooting like a foghorn."

"You run that plate?"

"No. I'm calling because I went to the doctor and now I'm conflicted about my sexual orientation and need some advice from somebody who's been there. Even though I now realize that there's no gift certificate in it for me to my favorite restaurant, yes, Logan, I ran your license plate. Because I love you, man."

"Maybe you are conflicted, Buzz."

"You ready to copy, wise guy?"

"Go."

"The plate belongs to a 2007 white Honda coupe. Registered to an address on Sea View Lane in the Mount Washington area of Los Angeles."

"Who's it registered to?"

"The owner of record: Richard no middle initial Smith."

My mouth went dry, the same way it used to just before I pickled a bomb or pulled the trigger on a target. *Richard Smith.* The same name on the stolen American Express card used to buy the Sawzall at the Home Depot in Phoenix.

Being the pro that he is, Buzz had gone one step further, looking up Smith's driver's license description: five-feet-eight and 178 pounds, with brown hair and brown eyes. He was sixty-one years of age, considerably older than any suspects that witnesses to Echevarria's murder had described to police. He didn't match the description of the suspect that Abnorman Buckhalter said he'd seen fleeing the house where Ortiz, the math teacher, was killed, nor did he resemble the man I'd seen on the Home Depot surveillance tape, exchanging heated words with Robbie Emerson before buying a power saw.

"What's the deal with the Honda?" Buzz wanted to know.

"The week before Echevarria got hit, there was another shooting, same address, one street over. Retired schoolteacher. A witness said he saw the shooter drive off in a Honda with that license plate. Richard Smith also reported his credit card stolen. That card was used to buy a power saw in Phoenix that might be connected to another murder linked to Echevarria's."

"You're thinking this guy Smith with the Honda took out the teacher *and* Echevarria?"

"That's the thing. Smith doesn't match up. Witnesses described a different shooter. I'm wondering if somebody else might've been driving his car."

"The same somebody else who was using Smith's allegedly stolen credit card," Buzz said.

"Read my mind."

"So why don't you go ask him."

"Maybe I might just do that."

"Good. That way, you can stop demanding favors from me every twenty seconds. You're worse than my kids. At least they remember me on Father's Day. You, I get nothing from but empty promises."

Savannah returned from the ladies room, drawing another round of lustful glances from the regulars.

"Hold the fort," Buzz said, "did you say *power* saw? What's up with that?"

"We'll talk later."

"What's wrong with now?"

"I love you, too, Buzz." I got off the phone as Savannah sat back down.

"I didn't know you loved anybody," she said.

"You'd be surprised."

"What're you, some kind of fuckin' narc or something?" the bartender said accusingly, having overheard my phone conversation with Buzz.

"Me? I'm just a simple country doctor."

Savannah sipped her drink and made a rancid face as the taste settled on her tongue.

"Yuck."

"You want wine? Go to the west side." He snatched Savannah's glass and dumped it out into the sink.

"Not to resort to clichés, amigo," I said, "but that's no way to treat a lady."

"This is my bar. I'll treat her any way I want."

"C'mon, Logan, let's go," Savannah said, sliding off her stool.

"We're not going anywhere until Lord of the Rings here apologizes to you for his crass behavior."

"You want an apology?" He reached under the bar and produced an aluminum baseball bat. "I got your apology right here."

I held my ground and stared him down.

"Please don't do this, Logan," Savannah said, tugging on my arm. "Let's just go."

"Listen to your bitch, Logan," the barkeep said.

"My *bitch*?" Something inside me snapped. "Now I'm afraid you're going to have to apologize twice."

"Bullshit."

He jabbed the bat at my face. I twisted it out of his grip and rammed the knobbed handle into his belly. He collapsed to his knees behind the bar, gasping for breath.

"Apologize to the lady."

"Sorry," he groaned.

"Again. This time with feeling."

"I'm really sorry for calling you a bitch."

I tossed the bat on the floor and followed Savannah out to her car.

"About damn time somebody put that turd in his place," one of the regulars said.

"Hell, I don't even know why I even drink here," said another.

The others all murmured in agreement.

<hr>

We drove up Mount Washington toward Richard Smith's house. Not much of a mount. More like a hill. Savannah acted like she was irked that I had resorted to violence defending her honor. And, while she wouldn't admit it, maybe a little flattered.

"I never realized Buddhists go around pounding people."

"Only when they deserve it."

She shook her head like she was disappointed in my behavior and downshifted.

"Well, anyway, I guess I should thank you."

"Just don't expect me to hold your umbrella or throw my coat down over any mud puddles. A man does have his limits, you know."

"I'll keep that in mind."

Sea View Lane was twisty and narrow, an eclectic hodgepodge of old and new homes, most with canyon views. Smith's house was a flat-roofed affair with stucco walls and metal-frame windows, cantilevered precariously over the lip of the canyon on wooden stilts that looked as if they might collapse with the mildest temblor. A black Lexus sedan with Nevada plates was parked out front, behind a VW Beetle with California tags and a bumper sticker that read, "Don't Forget to Floss." The white Honda coupe was nowhere to be seen. I tried not to look too obvious as we drove past.

There are thousands of Richard Smiths in America. And, as Czarnek had so astutely pointed out, the country is filled with white Hondas. So, yes, it was very possible that the Richard Smith who'd reported his credit card stolen, and whose Honda was purportedly observed by a crazy ex-cop leaving the scene of one murder, had nothing to do with another. But, I mean, c'mon. What are the odds?

Buddhists believe that events rarely happen by chance, that karma truly does govern the universe. As a budding Buddhist, I suppose I was about to find out. I directed Savannah to park down the street, around the corner and out of sight, which she did. I told her to stay put and got out of the car. She ignored my instructions and got out, too.

"You're not in charge of me, Logan."

"I'm not ordering you, Savannah. I'm asking. For your own good. Stay here."

"If this man was involved in Arlo's murder, I have a right to confront him."

"You have a right to get hurt, too. I don't want that to happen." And then I said, impulsively, "I care too much about you."

The expression on her face was something between disbelief and rapture. At least I think it was. Hell, I never could read the woman anyway.

"What did you say?"

"Nothing."

"You said you cared about me. Isn't that what you just said?"

"Yes, OK. I said I cared about you, Savannah. Can I go now?"

She smiled. "I care about you, too, Logan."

"If he has anything relevant to say, I'll come and get you."

"Just call me. We do live in the Digital Age, you know. Most of us, anyway. Some of us still live in the Pleistocene Era."

"Was that an insult?"

"Scientific observation."

I grinned and started walking.

<hr>

Richard Smith's doorbell chimed like Big Ben. No one responded. I pushed the button again and pounded my fist on the door because nothing says "You have a visitor" like pounding and impatiently ringing at the same time. I tried the doorknob. Locked. No one appeared to be home.

There was an attached two-car garage. I stood on tiptoes and peeked in through a narrow transom window at the top of the door. No vehicles inside. No newspapers piled up on the short driveway. Two large terracotta clay pots planted with pink geraniums flanked the front door. I checked the soil in the pots. Damp. I looked in the mailbox out front. Empty. The postal carrier would've already come and gone, this late in the day. Somebody had to have picked up the mail.

I called directory assistance. The operator said she could find no listing for a Richard Smith on Sea View Lane. I took out a business card from my wallet, jotted "I need to speak with you," and slipped the card under the front door.

My work was done.

I was on my way back to Savannah's Jaguar when a two-door white Honda Accord with black-tinted windows and a spoiler on the back cruised past me. Smith's garage door opened electronically. The Honda pulled into the driveway and rolled into the garage. A squat, middle-aged man in a brown UPS uniform got out of the car and retrieved two paper bags bulging with groceries from the trunk.

"Mr. Smith?"

He turned toward me, startled.

"Can I help you?"

"My name's Logan. I'm looking into a murder that occurred up in the Valley a few weeks ago. A witness said he saw your car leaving the scene. I'd like to ask you a few questions."

"A murder? There must be a mistake."

"That's possible, though the witness was pretty adamant he'd seen your car. This is your car, isn't it?"

"Yes, that's my car. But I just can't understand who would ever possibly say something like that. I mean—" he laughed nervously— "I'm no murderer."

"The witness is a former police officer."

"Really?" Smith was beginning to breathe hard. His upper lip glistened with sweat. "You a cop, too?"

I knew he'd be more willing to talk if he assumed that I was.

"What do you think?"

"Well, I really don't know what more I can tell you. I don't know anything about any of this, OK? So, if it's all the same to you, I'd like to go in now. I'm not feeling too good. Must've been something I had for lunch."

"Do you ever loan your car to anyone, Mr. Smith?"

"Loan my car? Umm, lemme think."

He set his grocery bags down on a woodworking bench inside the garage and licked his lips, running the back of his left hand across his mouth. Hand tools hung from a pegboard behind the bench, with various power tools stored on shelves below.

Among the tools was a Sawzall.

"It's possible I may have let my daughter's boyfriend borrow it when his car was in the shop, something like that but, you know, no big deal. That's his car, right there." Smith pointed to the black Lexus parked in front of the house. His hand was trembling. "He lives outta town, visits quite a bit."

"Mr. Smith, did you report your American Express card stolen recently?"

"What's that got to do with anything? Why are you asking me all these questions? I told you, there's been a mistake. I don't know anything about any shooting."

"I said someone was murdered, Mr. Smith. I didn't say anything about anybody getting shot."

"Oh my God." He slumped to the concrete floor, clutching his chest.

"Are you OK?"

"He told me it wouldn't come to this," Smith cried. "The Russian, he made him do it. Either he did what the Russian wanted, or they were gonna turn him in."

"Turn who in?"

"My daughter, her boyfriend. He said if we told anybody, they'd kill us, too. Jesus. I think I need an ambulance. Oh my God."

"Just breathe, Mr. Smith, try to relax. I'm calling 911 right now."

I was punching in the number when the door connecting the garage to the house opened, revealing a young woman in pink dental scrubs and the shadow of a tall, angular young man standing behind her. I heard her scream, "Don't!" as the man shoved her aside. All I saw was the nickel-plated semi-automatic he was raising up to fire at me. His right arm was straight, his hand flat, palm down, the pistol horizontal to the floor, the way gangsta rappers like to shoot.

Had it been Hollywood, I would've rolled to throw off his aim, bullets whizzing in slow-mo' inches from my face. But this was no movie. I held steady and reached for the little revolver tucked in the small of my back. *Instinct shooting is about smoothness, not speed.* I could hear Laz Kizlyak, my old firearms trainer from Alpha, talking like he was standing there beside me. *Grasp butt of weapon firmly, hand high on grip panels, and draw, not jerk, in single fluid motion. Trigger finger extends parallel to barrel, falling alongside frame above trigger as weapon is withdrawn.*

Something hot smacked me in the shoulder. I ignored it, elevating the muzzle of my gun as I extended my shooting hand, swinging my other hand up and locking both hands together just as the revolver entered my peripheral vision. *Wrap support hand around middle, ring and small fingers of gun hand, overlapping thumbs on backstrap of weapon. Do not clutch weapon. Clutching makes weapon shake. Face target squarely as weapon rises. Spread legs shoulder-width, assuming solid and braced firing platform. Bend slightly forward from torso and flex knees. Thrust hands out from the midline of your chest. Lock wrists, lock elbows, lock shoulders. Level muzzle just below eye level sliding index finger on shooting hand from frame of weapon onto trigger.*

Even without a stopwatch, I knew that no more than a second had elapsed from the moment I first glimpsed the gun in the man's hand to the moment I double-tapped my trigger.

Only after he was down and I had kicked his pistol away from his body did I realize that the man I'd killed was Lamont Royale.

TWENTY-FIVE

Everyone complains about hospital accommodations, like hospitals are supposed to be the Four Seasons or something. My stay at Cedars-Sinai couldn't have been more luxurious. Dinner the first night was a Caesar salad with pan-seared ahi, whole grain muffins, and chocolate pudding with real whipped cream. I had a private room with a thirty-two-inch flat-screen TV and a view of the Hollywood Hills, a fine bed that adjusted about a hundred different ways, and sponge baths administered by certified nursing assistants who, if I closed my eyes and imagined hard enough, resembled the kind of scantily clad Nubian princesses one would expect to perform such services. I would've stayed a month had they let me—especially considering Gil Carlisle was footing the bill.

"Almost makes getting shot worthwhile," I said to my menopausal battle-axe of a nurse as she changed the dressing on my wound.

"Almost," she said, ripping a strip of surgical tape off my skin.

The bullet had shattered my left collarbone and lodged in my shoulder. A fraction of an inch lower, the surgeon had told me almost breathlessly, and it would've severed my subclavian artery. I probably would have bled out in the ambulance. As it was, I could expect a full recovery after a few weeks' rest. The same could not be said for Lamont Royale. Two .357 slugs to the forehead have a tendency to do that to a man.

"By the way," Czarnek said, standing at the foot of my bed and watching the nurse work, "Royale wasn't his real name. His real name was London Bridges."

"Sure it was," I said. "And I'm the Empire State Building."

"I'm serious. London Bridges. I mean, who names their kid London Bridges?"

"My husband has a first cousin named April Showers," Nurse Battle-Axe said.

"I knew a guy in high school named Burt Nurney," I said.

Nobody laughed. Tough crowd. Czarnek cleared his throat and waited while the nurse finished patching me up.

"I know when I'm not wanted," she said. "Press the button if you need anything. I probably won't answer."

"Big surprise there," I said.

She gave me a wink and left.

As Czarnek explained it, London Bridges, aka Lamont Royale, was a young man with a past. He'd grown up in Miami, the youngest son of an African-American real estate developer and his Swedish-born wife, and dropped out of the University of Miami his sophomore year to attend culinary school, hitting the links during his off-hours to become a scratch golfer. But apparently he found criminal enterprises more entertaining. With multiple prison stints on priors ranging from burglary to assault, he eventually skipped out on parole and traded the Sunshine State for Las Vegas, there to reinvent himself, as so many others do. London Bridges became Lamont Royale, golf pro. While giving a private lesson one day, he taught my former father-in-law how to nail a fifty-yard bunker shot, then shared his secret recipe for beef bourguignon (applewood smoked bacon, heavy on the Côtes du Rhône). Within a week, Royale had quit his country club gig and moved into the penthouse to work for Carlisle full-time.

Somewhere along the way, Royale had also been recruited by Russian intelligence operative and oil broker Pavel Tarasov.

"Tarasov found out about his criminal record. He knew Royale was on the lam, so he blackmailed him," Czarnek said. "Anytime Tarasov wanted him to pull some little caper for him, all he had to do was threaten to rat him out and Royale danced like a puppet."

"How do you know all this?"

"Your new best friend, Richard Smith. Can't shut the guy up. A regular Chatty Cathy. He's down on the coronary ward. He feels damn lucky he and his daughter survived the whole thing."

It was Royale, Czarnek said, who'd introduced Tarasov to my former father-in-law, Gil Carlisle. There was a fortune to be made in the Kashagan oil field. All Tarasov needed was a willing investor with deep pockets. As soon as Carlisle's check cleared the bank, Tarasov intended to have him die "accidentally," after which he would take over the entire operation.

"Tarasov gets wind that Echevarria's doing some investigative work for Carlisle. He worries that Echevarria'll find out shit that'll squirrel the deal in Kazakhstan, so he decides to have Echevarria whacked. He sends Royale to Arizona with orders to convince a guy he knows out there who's on the Russian payroll to do the killing."

"Robbie Emerson."

Czarnek nodded. "Royale threatens to turn Emerson in to the FBI unless he agrees to be the triggerman, but Emerson can't bring himself to take the assignment. Commits suicide instead. So Tarasov orders Royale to do the killing."

"What about Ortiz, the retired math teacher?"

"I have to say, you pegged that one right, Logan. Royale told Smith he messed up on the address. Got the two streets confused. Went to the right house number but the wrong house. He shoots Ortiz thinking it's Echevarria, realizes later that he's screwed the pooch, goes to the right address a few days later, and this time does the job right."

"You told me the two murders weren't linked. Two guns, different calibers."

"I stand corrected. We found both guns in Smith's garage, where Royale had stashed 'em: The .45 he used on Ortiz and the Glock .40-caliber he shot Echevarria with—which, by the way, he also shot you with. We also found the Domino's shirt he was wearing the night he killed Echevarria. He hid that in the garage, too, including his receipt from the thrift store where he bought it. Not the sharpest tool in the shed."

The LAPD, he noted, had gone back to Echevarria's neighbors and run a photo lineup past them. Everyone picked Royale out of the six-pack.

"We showed the same six-pack to witnesses in the Ortiz homicide," Czarnek said. "They picked out Royale as well. The thing I couldn't figure out, though, was how Echevarria's neighbors could all say the shooter was dark-complected, when witnesses in the Ortiz homicide all said he was white."

"Helps if your killer's biracial," I said.

"Two for the price of one," Czarnek said.

Royale denied any involvement in the murder of Gennady Bondarenko, according to Czarnek, even though the bullet recovered from Bondareko's crispy critter remains matched the gun Royale had used on Echevarria and me. The story he told Smith before he died was that Tarasov had attempted to get Bondarenko to invest in the oil deal, and that he intended to have Gil Carlisle "permanently removed" as soon as the deal was finalized, thereby upping both Tarasov's and Bondarenko's potential shares. Bondarenko declined the offer.

"He told Tarasov he was done with that life," Czarnek said, "so Tarasov threatened to blackmail him. Bondarenko said if he tried anything like that, he'd drop a dime on Tarasov's plan to kill Carlisle. So Tarasov shot him. He cuts off Bondarenko's hands with the power saw he has Royale buy for him out in Arizona, steals a Winnebago, sets it on fire with Bondarenko's body inside, and tells Royale to stash the murder weapon. Royale hides it in Smith's garage."

"Like you said. Not the smartest tool in the shed."

The detective peeled the plastic off a fresh wad of nicotine gum.

"Where's Tarasov now?" I asked.

"On the wind. Possibly back in Russia. Arrest warrants were issued last night."

"What about for me?"

"What'd you mean, what about you?"

"I mean, prosecutors tend to frown on civilians who go around shooting other civilians with non-permitted concealed weapons, even in self-defense."

Even if by some miracle I got probation, I was certain that the FAA would pull my pilot's license permanently given all the trouble I was already in having violated the Vice President's airspace.

Czarnek assured me I had nothing to worry about.

"We take this to the DA, it gets leaked, pretty soon we got Washington stepping on our necks, calling every ten minutes. That's all this city needs right now. Besides, you did us a favor, Logan. You cleared three homicides and saved the taxpayers the expense of a murder trial. And I don't think you need to worry too much about your pilot's license. Some buddy of yours called me. Salty son of a bitch. Said he'd already talked to the FAA. Told 'em you were working some secret squirrel case. They're dropping their investigation in the name of national security."

"His name, by any chance, wouldn't be Buzz, would it?"

"How'd you know that?"

I smiled.

Czarnek patted my ankle and told me to get some rest. "You did OK, Logan. I apologize for every shitty thing I ever said about you."

He walked out. I closed my eyes for what I thought was a few seconds. When I opened them again, three hours had gone by.

Savannah was sitting in the chair beside my bed.

"Go back to sleep."

"I'm awake."

She studied my face.

"What?"

"I still don't know what exactly it was you did when we were together, your *real* job. But I do know what you did for Arlo, and my father. You saved his life, Logan."

She got up, leaned over and kissed me softly. Her lips, as the old expression goes, left something to be desired—the rest of her.

My gut roiled with warring emotions. I felt fulfilled and empty, like a million bucks and penniless. I remembered a literature class I took my senior year at the academy. We studied e.e. cummings: *Kisses are a better fate than wisdom.* I had no idea what e.e. was talking about back then, but I did at that moment. I turned and gazed out the window.

The sky was azure. Savannah was with me. More than anything, I realized, I was happy.

"You're ready."

"For real?"

"For real."

My one and only student, Eugen Dragomir, was grinning the way I would've grinned had Publisher's Clearing House ever delivered on that million bucks like they'd said they were going to in their letter.

"Four Charlie Lima, cleared for the option," the tower controller said through our headsets.

"Let's make this landing a full-stop," I said to Eugen.

He keyed the radio. "Rancho Bonita Tower, Four Charlie Lima, this one's a full-stop."

"Skyhawk Four Charlie Lima, Runway One-Seven left, cleared to land. Wind one-five-zero at six."

"Cleared to land, One-Seven left. Four Charlie Lima."

Eugen painted it on. Easily his best landing of the day. After clearing the runway, we taxied over to Larry's hangar. I told him to keep the engine running.

"Three touch-and-go's," I said, taking off my headset and unplugging it from the instrument panel. "Just remember everything we've practiced and have fun up there—and don't forget, do a run-up before you take off, OK?"

"OK!"

Eugen gave me a ridiculously enthusiastic two thumbs-up like he was John Glenn about to blast off into orbit or something. I exited the *Ruptured Duck* and made sure the copilot's door was latched, stooping to avoid the wing and turning my head to avoid the prop wash as he taxied back toward the active runway with too much throttle.

"Slow down," I said under my breath but it was a little too late for that.

Larry walked over, wiping the grime from his hands with a rag.

"Kid's first solo?"

I nodded.

Larry rubbed his knee. "Humidity's killing me. Your shoulder must feel like shit."

Worse than shit, but I kept it to myself. If the FAA found out, they'd probably ground me. Six weeks had passed since the shooting. The money I'd received from Savannah's father was more than half gone. I needed to continue earning a living.

"The shoulder's feeling great," I said.

We watched Eugen in the run-up area. The kid cycled the *Duck*'s control surfaces to make sure they were all working. Then he advanced the throttle to 1700 rpms, checking that the engine, gauges and instruments all functioned properly. He retarded the throttle and advanced the airplane to the hold-short line for One-Seven left. Though I couldn't hear him, I knew he'd changed frequencies and contacted the control tower to say he was ready to go.

I held my breath as the airplane rolled down the runway, past us. I always held my breath whenever I soloed a student. But I needn't have worried about Eugen Dragomir. He lifted off like he'd been flying forever. His pattern work was precise, his touch-and-go's solid. After he landed, I dumped water on him from a bucket that Larry let me borrow. Dumping water on a pilot after their first solo is one of aviation's most cherished rituals. Don't ask me why. An alternative ritual is cutting off the new pilot's shirttail (another "don't ask me why"). But, considering that Eugen Dragomir wore only T-shirts with surfboard logos on them, the shirttail option was a no-go. So I doused him but good. He declared it the greatest moment of his life, with the exception of when he lost his virginity.

"Flying all by yourself, just you, up there in a *freaking airplane*, it's like sex, but without the sex," Eugen said. "You know what I mean?"

"Sadly, all too well."

He said his father was wiring more money so he could continue taking flying lessons. Given that Eugen Dragomir was my only source of income—aside from my government pension check—I said I thought that was an excellent plan.

Kiddiot and I were sharing a studio apartment in lower downtown, close enough to the train tracks that I could look out my bathroom window and observe what the Amtrak passengers were having for breakfast. Neither of us was happy with our new digs. The passing trains kept us up all night and forced me to keep Kiddiot inside all day for fear he might get run over. For this, I was rewarded with mournful yowling that went on sometimes for hours. He was a cat unused to an existence of restriction. He missed hanging out in Mrs. Schmulowitz's oak tree. I missed her cooking.

A contractor was finalizing plans for rebuilding her firebombed garage. It would be better than ever, "a regular Taj Mahal," as Mrs. Schmulowitz described it, with a real kitchen and a Jacuzzi tub for me, and some sort of multi-level, super-duper cat jungle gym for Kiddiot. She wanted us to move back in as soon as construction was finished. Given Kiddiot's dissatisfaction with our current living arrangements, resettlement could not come soon enough.

She insisted I impart my blessings on the blueprints. I did so three days after soloing Eugen Dragomir, and was driving back to my railroad-convenient apartment when I glanced up in the mirror and there was a white Honda. Two door. No front license plate, tinted windows, rear spoiler. It was five lengths behind me.

There are a million white Hondas in America, Czarnek had said. Make that a million and one.

I slowed down to see if this one was following me. The driver backed off. I turned right onto Hendricks Boulevard and headed east. The Honda did as well. I accelerated, changed lanes. So did the Honda, still five car lengths back. He was definitely tailing me.

I reached instinctively for my revolver. Bad habits are hard to break. Then I remembered: the LAPD was still holding the gun as evidence. It would be returned, Czarnek assured me, after such time as the DA's office concluded officially that no charges were to be filed against me in the death of Lamont Royale.

A lot of good that did me now.

I turned onto the freeway, southbound, doing sixty-five. The Honda did likewise. I didn't care at that moment that I'd already received a traffic ticket for driving without a hands-free device. I dug out my phone and made a call.

"Rancho Bonita Police Department. How may I direct your call?"

"Detective Ostrow, please."

"One moment."

The Honda was now four lengths behind my truck.

"Detective Ostrow. How may I help you?"

"Detective, Cordell Logan. We spoke a few weeks back. You were investigating the firebombing of my garage apartment."

"Still am. How can I help you, Mr. Logan?"

"I believe the perpetrator may be following me as we speak."

"Seriously?"

I gave Ostrow my location and a detailed description of the Honda. He put me on hold. My pursuer was now five feet behind me. The driver wanted me to run. I slowed down even more instead. Sixty-five, fifty-five, forty-five, thirty-five. At twenty-five, he laid on his horn and began tapping my bumper like some New York cabbie gone berserk. *Someone*, I thought, *needs to work on their anger management skills.*

No more than a minute elapsed before a California Highway Patrol cruiser streaked into view behind me with his emergency lights on. A second CHP unit joined him, followed by three black and whites from the Rancho Bonita PD. I slowed to less than twenty mph as the cops formed a flying wedge of sorts across all three lanes of the freeway. With me leading the way and the police on his rear, the guy was boxed in.

"You, in the white Honda," an electronically amplified voice boomed from one of the highway patrol cars, "pull over now!"

The driver steered to the right shoulder and stopped. I did, too, careful to stay in front of him so he couldn't bolt. With pistols and assault rifles drawn, the cops took cover behind their open doors, ignoring traffic that was now stopping on both sides of the freeway.

"Driver, turn off your engine and throw your keys onto the road surface!"

A set of keys flew out from the driver's window of the Honda. "Now show me your hands!"

Two empty hands thrust out the window. Male hands. A white, long-sleeved dress shirt, crisply laundered, with gold cuff links.

"Driver, open the door from the outside and slowly step out of the vehicle!"

The driver exited as ordered.

Khakis, Ray-Bans, and a yellow ball cap with the image of a bull on it—the Lamborghini logo. I didn't recognize him until he opened his big, self-important mouth.

"I'm a lawyer! I know my rights! And that son of a bitch," he said, pointing angrily toward me, "has been trying to fuck my fiancée for months!"

His fiancée. Charise MacInerny. My former student. From an innocent kiss goodbye at the airport the day she'd decided to quit flying lessons, her lawyer boyfriend, Louis, had somehow gotten it into his insanely jealous head that I'd been jonesing for his lady. He'd chased me repeatedly in his tricked-out Honda—among the lesser members of his vast automobile fleet—torched Mrs. Schmulowitz's garage, and forced my cat to live in substandard housing down by the tracks. Felons in Texas get the needle for less.

The cops ordered him out felony-style, face-down on the pavement, and handcuffed him with his wrists pulled behind his back. He screamed police brutality. They were fucking with the wrong man, he warned them; he'd see all their asses in court.

I walked over.

"There's never been anything between Charise and me," I said as two CHP officers yanked him to his feet.

"You're a liar!" Louis seethed. "You took her to Paris!"

"I *what*?"

"You wrote it in that pilot book you gave her—'We'll always have Paris!'"

I started laughing.

"What, you think this is funny? Wait'll I get outta jail. I'm suing your ass, too, you miserable piece of shit!"

"Louie," I said in my best Bogie imitation which, truth be told, pretty much sucks, "this is the beginning of a beautiful friendship."

"What the fuck is that supposed to mean?"

I turned without answering and strode back to my truck.

The police dragged him kicking and screaming to a patrol car. They hog-tied his ankles when he continued to resist, and tossed him in like a bale of cotton. One of the cops told me I could give my statement at police headquarters at my convenience and said I was free to go.

I debated going home. I drove to the airport instead.

The *Duck* was waiting for me on the tarmac like a reliable old friend. We flew until day turned to dusk and dusk to dark.

The air was glass.